Brenda.

A House Full
of Women

A House Full of Women

Helen Upshall

PIATKUS

Copyright © 1990 by Helen Upshall

First published in Great Britain in 1991 by
Judy Piatkus (Publishers) Ltd of
5 Windmill Street, London W1

*Helen Upshall hereby asserts
her moral right to be identified
as the author of the work*

British Library Cataloguing in Publication Data

Upshall, Helen
  A House Full of Women.
  I. Title
  823.914 [F]

ISBN 0–7499–0040–7

Phototypeset in Compugraphic Times 11/12 pt by
Action Typesetting Limited, Gloucester
Printed and bound in Great Britain by
Butler & Tanner Ltd, Frome and London

For my sisters, Eileen, Ruth and Beryl,
with love, and remembering with affection
the sad and happy times we spent together
at No. 51, our special House full of Women

Chapter One

Fran rolled away from Henry, but with a grab he brought her back into the circle of his arm.

'No,' he whispered, 'today is your day and you're going to have an extra lie-in. Babe is still fast asleep and Katie won't be here for another hour at least.'

'There isn't time, Henry,' Fran protested as he slid his hand beneath her winceyette nightdress. 'Babe is going to stir any minute and you know I don't like a late start on Sundays.'

'Just a cuddle then,' he persuaded. He held her fast, his work-worn fingers rough against the smooth skin of her rounded belly. Fran knew by the moistness of his lips and the rising pulses of passion that he wouldn't give up until ... After bearing him five children she was weary of this part of marriage, but Henry Sheldon was an ardent and persistent lover. He knew how to make her weaken and in spite of her protests her body quickly reacted to his fondling. Her breasts were soft but firm and the nipples hardened. Then she was breathing quickly, arching her body to mate with his ...

'Now, Henry,' she begged. '*Now* – As he reached his climax, and she was gasping with ecstasy, he pulled free, spilling his unwanted seed where it could do no harm – and from the large cot on the other side of the room came a small voice, urgent in its appeal.

'Mummy, Mummy! I want to get up now, Daddy.'

A moment of fumbling, some ragged breathing from Henry, a guilty sigh from Fran as she slid from the huge double bed and the comfort of the feather mattress.

'What you doing?' Babe demanded, on the verge of tears.

'Just trying to wake up, dear,' Fran said. She put the side of the cot down, lifted the small four-year-old auburn-haired girl into her

1

arms and carried her into the next bedroom, where Ruby and Hilda slept in another double bed.

'You stay here with Hilda while I get washed and dressed. And you, Ruby, up, there's jobs to be done. You can clean the grate while Daddy gets the breakfast going.'

When Fran returned to her own room again, contented snores indicated that Henry had gone back to sleep. She stood looking down at him with a loving gaze. His dark hair was tousled against the starched white pillowcase, his weather-beaten cheeks relaxed with just hint of a smile — a smile that was so very dear to her. In sleep he looked younger than his forty-six years. She didn't often have time to stand still and reflect, but now memories of their youth flipped the years backwards to another time, another place, and a very different, younger — she had to admit it — a more handsome face. She felt herself colour guiltily as she hastened to get washed and dressed ready for church.

She chivvied Ruby to hurry along with the chores, clearing out the dead ash from the kitchen range before relighting the fire. Henry was soon down, whistling contentedly as he fried bacon and bread in the huge iron pan. By the time Fran had dressed the two youngest girls, eggs too were splattering noisily in the pan.

Kate, the eldest of the family, arrived before breakfast was over, and the mill house soon echoed to the sound of a happy family gathering on this special Sunday, Mothering Sunday 1931.

Kate was in service at Sherbrook House, where the Maitland family lived. They owned the village and acres of the surrounding land, including a stretch of the river Sher which flowed along the bottom of the mill-house garden. Not so many years ago the huge mill wheel had been driven by water from a tributary of the river which ran alongside the house. Weeks of wet weather meant that river and stream were running high, occasionally spilling over on to the garden and paths, making the ground soggy, but today winter had abated and there was the promise of spring in the bright morning sunshine.

Fran noticed how smart Kate was looking in a brown check skirt and patterned blouse. At sixteen she was attractive, her rich auburn-coloured hair coiled neatly in earphones, reminding Fran of herself at that age. Memories stirred, and Fran could feel again the excitement of all the staff as they made new dresses or remodelled old ones, ready for the annual servants' ball held every Christmas in the great hall at Lady Hinckley's where she had been Nanny. Such pleasant memories of doing a job she loved, with few worries. All that had changed since her marrying Henry. It was no easy

2

task keeping four girls well-dressed. She was always making do and mending, as well as cleaning and cooking. There were never enough hours in the day to do all that was necessary for a large family.

On their way to church Fran called at the small cottage next door to the mill house to take a cake to her mother, Gran Brown. Her father, the estate's shepherd, was out on the Dorset hills tending his sheep.

'The meat's in the oven, Ma,' Fran said. 'I don't expect to be much later than usual, though, so it should be all right, but when you're ready go round and baste the potatoes and joint if you will. I hope Pa will get in from the fields in time for dinner, being that Kate is home today. We'll have a nice family get-together.'

'He was out early this morning,' Gran said. 'Expecting the last of the lambs to drop. He's quite pleased with his flock, but I reckon he's getting past working all hours at lambing time.'

'Then he must tell Mr Maitland, Ma,' Fran said, a trifle impatiently. 'As long as Pa goes on doing it all by himself, they'll expect him to. He's sixty-eight, after all, time they started to think about the future.'

'Don't you say that to your father, Fran! He'll keep going till the rheumatics won't let him get up of a morning.'

'He looks so pale and gets so tired. He ought to be easing up.'

'But he won't want his sheep tended by anyone else, you know that.'

'Yes, he'll be stubborn to the last, I suppose, in spite of Dr Gibbs telling him that his blood is poor and he needs more rest.'

'Nice bit of raw liver'll do him good when the butcher calls next week,' Sara Brown said. ''Twill be a bit easier when the weather gets warmer and lambing's done with. Now you get on or you'll be late for church. I'll see to the dinner.'

Fran turned and left the small cottage. She knew that her mother would go to the window and watch Henry proudly leading his family down the lane to the bridge and out of sight. Although a short, dapper little man, Henry stood tall with dignified self-esteem. Farm labourer he might be but he had been to Canada logging, and would have returned there but Fran wouldn't leave her parents to accompany him. She was grateful that he had settled down in Sherbrook, though he was more in love with his shire horses than with his family, she sometimes thought. But he was a good man, hard-working, God-fearing, and although they were poor financially, they had much to be thankful for.

3

The service was a happy one, but when the vicar spoke of a mother's role as the pillar of the family unit, Fran felt a lump in her throat. She tried to do the best she could for them all but sometimes she was guilty of impatience. The atmosphere became warm, and the very fact that Fran was completely relaxed made her drowsy. The vicar's voice grew distant, monotonous, and her thoughts strayed back to the time just before she was married. She supposed it was seeing Kate looking so grown up that sparked off her reminiscences.

It was at Christmas in a distant past that the plans for her marriage to Henry were at last complete.

Henry had left his job at the brewery several months earlier to take up his work as carter on the Sherbrook House estate. He was living in the old mill house, preparing it for his new wife. Fran should have been at home in Sherbrook long before this, living with her parents in the small shepherd's cottage, getting everything ready for a summer wedding and helping Henry next door. But Lady Hinckley was determined to hang on to Fran for as long as she could. 'Just another week, my dear,' she kept saying, and one week had grown into six months. When the time actually came for her to leave the staff had decided to make Fran's departure a memorable one.

It was her last night at Hinckley Hall, and in four days' time, on Boxing Day, she would become Mrs Henry Sheldon. Music and laughter reached her ears as she descended the back stairs. She was late going to the servants' hall, having had some difficulty settling the children. Halfway down the dimly lit staircase she caught the sound of the door at the top opening. She turned, expecting to see one of the other servants. Instead, a tall, lean figure gazed down at her. She recognised him as one of the house guests, a friend of Mr Jonathan.

'This leads to the servants' quarters, sir,' she said politely. 'You've come down one flight too many.'

The man raised his eyebrows questioningly. He had been a frequent visitor to the house of late.

'I don't think so,' he said. 'This party sounds more exciting than the one upstairs.'

'But this is only for the staff, sir.'

His long legs brought him down to stand one step above her, and his haunting eyes mesmerised her.

'Forget the "Sir",' he whispered. 'I shan't be missed. What's your name?'

'Frances Brown, sir. Fran to most people.'

4

'You're Nanny, aren't you? I've heard them talking about you. Leaving to get married, I understand?'

Fran lowered her gaze to the dainty, blue dancing slippers that just peeped beneath her long, turquoise-blue dress.

'I ... I gave Lady Hinckley plenty of warning. In fact, we should have been married back in the summer.'

'My name is Luke,' he introduced himself, holding out his hand. 'Luke Hammond. Her ladyship tried to hang on to you, didn't she? Can't say I blame her.'

Fran blushed at his implication. His dark eyes seemed to bore right into her soul.

'Having trouble in replacing you, and young Andrew and the twins are loath to part with you, so I believe.'

'I realise it's difficult, but Andrew will be going away to school after next summer, and the twins will soon get used to someone new.'

Fran felt uneasy at the young man's scrutiny, as well as at holding a conversation on the back stairs with a guest who should be upstairs. She carried on down to the bottom with Luke Hammond following.

'Mind if I join the party?' he asked. 'I know it isn't the done thing, but it is your farewell one, isn't it?'

Fran didn't know how to answer. She was well used to house guests eyeing her inquisitively on the occasions when she had to take the children to the drawing room to say goodnight. This young man was no exception although he was so devilishly handsome that he had been the focus of servant gossip for several days. Fran had been pumped by the other girls to find out what she could, but all she had been able to glean was that he was a fellow officer in the Royal Navy, and a friend of Mr Jonathan.

'I really don't think it would be your kind of party,' she managed to say in a nervous whisper. Whatever would the others think if she arrived escorted by this young man?

He towered above her and, with a compelling hand at her waist, ushered her through the door. Fran was immediately drawn into the centre of her circle of friends, who showered her with confetti and petals made from crepe paper. They put them down her neck, and when she was pushed to the floor one of the bolder young men, with the help of Bessie the parlourmaid, with whom he was walking out, lifted Fran's petticoats and shook confetti into the tops of her stockings and up her knicker legs. Fran's screams brought Talbot, the butler, so they pulled Fran to her feet quickly and she was waltzed round the room in time to music provided by an

5

old Pianola. She went quite dizzy, and her long hair, so carefully arranged in her usual attractive style on top of her head, came loose until it fell about her neck and shoulders in a cascade of red-gold silk. They plied her with mulled wine and goodness knows what else. By the time she was thrown into the air six times, once for every year she had been with the Hinckleys, she hardly felt a thing. Her head spun and her feet were light as strong arms propelled her round the servants' hall. She felt as if she were floating on magical wings in time to a Viennese waltz.

Luke then took her to the long trestle table where a variety of food and drink was waiting to be consumed.

'I think it's probably time you had something to eat,' he said with a wry smile.

Fran had to cling to his arm for support, but nothing was going to stop her from enjoying the festivities.

No one questioned Luke Hammond's presence but his youthful, dashing appearance added lustre to the occasion, and Fran felt light-headed when he insisted she should partner him for ever dance.

After a rumbustious rendition of the Gay Gordons she was laughing up at him as if she had known him all her life. She saw him through a spider's web of fantasy as he picked her up and carried her to the nursery floor of the vast house. He set her down on the side of her bed, his eyes bright with anticipation.

Fran waved a finger at him. 'Sssch. Musschn't wake the children.'

Luke crossed the floor with a mere two strides to close and lock the communicating door. Fran watched, but his intentions didn't register so she made no protest. She giggled a great deal as he removed her clothes. Then her cheeks grew warm and her eyes burned. She lay back, looking into Luke's admiring expression as he scanned her nakedness.

'Mm,' he muttered. 'Such white skin − feels like porcelain.' He fingered her hipbone tenderly. Somewhere in the back of her mind she knew she was being outrageously brazen, but ever since the last time she and Henry had been together her body craved a man's touch. She was no longer a virgin. Once Henry had gone to live in Sherbrook their meetings had been infrequent, but increasing in passion, until Henry's impatience could not be supressed. Fran had been consumed with guilt but Henry had pacified her, excusing their impetuosity by blaming Lady Hinckley.

Luke's hands caressed with tantalising delicacy. Cupping her breasts, he lowered his face until his mouth met hers. A hesitant, gentle kiss at first until he realised that Fran was as eager as he.

She remembered little else except the height their passion reached, and then there was no going back. She recalled whispered promises and a declaration of love, but did it really ever happen?

The heat was stifling, probably because the sun was coming through the window directly on to the pew where Fran was sitting beside Henry. She moved slightly and opened her coat at the neck, her cheeks flushed. She sensed that Henry glanced down at her and then took her hand in his. He squeezed reassuringly while she wrestled with emotions she had tried to put behind her over the past nineteen years. The thought of how different her life might have been charged her with disloyalty to Henry.

During the singing of the last hymn the children all went up to the front of the church, where they were given a bunch of daffodils to take to their mothers. Ruby took Babe with her, and when they emerged into the sunlight outside Fran was holding three bunches of flowers.

'Good morning, Mrs Sheldon,' the vicar said, giving her a limp handshake. 'You've done well this morning, I see,' he added, nodding towards the daffodils.

'I'm going to take them to Lennie's grave, vicar,' Fran replied demurely, and walked on with Henry following. Conversation wasn't easy with the sound of church bells hanging in the valley, but when they were a little distance away she turned to Henry.

'You go on home with the girls and I'll put these on Lennie's grave.'

'Wouldn't it be nice to have them in the house, just for today?' Henry suggested gently.

'There's plenty coming on in the garden,' she said. 'And it would only mean I'd have to traipse down here tomorrow, and I've got enough to do with wash-day as it is.'

Henry recognised the signs of emotional uncertainty. For the most part Fran was a strong woman, but grief for her first-born, her only son, was always there just below the surface. In spite of her love for the girls, her obsessive love for Lennie seemed almost unnatural. He had tried to woo her back to reality. 'Life is for the living,' he told her on more than one occasion. He had tried to keep his own hurt private so as not to distress the girls. Fran's sorrowing had become an indulgence, but who was he to question a mother's love?

He patted her arm understandingly. 'Don't be long then, my dear.'

'Can I come with you?' Ruby chanted, and soon all the girls were hanging on their mother's arm.

'No,' Fran said firmly. 'Kate can come, she doesn't get the chance to visit her brother's grave very often. The rest of you go home with Daddy and see to the dinner.'

Fran wove a pathway through the headstones, glancing at the inscriptions and remembering villagers who had passed on long ago, including members of the Brown family. She came to a small mound beneath a holly bush.

'Mum,' Kate said in a perplexed tone. 'There's no room for any more flowers. The vase is full. You must have known . . .'

Fran felt herself go cold. She stiffened and clenched her gloved fist. Then with a shrug she pulled off her gloves, bent down and fussed with the beautiful bouquet of tulips and daffodils that did indeed fill the vase. She kept her face hidden, not wanting her daughter to see the guilt that she knew must be evident in her expression. *He* had visited Sherbrook again. Why couldn't he leave her alone and let the past die with Lennie? It was embarrassing. How could she explain away the expensive blooms obviously bought at a florist's shop? Was he deliberately reminding her of a brief lapse of fidelity? She wished Luke Hammond had never come into her life. She took some of the flowers out of the vase and said to Kate:

'Someone must have put these here by mistake. How could I afford such an extravagance?'

'You can't throw them away, Mum. They're too fresh and lovely.'

Fran nodded to the other side of the path. 'Take them to your great-grandparents' grave, then,' she said shortly.

She was grateful for a few moments in which to recover from the shock. It wasn't the first time she had found flowers here, but each time she experienced a strange tightening in her breast. On the first occasion, some months after Lennie's death seven years ago, a card had been attached to the flowers. No message, just a scrawled L.H. beneath the printed 'In Deepest Sympathy', reminding her of that brief interlude which should never have happened. As time passed she was to discover that Luke Hammond was not only a friend of Jonathan Hinckley but also of Nicholas Maitland, and the young naval officers sometimes came to Sherbrook House to spend a few days of their leave together. When Fran was aware of Luke's presence in the vicinity she remained at home, making

8

excuses for not going down to the church or village. Now she hoped Kate hadn't noticed her agitation, and she prayed that she might be spared from ever coming face to face with him.

She set the pace on the homeward journey, a pace that Kate recognised as being fast and furious, and she knew better than to question the reason. She wondered about her mother's change of attitude, though. It seemed quite illogical to her that a few flowers mistakenly placed on her brother's grave could cause such annoyance.

Fran felt an underlying impatience with everyone and everything for the remainder of the day. But Henry's happy-go-lucky nature eventually relieved the tension, and they all enjoyed a peaceful Sunday as a united family.

Three weeks after Mothering Sunday, Easter was celebrated and the girls eagerly enjoyed a holiday from school. It was a Monday morning and Fran was back in the usual routine of wash-day. As she pegged several blue-white petticoats on the line, she glanced up at the sky. After the long, wet winter it was something of a change to have a dry wash-day, but even as she looked she noticed that the sky was thickening, and over the Dorset hills dark clouds were lingering menacingly.

Gran Brown staggered over the damp grass with a wicker basket laden with clean washing.

'You should have left that for me, Ma,' Fran said.

'My feet are bad,' the old lady moaned. 'I wish I could get around like you do, but I can't and that's that.'

'That's why I suggested that you did the mangling instead. If we don't hurry up I reckon that storm's going to beat us to it.'

'It'll dry quickly while the sun's out,' Gran Brown mumbled as she picked her way across the uneven garden back to the outhouse where Ruby was helping. Together they folded the sheets, and then, while Gran fed them through the heavy wooden rollers, Ruby turned the big iron handle with one hand and caught the sheet with the other.

'Your mother thinks there's going to be a storm so we'd best hurry up,' Gran said.

Ruby smiled at her Gran sympathetically. Her mother's temper was short, especially on wash-day when there was so much to do. It was usually poor old Gran who received the butt end of her mother's tongue. Not that any of them escaped, except the two little ones, Hilda and Babe. Today, with the promise of warmer weather, her mother seemed in happier fettle, and the line, which

9

stretched right down the long garden at the back of the old mill house almost to the river bank, was soon filled to capacity with sparkling washing, billowing in the wind. Even when Gran had returned to her small cottage next door to get dinner for herself and Grandad, Ruby could hear her mother singing softly as she put the cold meat out ready for Dad to carve when he came in from the fields, and waited for the potatoes to boil.

While they ate their dinner, Fran kept a close watch on the weather through the window.

'I don't like the look of those clouds out there, Henry,' she said. 'I do believe the weather's on the change.'

''Tis early for the weather to be so warm, but the ground underfoot is still very wet and the wind's getting mighty strong. River's running pretty high, too, so I'd best get the sluice boards open before we go to bed tonight.'

After Ruby had helped with the washing-up, she was allowed out to play. She skipped off down the lane to a row of terraced cottages where a small group of children were playing on the grass verge. A tall girl of eleven came to greet her and together they went off round to the back garden to do what they considered were more grown-up things, like combing each other's hair into different styles, while they talked about the boys in the village.

'Can't do much with your hair,' Marion Belmont said. 'It's too long, Ruby. Why don't you get your mother to cut it off?'

'I keep asking her to, but she won't. We've all got to have long hair. Even our Kate has had to put hers up into earphones since she went to the big house to work. It isn't fair,' Ruby grumbled. 'And all because the children Mum was nanny to in service had long hair.'

They had been in the garden a little while when the wind suddenly seemed to whip up into a frenzy. The distant rumble of thunder could be heard, so they went up to Marion's bedroom. Mrs Belmont was a happy-go-lucky woman with much less stringent house rules than Fran, which made visiting Ruby's school friend a happy adventure. They got carried away with enthusiasm over Ruby's lovely long blonde hair. Without thinking of the consequences, Ruby allowed Marion to snip a bit here and there with some rather blunt scissors. When she looked on the bedroom lino she saw to her horror great locks of curly hair blowing about as the draught swept underneath the door.

'Marion!' she exclaimed fearfully. 'Whatever's our Mum going to say? And Dad? I'll get into terrible trouble.'

'Don't expect she'll notice,' Marion said nonchalantly. 'It'll soon grow again, anyway.' She stood back to admire her handiwork. Ruby, forgetting about the consequences for the moment, gazed into the mirror on the dressing table, feeling quite proud of the shoulder-length ringlets. The two girls giggled a great deal, and Ruby managed to put visions of her parents' fiery wrath out of her mind until Mrs Belmont suddenly opened the door.

'Think you'd best run home, Rub – Oh, my goodness, what *have* you two been up to? Marion, have you done this?' Her face was a mask of disbelief. 'Whatever is your mother going to say, Ruby?' Her pale cheeks turned pink with anger as she looked down at the hair lying on the lino. She lashed out at her daughter, cuffing round the girl's head while Marion shrieked in protest.

The wild wind howled in protest too, which reminded Prue Belmont why she had rushed up to Marion's bedroom. If only she had been ten minutes sooner, she thought in despair.

'Ruby, you get off home. There's going to be a nasty storm and your mother will be looking for you to help get the washing in.'

'Yes, Mrs Belmont,' Ruby said politely. How ever was she going to face her mother looking like this? The hour of reckoning had come sooner than she had anticipated but she did as she was told, said a hurried goodbye to her friend and ran back up the lane. Already large spots of rain were spewing out of the big black cloud. Through the garden gate she went, and round the side of the old mill house where water from the stream was seeping over the banks and spilling on to the path.

Fran saw her coming and called, 'Hurry up, Ruby! Help me, there's going to be such a downpour.' Even as she spoke it seemed as if the heavens opened and a deluge descended on them, the mighty roaring wind tearing the washing out of her hands and nearly pulling her away with it.

The line snapped and one end tore through the air, taking with it several petticoats. Fran and Ruby looked on helplessly as line and washing ended up in the swollen river. Ruby heard her mother's anxious voice carried away on the wind as she followed her gaze towards the swirl of water back upriver. A wall of dirty brown froth was cascading towards them at tremendous speed.

'Get in the house!' Fran screamed. Stopping just long enough to grab the basket overflowing with laundry, she chased Ruby into the mill house scullery. She had just slammed the door shut behind them when they heard the enormous roar of water as it tore along, bursting the riverbank, covering everything in its wake. Ruby went to stand on tiptoe at the stone sink to watch as the garden was turned into a lake in seconds.

11

By now the two little ones had come running from the kitchen into the scullery and were crying with fright. 'Come along,' Fran said. ''Tis all right. A bad spring tide – no worse than we've had in the past. Let's go next door to see Gran.' But water was seeping underneath the back door. 'Help me, Ruby. Fetch that pile of newspapers in the box by the range. Hilda, give me the old towel on the copper.'

Together they rolled newspapers up and laid them along the floor and on top of that placed towels and old sheets kept for the purpose. Fran went to the front door, which was seldom used except when the vicar called. Lifting the letter box from inside, she saw that the path was just about visible in the front where the ground rose slightly.

'We'll have to put galoshes on, and our macs,' she said, trying to sound calm, but Ruby detected a croakiness in her voice which warned of her mother's fear.

They dressed up against the wind and rain before Fran dared to open the front door. When she did, it was almost ripped from its hinges. She held on as firmly as she could to Hilda and Babe, then gave Ruby a push so that she could pull the door behind her.

'Ruby, you go on ahead while I bring the little ones with me. Hold on tightly to the front wall. The wind is that strong, it'll blow you over if you don't take care.'

Hilda was crying, and Babe's frightened screams could be heard above the roar of the storm. They clung frantically to Fran's mac as she inched her way along the low garden wall behind Ruby. She must be mad to bring the children out in this, Fran thought, but her mother needed her as well. Normally, the short journey next door took a few steps, but now the little terrified party took three steps forward and were blown back two. Gasping for breath, soaked to the skin, and with water swirling round their galoshes, they finally reached the cottage door. Fran banged noisily, shouting: 'It's me, Ma. Let us in, we're like drowned rats.'

They heard the bolts being slid back and Gran opened the door, pale-faced and frightened.

'Fran! Oh, Fran, whatever's going to happen? Your father and Henry – they were going to try to get the stock up to the top field. Pray God they got up there in time.'

'Now don't fret, Ma. They'll have got up there all right. But it's a bad storm and no mistake.' Fran hurried the children inside and with her back heaved against the door to get it shut. 'We may as well stay with you till it calms a bit. I'll put the kettle on.'

They carried their dripping galoshes and macs through to the

12

scullery and then Fran filled the kettle with water from the single cold-water tap. With Babe still clinging to her skirt she carried it to the fire in the back kitchen. The rain beat against the small windows and the wind howled round the chimneys. She joined Gran at the window and watched the trees swaying crazily.

'I never ever saw anything like it before,' Gran Brown said with a tremble in her voice. 'I've seen the river rise and known gusts of wind howl round the cottage like a pack of angry wolves – but I ain't never seen a wall of water like that afore.'

'Spring tides, I suppose,' Fran said, but her thoughts were out on the land with the men. Cattle and sheep were most likely frightened out of their wits. Goodness knows where they'd end up if they started to panic and run this way and that. At sixty-eight, Pa wasn't as nimble as he used to be. He'd have his work cut out to control his flock with only the help of old Sukey, the sheep dog. Perhaps the other men on the estate would go to give him a hand. There was all the livestock to get to shelter and Henry would have his own job to do. But they were well used to the elements, she consoled herself. Her father knew no other way of life than here on the Dorset hills, and Henry had plenty of experience, having been raised on a big estate near Blandford where at the age of twelve he had been put to work in the stables. Fran tried not to dwell on her fears but she silently prayed for the men's safety.

When they could tear themselves away from the window, Fran got out the Halma board and the packet of Snap cards to amuse the children. Unable to concentrate, she left them to their own devices while she sat by the fireplace opposite her mother, sipping some much needed tea. They seldom spoke as they gazed into the red coals, each with her private anxiety, both too frightened to voice their alarm.

Fran got up hurriedly and lit the lamp on the table. Darkness had thrown a shadowy blanket round the cottage, shutting out the ferocious winds and the blinding rain from view. But nothing could blot out the noise of the storm. The children liked being in Gran's cottage but soon tired of playing games. Ruby watched at the window until it was too dark to see any more, then she let the curtain drop disconsolately. 'Daddy ought to be home soon, didn't he?' she questioned. 'And Granddad. Whatever can he be doing with sheep at this hour?'

Fran tried to motion her to silence, and by the unspoken fear that each saw in the other's eyes they acknowledged some sort of understanding. As they made fresh tea and set out the cups, Fran

13

suddenly noticed Ruby's hair. After getting a soaking it had become plastered to her head, but now that it had dried and fluffed up it was curly and unmanageable, barely reaching her shoulders.

'Why you ... you *naughty* girl – you've cut your hair!' she raged. 'Now what'll your father say? You'll be for it, my girl. No play for you and twice as many jobs.' Anger afforded an outlet to her worry.

Ruby began to sob. 'Marion did it. I didn't mean her to cut so much off.'

'Don't make excuses, I dare say you were equally to blame.' Fran turned to her mother. 'That wretched girl! Still, I suppose I can understand Prue Belmont, not having any children of her own. Trouble is, when you adopt a child you can't know what sort of background its real parents had. Prue's a good sort and she loves children so I suppose it's only natural that she's spoilt Marion – quite uncontrollable she is, but Prue only laughs.' Fran was red-faced with indignation.

Gran wasn't really listening, and after more reproach from her mother Ruby remained subdued. Even though the storm hurled its fury on the land, bringing down trees and old wooden buildings as well as the river torrents rushing over the landscape, she was too frightened of what her father was going to say about her hair to worry about the storm any more. He was so proud of the girls' hair and of the way Fran groomed and cared for it. Babe and Kate both had rich auburn-coloured hair like Fran's, but Hilda's, while jet black like Henry's and Lennie's, had a softer and silkier texture.

Suddenly there was a loud banging on Gran's front door.

'That'll be Henry and Dad,' Fran said, rushing out into the front parlour. 'I expect the water's too deep to get in at the back.'

Ruby felt quite sick at the prospect of what her father was going to say once he set eyes on her. And he'd notice – nothing ever escaped his keen, observant eyes. The sound of hushed voices wafted into the kitchen, where Gran pulled herself out of the armchair near the fire. She suffered from corns and calluses, which made her feet painful to walk on, so she couldn't hurry anywhere. Then Fran's voice echoed louder and with deep consternation. Ruby forgot about her hair. Dad! Granddad! Something was wrong.

It was the estate manager who brought Fran back into the room and looked at Gran with a solemn expression.

'Mrs Brown, we're all so sorry ... Henry did everything he could to save Edwin, but the sheep panicked and ran towards the rope bridge. Edwin was faithful to the last, trying to save the silly

14

creatures, but they were swept away in the current and Edwin
with them. Henry dived in after him but the river's a cruel force
to reckon with during a spring tide.'

'You mean – oh, you can't mean – not both of them! They'll
cling on somehow, they'll swim for survival – surely?' Gran gasped,
clutching the bib of her apron. Her pale cheeks turned quite pink and
then back to an ashen colour.

Ruby knew by the grave look on Mr Fry's rugged features that
it was too late for her dad and granddad. Poor Gran, she was
desperately fighting for self-control, and when Ruby looked at her
mother, she saw that her chin was trembling as she too tried to take
in the awful news.

The cottage and the old mill house, no longer used for grinding
corn, but a dwelling place for Henry, Fran and their children
for the past eighteen years, became a silent shrine of mourning.
Throughout the night Fran did her best to console her mother
while she struggled with the pain within her own breast. The past
seven years had taken their toll as she had been forced to come to
terms with her son's death. It wasn't fair, her heart cried out, to
lose her only boy, and now her father and husband in one day.
She couldn't bear it. Wasn't it more than a body could stand? For
hours she paced the floor, going to the girls when they cried out
in their sleep, brewing tea to try to ease their sorrow. Ruby had
taken it the hardest. She had screamed hysterically at the realisation
of what had happened to her father. Mr and Mrs Maitland from
Sherbrook House had visited and brought Kate home with them.
They had spent time talking with Gran, while Fran had explained
to the girls what had happened. Eventually she had persuaded them
to go to bed. Fran felt as if her insides had been gouged out of her
body. The emptiness was indescribable – yet the house was full of
sickened, heart-broken women.

Chapter Two

It was a cloudy morning when Fran went into the back bedroom to pull back the floral curtains.

'Draw them along again when you've dressed,' she said in a quiet voice and the two older girls remembered that today was the day of the funeral. 'Ruby, you'll have to wear Katie's old dark-blue coat — I know it's still a bit long for you but we must make do. Mrs Maitland has given me a grey coat of her mother's for you, Katie dear, and I've sewn the black diamonds on the sleeves for both of you. Now hurry up, and when we've had a cup of tea we'll all go and say goodbye to Daddy and Granddad.' Her voice broke and she hurried downstairs.

There was no conversation between any of them, only a still, silent thickness which seemed as if it would choke them.

Fran had her work cut out to get Gran ready. She wept and wailed persistently until Fran lost patience with her.

'We *must* get ready, Ma!' she shouted. 'The others will be here in a minute and you don't want Eric and Annie to get here and find you still in your petticoats.' Cruel though she knew it was, Fran realised that to mention her brother was the only way to make her mother move, and when she had fastened the row of buttons on her long serge jacket which nearly covered her full-length black skirt, she brushed her mother's white hair and rolled it into a bun before setting her black felt hat on the top.

'Make sure you've got a clean handkerchief in your bag, Ma, and you just sit quiet until Eric and Annie get here. The train should just about be getting into Blandford station now. Mr Maitland has kindly sent cars for all the family. I can't imagine how Henry's mother has taken it. After losing three sons in the war, now Henry — it only leaves Nathan and Sissie . . .' She had to rush away to hide her own grief. If only she could get away somewhere by herself and give way to her pent-up emotions, which she felt she must bottle up for the sake of the children. She had to be strong for the rest of them.

As soon as the cars arrived, bringing the relatives, Fran was caught up in the event, feeling as if it was happening to someone else. She did all that was required of her, feeling numb. Sherbrook and the surrounding villages were a close-knit community and stood by one another in times of trouble. Everything looked black as they prepared to take Henry and her father on their last journey. There were no motor-drawn hearses for Edwin Brown and Henry Sheldon, whose lives had been so dedicated to the land and farm animals, even though Mr Maitland had offered to arrange it. The local undertaker, a distant cousin of Edwin Brown, had been only too glad to offer his services with horses and carriages. The dark horses, their black plumes waving in the breeze, started the slow descent down the hill. Only the beautiful floral wreaths covering the two coffins, and on top of the large hearse, afforded colourful relief from the sombreness. When someone mentioned rain, Fran looked up and saw purple clouds in the angry heavens, and she wondered what could possibly have made God so displeased with her that he had taken two devoted men from the same family at the same time.

Tears fell unhindered during the emotional service and then the sorrowful procession made its way to the open graves in the church-yard. Fran was glad that her brother Eric was there to support their mother, and Nathan and Sissie to show compassion to Henry's parents, while she gave and found comfort with her arms around Kate and Ruby.

She felt a sob catch in her throat as the gravel fell on the coffins.

'Dust to dust, earth to earth, ashes to ashes ...'

Life seemed to have stopped for Fran, and yet it continued. The weeks passed with much weeping; both she and her mother had a lifetime of memories to sort out. Fran had of necessity to be the strong one and make unpleasant decisions, but she was able to vent her bitterness on much of the old worm-eaten furniture she had grown up with, which ended up on a bonfire in the garden. She guessed that some of the villagers would think she was a heartless creature, but she knew she couldn't afford to rent a large enough house in Brimdene to take the contents of two homes.

The Maitlands were kind, promising that there was no urgency for them to move, but Fran knew that the mill house and the shepherd's cottage were required for the new men and their families. She tackled the problem philosophically, grateful for the help given by Henry's parents and brother Nathan, who found the house they were to rent in Brimdene. It was the girls' future she had to consider now. Jobs would be easier for them to find in a town than here in the countryside. It was what Henry had always wanted for his beloved girls, but Fran had been reluctant on account of her elderly parents. Now here she was having to uproot her mother as well as herself and the girls.

No one would ever know how difficult each day was. Some days when she found herself alone she just sat and wept.

One Saturday morning, on a perfect June day, the sun brilliant in a cloudless sky, Fran looked out of the scullery window down the long garden towards the river where Babe was playing. It was difficult to believe that this was the scene of such a dreadful event only a couple of months earlier. She could still hear the roar and see the frothy wall of water as it coursed its treacherous avenue of greed. The only difference was that Ma's curtains were fluttering in a gentle breeze on the line today instead of the girls' petticoats, and the river was meandering along as if it was incapable of causing so much havoc. They were all going to miss it, as well as the peaceful sounds and smells of the countryside.

Fran strolled out into the sunshine and down the path to the water's edge. Babe was sitting in the long grass entwining reeds together, chattering non-stop as if she hadn't a care in the world. Fran couldn't understand why she hadn't wanted to go with Ruby and Hilda to play with Marion Belmont, but she had been adamant that she wanted to stay at home. Fran wondered what was going on in her mind. She had shown little reaction to her father's and grandfather's deaths. Come to that, so had Hilda. Perhaps they were too young. Nature had its own way of softening blows for those too weak to accept life's knocks. Ruby had taken it badly. She had nightmares as well as periods of hysterical screaming. Fran felt the wave of nausea churning in her stomach again. It crept up on her just when she thought she was getting the better of it, with the realisation that she had to shoulder all the responsibility alone, and that the change in circumstances would alter their whole lives.

The children had been Henry's life. He had adored each of them, and now he was no more ... swallowed up by the merciless tide and carried away, every breath sucked out of his lungs to be replaced by dirty water. Fran felt herself swaying at the picture, which refused

18

to fade. She'd be glad to get away from the river, whose cruel force tormented her, drew her into its very depths. Faces, not quite manifesting themselves in the ripples of water, blurred, disappeared, taunted her again ... In the distance she heard footsteps crunch on the nearby gravel path, then strong hands gently guided her backwards, away from the water's edge.

Strange flutterings murmured in her stomach and she blinked away torturous memories of the past weeks and months as she looked up at the stranger supporting her.

'Are you all right, Fran?' he asked with concern.

She stared in disbelief. 'Luke?' she managed to say, then laughed nervously. 'Heavens! Where did you spring from? I wasn't going to − do anything silly.' She tore herself from his grasp. 'I was daydreaming,' she said hurriedly. 'It's so lovely this morning, and the river is so calm − it's hard to believe that it can change its moods so quickly.'

'Fran.' His voice was gently scolding. 'I'm so dreadfully sorry. I know what you've been going through, but this isn't the answer.'

Babe placed herself between Luke and Fran, holding her mother tightly as if protecting her from this tall, arrogant stranger.

Fran faced Luke, embarrassed and indignant. 'Can't a woman stand and stare in her own back garden without some busybody thinking she's going to ... to ... run away from her responsibilities?' she said. 'I've got four girls who depend on me.'

'I'm aware of your situation, Fran, and that's why I came: to ask if there's anything I can do to help.'

Flushed and upset at his insinuations, but at the same time impressed that he should visit her, she said quietly: 'You'd best come inside.'

Luke followed her along the path and in through the back door. Fran went straight to the window to check that Babe hadn't followed too, then she led the way into the kitchen, where she turned on Luke. 'You shouldn't have come here,' she said heatedly. 'Whatever will people think?'

Luke looked nonplussed. 'That I've come to pay my respects in the very sad loss of your husband and father, Fran, I should think.' He took a step nearer her, but she placed her hands on the back of one of the high-backed dining chairs, indicating that he keep his distance. 'Fran,' he said, with genuine concern in his tone, 'I am *so* very sorry. It was a terrible tragedy for you and the children, and your mother.'

Fran gulped awkwardly, playing for time. 'A tragedy it certainly was,' she conceded, then covered her face with her hands, trying to

19

shut out the mental picture. 'I've never seen anything like it before,' she said in a trembling voice.

'The Maitlands told me about it. The elements can be so cruel, but I imagine it's not the first time you've been flooded here at the mill house?'

'We've had it lapping at the doors a few times and in a bad winter it saturates the garden, but I've never seen such fury in a tide before. Henry had just said that the river was running high, and as soon as he'd gone back to work the heavens opened and a wall of water came rushing down into the valley. It was like a bad dream.'

'You've had a rough time. And all the clearing-up to do when the river subsided.'

'I can't remember much about the clearing-up,' Fran said slowly. 'There's always silt left after a flooding. I ... I just don't recall who ...' She passed her hand over her brow, her eyes filling with salty tears.

'I'm sorry if I've brought it all back, Fran. The memory of that day must be horrifying. The water soon went down, according to Mr Maitland. It was a freak tide.' She hadn't thought to ask him to sit down but he pulled out a dining chair from under the whitewood table. 'My ship was due to sail a week ago, but more maintenance work needed to be done in dock so it gave me the chance to visit you. As soon as I heard of the tragedy I knew I had to come.' He sat down as if he meant to prolong his visit. 'I hope you won't think it's in bad taste to approach you so soon after Henry's death? Time is never on my side as I'm away more than I'm in this country.' He paused before saying: 'My thoughts are always with you, though, and what might have been – what should have been.'

'In poor taste!' Fran almost screamed the words at him. What was he suggesting? 'I'm grateful for your sympathy,' she acknowledged. 'But how can you dare to presume that I'd ever want to see you again after what you did?'

'That was years ago now – eighteen, nineteen – and we've both matured since then. I found it difficult to forgive you for marrying Henry and bearing his children after what we experienced that night. I thought you might at least have postponed your marriage to him until we had time to talk.'

'There was nothing to talk about then, and there's nothing to talk about now,' Fran said adamantly. 'I'm sick of you stalking me – yes, stalking me. Every time I go to the churchyard to place flowers on my son's grave you've been there before me. Why?'

'Why shouldn't I? Lennie was my son, not Henry's, and well you know it.'

'*Your* son?' she questioned. 'Don't flatter yourself, Luke. He was every bit Henry's son, dark-haired like Henry, with brown eyes.'

'But Henry had a sallow skin, and Lennie was pale-skinned like me. I have brown eyes too – he could easily have been mine.'

'I can't think why you haven't married and had children of your own,' she retorted impatiently. 'Why must you be so obsessed with my son?'

'Because I just know he was mine too.'

'I thought you had more intelligence than to build up such a fantasy, coveting what doesn't belong to you,' she said angrily, 'Lennie's been dead for seven years, and now my life is in a turmoil and you have the audacity to come here to torment me even further.'

'Fran, you know that isn't true. I came here to offer my heartfelt sympathy, and I mean that sincerely.'

'Now go, then,' she snapped.

'I realise how hard things are going to be for you,' he continued patiently. 'You have your mother to consider, as well as bringing up four girls by yourself – I only want to help.'

'You'll do that best by leaving me in peace. We're moving to Brimdene to be near my in-laws.'

'Then let me keep in touch,' he pleaded, crossing his knees, indicating that he had no intention of leaving just yet.

'I don't know where we'll be living. It's early days, and there's still a lot to be arranged.'

'Isn't there any way I can help you before I go back to sea?' he begged.

Fran gripped the chair-back with renewed ferocity. 'Go back to sea and forget me – that's what would help me most of all. Forget, Luke, *forget*!' she shouted, her voice trembling.

He gazed with deep affection into her beautiful blue eyes. God, how the memory of this petite, high-spirited woman had taunted him over the past few years. He admired her sense of loyalty, and he loved her all the more for her rejection of him now. It was surface rejection. The expression in her eyes told him that she wasn't averse to his attention although she would never admit it.

'I shall never forget you, Fran,' he said calmly. 'I'm sorry about Henry, of course I am, but hasn't fate intervened?'

'No!' Fran's voice was alarmingly loud. 'Just because of what happened when we were young and silly doesn't mean you can walk in here –'

'I have every right to walk in here and claim what's mine,' he interrupted. 'You were mine, Fran, before you were Henry's wife, and Lennie was proof of that.'

Fran's cheeks were bright red. She felt so angry she was sure she could have strangled him with ease. Yet the manner of the man was such that she knew she could turn to him for comfort.

'Indeed he was not,' she argued. 'Lennie belonged to Henry and me. You should never have come here, you have no claim on me at all.'

'It's sad that you'll be moving away from here, but I shall continue to place flowers on Lennie's grave whenever I visit Sherbrook. At least it proves my love and devotion to you and my son.'

'Don't you realise the embarrassment it causes? Haven't you any discretion? People notice things and are quick to gossip.'

'I'm not ashamed of my feelings for you. Maybe I am being too previous, but I want you to consider letting me look after you and the girls. I can give you more than Henry ever could – and I want to, Fran, I really want to.' Luke stood up suddenly and went to her, placing long elegant fingers on her shoulders as he looked deep into her eyes. Then Babe appeared from nowhere and leapt forward to get between them again.

'Hullo, Copperknob,' Luke said kindly, ruffling her curls. 'It's all right, I'm not going to hurt your mother.' He laughed sardonically, which only made Babe cling to her mother.

'You'd better go before the others come back,' Fran said in a low voice. 'It was kind of you to pay your respects.' She placed her arms loosely round her youngest daughter's shoulders. 'Times will be hard but we shall get used to managing alone.' She made her way pointedly to the front door.

Luke walked slowly behind her. He looked down at the red-headed child and jingled the coins in his pocket before offering some pennies to Babe. She smiled shyly, doubtfully.

'Go on, Copperknob, take them and share them with your sisters.'

Fran nodded, so Babe took the money while Luke searched his other pocket and found some sixpences.

'Here's one each for your money boxes. If you go to Brimdene to live you'll be able to buy ice creams at the seaside.' He took a step nearer Fran, but she countered by stepping back a pace. He smiled as he held out his hand, and when Fran hesitantly placed hers into his he kept hold of it tightly while he tried to pull her closer. Babe jammed herself against her mother's stomach and with a laugh Luke let go.

22

'You're well protected, Fran. But this isn't goodbye. I'll find you sooner or later, wherever you go. I suppose your brother will have your mother to stay with them once or twice a year?'

'I doubt that,' Fran said. 'Annie didn't want to have her now. Their lives mustn't be upset.' She sighed. 'We shall be all right. Ma will be a help with the girls.'

'And together your pensions will pay the rent? Is that the plan?'

'I dare say we shall manage our financial affairs satisfactorily. Mr Maitland has been very kind to us, but no amount of money will make up for the loss of my husband and my father,' she said. 'My task now is to do the best I can for my girls, to bring them up as their father would have liked. I worry about moving to Brimdene, of course I do,' she confessed. 'This is my home, where Henry and I have been happy — and had our sadness, too.' She sighed, finding comfort in being able to talk to someone other than the girls. 'If only I could have stayed on for a year or two ... But I appreciate the situation Mr Maitland is in. He needs the house for the new farmhand and Ma's cottage for a shepherd. It's just that ... well, this was one situation we could never have anticipated.' Fran groped in her pinafore pocket for her handkerchief. 'The hand of God ... and all that ... I suppose it could be His justice — although I didn't want — God knows!'

'That night, Fran, you wanted me as much as I wanted you,' Luke said slowly with emotion. 'If only we had met sooner! But you can't expect me to forget what happened between us now, any more than I have done all these years. You've been beside me in my dreams as well as in my waking thoughts.'

'There's such a thing as love, Luke Hammond. All you wanted was my body. There's also such a thing as class difference. There was never any question of a match between us.'

'Obviously not you you — but I went away and dreamed that one day we would belong to each other.'

Fran's cheeks were scarlet with fury. How dare he come here and talk so brazenly? And in front of Babe, too! Still, she was too young, thank goodness, to understand what he was saying.

'I think it's time you went.' Her voice was low, yet indicated the anger she felt.

Luke inclined his head. He was getting to her. He recognised all the signs of her weakening just as she had done before her wedding. If only he had been able to stop her marrying Henry! He didn't doubt for one moment that she had loved the good-looking little man from the brewery much more than she had ever loved him — then ... There was a lifetime, though, for him to make her change her mind. 'Please promise me that if ever I can be of assistance to you, Fran, you'll contact me. You've suffered enough – it grieves me to think of you having to struggle financially.'

'I told you, Luke, we'll manage. In the town the girls will have a good education and the opportunity to earn a decent living.'

'And you? What will you do? Go out to work?'

'At my age? What could I do? I can sew, and it will help if I just continue to make all the girls' clothes as I have done in the past. I'm forty-two years old, for goodness sake, and not always in the best of health.'

'You're very pale. Make sure you see a good doctor as soon as you settle in Brimdene. I shall find you, Fran, never fear.' He looked down at the small child clinging to Fran's apron. 'This one is a miniature of you. Her hair is a superb colour, and she has an abundance of it. As she grows older it'll get darker in shade similar to yours. Have none of the children eyes as blue as yours?'

Fran shook her head. 'No, they all have dark-brown eyes like Henry's' Her throat went tight and she felt herself swaying. She gave Babe a gentle push. 'Go out in the garden to play, Babe, it'll soon be dinnertime.'

The little girl seemed unwilling to leave her mother alone with the stranger, but she knew better than to argue, and after hesitating she skipped away, her lovely hair dancing down her back.

'I'll be staying overnight with the Maitlands.' Luke explained. 'Nicholas Maitland is coming from Portsmouth to visit his parents so I shall return there with him. It's been most fortuitous to have a close friend here at Sherbrook and I have been very discreet always, Fran. No one has ever seen me place the flowers on Lennie's grave. People sleep most deeply between one and three in the morning. I suppose I might have been in danger of being caught as a poacher, but sleeping ashore doesn't come easily after months away at sea.'

'Find yourself a nice woman from your own class who'll make you a good wife,' Fran scolded, reasserting herself. 'You're still in your prime, Luke, but you're deluding yourself if you imagine there was anything lasting between us, so go away and forget about me. Let me get on with the job of bringing up my children and looking after Ma.'

Luke shook his head sadly. 'If only you'd let me help – I really want to, Fran. I mean everything I say.'

'*No*! No, no, *no*!' Fran shouted in a sudden fit of temper.

Luke opened the door and left without another word. Fran sat down on the chaise longue – one that had seen better days, given to her by her previous employer, Lady Hinckley. She buried her head in her hands and wept as if her heart would break. For weeks now she had bottled up the real deep-rooted grief. Why should it have been Luke Hammond who caused the floodgates to open? She had suffered immense pain because she tried to hide the anguish of her loneliness. Even when she wept silent tears in the dead of night Babe would stir, sometimes cry out and cling to Fran as if she knew the awful despair she was experiencing. Now her tears were not only for Henry and her father, who, she could scarcely realise, would never be coming home again, but for the wrong she had done nineteen years ago. One night of lying beside Luke Hammond, did it really warrant such a ransom? Almost everything she loved had been taken from her now except her four girls. Her atonement must be to care for them, bring them up to love God and respect their fellow beings, to make something of themselves and to obey God's commandments. Tears and recriminations drained her, but she got up, dried her sore eyes and went out into the garden to fold the washing and peg it over the line to air in the warm summer sunshine.

Chapter Three

The move was arranged to take place at the beginning of the summer holiday when the school term ended. Ruby, Hilda and Babe were all excited at the prospect of going to live in a seaside resort but Fran's dread grew daily. She fretted for her mother, knowing the heartache such an upheaval would inevitably cause. There was Kate, too. It just wasn't wise to take her away from a secure position with the Maitlands until Fran was sure that work was available in Brimdene. She slept hardly at all from worry, and then only from sheer exhaustion. Night after night she stood at the bedroom window in her long nightdress, her hair in a plait hanging over one shoulder, her eyes filled with tears as she stared at the stars in the summer sky. Why should this terrible thing have happened to them?

The moonbeams glistened across the black water of the river and it seemed as if she could see Henry's face in one of the bramble bushes on the far bank. She knew it had to be a figment of her imagination, but he often came in the darkness of night, smiling his loving smile with arms outstretched to her. She regretted the times when she had rejected him. It was strange how, after all these years, she now experienced nights of longing, wanting to feel Henry's strong arms holding her, his exploring fingers arousing her latent passion. It was difficult to comprehend that she would never know such intimate union again. And it was even more difficult to realise that in another two days she would be gone from here for ever. She wanted to savour these memories. She clutched the front of her nightdress and drew in great gasps of breath, fighting for control. She mustn't give way, she must be strong for the sake of her children, but oh, the pain, the anguish, yes, and the bitterness. Wasn't taking her first-born enough? she demanded of God. Hadn't she suffered enough grief already? She clung to the brass knob at the foot of the bed and her body shook with violent sobs. No longer could she restrain them so she went in bare feet round the bed to the door where a shaft of moonlight guided her to the spiral staircase. Babe had stirred and she didn't want to waken her so she tiptoed down to the kitchen where she sat at the scrubbed whitewood table, rested her head on her trembling hands and let the tears flow in an unhindered stream. It seemed in her distorted vision as if they ran down the long garden, over the bank and into the river where they were caught up in the same current that had swept Henry and her father away from them for ever. Chilled, and weary with emptiness, she watched the pale pink dawn rise across the meadows and only then could she bear to go upstairs and lie beside the sleeping Babe.

Gran Brown watched the preparations for the move with trepidation. Moving from Sherbrook was going to be a dreadful wrench to her. She had lived in the village all her life, and her forebears had been faithful workers for the Maitland family over several generations. The girls all thought it was an adventure, but the mere thought of living in a town filled Gran Brown with fear. She tried not to let it show, but she wept many a silent tear during the lonely days following Edwin's death.

People were kind during these difficult days. Kate was allowed the day off to help Fran and Ruby as packing cases and furniture were removed from the two houses and put in the removal van. At sixteen Kate was old enough to experience a great deal of emotion at all that had happened recently. She was deeply hurt that she wasn't allowed to go with the rest of the family. It was all right at the Maitlands' and she had some good friends in the village but, like her dad, she yearned for a more exciting life in town. She was afraid for her own future as well as her mother's. Whispered conversations about her mother and what fate might have in store gave Kate cause for concern. Her worst fear was that having been left behind she would quickly be forgotten.

Fran placed an arm round Kate's shoulders as they watched the loaded van set off down the hill. 'Seems like the end of everything,' she said solemnly.

'A new beginning, Mum,' Kate said bravely. 'That's the way Mrs Maitland said we must look at it — but oh, Mum, you will let me come too, as soon as you can, won't you?' Kate's tears would not be suppressed any longer. She clung to Fran, crying hysterically, burying her face in her mother's bosom. Fran allowed this display of emotion to last a few seconds and then she pushed Kate away from her.

'Come on now, dear, this won't do. Prue will be expecting us for dinner. Wasn't it thoughtful of her to give us a meal before we go off to catch the train? After we've eaten I'll walk down as far as the church with you and visit Lennie one last time.'

'But you'll come back here sometimes, surely?' Kate asked with bloodshot, puffy eyes.

'Of course, whenever I can, but there won't be much money to spare, dear. Besides, Gran is the last of the Browns. There's no family left except us, and once we're gone the Brown family will be forgotten.'

Kate hadn't realised the wider implications of 'family' before. Now she vowed that she didn't ever want to be married and have family if it meant goodbyes. Splitting up like this was too painful. She couldn't bear it, and when they reached Prue Belmont's cottage, one on each side of Gran to help her along over the rough ground, she turned to her mother. 'I think I'll go on, Mum. Say goodbye to Hilda and Babe for me.' She turned to hug Ruby. 'You help Mum, mind, Ruby. I'll miss you all so much.' She kissed Gran and her mother, and without a backward glance hurried on down to the bridge. There she turned. They were all standing at the gate. She picked up the skirt of her coarse grey dress and wiped her eyes, then waved with both hands before continuing on her way.

Prue was sympathetic to Fran's plight. She was a cheery woman whom everyone loved, the local midwife. Now she did her best to comfort Fran and her mother, and later, after dinner, when the taxi came to take them to the station, she hugged her friend.

'Take care, Fran, and don't worry about Kate. I'll keep my eye on her. She can always come down to us on her day off. Brimdene's only twenty miles away. 'Tisn't the other side of the world. She'll have to get herself a bicycle. That way she won't have to spend out on train fares when she visits you.'

'We're going to miss you,' Fran sobbed. 'And ... and ... everyone ... and Lord knows how I'm going to manage with rent to pay and everything so much more expensive in the town.' She pulled away, her heartstrings taut with the strain of parting, but Prue held on to her hands.

'Sam and me, we meant what we said, Fran. If there's ever anything we can to to help, you know we will. Babe would be happy here with us if things get rough. You know we'd be good to her − it won't be easy for you until the girls leave school and get work.'

28

'But we'll stick together,' Fran said, bravely. 'Henry would expect that of me. The girls were Henry's life and now 'tis my job to raise them the best way I can. His dream was to move to the town, and we'll have Kate with us as soon as it's possible.'

As the taxi drove past the big house, Fran looked for some sign of Kate. Leaving one of Henry's girls behind was enough. She'd never part willingly with any of them.

Fran was agreeably surprised at the house her in-laws had found for them, but it took days to get it into good shape. It was modern with a lavatory and bathroom inside. Open grates instead of the usual kitchen range meant no more black-leading but she scarcely thought about the benefits. Would she ever get used to this being 'home'? It was as if she was on an extended holiday and any minute she would find herself going home to Sherbrook.

The roads were all well-kept, the houses neat with tidy gardens full of flowers and shrubs, and she knew that Henry would approve of the high position of the house even if the hill leading to it was a drag. She supposed her in-laws had remembered the flooding at the mill house when they chose this particular spot. They had been so good to her and at least she had been relieved of the worry of finding somewhere to live. Granddad Sheldon had even paid the first month's rent so that Fran could get herself and her finances sorted out.

It was amazing how quickly they drifted into a routine. Ma seemed to have accepted that her one room upstairs at the back of the house overlooking the garden was her final abode. She seldom complained except about her feet, and once she came downstairs in the morning she stayed there until after dinner was over and the washing-up done, and then she returned to her own room for a nap and quiet time. The break was not without distressing moments and Fran knew that she took some of the bitterness out on her mother, but she also knew that she couldn't manage without her. She was always on hand to help with the dishes and preparing vegetables, and in the evenings she sat and mended socks and repaired tears in the girls' underwear, while Fran cut out and stitched, tacked and fitted so that the girls were well-dressed. But the pain for each one of them remained. Ma wept openly when she was unable to hide it any longer. Fran could only give way when she was alone in her bedroom after a hard day's work when nothing seemed to have gone right.

The girls settled down in Brimdene quickly. August remained hot and dry and they were able to visit the beach on their own. Fran only accompanied them on rare occasions. While they were out of the way she could spend the afternoons sewing, making gymslips and blouses ready for the autumn term at their new school. But on the last bank holiday of the year they were all up early, packing bathing costumes and caps, food and drink to enjoy a day at the seaside with Prue and Marion Belmont, who were coming with Kate. They were all to meet at the Pier Approach and Fran felt a measure of excitement that Kate would be home for a whole week.

The day was bright with colour and seeing Kate again helped to put Sherbrook with all its past tragedies out of Fran's mind. Ruby and Marion were soon gossiping like a couple of hens while Kate was overjoyed to have Babe and Hilda skipping along at her side.

They walked along the promenade, away from the crowded pier, to where there were fewer people. When they found a nice clean space on the sandy beach, the girls dug a large hole in which to dangle their legs as they sat round the edge to eat sandwiches and drink lemonade, while Fran and Prue sat in deck chairs, catching up on all the latest news over a cup of tea.

'You won't be able to go into the water straight after eating,' Fran warned. 'Ruby, you and Marion can take the two little ones along to find the Punch and Judy show. It's near the pier. Babe will enjoy that. Here's a penny to put in the box, unless you can come away before the man comes round.'

Prue delved into her bag. 'Here you are, Marion, here's a penny for you as well, and on the way back buy ice creams for yourselves, and bring one back for Katie.' She put a shilling into a small cloth bag which Marion was wearing round her neck, and the girls set off.

Fran and Prue talked about everyday matters until Katie went down to the water's edge, and then Prue asked: 'How have the girls settled down, Fran?'

'Babe and Hilda don't seem too bad, but I can't do much with Ruby. She's persistently naughty, and aggravating beyond endurance.'

'She's the middle one, Fran. She'll grow out of these tantrums in time. She wants to grow up too quickly, like Marion. Poor mites, I think of you all so often, and Kate has looked so forlorn when I've seen her in the village. She was that excited today I thought she'd burst.'

'Any news from Sherbrook? I suppose our house is occupied?'

Prue fell silent and looked out to sea at the mist which hung on the horizon. She sighed. 'Yes, the new families settled in just a week ago. They seem nice enough folk. The shepherd is in his early forties, I should think, with two children, the girl is fourteen and the boy is seventeen. They say they're both clever, especially the boy.'

'The age to start work, then.'

'The boy helps his father during the school holidays, otherwise he's at some college or other. Haven't found out yet what he's studying for.'

'What about the girl?'

'They're trying to get her in at the big house. From what I've seen of them they think they're above letting her go into service, but what else is there?'

'I do want to have Kate come to live with us, Prue. She might be a good influence on Ruby. At least she'd be a help to me.'

'Have you made enquiries about work in the town?'

'There's always shop work, of course,' Fran said slowly. 'Then there's domestic work. Sissy works for the Neale family. They're the owners of the main shop in Brimdene, and they own a hotel as well. Sissy's going to put a few feelers out to see if there's any suitable job going for Kate, but don't say anything to her just yet. I don't want to build her hopes up if nothing comes of it.'

'I hope it does for her sake. She feels so left out.'

'I suppose boys will be the next problem with her. With Henry to take the responsibility it wasn't such a worry, but now I can't imagine how I'm going to cope with four of them.'

At that moment Kate came running up from the water's edge, waving to the other girls returning from the Punch and Judy show. On such a hot day the ice cream in the cornets they had bought was melting fast, dripping down their fingers as they quickly licked at each one in turn.

'I've had to lick some of yours up, Katie,' Ruby said, handing it over.

'You should know better than to do that,' Fran said sharply. 'Don't you understand we all have germs?'

'It's all right, Mum,' Kate soothed. 'If she hadn't I wouldn't have an ice cream left at all.'

Babe screamed as a wasp buzzed round her head.

'Kate, get her into the sea quickly. All of you, go on down to the water's edge and finish those messy things before you get stung.'

Prue got to her feet and helped Babe hurry down the sand and into the water. She had removed her shoes and stockings and was delighted to have an excuse to paddle with Babe, while Fran looked on somewhat disapprovingly. After that, the girls changed into bathing costumes with much giggling as they wriggled beneath large towels, and then they ran into the sea.

'Now you watch the little ones, Ruby and Kate,' Fran called, and at last she was able to relax in a deck chair to chat to Prue about Sherbrook, old friends, neighbours and memories.

Ruby and Marion returned to fill buckets with sand and water in order to make a sand castle, while Kate wandered off looking for shells. Fran and Prue dozed in the afternoon sun but woke with a start when Hilda started to shake her mother.

'We can't find our Babe,' she said. 'Mummy, wake up! Auntie Prue, Auntie Prue, Babe's gone!'

The two women were up in an instant, shading their eyes from the heat haze as they scoured the beach for any sign of the small red-headed child.

'Kate, you go left towards the small rowing-boat jetty, and you, Ruby, run along to the pier. She might have gone back to look for the Punch and Judy man again,' Fran said.

'Don't worry, Fran, she can't have gone far,' Prue consoled. 'I'll walk along too, and ask round among the people sitting on the beach.'

'Supposing she went out too far — out of her depth ...' Fran panicked. 'It's all Ruby's fault, I told her to watch out for the little ones.'

Her heart thumped anxiously against her chest and she felt as if she would explode. Henry would never forgive her if anything happened to his Babe. But there was no Henry. Fran caught her breath. Dear Henry, please find my baby, she begged, and then, feeling guilty, she found herself pleading to God. Waiting seemed like an eternity, and she dared not move in case Babe returned. Besides, there were their things to look after. Other people who had been sitting nearby joined in the search and Fran lost sight of Prue and the girls. It was amazing how quickly they merged into the kaleidoscope of colour and activity on the beach. Surely Babe would be quickly spotted by her hair? But there were several red-headed children playing on the sand.

Ruby ran, frantically looking this way and that. There was no sign of the Punch and Judy show and she stood gazing round, searching for the place where it had been. She was on the verge of tears.

'The Punch and Judy show man packed up and moved along to the Chines.' The delicate voice came from nowhere. Then Ruby found herself grasping the side of a long wicker carriage, something like a large pram. It took her a few moments to comprehend that in it lay a girl of about her own age who had spoken. 'And if you're looking for a little girl with bright auburn hair, she's just gone investigating beneath the awning round the pierrots' stage.'

Ruby couldn't help staring. How awful to be confined to one of these things, she thought, forgetting about Babe.

'Didn't you ought to go and fish her out?' the girl said with a bright smile. 'Don't look so worried. Children go missing all the time on the beach.'

'Thank you very much,' Ruby mumbled and went to where the pierrots' theatre was set up on the sand.

The man wouldn't let her go in the entrance without paying.

'I think my little sister's got in underneath,' she explained.

'Blinkin' kids,' the big man grumbled. 'Go on then, you can take a quick look, but be sharp, mind.'

Ruby felt acute embarrassment as she stood behind the row of canvas chairs set out for the audience. There, down by the stage, stood Babe, looking up in wonderment at the performance in progress. Outside, with the noise of people on the beach, it had been impossible to hear the out-of-tune piano that accompanied the pierrots, who sang and danced in their all-in-one costumes of white material, decorated with huge coloured pom-poms. Their tall dunce's hats bobbed, making the pom-pom at the end look as if at any moment it would fall off. Ruby was spellbound, too.

'Get a move on, missie. Is she there or ain't she?' the man asked roughly.

'Yes, but she's right down in the front,' Ruby whispered in a frightened voice.

'Just wait until this act has finished, then you can get her – but don't make a habit of this, mind. Next time you'll have to pay like honest folk do.'

If Ruby hadn't been so scared of the man, she would have enjoyed watching the pierrots, but she was thankful when the song ended and she could run down to grab Babe.

'Mum's ever so cross with you,' she chided. 'You mustn't go off by yourself.' As the big man held the rope aside for them to go out, he smiled and patted Babe on the head. Ruby pulled Babe along hurriedly to return to face her mother's anger. They passed the spinal carriage again and the occupant smiled cheerily.

'Thanks very much,' Ruby stopped to say.

'That's OK. You'd be surprised what I see from this position. Can you come back for a chat? I get lonely with no one to talk to, and people think I'm dumb, stuck in this thing.'

33

'I'll ask Mummy,' Ruby said, and she kept a firm hold on Babe as they ran back along the beach.

Fran didn't know whether to cry with relief or lash out at both Babe and Ruby.

'She was watching the pierrots, Mummy,' Ruby explained apologetically.

'You naughty girl,' Fran scolded. 'Don't you ever go off by yourself again. And you just keep a watch on your sisters better in future, Ruby.'

'She's found, and that's all that matters,' Prue said calmly. 'Nothing like getting a free view, is there, Babe?'

Ruby went on to explain about the girl in the spinal carriage who had watched where Babe went.

'I hope you thanked her properly,' Fran said, shading her eyes against the sun to look along the beach. 'Poor girl! It must be awful to have to spend a lovely day like this in one of those things.'

'I wonder what's wrong with her,' Prue said. 'Might be disease, or even a spinal injury caused through an accident.'

'She asked, could I go back to talk to her.' Ruby broached the subject hesitantly. She thought she knew by her mother's expression what the answer would be, but when Fran looked down at her she managed to smile faintly.

'Well, just for a little while. It must be so frustrating to watch other girls playing in the water and on the sand, and not be able to join in yourself. Mind your manners now, Ruby. Just for quarter of an hour and then come back. We don't want to have to go looking for you as well.'

Ruby could hardly believe her luck to be allowed to go away by herself and not have to look after the younger ones. So far, since they had lived in Brimdene, they were hardly allowed outside the front gate except when they went to visit the grandparents, or to go shopping. Ruby got the impression that her mother thought all kinds of danger lurked round each and every corner in the suburban area of Brimdene where they lived. She retraced her steps to where the carriage had been placed, just at the foot of a slope down to the silver-white sand. To her surprise the girl was now lying on her back.

'Hullo,' Ruby said. 'Can you turn yourself over, then?'

'No, my nurse or parents have to do it. I have to have an hour on my front every four hours. I prefer it on my front as I can manage to lift my head to watch what people are doing, but this way up all I can see is the sky. Come up this end so that I can see you. Did you get into terrible trouble or something? You looked scared to death.'

34

'No. I do usually get blamed for everything, but we were all anxious this time.'

'What's your name?'

'Ruby Sheldon. What's yours?'

'Anita Feltham. I'm thirteen, how old are you?'

'Ten, nearly eleven.'

'I expect you're wondering what on earth I'm doing in this thing – everyone does, but you're too polite to ask, so I'll tell you. I have a disease of the spine, which is why I have to live almost entirely out of doors. I have to lie flat all the time – but I am getting better, and soon, I hope, I'm going to learn to walk again.'

'How long have you been like this then?' Ruby asked, wide-eyed with curiosity.

'Six months. They thought I was going to die at first.'

'How awful!'

'I don't remember much about the beginning, I just found myself in hospital. I'll be half afraid to walk again, but it would be lovely to be able to swim and play ball on the sand like other girls.'

'Gosh! Can you really swim?'

'Of course, silly. Can't you? Whatever school do you go to?'

'We've only just moved here from Sherbrook. We went to the village school there, but here we're going to Cumberland Road Elementary School for Girls.'

'Then you must live quite near us. I started at the Infant's School in Cumberland Road.'

They exchanged details about each other and were joined by two women who had been sitting in deck chairs on the promenade.

'Hullo,' Mrs Feltham said, with a warm smile. 'It's so nice of you to come to talk to Anita. But I'm afraid we're going to have to go home now, dear.'

'This is Ruby, Mum. They've moved here from Sherbrook and she's going to Cumberland School. She lives a few roads away from us so can she come and visit, please?'

'Of course, dear – if her parents agree.'

'She hasn't got a dad. He was drowned in that dreadful spring tide we read about.'

Ruby began to feel awkward, but Mrs Feltham, who had appeared somewhat aloof to begin with, suddenly put her arm round Ruby's shoulders.

'Oh, you poor dear! It was a terrible tragedy – you're one of four girls then?' Ruby nodded. 'I'd like to meet your mother one day when you've settled down in Brimdene. Of course you can visit any time you like. You'll be good company for Anita until school starts.'

The other woman, who Ruby could see was a nurse, started to push the carriage up the ramp.

'Do come to my house soon, Ruby,' Anita begged.

'I will if I can, but I have my two young sisters to look after and I have to help Mummy too.' Ruby waved and skipped off down to the sandy beach again and back to where Fran, Prue and the others were packing up.

'Oh, have we got to go home already?' she asked.

'Afraid so, dear. Auntie Prue mustn't miss the train. I expect the trams will be crowded, it being bank holiday.'

They started the long trail back along the promenade to the pier-head again.

'It's been lovely to see you all, Fran dear,' Prue said, kissing her friend lightly on the cheek. 'Everyone in Sherbrook will be anxious to know how you are. You must come and visit us very soon.'

Fran sighed, and her chin trembled. 'It's a bit soon, Prue. I know I'll have to make the effort but I haven't got the courage just yet. There's still a fair bit to do in the house, and there's the girls' clothes to get ready for school. I don't like to leave Ma on her own for long, but thanks for the invitation.'

'Sam said I must be sure to invite you. You'll always be welcome at any time, and I know you'll want to visit the graves.'

'That's been the worst part of moving, leaving my family behind, but it gives me a reason for wanting to go back to Sherbrook — eventually.' They waved Prue and Marion off on the tram to go back to the railway station, and boarded another tram which took them nearest to where they lived.

This was the tiring part, Fran thought, when they reached the terminus. The children were very tired and hot, and the walk seemed endless, especially up the last hill. Their footsteps began to drag and Fran was forced to keep stopping to urge on Ruby and Babe who lagged behind while Kate and Hilda were way out in front. At last they reached the garden gate and Fran recognised her brother-in-law Nathan's bicycle propped up against the wall outside. He was a constant source of support, ever ready to advise. Just being able to discuss problems with him was a comfort.

The girls found extra energy when they realised that Uncle Nathan was there. They hoped he had brought one of their cousins with him on the seat attached to the crossbar, but when they went inside he was sitting on the sofa alone, talking to Gran Brown.

Nathan was Henry's double in many ways. He was a stockier

36

man and slightly taller, but his eyes always held the same magical, mischievous expression and the girls loved him dearly. It was the next best thing to having their dad back again, and he was quickly surrounded by them.

'Where's Sybil and Jenny?' Ruby asked.

'Has Andrew come with you, Uncle Nathan?' Hilda and Babe chorused.

'No, Andrew's in bed, and Sybil and Jenny have gone to a church picnic – they should be home by now. Kate, let me look at you – my, you're as pretty as a picture! 'Tis nice to have you home. Have you all had a good time at the beach? You're as brown as berries.'

Nathan enjoyed a playful frolic with them before Fran sent them off to bed, while Kate put her small case down and stood and stared. There was so much for her to explore, the house and garden – even the garden shed. 'Whose bike is this?' she asked enviously.

Nathan went out to the yard and looked lovingly at her. 'Yours, Katie. A present from your grandparents and me, to make up for not being able to come home to live just yet.'

'For me?' she questioned in disbelief. 'I . . . I can't believe it! Mum, is it true?'

'Yes, Kate – aren't you lucky?'

Kate thought there was a hint of disapproval in her mother's tone, and the frown prompted her to respond quickly with: 'Oh, *thank you*, Uncle Nathan. But I can't ride – will you teach me?'

'That's why we got it now, so that you can learn this week while you're home. It'll be up to your mother whether you take it back to Sherbrook or not. You can always take it on the train and it'll save you that long walk at the other end.'

'It's lovely – and it's really mine!' she breathed proudly.

Nathan helped her to sit on it and adjusted the saddle to suit her height. 'You must be able to reach the ground with your toe in case of emergency,' he said. 'I'll probably have to go on adjusting it until you've finished growing. I'll come and take you out each evening this week until you feel confident. Haven't you ridden at all before?'

'Only on that little bike your Sybil and Jenny had.'

'You'll soon get the hang of it.'

Her determination helped, and a few days later she was popping to visit her grandparents and going to do the shopping on her bicycle. She taught Ruby to ride as well, but the saddle was too high so she could only manage standing up. But that was good

37

enough to get her to Anita's house in the mornings when she had finished the jobs in the house, and their friendship blossomed.

The week's holiday passed much too quickly for Kate. If only she didn't have to go back to Sherbrook. But she knew it was no use to plead with her mother. Everything was different. She envied her sisters living in the town. Being parted from them all made her feel isolated, and she had to fight back the tears on Sunday at teatime when Uncle Nathan went with her to the railway station to see her off.

Nathan went straight back to Fran to reassure her.

'I just thought I'd look in on my way home to tell you that I put the bike in the guard's van, and saw Katie safely in a carriage with two elderly ladies,' he said. 'She'll be fine, Fran — don't worry.'

The tears began then, and Nathan gathered her in his arms. His jacket smelt as Henry's had done, of horses, hay and earth, and when the crying lessened she could feel his warm breath on the side of her wet cheek. He held her fast and she was grateful for the comfort of his embrace.

'I ... I'm sorry, Nathan — I shouldn't have ...'

'Isn't that what brothers-in-law are for?' he whispered softly.

She gave a small, weak laugh and pulled away, dabbing at her eyes furiously. 'It's just that I feel so guilty at having to send Kate back. Bad enough Henry and Pa missing without Kate not being able to stay here with us. I do hope Sissy will soon hear of something for her in town.'

'There's plenty of time, love. You've hardly had time to get your thoughts together yet, and at least Kate is safe enough with the Maitlands.'

'Sometimes it all comes over me like a great black monster,' Fran said. 'How on earth am I going to manage without Henry? I'm just not strong enough, Nathan.'

''Course you are, Fran, and we're always here to help. That's what families are for. We all miss Henry, but we'll stand by his wife and kids, that's for sure.' He kissed her tenderly, gave her a really warm hug and then turned and hurried out of the back door.

Fran stood there for several seconds. Poor Nathan, he had lost the last of his brothers, and his duty, after caring for his own wife and children, was to his ageing parents. There was Sissy, but Nathan was now the only man in the family to bear the family's burdens. He would have to be guide, comforter, even protector for Fran and her girls as well. It was good to know that he was thoughtful enough to be available whenever she needed him.

She didn't hurry to bed, although Sunday was the one night she

38

normally did. Knitting, sewing and mending were all put out of sight on the Sabbath and she hated Sundays of all the days of the week. It used to be the one day Henry had been able to spend with his family, so that day she missed him most of all, and the day of rest became a day of silent mourning. She eventually locked the doors, put out the gas lights and, with a candle to light her way, went upstairs. She knocked lightly on Ma's door and opened it a crack. ''Night, Ma. Sleep well.'

There was a pause and then a shaky voice answered: ''Night, Fran – and you, my dear.'

Another lump restricted Fran's throat. She knew she ought to go in and apologise for the harsh words she had spoken on so many occasions throughout the week, but she wasn't one to show affection easily. She closed the door softly and peeped in on each of the girls. At last she stood in front of her dressing table and peered at herself in the flickering candlelight. Her eyes were red, her cheeks pale and drawn.

So many cruel thoughts invaded her mind at times like this. Her mother might fall ill, or one of the girls, and what would happen to them if she should be taken ill? She turned to look at the sleeping baby of the family. She didn't like the idea of Babe occupying Henry's place in the big double bed, and she had tried to persuade her to sleep in the small room, which was really Kate's, but Babe had only stayed there for a couple of hours and then stealthily crept back to the comfort of her mother's arms. It was too soon for all of them to adjust to life without Henry. She had never thought what life would be like without the support of her man, but what wife did? Only perhaps a wife who was treated cruelly by her husband, and now she realised how very fortunate she had been. So often she had taken the decisions, cajoled Henry into doing things her way, and been the dominant one, but, oh, what wouldn't she give to have her man back to head the family as was his right? She had taken everything for granted and now regretted it. She undressed and lay on the top of the bed. It was a hot night, too hot to sleep, and she wondered how Kate had fared on her return journey. So much responsibility with so many of them dependent on her.

Sleep came in fits and starts, every sound magnified to startle her – the town sounds were vastly different from country noises. People would soon get to know that there was no man in this home. What would she do if an intruder forced his way in? A house full of women – it was a demoralising thought.

Chapter Four

The girls found the large town school awe-inspiring, but they soon settled down and within a few days Babe announced that she wasn't going to answer to 'Babe' any longer.

'My teacher says Barbara is much too nice to be shortened,' she said to Fran. 'You can call be Babs if you like, but at school I'm Barbara.'

Fran turned away with an amused expression. She remembered how besotted Henry had been with his darling Babe from the moment she was born. Now, here she was going to school and he would miss her growing up.

Hilda was the only one who appeared not to like school very much and she knew she could easily play on her mother's sympathy with imaginary aches and pains. Fran indulged her. She was the baby who had taken Lennie's place in her affections at the time of his death. Dark-haired, dark-eyed, she was so much like Lennie that Fran doted on her, and during the autumn months when loneliness overwhelmed her she was glad of any excuse to keep Hilda home.

Christmas was drawing near and Fran dreaded it. She wished she could go away somewhere and forget that it was the festive season, but she must do the best for her family just as Henry would have wanted.

'You seem a bit preoccupied, Fran,' Nathan said to her one evening. He had made a habit of calling in to see if everything was all right once or twice each week and Fran was grateful for his concern.

Hilda and Babs were in bed and asleep. Gran Brown and Ruby were finishing their Ovaltine. They said good night and went upstairs, leaving Fran and Nathan alone.

'There's a lot to think about,' she admitted. 'Ruby's in the Christmas play and needs a costume made, and Babs is going to be a cracker so we've got to concoct a crepe-paper outfit for her.'

'You'll manage, I dare say. You always do; in fact, you thrive on having plenty of sewing to do. You don't get out enough, Fran. It's good that you can make the girls' clothes but it gives you time to sit and brood. You should get out and about more.'

'Doing what, for goodness sake?'

'There's the pictures — that's all the rage nowadays.'

'Pictures!' Fran exclaimed. 'Nathan Sheldon, are you out of your mind? Can you imagine Henry allowing such a thing? He considered they'd be the downfall of this country.'

'Henry would have come round to it in time. He wasn't one to let the world pass him by, Fran. He loved life and everyone in it.'

'I don't need you to lecture me about Henry's likes and dislikes,' she said pointedly. 'Henry had strong principles, and we shall go on observing them just the same as he would have done.'

It wasn't the first time she and Nathan had disagreed. It seemed to lessen the tension that Fran could sense often existed between them. A long silence ensued before Nathan stood up, saying: 'Henry wouldn't have wanted you to fret, love. We must do what we can to give the girls a happy life, but you're still young enough to enjoy yourself too.' He squeezed her affectionately and made her prick herself.

'Oh, Nathan, careful,' she grumbled.

Nathan pulled the sewing out of her hands and tucked his fingers in the hollow of her armpit until she was wriggling helplessly.

'I can still make you laugh, Fran. Never forget that.' He kissed her cheek lightly, his dark-brown eyes boring into Fran's blue ones with an intensity that made her look away. He reached out and held her chin, forcing her to look back at him. 'We're kinsfolk, aren't we?'

Fran couldn't bear the expression in his face, which reminded her so much of Henry. She experienced a moment of unease, so she got up and went to the kitchen to make some hot chocolate, and they chatted about the Christmas preparations and arrangements for family gatherings. Nathan stayed on, sitting in the armchair opposite her. It was almost like being back at the mill house with Henry giving her his special persuasive smile. Fran tried to shut the memory out by glancing up at the clock. She noticed that Nathan followed her glance, his smile deepening. She wished that he would make a move to go home.

'Better think about bed, I suppose,' she said.

There was an intense silence. 'Then we'd better get on with it.'

41

Nathan's face was wreathed in smiles, his eyes a reflection of his thoughts. 'You must miss Henry, Fran,' he suggested.

'You know I do,' she answered shortly.

'I don't mean like that,' he said. 'I mean – well – you know ...' Suddenly he was kneeling down on the floor in front of her, his hands on her knees, pinching and groping. 'A lovely little woman like you, Fran, was made to be loved. I get all I want from Laura, but there's more to spare – let's call it comfort.'

'Nathan! Stop! For pity's sake, *stop*!'

'Ssh, your ma'll hear. Just a little harmless fun, Fran. Come on, you know you like it ...' He pushed her dress up to her thighs and struggled to get to her knickers. She fought wildly but somehow he found his way up inside the elasticated leg and with a snap the elastic gave way. There was no stopping him. He buried his head on her stomach to keep her still and with the other hand he pulled her knickers down. He was incensed with desire, urged on by the fact that she was unable to prevent him from thrusting his fat fingers inside her. No matter how much she cried out he refused to let her go. With every attempt she made to get out of the huge leather armchair his passion increased. She pushed against his massive shoulders but, like Henry, he had such power in his masculine body that she made no impression.

'Henry ... Henry ...' she implored on the verge of tears. Nathan paused, his breathing irregular as he stared up at her stupefied.

'Fran, 'tis me, Nathan – Henry's gone, love ...'

There were several seconds of anguished silence.

Fran, realising that her mistake had been a fortuitous one, pushed her skirt down and stood up so that Nathan's hands fell away. She gave him a contemptuous shove. 'Get up, you foolish man, and don't you dare try anything like that on again.' She calmly went to the couch where he had placed his overcoat and held it out to him.

'Go home to your wife, Nathan,' she said huskily. 'I just can't imagine what got into you, but you hadn't better try that on again.'

Nathan looked suitably rebuked as he took the overcoat and placed it over his arm. 'Fran, Fran,' he said penitently. 'Aren't we as good as related?'

'Only husbands and wives do what you had in mind. Where's your discretion, for goodness sake? My marriage was sacred to me, and Henry's memory will last much longer than a few months, a year, two years – for ever, I hope.'

He smiled as only a Sheldon man could. It would have been so easy ... For a second she had believed that it was Henry up to his old tricks, and her reaction was justified. First, the protests, then the surrender ... Dear God, how would she ever survive?

'I ... I thought you must be near crazy for it by now,' Nathan said half apologetically. 'And – if you ever feel the need ...'

'I shan't betray my sister-in-law's trust, that's for sure, Nathan Sheldon. You just get off home to her and realise how lucky you are. I had a good husband, and I bore him five children. These days, I've got too much else to think about to hanker after *that*!'

Nathan fingered the cloth of his heavy coat. 'You won't tell Laura, will you, Fran?' he asked sheepishly.

'I ought to, but as long as you behave yourself in future and be good to her as you've always been in the past, as far as I know, no one will ever hear anything from me.' She grabbed his coat from his hands, and held it out so that he could put his arms through the heavy sleeves. He took ages to do up the buttons, by which time Fran had gone to the scullery and was turning the handle of the back door. Nathan walked past her, barely touching her arm by way of acknowledgement. She closed the door after him and turned the key. She listened for the crunch of Nathan's boots on the gravel outside and after they had died away there was an eerie nothingness. She was trembling, partly with rage, partly with fear. She put the guard round the fire, intending to prepare for bed. If only Nathan knew how much her body did crave a man's touch, but not in that coarse, illicit, clumsy way. She needed to be loved tenderly for herself. To have someone share the burdens of everyday living. Someone to talk to in the evenings when the girls and Ma were all in bed. How could she feel so unutterably lonely in this house full of women?

Preparing for Christmas was little different from previous years. Only the surroundings had changed. Everyone rolled up their sleeves and gathered round the kitchen table skinning almonds, chopping cherries, picking over washed currants and sultanas, and seeding the raisins. Babs was doing the job she loved best, that of rubbing bread between her small hands to make the breadcrumbs. When she tired of being helpful she crawled beneath the table and secretly begged a currant from Gran Brown, who sat down to do her share.

In the midst of the activity there was a loud knock at the front door and Ruby was sent to answer it. Immediately the door was open, the sound of the Salvation Army band filled the house and all except Gran rushed into the hallway to sing along with the carols, while Fran cleaned her hands on her apron and hurried to find her

43

purse for a few coppers. This was a new experience for the girls and they loved it. Fran was apprehensive about the new experience for her of baking the large fruitcake in the gas oven.

'Won't be such a good cake, having to cook in that thing,' Gran Brown said, disparagingly.

'We've managed not to ruin anything since we came here, Ma, so I expect the cake will turn out all right,' Fran said.

To everyone's delight it did, in spite of Fran having to sit up until nearly midnight waiting for it to cook through. With the delicious smells that pervaded the house during the following days, and the buying and surreptitious wrapping of presents, the spirit of Christmas affected the entire household. Fran was kept so busy she had no time for self-pity or concerns for the future. The costumes were completed in time and the school concert, which took place on the last day of term, was a great event. Fran was quite proud of Ruby's performance, and Babe's too.

On Christmas Eve Fran took the girls into town. They visited the large stores crammed with people enjoying a spending spree and admiring the sparkling Christmas lights. Granddad Sheldon had given each of the girls the required sixpence to visit Father Christmas's grotto in make-believe Lapland, and they came away with small gifts.

If Fran felt a hollow emptiness at Henry's and Kate's absence over the festive days, she didn't let the others see it. She even bought a clockwork clown to hang on Ma's doorknob for Christmas morning just as Henry had always done. It was a small gesture of fun to please the children, and to carry on the tradition of Father Christmas visiting everyone. Thanks to Nathan, Fran found a net stocking at the foot of her bed containing some scent and soap, secretly placed there by Ruby who was taking on the role of elder daughter and trying her best to please her mother.

It was a happy occasion when Kate arrived home on Sunday morning just before morning service. Her cheeks were rosy but chafed, and her fingers were frozen after the long cycle ride from Sherbrook. Fran insisted on a drink of hot cocoa before they set out.

'I suppose they've kept you busy all over Christmas,' she said. 'Never mind, perhaps this will be the last Christmas you'll be there.'

'Oh, Mum, I do hope so,' Kate said eagerly.

'You mustn't bank on anything, though, Kate. There aren't too many jobs going at present, but Aunt Sissy is keeping her eye and ear open just in case. Now we'd best be off or we'll be late. There'll be a full church this morning, I expect. You can tell me all the news as we go along.'

Fran wondered about Luke Hammond and whether he would be home on leave at the Maitlands' for Christmas. She recalled treating him rather harshly when he had visited her after Henry's death, but it had been too soon – much too soon. Nathan had revived emotions and feelings of frustration, and the fact that she was still attractive to men brought a faint glow to her cheeks.

'I quite enjoyed the cycle ride,' Kate was saying. 'It was a bit cold this morning, but better than waiting about for trains. It's much quicker and I can go back whatever time I like.'

'But you mustn't leave it until it's dark, Kate. I don't want you about in the lanes late at night. You don't have to cycle back to Sherbrook. You can go back by train after tomorrow when they're back to running normally. Put your bike on the train, like you did when Uncle Nathan first got the bike.'

'I've only just got home, Mum.' Kate laughed. 'Don't let's think about having to leave just yet.' She pushed her gloved hand through Fran's arm and squeezed reassuringly.

Kate's time at home passed by all too quickly, and as a special treat Fran took the other girls to the station to see her off on the train. When they had waved her out of sight they went for a walk along the clifftop before going home through the park.

By the time the girls returned to school, the weather had become more severe with heavy overnight frosts, and often when Fran got up in the morning the mains water was frozen. Candles were lit and placed beneath the pipes to thaw them out, and small oil stoves helped to increase the temperature in the bedrooms. Fran's first job every morning, after a cup of tea to warm her up, was to clean the grate and light the fire downstairs. At least winter in the town didn't seem quite so bleak as in the country, and yet Fran missed being able to look across the river at the white-sheeted meadows. Icicles, like Christmas decorations, hung from gutters, and Jack Frost left delicately drawn patterns on windows everywhere, but the scenes were not as picturesque as in the Dorset countryside, where trees wore their winter-whites and tapering fingers of ice dripped tears in the weak midday sun.

Fran often woke in the mornings convinced that she heard the cows mooing as they went in for milking. It was usually five o' clock, the exact time when country people would be stirring to start the day's work. Somewhere inside her lurked the timetable she had been brought up with and every now and then it served to remind her of a pattern she was no longer part of. Whenever she

45

saw the corporation cart horses going back to the depot or setting off pulling ash carts, she thought of Henry and his love of horses. Not that she needed reminders; Henry was beside her wherever she went, whatever she did. She felt his influence and constantly used it to correct the children, but Sherbrook was slowly receding into the deepest crevices of her mind. She missed the river, and often imagined she could hear the rush of water on a rough day, yet at the same time she felt aggressive towards it, even hating it. She had felt tied to the gentry's way of life and had longed to be free of it, but there were times now when she wished she could go to the big house and ask for some minor repair to be done, or seek advice over some legal matter.

There was always Sissy, though, a tower of strength, more like a close friend than a sister-in-law. When one of the girls went down with a fever it was Sissy who came to her aid.

In spite of everything, Fran realised that she had a great deal to be thankful for, a nice home and a good family.

At last the dark days of winter began to give way to brighter mornings. While the wintry weather had given her a valid excuse not to return to Sherbrook, Fran knew that both she and her mother must find the courage to visit the churchyard on the anniversary of the tragedy.

It was a time of mixed emotions, each mile taking them back ... back in time to the day of the awful storm and freak tide. Fran worried that it would be too much of a strain for Ma, but Prue and Sam Belmont welcomed them warmly, and over dinner they never stopped talking.

Later, when they walked down to the graveyard, Fran felt a strange emptiness envelop her at the sight of the bare grass covering the mounds of dry earth. Previously she had experienced antagonism when finding evidence of Luke Hammond's visits to Sherbrook, but now it was as if even he had forsaken both her and Lennie.

There was nothing to remind anyone that any of them had ever been a part of this village except the black lettering on cold marble. LENNIE SHELDON, aged 10 years. HENRY SHELDON, aged 46 years. EDWIN BROWN, aged 68 years.

Some might say that Edwin Brown had lived the best years of his life, but sixty-eight wasn't old. Some country folk lived to be ninety and more. Forty-six was too young to die. It was cruel to take a man when he had his wife and children to provide for. And ten-year-old Lennie ... Fran openly wept as she savoured memories of her first-born, her only son. A tall lad for his age. Pale-skinned and dark-haired, quick-witted like his father, but a deep thinker. In solemn emotional moments Fran was almost glad that he had been spared the world's crude experiences. He had been too delicate, too caring to withstand the harshness of a cruel world.

When the fresh flowers were in position, brightening up the family corner of the churchyard, Fran suggested that they all stood in a circle round the graves, holding hands, vowing never to forget.

Inevitably some things had changed, but the visit was not as traumatic as Fran had feared. She could appreciate now that her town house in Brimdene was a vast improvement on the old mill house. She knew it was harder for her mother to accept, but even she must be grateful for the amenities of town dwelling. Fran and the girls were young enough to adapt to the new way of life – something Henry had hankered after. It was a sobering thought that through his death she now had what he had sought.

While the girls took themselves off to meet old friends, Fran was glad of the opportunity to ask after her eldest daughter.

'Is Kate well, Prue?' she said. 'Has she got over the fact that she had to stay in Sherbrook, d'you think?'

Prue made a grimace of doubt. 'She seems happy enough, but I fancy she harbours a grudge, Fran, which is only natural, poor child. Bad enough to lose her dad without the rest of her folks deserting her as well. It hasn't been easy for her.'

Fran wished with all her heart that circumstances and miles hadn't distanced them from one another. Kate was maturing rapidly. Of necessity she had become independent and Fran felt concerned for her and what effects the separation might have. She was the eldest and, with Henry gone and Gran's years advancing, Fran needed Kate as a friend now as much as a daughter. Kate must feel she didn't belong anywhere. She wasn't a schoolgirl any more but she wasn't really adult either. Where did she fit in?

'Does Kate visit you sometimes, Prue?' Fran asked.

'Quite often, and we see her in the village and at church. She misses you all. She's had no one to share her grief with.'

Fran sighed and went to stand outside the back door, watching the girls take turns on the swing at the end of Prue's garden.

How could anyone share their grief? It was a torment for each of them in a different way. She had to try to keep the hurt she felt from the girls, while at the same time understanding her mother's deep sorrow. The two little ones didn't seem to care, and that worried her as much as Ruby's rebellion or Kate's silence. It all seemed to fall on her shoulders. How she wished that she could

47

demonstrate her love to each of them better, to make up for their father's love as well.

Prue joined her in the doorway, and they strolled down the garden and across the meadow, still exchanging local news and remembering old times, until it was time to return and prepare tea.

Kate had come down from the big house on her bicycle so she set off immediately after tea so that she reached the station before the taxi bringing the rest of the family.

'You shouldn't have come all this way, Katie,' Gran said as they stood on the platform.

'I wanted to see you off,' Kate said. 'I like riding my bike and I shall be able to cycle all the way to Brimdene now that the weather is getting better and the lighter evenings are coming.'

'Everything all right up at Sherbrook House?' Fran asked Kate. 'We don't seem to have had much time to talk, dear, but now that we've been once we'll come again soon.'

Kate hugged her mother when they heard the train coming. 'I do want to come to Brimdene to live, Mum.' She had the distinct impression that her mother had shelved that idea for good. 'But it was nice that you all came to Aunty Prue's. Nothing's the same here, though. Mrs Maitland is very kind to me but I'd rather be with you. I'd like to get a proper job.'

'You've got a job, Kate, and that's important. You're much luckier than many of the town girls. I shall find it difficult to place Ruby when the time comes.'

With that Kate had to be satisfied. She kissed her sisters goodbye and waved the train out of sight. She didn't weep any more. It only made her feel thoroughly wretched, but she hated being the only one left in Sherbrook. Now the two-mile cycle ride gave her time to think.

She felt the separation acutely. It had been hard enough when the rest of the family lived at the old mill house, but now twenty miles seemed to isolate her completely. She knew she was lucky to have Aunty Prue, Uncle Sam and Marion, but they weren't real family, even though their cottage was the happiest place in the world. Aunty Prue was lenient with Marion, but they enjoyed a different type of friendship and were more like sisters, Kate thought. Kate wanted desperately to be close to her mother, to ease her pain and help her with family problems, but she only commanded obedience and respect, which kept Kate at arm's length.

Dusk was falling as she left the outskirts of Blandford to take the lonely country road that led to Sherbrook, and before long she had to get off her bicycle to switch on the front and rear lamps. To her dismay the rear one wouldn't work. The battery must have run out. Had she left it on inadvertently? The view of the deserted lane ahead of her was disconcerting. She didn't fancy walking; besides, it would make her late reaching Sherbrook House and both Mrs Maitland and Mrs Sturmey would be concerned. Despite the bangs she gave the lamp, twisting the knobs and removing the battery before trying it yet again, it still wouldn't work, so there was nothing for it but to ride on regardless of the consequences. The village policeman wasn't likely to be out at this time of the evening. He usually did his cycle round when the pubs and local inns closed, so she felt fairly safe to pedal away.

She hadn't gone far when she heard a hiss, the front tyre seemed to disintegrate and she realised the rim of the wheel was crunching on the ground. A puncture! It was her first experience of one. She gallantly pumped up the tyre with her pump and rode on for a few yards, but it quickly went flat again so there was nothing for it but to walk.

The lane became eerie. The leaves on the tall trees on either side of the lane, except where she passed an isolated cottage, rustled mischievously and occasionally the wind howled as if to torment her. She walked on, keeping in the centre of the road, all the while watching for hopeful signs of life where lighted lamps shone from cottage windows. She had never needed to be out alone during the hours of darkness when her father was alive. He had escorted her to and from Sherbrook House, but now she had to be brave and try not to be scared.

Surely the end must be in sight. The lane had never seemed quite so long as it did tonight. Then, out of the darkness, she heard the soft sound of movement behind her. Before she could look round, bicycles drew up, one on either side of her. She prayed that it would be the police constable, at worst a lad from the village, but she found herself looking at two boys with unfamiliar faces.

'What have we here then? Pretty little maid out on the prowl at this hour?' one of them jested.

'My rear lamp won't work, and I've got a puncture as well,' Kate said. She hoped that her voice didn't indicate her fear.

'What a stroke of luck, Maurice,' the other boy said. 'She can't escape and if she runs we can catch her easily on our bikes. You should make sure your bicycle is roadworthy before you go off to meet your boyfriend late at night.'

'If you must know,' she said hotly, 'I've been in to Blandford to see my family off on the train back to Brimdene.'

The boys laughed. 'A likely story! So why haven't you gone with them?'

'Because I work at Sherbrook House – that's why!' she declared impatiently. 'And they'll come out looking for me if I don't soon arrive there.'

'Another likely story.' They started to circle round and round her. 'Gentry folk don't pay too much attention to what their servants get up to. If you go out looking for trouble they can get rid of you and find someone else.'

'The Maitlands aren't like that,' Kate protested. 'They've been good to me and my family, especially when my father and grandfather drowned in the river.'

This seemed to silence the young men, but they still persisted in circling round her, getting as close to her as they dared. One of them tipped her hat forward, the other caught her back wheel and held her back.

'Oh, please, do stop,' she pleaded, trying to keep her voice steady. 'I don't even know you, so why can't you go on your way and leave me alone?'

One of them dismounted. He was very tall and lean with rugged features. He peered into her face. Kate tried to keep her bicycle between herself and him. 'Because we ought to get to know you better, miss. No girl who values her reputation would be out alone after dark. Come on, how about a roll in the hay? 'Course I can't pay you but I bet your boyfriend didn't pay for it either.' He leered towards her and laughed sadistically.

'You're only silly schoolboys,' she said crossly. 'What would you know about such things?'

'O-oh? What an invitation, Maurice! Let's show her, shall we? I'll hold her down while you get in, and then I'll have a go.'

'Don't be so coarse!' Kate snapped, but inside she was trembling, and in a moment she knew tears would be evident. She mustn't give way. She must show strength even if all she possessed wasn't sufficient to fight off these two burly farm labourers. The boy threw down his bicycle and made a grab for Kate, but she pushed her bicycle into his stomach.

'Come on, Maurice, let's get her down. What the devil are you waiting for?'

'No, Felix, *no*!' The other boy put himself between his friend and Kate. By his broad back Kate knew that he was the stockier of the two, but by his voice he sounded much less aggressive. 'Sorry, miss. We didn't mean to frighten you. Felix doesn't hold his drink very well. I'm sorry we can't help you with your bike, but it isn't far now to the big house.' He picked up his friend's bicycle and by his actions demanded that they should continue on their way, much to the disgust of Felix.

Kate just remained standing where she was. Her heart was thumping with fright when she considered what might have happened. She felt very alone and vulnerable, but thankful that one of them had come to his senses in time. She couldn't imagine who they were or where they were going, but the one called Maurice had mentioned the 'big house', which must mean he had connections locally.

After that each sound, each whisper of wind caused her to panic inside. However much she tried to hurry, her legs were wooden, refusing to be pushed at a faster pace. She didn't believe that the lane could stretch so far, but at last she was passing the woods that skirted the big house on three sides. Home was in sight somewhere beyond the trees. Suddenly she thought she saw a dim light in the distance. Perhaps it was the policeman going home after his round. In case it wasn't, she put a spurt on to reach the entrance to Sherbrook House before the rider, coming towards her quite speedily, did. The light grew brighter, and Kate caught her breath, fearful that it was this Felix returning to get what he had been denied before. No way now could she reach the entrance before the cyclist. Should she hide close up to the hedge? Would she be lucky enough to find a gap through which she could squeeze? Fear gripped her with such ferocity that she found she couldn't go another step. She just stood still and waited as the man emerged out of the darkness and skidded to a halt in front of her.

'Look, miss, I know just how scared you must be.' She almost sighed with relief that it was the young man called Maurice who had returned and not Felix. 'I'm sorry about Felix — sorry that we behaved so badly. I want to make it up to you by escorting you to Sherbrook House, if I may?'

'Humph!' she retorted. 'And what makes you think I trust you?'

'I realise how damning our behaviour was and I'm truly sorry. It's one thing to play a prank — but I've got a sister a bit younger than you, only fourteen in fact, and I would throttle anyone who did to her what Felix and I just did to you. It was unforgivable — you all alone on such an isolated road. I'll walk in front of you, or behind, whichever you prefer, but at least I'll be company for the rest of the way.'

'Not *my* company! Please yourself where you walk or ride, but I want nothing to do with you at all. Just keep your distance.'

He chose to walk on the other side of Kate's machine. She was breathing quite rapidly, and he must surely be aware of her fear.

They walked in silence, each with their own thoughts. Kate was wondering who he was, with his rather posh way of talking. He couldn't be of Dorset stock, she thought.

'My name is Maurice Lambert and my father is the new shepherd on the Sherbrook estate,' he said after a while, as if he had read her thoughts. 'I believe we live in your grandparents' cottage; well, my parents do with my sister. I'm away at college for most of the time. I'm still on Easter holiday at present.' He paused, evidently hoping that Kate would say something, but she remained mute until they reached the entrance to Sherbrook House. He placed his bicycle across her path.

'I've said I'm sorry and I meant it,' he said with hurt in his tone. 'You must be Kate Sheldon; I've seen you once or twice in church, though I would rather you'd introduced yourself. It may be a poor effort, but really, I am trying to make amends for myself and Felix. He's not so bad once you get to know him and as long as he hasn't been drinking.'

'I don't have anything to do with young men who drink,' Kate said haughtily.

'But we were out celebrating, in a mild sort of way. Felix lives in Croydon. We're mates at college in London, and he came home with me for a couple of days as we've just heard that we've passed the last set of tests we took before the vacation. It's been jolly hard work, I can tell you. Only natural that we were on the look-out for a bit of fun. There was no one interesting at the King's Head so I suppose we drank one to many – or at least Felix did.'

'I'm really not interested. What you do for fun is no concern of mine – or hadn't better be. The Maitlands are my guardians as well as Aunt Prue and Uncle Sam – and if *he* should hear about this you'll get a good hiding, most likely.'

Maurice didn't reply, but in the night light Kate could see two sparkling eyes which seemed to be laughing at her. She tried to push the bicycle round him but he moved with her.

'There is one thing I can do to make amends, and that is repair your puncture and get you a new battery for your rear light. Felix goes back to Croydon tomorrow so I'll be at a loose end. Please let me, Kate?'

His plea sounded so genuinely earnest that she was tempted to give in. 'Uncle Sam will soon fix it for me,' she said quietly.

'No, I want to. I insist, *and* I'll tell Sam Belmont how we met. If he gives me a good hiding, then so be it. I reckon I most probably deserve it, but knowing Sam, he'll understand. Oh, he'll rant and rave, but Sam knows I wouldn't be party to hurting any girl, much less do what Felix was suggesting. You're a pretty girl. Can't we at least part friends? I'll mend your bike and bring it up to the house tomorrow or the next day.'

Kate reluctantly allowed him to wheel her bicycle away alongside his own. At least she knew now who he was, and if he didn't return it in two days as promised, she'd tell Uncle Sam.

When she went in through the back entrance, Mrs Sturmey quickly accosted her with a few harsh words, but when she heard of the puncture she showed some sympathy. Kate went up to her small room in the attic and prepared for bed. After the fright came the anticlimax, and with it a strange feeling she hadn't experienced before. She washed her face and brushed her teeth at the small marble-topped wash-stand in the corner. She was getting so tall that she was outgrowing the little attic room, but it was the place she thought of as her own home. Here there was no one to spy on her. No one to know that when she took all her clothes off at night she stood before the cracked mirror on the back of the door to learn about her own body. She didn't need anyone to tell her that it was shapely. Her rich red hair, when let down from the earphones, fell over her naked shoulders and almost covered her firm, round breasts. Her dark-brown eyes burned uncomfortably as she found herself ruminating on Maurice Lambert while she brushed through her thick tresses. Why was she thinking about a young man who might have been excited enough through drink to take advantage of her? She began to think less angrily about him. He had, after all, returned to make sure she got home safely. He had a pleasant voice, he was nice looking ... Kate jumped happily into bed, curling up inside her winceyette nightgown, and enjoyed dreaming dreams ...

Chapter Five

The next day Kate found herself singing softly as she went about her work in the large mansion house. She didn't notice that Mrs Sturmey and one or two of the other servants eyed her suspiciously. She hadn't even been aware of how unhappy she had been over the past year, but now, all of a sudden, it seemed to the other staff that Kate Sheldon had shed her grief, or come to terms with the loss of her father, and had decided to make the best of her life. Perhaps, they thought, the fact that her mother, grandmother and sisters had paid a long-awaited visit to Sherbrook had made all the difference and they were pleased for Kate. A few days later, though, when a respectable young man knocked on the door of the servants' entrance and asked if he might see Kate for a few minutes, speculation changed.

'Only five minutes, Kate,' Mrs Sturmey said sternly.

Kate slid shyly through the door and closed it. 'You shouldn't have asked for me,' she whispered frantically. 'You could have left my bike at the Belmonts'.' She dared to face him and liked what she saw. He had a fresh complexion and was well-dressed, not spotty and dishevelled like so many of the estate boys. He was hatless, revealing a shock of black wavy hair with a high forehead — sign of intelligence, her mother would say.

'I've cleaned and polished it all up.' Maurice seemed to be nervous too, and for a few seconds they remained motionless, staring straight into each other's eyes. 'What time do you have off?' he blurted.

'Not much,' she said.

'I'm only home for the rest of this week. I'd like to meet you when you finish work tonight. We could go for a walk, couldn't we? I realise it can't be very nice for you, knowing that my family live in your grandparents' cottage, but I'd

54

like you to come home with me. Mum would make us cocoa.'

Kate shook her head. 'Mrs Sturmey doesn't like us to go out after dark,' she said.

'Then this afternoon. You get some time off, don't you?'

Kate didn't answer immediately. Then, throwing caution to oblivion, she said quickly, 'I must get back to work. This afternoon when I've written to my mum I shall go down to the post office in the village.'

She opened the door. They heard the crackle of a starched apron inside and Maurice whispered: 'What time?'

'Three o'clock. Thank you very much for mending my bike.' She shut the door decisively.

'And what did that young man want with you, may I ask?' Mrs Sturmey asked.

'He stopped last night to see if there was anything he could do to help. He walked me home, and then took my bicycle away to mend it, Mrs Sturmey.' The housekeeper grunted disapprovingly. 'He's the boy from the family who live in Granddad's cottage,' Kate explained.

'I know well enough who he is. Not the boy for you to associate with, young lady. He's a college lad. No good hobnobbing with clever folk who soon get above themselves. Don't do anything your father wouldn't like, Kate.'

'He only brought my bike back, Mrs Sturmey,' Kate replied indignantly.

'Good. Now you can get back to work, then.'

For a while Kate felt downcast at the housekeeper's attitude, but who was she to advise her about the choice of friends? The prospect of a further meeting with Maurice helped the morning along, and when the luncheon things were cleared away and the staff had eaten their own dinner, Kate went up to her room to write to her mother. In her neat, round handwriting Kate quickly filled a whole sheet, giving graphic details of her encounter with Maurice and Felix, until she came to the part where the unsavoury suggestions had been made. With flushed cheeks she tore the letter into shreds and began again. She mustn't say anything to upset her mother, so she related the incident in a casual way, explaining that she had a puncture on the way home and that the young man from Gran's old cottage had mended it for her.

Kate took special care with her appearance as she put on her warm coat and felt hat to walk down the road to the village. Even before she reached the bridge she could see Maurice waiting for her there, and as soon as he saw her coming he began to walk towards her.

His smile was full of genuine warmth as he greeted her. 'Hullo, Kate. I'm glad you came. I thought you might not.'

'I had to write to Mum so I had to come to the post,' she said indifferently.

'It's quite a nice day. Could we walk by the river?'

Kate shrugged. 'I s'pose so.'

'Oh! Was that thoughtless of me, Kate? It's a year since the accident. You must hate the river.'

'I often walk by the river because I can feel Dad with me.'

'You're very brave. I think I'd die if anything happened to my dad,' Maurice admitted honestly.

'It's a terrible experience — but you just have to get on with living. I thought I'd never get over it. I wanted so much to move to Brimdene with Mum — but I had to stay here. I shall eventually go when they can find me a job to do.'

'The Maitlands can't take my sister Carol yet. They told my parents that you might be moving away and then Carol could have your job.'

'Well, I'm sorry, I'm sure, if my staying interferes with your family's plans.'

'No, no, I didn't mean it like that, Kate. Gosh, you are touchy! It's just that Mum doesn't like her having to cycle into Blandford every day, but at least she's got a job, even if it's only cleaning for the family who own the brewery.'

Maurice waited outside while Kate bought a stamp and posted her letter, then they retraced their steps to the bridge, which they crossed. It seemed natural to take a leisurely stroll through the churchyard and out along the towpath.

'I can walk back to Sherbrook House this way,' Kate said, and Maurice asked about her work with the Maitland family.

The first signs of the late-arriving spring were everywhere. Along the bank primroses were in bud, and lamb's tails hung from trees alongside pussy willow. Birds displayed, mated, and called to one another in the sunlight while the smell of fresh growth rose from the earth. It wasn't long before Kate was talking amicably to Maurice with little hint of antagonism. The path wound through meadows and fields belonging to the Sherbrook estate, and finally they came to the lake.

'I'll have to go in now,' Kate said. 'You're on private property and no one must see us.'

'We aren't doing anything wrong, and I've asked Sam's permission to walk out with you.'

'Hmph! Cheek!' Kate exclaimed. 'How d'you know I want to walk out with you?'

Maurice smiled, a knowing, cheeky smile. ''Cos I says you do,' he said, with winning confidence. 'When can we meet again, Katie?'

'I . . . I don't know,' she said.

Maurice looked all round at the scenery, then he nodded. 'Is that a boat-house over there?'

''Course.'

'Then we'll meet there tonight at nine o'clock.'

Kate shook her head. 'No, I can't,' she said.

'Yes, you can.'

Kate couldn't explain why she didn't argue, and that evening was the first of many spent in the small wooden boat-house. They chatted about their respective families, and Maurice told her all about his life at college where he was studying to become an architect and surveyor. On the last day Maurice was at home before returning to college they spent Sunday afternoon together and Kate was invited to his home to tea. At first she felt uneasy, there were so many memories of her grandparents here, but Mr and Mrs Lambert understood. They were a happy family, doing everything to put Kate at her ease, and she was soon experiencing the loving warmth of her new friends. When Maurice walked her back to the big house after the evening service at St Stephen's Church, he pulled Kate back into the rhododendron bushes and held her tightly. One kiss led to another until she felt his passion igniting flames of desire in her.

His mouth sucked hers until it was submerged in the heat of his violent wanting. He urged her close to him until she felt something hard and throbbing pulsating against her body. With large, compelling hands he smoothed her back and caressed her young tender breasts. Then one hand groped beneath her clothes, clumsily seeking out the tops of her stockings until in fury he was tugging at her knickers.

'No! *No*!' Kate whispered frantically. 'What d'you think you're doin', Maurice Lambert? You aren't any better than your friend.' She tried to pull free, but with great gasps of breath he clung to her.

'Katie . . . Katie . . . I want to do it. I . . . *must* . . . oh, my God!'

Somehow his fingers found her bare flesh. Control was lost as he anguished inside the tightness of his trousers. Kate slapped his cheek in innocent confusion.

Maurice groaned. 'Katie, hasn't anyone told you how it is with a man?' he said after a few seconds.

'Man?' she questioned indignantly. 'What makes you think you're anything more than a boy? Just because you go to college doesn't mean you can take liberties.'

'I do have feelings just like any other man or boy of my age. Doesn't matter what you call me, Kate. Now I'm in a mess – it had to come, Kate. The feel of your skin – 'twas like velvet. Let me touch you again – please?' he begged.

In the fading light of the spring evening Kate's cheeks were scarlet as she said: 'No!' but with less protest than before. ''Tis wrong, Maurice. My mum would be furious.'

'She doesn't have to know. For goodness sakes, Katie, you've got to learn somewhere. I know you like me and I like you – more'n a bit. There'll be no harm – I can't do it again for a while – and I promise I won't take advantage. I'd never force you. I stopped Felix, didn't I? There were two of us that night. 'Twould have been easy enough – you must see that – but I like to treat a girl tenderly. I want her to want me. You've never complained when I've tickled you, or run my fingers up and down your bare arms.'

'That was different,' Kate snapped.

'So you only want the fun without getting serious? If you think anything of me, Kate, you'd want me to get some pleasure too. Let's go down to the boathouse – 'tis my last night.'

'No!' Kate paused, and the thought of not seeing Maurice for several weeks made her sad. She did like him a great deal. She wanted him to do all the things her imagination could dream up, but she had considered that they were her very private desires not experienced by anyone else in the whole wide world. 'We-ell,' she began, 'if you promise not to –'

'I won't do anything you don't want me to,' Maurice said, and with hands held tightly they found the narrow path which skirted all round the huge garden. A wooden seat spanned the back wall of the boat-house, and as they sat side by side and kissed in the darkness, the only other sound was the gentle lapping of the water against the sides of a rowing boat housed here.

'We could lie in the boat, Kate,' Maurice suggested.

Kate giggled at the suggestion and while Maurice steadied the boat Kate clambered into it.

'Take your knickers off for me now, Katie,' Maurice urged, but Kate shook her head coyly. She didn't object when he gently did it for her. As his slender fingers caressed the lower part of her abdomen she gasped with pleasure at the strange fluttering feeling inside her. Something far away was telling her that this was wrong but she had no inclination to ask Maurice to stop. It was as if something

58

very precious of Maurice's was being passed on to her. No one had ever touched her intimately before, though she had seen one of the estate men with his hand up a girl's skirt. Now she understood why the girl had writhed about on the barn floor, why the laughter had changed into heavy breathing and why the man had started to undo his breeches. In embarrassment she had left the barn then and tried to forget the incident, believing it was just the way men and women frolicked about the way her parents had done in the past.

As Maurice explored, Kate's breath ebbed away. She stretched her legs, then drew one up as the boat rocked precariously. Maurice forced her legs apart, placing one of his knees over hers. She quickly pulled her other leg in to collide with his, but he as urgently knocked it back and pushed it to balance on the edge of the boat.

'You won't feel anything with your legs together,' he whispered.

She couldn't believe anything could bring about such a warm glow to that part of her body. His actions were gentle, giving her a tingling sensation both inside and out, and then his fingers delved further . . . She arched her body to gain the full ecstasy of his caressing and suddenly she was wanting too – desperately, frantically – but she didn't know what, until she felt as if she were climbing a mountain where at the summit she panted, ached, enjoyed . . . and found herself losing control as she reached the pinnacle of excited frenzy. She moaned as if in a mystic trance as Maurice kissed her, still pleasuring her with the gentle rhythm of his fingers which had penetrated deep into her unknown depths. For several minutes they lay together in complete harmony.

'Can I do it now, Katie? I need to be inside you – let me have a memory to take back to college,' Maurice pleaded.

Kate struggled to sit up. 'A memory is one thing, Maurice, but you aren't going to leave me with more! You'll have to be patient – there's such as thing as marriage, you know.'

'I can't wait that long – and neither can you.'

'I'm not that kind of girl, Maurice. 'Twould be wrong – a terrible sin –'

'Not if we love each other.'

'It's too soon to say that.'

Maurice sighed. 'I respect you, Kate, and I'm sure I love you.'

'Only my body,' she said haughtily, suddenly realising just how far the petting had gone on this, their last evening together. 'We must be patient,' she said again.

He pulled her into his arms and she gave in to his cuddles. Passionate kisses were exchanged, but when the exploring began

59

again Kate put a stop to it. 'No,' she said. 'I shall bleed and then there'll be some explaining to do.

'Promise me that we will when I come home again? I'll bring a French letter with me, then you'll be safe.'

'Whatever's that?'

Maurice chuckled gently. 'A thing men wear to prevent a girl falling for a baby. It's a good thing I came along, Kate Sheldon, or you might have got yourself into real trouble with the first man who tried it on.'

'Like Felix?' she taunted.

'Felix won't ever touch you again. You're my Katie – *my* girl – agreed?'

They sealed their pact with a loving kiss. Kate put her knickers back on and Maurice escorted her as near to the house as he dared, then Kate ran under cover of shrubs to the servants' door at the back of the house. With a last wave to the void in the dark she let herself in, took her shoes off and crept up the stairs to the attic. She climbed on to the small wooden chair and peered through the lattice window towards the towpath where she knew Maurice would be walking home. She spotted his jaunty figure and when he turned and looked back towards the house Kate waved her white handkerchief. They went on waving until he was forced to carry on out of sight.

With mixed feelings of guilt, excitement, and disappointment that she wouldn't see Maurice now until the summer, she vigorously washed herself before getting into the narrow bed. She couldn't sleep as she relived the events of the evening. She thought of her mother's words about men taking advantage of her, but that was what Felix had wanted to do. Maurice was too kind to treat her brutally. He had saved her from Felix. What she and Maurice had done was natural if you felt anything for one another, so Maurice had said, so it couldn't be wrong. She could hardly believe that he had given her such ecstatic feelings, feelings that quickly rose to the surface even now when she thought of his hands caressing her. Feelings that were indescribably beautiful ...

Kate drifted into a happy sleep, and from then on watched and waited for the postman to bring her a letter from Maurice.

It was over a week later that Mrs Sturmey came downstairs at breakfast-time and handed Kate two letters.

'Your ma's from Brimdene, and – this one.' The housekeeper eyed Kate suspiciously. 'Hope you haven't been up to no good with that young Lambert boy?' she said, watching Kate's reaction.

Kate's cheeks burned uncomfortably as all eyes rested on her expression. 'I've only just met him,' she said nonchalantly.

'You behave yourself, my girl. Remember you're in my charge. Any trouble you get into is a reflection on us, especially Mrs Maitland. Think of your dear departed father, Kate. Don't do anything that would vex him or your ma.'

'There's no harm in just writing to a boy, is there?' Kate demanded.

'If a boy writes to a girl it usually follows previous assignations. Oh, I saw you skulking down to the boat-house with him a time or two.' Mrs Sturmey sniffed. 'Still,' she went on, 'it'll be light evenings when he comes home again so you won't get the chance to canoodle in the dark.'

She turned to leave the kitchen and Kate made a face behind her back. She wished that Mrs Sturmey hadn't mentioned her father, though. Somehow it took all the gilt off the happiness she had felt since getting to know Maurice better. She supposed she had better tell her mother that she was walking out with Maurice. It would be easier to explain in a letter, and suddenly the idea of being found a job in Brimdene lost its attraction.

Fran decided to take the girls to Sherbrook for the Whitsun Bank Holiday. She was eager to see Kate again as guilt heaped upon guilt each time she saw her. The desperate unvoiced plea of 'When am I coming to Brimdene to live?' was so evident in her expression. Fran felt the pain for her as her daughter's lovely brown eyes filled with unshed tears when goodbyes had to be said. She was fearful that Kate would harbour a grudge at having to stay in Sherbrook, away from the rest of the family. Now she had an ideal opportunity to go off for a days outing because Ma had gone to stay with Eric, Fran's brother, his wife Annie and their daughter May, who lived in Stockclere, on the Hampshire-Berkshire border.

The girls danced with joy to be back again so soon in their old village, and Prue hugged Fran, nearly suffocating her.

'I'm so glad you could come,' she enthused. 'There's so much news to catch up on.'

'Really? It's only six weeks since we were here before,' Fran said wide-eyed. 'Nothing ever happens in Sherbrook, so we always said.' Her face clouded briefly, remembering that something terrible had happened in Sherbrook, then she hastened to add: 'Is Kate all right?'

'Kate's in love,' Prue told Fran. They were sitting at the kitchen table enjoying coffee before going up to the barrow for a picnic.

Fran laughed. 'That all? Suppose it had to happen eventually. As long as she's not serious.'

'Your Katie is seventeen, eighteen come Christmas, Fran. Most of us were walking out steady by then, you know.'

'But not my Kate. She's keen to come to Brimdene to live. She'll meet lots of nice young men there. Who is this boy?' she demanded to know. 'I can't think of anyone local who would be suitable.'

'They're a very nice family, Fran. Come on, the girls are ready now so we'll talk as we walk.'

Each one was given something to carry and they went down the long garden, across the stile and along the narrow bridle path that led up to the barrow. Prue had reckoned that Fran wouldn't want to face going past the old mill house and the shepherd's cottage today.

'Come on then,' Fran pursued. 'Who is this boy?'

'The shepherd's son, Maurice Lambert. Poor Kate, when you were here last time she had a puncture coming back from the station. This young lad walked with her as it was getting dark, and then he mended it for her. It seems they hit it off right from the start and he came to speak to Sam about it before he invited Kate to their home for tea.'

'She didn't go, of course?' Fran retorted.

'Well, we didn't think you'd mind, Fran. It seemed better to agree than to have them meeting secretly. The Lamberts really are a very good family. Maurice is at college, he's very clever. Anyway, you'll be able to decide for yourself later on. He's home for a few days and he's coming up to the barrow with Kate so that you can meet him.'

Fran sighed. 'Goodness knows how I'm going to cope with all this on my own, Prue.' She tried not to think too much about her own courting days, and the unfortunate meeting with Luke Hammond just before she married Henry. Suddenly she felt afraid for Kate, but she knew she had to guard against being overprotective.

An old mackintosh of Sam's was spread out on the grass and then a rug. Prue began to unload the basket of food, and when Ruby shouted that she could see Kate coming up the hill Fran stood up to get a glimpse of this boy called Maurice. She felt wary of anyone new, and instantly began to wonder how Henry would have reacted at the news. 'No boyfriends for my girls until they're seventeen,' she remembered him telling a neighbour once. Kate was seventeen. A pretty seventeen at that, far too pretty for the stocky young man who presented himself to be introduced.

He offered his hand politely. 'Pleased to meet you, Mrs Sheldon,' he said in a quiet voice.

'This is Maurice, Mum,' Kate said breathlessly. 'They live in Gran's cottage. He mended my bike for me.'

Fran smiled, hugged and kissed her daughter. She was growing up and no mistake. There was a new bloom about her even since Easter. Whatever reprimands Fran had conjured up to try to end this friendship before it went too far, slipped unvoiced out of her mind. It was enough to see Kate happy, without the pain of rejection in her eyes. And even when the brilliant sunshine began to fade and Sam came up the hill as far as he could with a horse and old wagon to take them back to the station, there was no sign of tears or disappointment. The all climbed in and sang happily as they bumped over the gravel track down to the bridge. There they paused while Fran went alone to the gravesides of her departed family. No florist's bouquets again this time, reminding her that Luke Hammond must still be away at sea. Salty tears overflowed as she placed flowers in the vases. Some late tulips and lily-of-the-valley from her own garden in Brimdene. 'Not a very good show yet,' she whispered to Henry. 'The soil needs attention before we can get good crops. Never been cultivated before, you see, but I'll grow lots of flowers and vegetables. Be near me, my darling. I can't go on without you ...' Birdsong drowned out her sobs as she beat at the bare earth with her fists.

Kate wished the summer would last for ever. Maurice had come home to Sherbrook for six long weeks. He helped his father with the sheep, or Sam at the forge, and in the evenings he and Kate went for long walks by the river. They sometimes cycled far away from Sherbrook where prying eyes didn't see them lying together on the coarse dry grass. Kate learned to respond to his youthful kisses. She was frightened to let Maurice become too intimate even though her inner self longed for something more to happen. She didn't know what it was. She only knew that she was blissfully happy in Maurice's company, and grew close to him in spirit. When she wrote to her mother every week she mentioned Maurice in passing, but didn't enlarge on their growing friendship. Whereas once Kate had begged to be allowed to join the rest of the family in Brimdene, now Maurice had provided her with a very good reason for being content to remain working at the big house.

At the beginning of August Kate went to Brimdene to spend the bank holiday with the family on the beach. Maurice accompanied her and enjoyed the day's outing, but Kate stayed on for her week's holiday, and as the days passed she became impatient to return to Sherbrook.

Kate realised that there was something to be said for keeping her independence by staying in Sherbrook. Her mother made it quite plain that she considered Kate too young to be thinking seriously of Maurice Lambert.

'What do you think you know of young men?' Fran said derisively. 'You'll need to meet a few more chaps before you can make a choice – and you're far too young anyway. Your father certainly wouldn't approve.'

Kate had lapsed into silence. By Christmas she would be eighteen. Lots of girls were married at that age. She and Maurice talked earnestly about the future, but mainly in the light of Maurice's career. He had a few more years at college yet so marriage was out of the question. There was no rush except that they longed to be together for always. Aunt Prue said that it was a good thing that they couldn't be together all the time, that they must prove their maturity by controlling their feelings. She had even suggested that to go to work in a hotel in Brimdene might be just the thing for Kate, as with tips she could earn a better living with some to spare to save for the future.

'Your dad would be proud of you then,' Prue Belmont had said, and Kate could see the logic of that. Unfortunately, Aunt Sissy seemed to be a long while finding her a job, so meanwhile Kate had to be satisfied with things the way they were. She was content to return to Sherbrook after her holiday and not only because of Maurice.

'Mum's always going on about something,' she grumbled to Maurice. 'If she isn't nagging Gran, then she's on at Ruby or Babs. I know how hard life is for her, but Gran and Ruby do all they can to help.'

'It can't be easy for her, Katie,' Maurice said. 'I'll hate it if you go to live in Brimdene, but it won't be the end of the world.'

'Mum doesn't really approve of us walking out, you know. She'll always be watching us. I want to work in the town to earn more money, but at least we can do what we like here.'

'Not quite, my Katie,' Maurice said. 'We must think of our families. We're lucky in having good parents. Not like poor old Felix.'

'*Poor* Felix?' Kate echoed. 'I didn't like him much. Can't understand why you chose him as a friend, Maurice.'

'You don't understand, Kate. He's had a really rough time. It's made me appreciate my parents more than I did. His parents have split up, but no one likes to mention divorce. It leaked out at college, and some of the chaps have given him a hard time, which makes him aggressive. He's on the defensive all the time. He naturally feels let down. On the other hand he blames himself, thinking that it's something he's done that has caused the rift between his parents.'

'If he treats everyone badly he shouldn't expect sympathy.'

'He's not too bright, and finds college work difficult. His father expects too much, putting the pressure on all the time. I feel really sorry for him so I've done my best to be a good friend to him. I've tried to understand, but it's not easy with someone who picks a fight at the least provocation. He's taken to drinking too much and he can't hold his drink. One drink too many and there's always trouble.'

'As long as you don't get like him,' Kate whispered, and they indulged in meaningful kisses and petting until they were forced to go home.

The summer was over, yielding to autumn with strong winds and rain-filled skies, and Kate was left with nothing but happy memories. She exchanged letters with Maurice, bringing contentment which had to last until Christmas.

One day she was given an unexpected day off to go to Brimdene. Mrs Maitland, the lady of Sherbrook House, was too unwell to make the trip herself to fetch a new dress she'd had made at an exclusive dressmakers in the town.

'Mrs Maitland says you may visit your mother, Kate,' the housekeeper, Mrs Sturmey, said. 'You're a good girl and we all know how much you must miss your family. Take great care of the parcel, though, and don't leave it too late getting back as you'll have to walk from the station.'

Kate set off in high spirits. Mrs Maitland had given her a warm tweed cape which she had finished with, mainly because it was out of fashion. The neck edge was trimmed with fur and Kate found the matching fur hat at the church jumble sale.

Mrs Maitland got up from her sickbed to give instructions to Kate and was agreeably surprised at the young housemaid's appearance.

'My word, Kate, you do look smart,' she said. 'It's important to look nice as you're to visit my dressmakers, and I'm sure your mother will be pleased to see how grown-up you look. I've got just the thing to brighten up the outfit. You're only young, perhaps tweed is a trifle too mature for you.' She went away, to return a few moments later with a colourful square scarf.

'I want you to have this, and the brooch for your birthday, Kate dear. I know you won't be eighteen until nearly Christmas but you may as well have it to wear today.'

Kate could hardly believe how lucky she was. The brooch was gold, circular in shape, inset with brightly coloured stones.

The carter from the estate, on another errand for Mr Maitland, took Kate as far as the station in a horse-drawn wagon. Kate sat up beside him, fingering the beautiful brooch and feeling quite grand. If only Maurice could see me now, she thought.

It was one of the happiest days of her life. Fran was so surprised and delighted to see her that she gave up all her attention to her, making her feel really special. The girls were at school until teatime, by which time Gran had made a light sponge cake as a treat for them all. Ruby was envious of Kate's new clothes and such was the excitement that Kate almost forgot she had a train to catch. Hasty goodbyes were said as she hurried off to catch the tram, carefully guarding her precious parcel for Mrs Maitland.

Dusk was descending and the evening air was chill and damp by the time Kate reached Sherbrook. A fault in a signal box somewhere along the line had delayed the train by nearly an hour. She didn't relish the walk back to the big house, and wondered how angry Mrs Sturmey was going to be. She had promised that she would be home well before dark. She wished now that she had used her bicycle and left it at Mr Cutler's garage so that she could ride home from the station, but Mrs Maitland had said she looked too well-dressed to ride her bicycle. The real reason, Kate knew, was that Mrs Maitland thought her expensive new dress might get damaged if it fell from the handlebars. Kate thought she might have enough money for a taxi, but somehow that seemed wasteful, or she was sure her mother would consider it so.

By the time Kate crossed the bridge over the river in Blandford it was really dark. She looked down into its murky depths and felt a quiver of fear as she thought about the lane along which she must walk until she reached the gates of Sherbrook House. She wouldn't glimpse the river again until she was safely back in her attic room. It wasn't really late, she consoled herself as she stepped out bravely. She had anticipated that other people would be walking the lane too, and hoped that someone might offer her a lift in a cart or taxi, but tonight she was the only person going in the direction of Sherbrook.

She hurried along without meeting anyone. Then she thought she saw a dark figure ahead darting in and out of the hedge. It could be one of the farmer's lads out looking for a lost sheep or dog, but when she reached the place all was quiet and there was no one about at all. She breathed a sigh of relief when she came to the five-barred gate that led into the estate's home farm. Soon she would reach the wrought-iron gates to the main entrance, then she would be safe. A swift movement behind her as someone jumped the five-barred gate made her reel round anxiously.

A hand grabbed her arm in a vicelike grip. 'Hullo, Katie. It's me, Felix. Maurice's friend.'

A cold sweat broke out over Kate. Shock at the sudden appearance of anyone, fear when she realised who it was. Maurice didn't think so badly of Felix, she remembered, as long as he hadn't been drinking.

'W – what are you doing here?' she stammered, wishing he would release his grip from her arm.

'Just, um, paying a visit – to see you actually.' He was close enough to Kate for her to smell his breath, which confirmed that he had been drinking.

She had a horrible premonition that history was repeating itself, only this time there was no Maurice to protect her.

'I'll have to go in, Felix. Mrs Sturmey will be very angry as I'm so late.'

'But it isn't that late, Katie.'

Kate prickled at the use of her familiarised name. It sounded provocative coming from him, quite different from the way Maurice said it.

'It's late, and it's dark, and I'm tired so I'm going in.' She tried to assert herself, but instantly knew she hadn't a hope with Felix. He tightened his grip on her arm, and no matter how frantically she tried to free herself, she was ensnared. His strong arms encircled her until she could hardly breathe, and then he guided her across the lane to where a narrow bridle path led into an overgrown copse. 'Felix!' Kate yelled. 'For goodness sake don't be such an idiot!' Her cape hatched on a bramble bush, but he pulled her along, regardless of the ripping sound, until they were enveloped by tall trees and bushes. Her hat tumbled away on the damp grass as she fought in vain for freedom. The whites of his cold, venomous eyes showed clear in the night gloom as he flung her to the ground, falling on top of her heavily, winding her.

'This time I'm going to get what I want, so it's no use you fightin' and screamin', my darlin'. If Maurice can have it, then so can I.'

'Felix, you're hurting me. *Ple – ease,*' she begged, panting for breath, 'let me get up. Maurice hasn't – we haven't ...'

His reply was a fierce, wet kiss on her trembling mouth. She was pinned down, her arms useless under the weight of his knees. He pushed her cape upwards until it was a crushed heap across her chest, then, as his mouth ravaged hers, his hands groped and tore at her clothes. She was helpless, and gave a frightened scream as he pulled off her knickers. It was as if the lower part of her body had been severed from the rest of her, yet the pain was real enough.

Feeling Maurice's hardness through his trousers was exciting, she had learned, but the hairy, throbbing organ that invaded her filled her with terror. His pumping action seemed as if it would never end and the animal cry that accompanied the final thrust pierced the still, dark night.

Kate wept with humiliation as he flopped down on her exhausted. Her body, reviled with the warm, sticky substance of his lust, fought back, and in a new effort to rid herself of this violation she pulled the brooch from her cape and tore wildly at Felix's face with the long, sharp pin. His fearful cry as he rolled away from her remained with her all the way back along the bridle path. She raced across the road and up the drive to the big house, convinced he was chasing after her. Her first impulse was to bang on the front door, but some sort of sanity was returning in a hazy kind of way. She ran on again to the servants' entrance, then stopped short by the coal cellars and outside lavatory. No one must ever know what Felix had done to her.

Irrational thoughts twisted and turned until her brain felt weary and she slipped into the lavatory and bolted the door. Never could anyone have been so grateful for this new amenity as Kate was in that moment. It was one of the old wood stores converted for the use of the men who worked outside. Kate sat down on the wooden seat with an urgency to flush away all the contents of her inside, especially that which Felix had so cruelly bestowed on her.

She was so cold that her body shook uncontrollably, and then she held her breath as tiptoeing footsteps stealthily reached her keen hearing. Dear God, she thought, now I shall have to stay here all night. It had to be Felix. Prowlers were unlikely to creep about this early on a damp, miserable night, and the staff would be walking more briskly than this person. She waited, holding her breath in the total darkness, thankful that there was no light in the lavatory to give her presence away. From inside the house the sound of one of the dogs barking could be heard. The latch on the lavatory door was tried in agitation, and when Kate heard the back door being opened the footsteps rushed away.

'Anyone there?' Kate heard Mrs Sturmey's shrill voice distantly. A loud slam followed, and she breathed a sigh of relief that the dog had not been sent out to investigate. Mrs Sturmey would be expecting Kate, of course. Now what should she do? She called up all her reserves of courage, and decided that she must excuse her state of dishevelment by saying that she had fallen down. The precious parcel and her hat were left behind somewhere on the bridle path or in the copse. Mrs Sturmey would want to send someone to find them. What explanation could there possibly be for them to be on the bridle path? Kate knew that Mrs Sturmey was much too astute to be fobbed off with lies — and Kate had never told a lie before so she knew she wouldn't be very convincing.

The minutes ticked by. Kate became accustomed to the dim light seeping through the notched top of the door. There was even a wash basin here, so with a wad of toilet paper she managed to rid herself of the smell of Felix before she faced Mrs Sturmey. She couldn't bring herself to venture outside, but at length she knew she must.

With her ears tuned to even the slightest sound, she waited after drawing back the bolt. All was quiet, the loudest noise her own breathing, and she was sure her heartbeats must echo right out to the road. She closed the lavatory door behind her as quietly as she could, still trying to solve the puzzle of what to tell the housekeeper. Then, as she took a step surreptitiously along the wall of the house towards the back door, she fell over something. She went down clumsily on the gravel path, uttering a cry of fright, tearing her stockings and grazing her knees. One calamity after another, she thought, despondently.

As she pulled herself up she was amazed to discover that what she had fallen over was the parcel with her hat as well. She offered up a silent prayer of thanks. No lie was necessary now — she really had fallen over! But what of Felix? Had he known that she was in the lavatory or was he looking for somewhere to hide? The college term hadn't ended, so what was he doing here in Sherbrook? Kate was baffled, and terrified that he would seek her out again. Suddenly the back door burst open, spilling light out on to the path.

'That you, Kate? Where on earth have you been until this hour, child?' Mrs Sturmey's voice was high-pitched with annoyance. 'And what are you doing kneeling down there, for goodness sake?'

Kate struggled to her feet. She hadn't realised that she had only got as far as her knees. 'I ... I fell down, Mrs Sturmey,' she stammered. In spite of herself, Kate burst into tears.

'There, there, child. You aren't a baby now. Come on in and let's see what damage you've done to yourself.'

The housekeeper wrapped her shawl closer round her shoulders and came outside to help Kate.

'I ... I've had a dreadful journey, Mrs Sturmey, that's why I'm so late.'

'Oh, only your knees grazed,' Mrs Sturmey said unsympathetically. 'I expect you're chilled, and tired. I certainly am, waiting up for you. Just look at the state of you. How on earth did you manage to rip this lovely cape the missus gave you?'

'I ... I ... walked too near the hedge. It was a bit eerie down

69

the lane tonight. There was no one about.' Kate felt guilty that lying came so easily after all.

'Then no reason for you to be so scared, Kate.' She walked over to a tall kitchen cupboard and took out a bottle. 'Here, child. Put a couple of drops of this in the water and bathe your knees well. Better have an aspirin, too. Not like you to be so scared.' Now in the kitchen light Mrs Sturmey took closer stock of Kate, and made no secret of her concern by the fear in the young girl's eyes. 'You sure you're all right? No one made advances on the train, I hope?'

Kate shook her head. 'No, the guard kept his eye on me. I got worried when the train was so late starting off. I ... I thought about having a taxi home but Mum would have thought that extravagant.'

Mrs Sturmey sniffed haughtily. 'Should think so indeed! You know the lane is safe enough. You've walked it plenty of times. Now get off to bed so that I can do the same. Take your things up and then come down again and I'll have your cocoa ready. You can carry it up to the attic tonight for a treat. I'll have your hot-water bottle ready too. That'll warm you up a bit.'

Kate's knees felt stiff as she climbed the narrow attic stairs for the second time. She couldn't believe her luck in being given a hot-water bottle. Now at least she would be able to wash herself properly. She unscrewed the knob on the stone bottle and poured the water out into her china basin. She started with her face, neck and arms and worked her way down, horrified at the dried blood stuck to the tops of her stockings. She scrubbed every inch of herself with two lots of soap, and even then she didn't feel really clean. She put the empty bottle between her sheets to glean the last ounce of warmth from it, and, when she had taken the aspirin and drunk her cocoa, she blew out the candle and snuggled up in bed. But not to sleep for a further hour as she relived each horrible minute of Felix's rape of her virginity. What was Maurice going to say? He often talked affectionately of her youthful innocence, and how he longed to be the one to claim her as his very own, by breaking the last barrier of her maidenhood. Now she wasn't pure any more, and through no fault of her own. If her mother should ever find out ... Kate turned over, closed her eyes, covered her face with her hands and prayed God that she never would.

70

Chapter Six

Kate woke with a monstrous headache next morning. But still she got up at six o'clock and went downstairs for a jug of hot water. In the privacy of her attic room she scrubbed herself all over yet again before putting on clean underwear and the coarse dress and white cap and apron ready for the day's work. She had found her knickers tucked inside her bag. Her first instinct was to throw them away, but someone might discover them and questions would be asked. She thought of tossing them into the river but that idea was no better. Clothes were too expensive just to cast aside when they were perfectly wearable, so she put them in the bottom of a drawer until she could bring herself to wash them. She couldn't bear to look at them. They were a symbol of her lost virginity, a reminder of the hateful Felix. How on earth had Maurice, who was decent and kind, have ever got mixed up with such a fellow?

Kate went about her work in a daydream. Unexpressed anger added to her distress. She was afraid to leave the house or even go out to fill the coal scuttle lest Felix should be lying in wait somewhere. Then she remembered the brooch and the savage way she had scored his face. Revenge, such as it was, was sweet, even though a scratched face didn't make up in any degree for what he had done to her. She would never wear the brooch again, she vowed.

Her letter to her mother was short and strained that week, and she couldn't bring herself to write to Maurice. Even though she had received a letter from him the day before she went to Brimdene, when he failed to receive her usual reply he wrote again, hoping that she was all right. He added a postscript saying that Felix had been in trouble at college and had run away. No one knew of his whereabouts and the police had been informed. Maurice indicated that they were fearful that he might attempt suicide.

Oh, if only he were successful, Kate thought, and then in guilty desperation she knelt beside her bed and begged God's forgiveness. Maurice was concerned for his friend, and, after all, there must be some good in Felix since he had returned her belongings. Her only grain of hope was that he had taken himself as far away as possible from Sherbrook. In the kitchen she heard talk that the police had visited Maurice's parents in their search for Felix. Outhouses, barns and stables were all searched, and everyone in the village was advised to keep a lookout for anything suspicious.

Kate even found herself worrying about Felix. He knew about the bridle path and copse. Was it possible that he had made himself a hideout there? But if he had, what would he eat? There would soon be signs of pilfering from people's kitchens, she supposed. The concern for him seemed to overshadow what he had done to her. She would never, ever forget – how could she? – but as time went by the humiliation at least lessened, until, one morning early in December, she got out of bed and was suddenly sick. She gazed at herself in the mirror, waking up to the fact that what she saw was a mother-to-be!

In her wretchedness Kate contemplated suicide herself. How could she tell her mother? And, dear God, if ever she needed her mother it was now. She went alone to the graveside of her father and wept. How vexed he would be, but somehow she felt that he would understand. Her mother wouldn't. Kate could envisage her anger. She would be embittered at the disgrace Kate had brought upon the family. Kate's story would never be believed. All her mother would worry about was what the neighbours would say. Rain beat down on her head as she remained kneeling on the wet ground. Perhaps she could run away – but where could she go? And who would employ her carrying an illegitimate child? What was she going to do after it was born? The questions went round and round in her tired brain, but there were no answers.

'Katie?' At first Kate didn't hear the voice, then her name was called a second time and she looked up into Mrs Maitland's face. 'Kate, whatever d'you think you're doing kneeling on the damp grass, my dear?' Kate allowed herself to be helped up. Her hot, unhappy tears flowed thick and fast. 'You're shivering with the cold and you're soaked to the skin. Come along, let's get you back and into a hot bath.'

'It ... it's all right, Mrs Maitland, really. I meant to call on Aunt Prue ... b – but I stopped at D – Dad's g – grave ...'

'You can't go anywhere in this state.' Mrs Maitland placed protective arms round Kate's shoulders and hurried her through the churchyard back to the house. Mrs Sturmey rushed to greet them with motherly concern.

'Oh, my dear child, whatever 'as happened to you? Have you fallen again?' Kate was persuaded to sit on a whitewood kitchen chair near the range while Mrs Sturmey pulled off her shoes and stockings. 'These are wringing wet through, child,' she scolded.

Kate felt so utterly despondent that she wept and wailed as only her sister Ruby usually did.

'It's all right, dear. Best have a bath to prevent you catching a chill,' Mrs Maitland said kindly. Then, after an uncomfortable pause, she added: 'Is something wrong, Katie? Mrs Sturmey has already told me how worried she's been about you lately. You've been tired and listless, and unusually pale. It's more than grief for your father now, isn't it?'

With eyes and nose running profusely Kate looked up at her employer with a frightened expression.

'I ... I'm all right,' she said in a timid whisper.

Mrs Maitland sat herself down in the rocking chair opposite Kate, and Mrs Sturmey perched on the edge of the kitchen table.

'Come now, Kate, you aren't all right. You've been vomiting in the mornings. And I have reason to suspect that you haven't seen anything for well over a month. You haven't have you, Kate?' Mrs Sturmey pursued her questioning accusingly.

Their positive diagnosis, without Kate mentioning a single word to anyone, came as a shock to her. It was no use trying to hide the truth now.

'I − I don't want my mother to find out,' she said tearfully.

'Has that young Maurice Lambert taken advantage of you, Kate?' Mrs Maitland asked gently.

Kate shook her head vigorously. 'No! *No*! He hasn't been home. It doesn't matter who ... It was − an accident.'

Mrs Sturmey sniffed indignantly. 'Accident indeed!' she scoffed. 'Takes two, young Kate, and I must say I'm surprised at you. No wonder you don't want your mother to find out. She'll be that vexed, just as your dear departed father would have been.'

'You've betrayed my trust in you, Kate,' Mrs Maitland said with slow deliberation, and Kate looked up into the older woman's reproachful expression, knowing that she was being condemned for something that was not her fault. 'Your mother will blame us and so will Mr and Mrs Belmont. It's a bad business. You'd better tell me exactly how it did happen.'

Kate hung her head in shame. She had blamed Felix, but maybe she was the one who did wrong after all. She was confused, and now that the attitude of those she thought were trying to help her had changed, she felt as if she were on trial.

'I ... I can't say ...' she faltered.

'Why won't you name the young man? Why are you shielding him? You may be equally to blame, Kate, but he must share the responsibility. There'll be a baby to provide for in a few months' time. You won't be able to work, child,' Mrs Sturmey warned. 'How are you going to manage, I'd like to know?'

Kate continued to weep great tears of misery, which softened the hearts of both employer and housekeeper.

'I knew it,' Mrs Sturmey said, getting off the table suddenly. 'It was that night you came home late, wasn't it? What did you get up to, young Katie?'

'I – I was ... I – I ... was raped!' The words finally came out, and she cried uncontrollably.

'There, there, Kate dear.' Mrs Maitland tried to console her. 'We'll do all we can to help you – but you must tell us what happened.'

Kate shook her head. It was bad enough that she had been so ill-used – she couldn't bring herself to tell the story to anyone, let alone her employer. 'I can't tell you anything,' she sobbed. 'Please help me – *please*, Mrs Maitland – how can I get rid of it?'

Through her tearful gaze Kate saw Mrs Maitland look questioningly at Mrs Sturmey. They seemed to be communicating without uttering a sound.

'You go off to the bathroom, Kate, and have a good soak to get the chill out of your bones while Mrs Sturmey and I try to think of ...' Her voice trailed away almost guiltily. She ushered Kate to the door, and as Kate climbed the back stairs she heard the door close decisively behind her. They would have to send her home to her mother, of course. Instead of feeling relieved that the truth had spilled out about her condition, she felt in a worse dilemma than before. Never could she face her mother – never!

In a daze she went up to the attic room and fetched clean clothes, then she crept back to the lower landing where one of the bathrooms was situated. Hot water flooded out of the huge taps, creating a room full of steam. She took off all her clothes and paused while running cold water on top of the hot. She held her belly gently, then squeezed and with an anguished cry told her unborn child, 'I hate you, I hate *you* ...' and without thinking she stepped into the bath of hot water. The pain of scalding toes caught her breath, but she fought back any further cries as she endeavoured to sit down in as hot water as she could bear. Maybe, just maybe this would do the trick. She had heard some of the girls talking once about how to get rid of an unwanted baby. It was all too common an occurrence in service and hot baths were usually tried – but in vain, if the dismissal of Dottie and Mavis was anything to go by. Mrs Sturmey had given them all a good lecture after that. Instant dismissal, she had warned, and here was Kate in the same predicament.

The brass bell jingled noisily in her attic room while she was dressing and brushing her hair. She made haste to return to the kitchen to learn her fate, but there was quite a commotion going on between Mr Withers and Mrs Sturmey when she entered.

'Ah, Kate, be a good girl and lay up in the dining room quickly. Mr Nicholas has returned with Captain Hammond and some other friends. There's to be a dinner party. We're cooking dinner earlier so there's plenty to be done and not a moment to be wasted.'

Kate's condition evidently meant nothing now. Well, at least she wasn't being turned out on the streets immediately. There was little time to feel sorry for herself during the next couple of hours. Mrs Sturmey kept everyone running hither and thither while Cook became red-faced and harassed, her cap askew and flour settling like fine snow all around her. Kate was detailed to help Tilly in the dining room and for the first time was to help wait at table.

'Here, child,' Mrs Sturmey commanded, pushing a black dress in Kate's arms, 'try this dress on for size. Here's the apron and cap, then let me look at you.'

A few minutes later Kate reported to the housekeeper.

'Oh, very good,' Mrs Sturmey complimented. 'Very nice indeed.' Then she looked directly into Kate's deep-brown eyes. 'Oh, Katie, why have you let us all down so? You had a good position here – still, all is not lost. When you have your cocoa tonight I'll give you some herbal medicine. If that doesn't work, nothing will.' She waved a warning finger at Kate. 'I'm only doing this for your poor mother's sake, but, like the missus says, she'll most likely blame us for letting you go astray. How could you do it? You're nearly eighteen, old enough to know better, my girl. Now, be off with you and watch your manners, mind. If you get flummoxed, ask Tilly.'

This was the day Kate had dreamed of. A neat black dress with a white frilly apron and small cap to adorn her auburn hair, and the most grown-up thing of all were the black stockings. She kept asking Tilly to check that the seams were straight, and just before the gong sounded Tilly went over all that she thought Kate should know about serving at table.

They stood straight and still in front of the long oak sideboard as the family and guests came in for dinner. Captain Hammond accompanied Mrs Maitland, with Mr Maitland and a young lady walking behind. Mr Nicholas Maitland, the eldest son, was laughing amiably with a tall, very elegant young lady, and Gordon Maitland, the youngest of the family, followed with his sister Virginia. Dr Gibbs came last with another young woman on his arm, whom Kate hadn't seen before. Kate wondered if Mr Nicholas was about to announce his engagement or something since they all seemed in high spirits and were dressed up for the occasion. But nothing in the conversation indicated such a celebration. Mr Nicholas and Captain Hammond were simply pleased to be back in England in time for Christmas, and it appeared there was going to be quite a house party during the festive season.

Course followed course so that Kate and Tilly were kept busy. Their feet ached and Kate longed to kick off her shoes, but she knew she dared not, though no one would have noticed, she felt sure, because they were too busy laughing and chattering.

At last the men retired to their port wine. As Dr Gibbs passed Kate, he paused to light his pipe. Shaking the match to extinguish it, he looked at Kate and smiled. 'Well, young Katie, you seem to be doing very well, and how's the family? Your mother well?'

Kate bobbed a curtsey. 'They're all well, thank you, sir,' she said politely.

Dr Gibbs walked on towards the drawing room and Captain Hammond came up to Kate. 'I believe you must be one of the Sheldon girls,' he said. Kate noticed a twinkle in his eye, but not for her; it was just the effect of the many glasses of wine he had drunk with the meal.

'Yes, sir, I'm Kate Sheldon,' she answered demurely. Surely he must know that it wasn't ethical to address one of the servants? But there was something about this man's manner that suggested he was a law unto himself.

'You don't live with the family?' he asked.

'No, sir, not yet. I wanted to go to Brimdene with them, but work there is scarce.'

'Your mother has been through a very rough patch, Kate. Please give her my kind regards when you go home next time.' He sauntered on to catch up with the others. Kate heard Mr Nicholas make some remark about hobnobbing with the staff, after which there was loud laughter and then the door was closed, so Kate heard nothing more.

The clearing-up took the rest of the evening. She longed to go to bed. Hearing the family discussing Christmas arrangements had made her realise that she would soon be going home and her mother would notice that something was wrong. Her thoughts wafted to

Brimdene and her own family as they prepared for Christmas. Ruby, Hilda and even Babs would all be helping to prepare the fruit for the cake and puddings. Gran would seed the raisins, and her mother would wash and then push the small silver charms into the big family-sized Christmas pudding. There would be the usual rush to write cards, buy and wrap presents secretly, and decorate the house with holly and paper chains. And all the time the festivities would be marred by the fact that Kate Sheldon, eldest daughter of Fran Sheldon, was pregnant.

Kate thought she had never felt so weary in all her life, and in three days' time she would reach the age of eighteen. There was no anticipation, though, of a happy birthday this year. Her desperate longing to join the family in Brimdene to live had been overtaken by her friendship with Maurice, but now she was consumed with guilt and fear. She would open her cards and presents and have to pretend that she was happy, but no one, not even Mrs Sturmey, could know the heartache that was ripping her apart. Instead of looking forward to going home, she dreaded it.

At last all signs of the dinner party had been cleared away and the staff sat down to their own supper. Game pie had been on the menu and there was a good portion left, which was to be divided among the staff, but the mere smell of it made Kate feel nauseated.

'I'll keep a bit back for you, Kate. I'm afraid you caught a chill when you went out in all that rain today,' Mrs Sturmey said, covering up for her. 'Before you go up tonight I'll give you some medicine.'

'Can't miss an opportunity like this,' Tilly said enthusiastically. 'Never had no more than a morsel of game pie before.'

'And that you pinched,' Mr Withers said dryly.

Kate was too tired to eat much, but she pushed some food down to save any embarrassment. Later, when the rest of the staff had retired to their quarters, Mrs Sturmey gave Kate some revolting-smelling liquid to drink.

'Now you'll have to be on your guard, Katie,' she whispered. 'It may take a day or two to work and when you come on you'll have a flood, so be prepared, dearie.'

Kate closed her eyes and swallowed the potion in one go. She retched and had to swallow hard to prevent it from coming up again, but Mrs Sturmey had a piece of dry bread at the ready. 'Eat this quickly and the unpleasant taste will soon go off.'

'It won't do me any harm, will it, Mrs Sturmey?'

'Gracious, no, child. 'Tis only herbs. I can't promise that it'll do any good though. Depends how far on you are. If it happened that night you were so late home 'tis only about six weeks so you should be safe enough.' Mrs Sturmey sniffed and placed a restraining hand on Kate's arm. 'Whoever did it to you, Katie, don't you think it's wrong to let him get away with it? He'll try it on with some other innocent young girl. And if he's some wicked blackguard preying on young girls he'll stop at nothing, and 'twill end in murder.'

'He'd been drinking,' Kate said, then she turned quickly and made for the back stairs.

When she said her prayers that night she begged forgiveness for all the wrong she had ever done, and then asked God to make the potion work.

Kate enjoyed her birthday, feeling brighter and more hopeful than she had done for some weeks, but after three days there was still no sign of the medicine having done any good. Cook baked her a birthday cake with eighteen candles. She blew them out in one almighty puff, wishing that soon she would be relieved of the worry of an unwanted pregnancy. If only it would happen before she went home for the weekend ... The staff sang 'Happy Birthday', there were cards to look at and presents to open, and Mr Withers gave them all a drink of port wine to celebrate the occasion. Kate felt slightly light-headed by the time she climbed the attic stairs and she was soon drifting towards dreamland, trying to imagine the real birthday party she expected to have when she went home to Brimdene, and forgetting her condition and how she would find the courage to break the news eventually to her mother.

She woke suddenly, in intense pain. She felt cold, yet her body was wet with perspiration and she knew she was bleeding profusely. She sat up and with trembling fingers lit her candle. Blood was everywhere, far more than she had ever seen before, and she was terribly frightened. It felt as if her very lifeblood was being pumped out of her body. She must seek the housekeeper's help. Somehow she managed to totter down from the attic to the half-landing where Mrs Sturmey's room overlooked the side of the house.

'Mrs Sturmey, Mrs Sturmey! Help me, please,' she cried as she banged on the door.

Mrs Sturmey came out in her nightgown and switched on the electric light. It was a new innovation at the big house, which had not been extended to the attic rooms. The housekeeper appeared less sleepy than Kate had expected. She took one look at Kate and put her hands to her mouth. 'Dear God, Kate! I told you to be prepared. It looks as if someone's tried to murder you.'

She fetched a large bath towel and wrapped it round and between

Kate's legs, but still the blood poured down, staining everything in its wake. The last thing Kate remembered was thanking God for answering her prayer, and then Mrs Sturmey got smaller and smaller. As she receded into the background, Kate tried to find her voice to beg her not to leave her, but she could make no sound, and then there was nothing ...

From time to time she rallied enough to know that Dr Gibbs gave her an injection and Aunt Prue was with her – dear Aunt Prue, everything would be all right now. Voices, faces subdued in the half-light, Mrs Maitland's and Captain Hammond's coming out of the confusion.

'There's no time to wait for the ambulance,' he said. 'I'll take her in my car – maybe I'll meet them halfway, ring them and tell them to watch for me.'

'Aunt Prue,' Kate said weakly. 'Don't leave me, please don't leave me.'

'I won't, Katie dear. I'll go to Brimdene with you, never fear.'

Kate felt awful, but at least everything was going to be all right now. She drifted into unconsciousness again until voices began to haunt her. She felt herself being lifted and tried to protest.

'It's all right,' Aunt Prue assured her. 'You're being transferred to the ambulance. It won't be long now until we reach the hospital.'

'Kate, dear, can you hear me?' It was Captain Hammond's voice. Kate nodded, but she couldn't seem to open her eyes. 'I'll fetch your mother. Can you tell me her address?'

'It's all right, it's all right, I know it,' Prue said. 'I'm going with Kate anyway.'

'I want to fetch Mrs Sheldon immediately. She'll want to be with Kate, won't she?'

Prue had to agree with the captain, though why he was being so concerned she couldn't imagine. As she soothed Kate's brow and watched over the frightened, pale young girl, Prue could only wonder how much more Fran could take. She was a strong woman, no one could deny that, but the dreadful things that seemed to happen one after another were enough to put her into a mental institution. And this situation to a woman of Fran's integrity was the last straw. Girls of eighteen didn't haemorrhage to this extent unless a miscarriage was the cause – and Prue's midwifery experience told her that Kate was in a serious condition. She was losing her lifeblood – pray God they would reach the hospital in time.

Fran rubbed her fingers until the blood circulated faster. It was a cold, bleak December morning. When she let the blind up she saw that Jack Frost had been busy turning cobwebs into picturesque lace hanging from the roof and windows. Babs was still asleep, and it being Saturday morning she left her there while she went downstairs to clean the grate and light the fire.

'Can I help, Mum?' Fran was surprised when Ruby appeared behind her.

'My goodness, what's got you up so early this morning, and without being called even?'

'Brrr ... it's so cold, and there's a lot to do to get ready for Kate's party. I'm so excited, Mum. It seems ages since she came home.'

'I'll empty the ash-can, you lay the paper and sticks and get the fire going.' Fran managed to give Ruby a warm smile at her enthusiasm for her older sister. 'At least there's no black-leading to do,' she said meaningfully.

Fran put on an old overcoat of Henry's and went out into the back yard to the galvanised dustbin, where she emptied the ashes into a large, round sieve. She was shaking it vigorously when she thought she heard a car stop outside. Someone for Mr Blake, she supposed. Then came the unmistakable click of the front gate. This was followed by loud, urgent knocking. Kate? So early? No, couldn't possibly be, she thought, so she went on with wI.at she was doing, leaving Ruby to answer the door. A vague suggestion came into her head that it might be the gypsies who often called on a Saturday morning, selling lavender, pegs or flowers, but it was far too early even for them.

The back door opened. 'Mum, there's a gentleman to see you,' Ruby whispered frantically. 'Says it's very urgent. I've shown him into the front sitting room.'

'Good Lord!' exclaimed Fran. 'Who on earth would want to see me at this hour? Even the landlord wouldn't be this anxious.'

'No, Fran, I'm not the landlord.' The voice, usually so smooth and cultured in Fran's memory, though satiny soft now, held a more compelling appeal. 'I'm sorry to come at such an inconvenient time, but I happened to be at Sherbrook House when your daughter Kate was taken ill.'

'Kate? Ill?' Panic urged Fran to leave the ashes and rush inside the house, shutting the door firmly and standing with her back to it. She must be dreaming. Luke Hammond was here, tall and good-looking as ever, standing in front of her and telling her some unlikely story about Kate being ill. 'She can't be!'

'Fran – I'm sorry. Make haste and I'll take you to the hospital. Mrs Belmont is with Kate. She's had a bad haemorrhage, lost a great deal of blood. I just happened to be there ... She's your daughter so I wanted to help.'

'Ruby, go tell your gran and the others. See to the breakfast. I ... I'll ...'

'Fran, dear, you look as if you don't believe me. It's true — there isn't a kinder way of telling you. Kate needs you. Hurry, please.'

Fran found it difficult to get her thoughts in some semblance of order of importance. The shock of Luke arriving was enough on its own without the added worry of news about Kate. She pushed past him. Upstairs she quickly changed her clothes to something more suitable for hospital visiting, and then, picking up her bag, she hurried along to her mother's room.

'They've come for me, Ma. Our Katie's in hospital. I must go at once. Ruby's seeing to breakfast.'

She didn't wait for any reaction but joined Luke at the front door.

'I'm so sorry to be the bearer of bad news, Fran, but I want to be with you to support you. I'm sure she's going to be all right.' He ushered her out to his car, and, as they drove along the streets, deserted except for the milk cart and a coal cart starting on his round, Luke explained briefly what had happened. Fran barely spoke, except to give him directions. Shock had brought about some kind of stupor, while inwardly she was willing the car to go more speedily to the hospital.

'It's lucky you were at Sherbrook House,' she managed to say at last as the hospital came into view.

'My dear Fran, we invariably find ourselves in the right place when we're most needed. The Maitlands would, of course, have done everything possible for Kate, but I was there, and as I've told you before, sleep doesn't come easy after months away at sea. I like to think I would have acted the same way whoever was in trouble. Fortunately I heard the commotion and went to investigate. Dr Gibbs was already awake — no time was wasted.'

He pulled into the forecourt of the old Victorian hospital and a porter appeared at once to open the door. With a hand at Fran's elbow Luke guided her through the long corridor, following the porter's instructions to the ward where Kate had been taken.

A nursing sister met them at the door. 'Mrs Sheldon?' She was a petite young woman whose smile transformed an otherwise colourless face to warm radiance. 'You're just in time to see your daughter before she goes to theatre.'

'Theatre?' Fran echoed, her stomach muscles knotting painfully. 'What for?'

'Plenty of time for questions later, Mrs Sheldon. Just pop in and have a quick word. Kate is very weak as she's lost a great deal of blood, but she'll be pleased to see you if she's still conscious. She's had her pre-med, you see. Would Mr Sheldon like to come in too?'

Fran felt herself go suddenly cold, then her cheeks turned pink. 'Not my husband,' she said quickly. 'A very kind friend.'

'It's all right, Fran, I'll stay outside and wait for you.'

Fran turned back to face Luke. 'There's no need,' she said quietly. 'I'm so grateful, Captain Hammond, but I'll be all right now.'

He half raised a hand. 'I'll wait,' he answered positively. The sister led Fran into the long clinical ward to some screens just inside the double doors on the left-hand side.

'Katie? Oh, my poor Katie! Are you all right, darling?' Fran had the utmost difficulty in keeping her voice steady. The sight of Kate with cheeks drained of colour, contrasting against her chestnut-red hair framing the still, girlish face, gave her a dreadful shock. Kate's eyelids flickered, opened briefly and then closed again. But as Fran looked down at her daughter she noticed tears oozing from beneath her dark lashes. That was what made her girls so special, she thought in a moment of maternal admiration. Kate and Babs both had rich auburn hair like her own, but eyes and lashes as sable-black as Henry's. Fran placed her hand over Kate's and squeezed. 'I don't know what's wrong yet, Kate, but I'm sure everything can be put right,' she whispered in a trembling voice. The sister urged Fran away but Kate was grasping Fran's hand desperately. 'God be with you,' she added as her own strength surpassed Kate's.

'We're going to take her down now, Mrs Sheldon, so perhaps you'd like to come to my office.'

Fran followed meekly, her thoughts at last beginning to grasp the situation. Kate had suffered a massive haemorrhage, and the awful truth was dawning: her Kate — a miscarriage? It seemed the only explanation and yet she dared not, could not, would *not* believe it of her.

Outside in the corridor Luke was sitting on a bench beside Prue. Her friends were there to support her, that was a comfort — even if Luke Hammond was the last person she had expected to see. He raised his eyebrows in sympathy before she disappeared into the office.

'Sit down, Mrs Sheldon. Obviously this has been an enormous shock for you so a nurse is bringing a cup of tea — and one for your friend as well.'

'Is Kate going to be all right, Sister?'

'The surgeon will investigate her condition and do all that's necessary. I ... take it that you probably didn't know that Kate was pregnant?'

Fran shook her head solemnly as tears threatened. She wished the truth could have been delayed. She needed to hear it from Kate's own lips — and yet she knew that these medical people were hardly likely to make a mistake. 'I — I didn't know,' she sobbed, and the sister placed an arm around Fran's shoulders and patiently waited while the shock flushed out with hot, emotional tears.

'She could have lost her life,' the sister went on gently. 'But, thanks to prompt attention and a speedy journey here, she will be all right. As yet we don't have all the details. Kate is too weak to be questioned except for the relevant details, and we'll know more when the surgeon has completed his investigation.'

'I just can't believe it,' Fran said at last, and in faltering sentences explained her situation to the sister, who was deeply moved by the tragedy that had necessitated Kate's staying in Sherbrook.

'You mustn't blame yourself, Mrs Sheldon. Kate is eighteen, after all, and it does happen frequently.'

'Not in my family!' Fran exclaimed vehemently. 'What will my in-laws say and think? And my friends and neighbours?'

The sister was silent for a few moments, then she said: 'In cases like this we have to record the truth of course, but for the sake of propriety you are at liberty so say that Kate required an emergency appendicectomy.' The sister smiled. 'I'm sure that's the best idea.'

'I hate lies and deceit,' Fran mumbled. 'My husband wouldn't tolerate it.'

'But it's for Kate's good in the long run. She's the one who has to live with it.'

'She should be ashamed,' Fran spat out. 'I hope she'll have the grace to feel guilty.'

'Right now, Mrs Sheldon, she's lucky to be alive. I'm sure your late husband would be thankful that Kate's life has been spared.'

Fran's chin trembled. She felt sick inside. Of course she was thankful that Kate was alive — and Henry would have been philosophical in such a situation. There were things she needed to know, but that could wait until later. 'When can I see the doctor?' she asked humbly.

'Right now, Mrs Sheldon, I think it would be better if you went home with your friends. Give yourself time to get over the shock, and perhaps tomorrow when you visit Kate you'll be able to have a word with Mr Radcliffe, the consultant. Don't worry, Mrs Sheldon, Kate is in good hands. Now, do you feel up to giving me a few particulars? Kate's full name, your address, her date of birth and where we can contact you, should we need to?'

Fran's mind was not at all clear, but she gave the sister the necessary details. Then Luke and Prue helped her along the corridors and out into the forecourt, where the cold northeasterly wind chilled her cheeks and brought fresh tears to her eyes. She sat in the back seat with Prue but hardly spoke a word until Luke drew up in front of the house. Ruby ran to meet her mother at the gate.

'Is Kate all right, Mum?' she asked anxiously.

Fran reasserted herself. She wanted to rest her head against a masculine chest and weep for ever, but she was the head of this household and needed to show strong courage.

'We'll have to pray that she will be, dear,' she said with a calmness she didn't feel. 'An emergency appendix — she's in the operating theatre now.' She turned to Prue and glanced at Luke. 'You'll come in for a bite and something warm, won't you?'

They followed her in. She showed them into the back kitchen, where coals glowed red in the grate and a log hissed and spat.

'I'll put the kettle on,' she said. 'Please make yourselves comfortable. The front room is too cold to sit in.'

Ma was peeling potatoes, and Ruby set out the best china cups and saucers on an oak tray, while Hilda and Babs went to greet Aunt Prue and survey, not without some suspicion, the stranger.

Fran's energies would have been better spent, she felt, on swearing vengeance on that Maurice Lambert, who she felt certain was responsible for Kate's condition, but with the younger girls around she played the role of hostess to the best of her ability. An Irish stew prepared the previous day was simmering on the stove and Fran invited her guests to eat with the family.

'It isn't much,' she said. 'At least it will keep out the cold before you start back for Sherbrook. We were preparing a birthday tea for Kate, but we shan't be needing that now.'

'I'd like to wait to hear news of Kate to take back to the Maitlands,' Luke said. 'I'll be happy to take you back with me, Mrs Belmont.'

'I feel Fran needs someone,' Prue said. 'I could stay overnight if you need company, Fran. Sam and Marion can manage without me, same as they have to when I get a difficult delivery.'

Fran sighed. She knew they meant well, but what she really wanted was to be by herself to think and try to come to terms with what had happened. 'If only Henry were here,' she murmured disconsolately.

Ruby went to her mother's side and put her hand in Fran's. 'Kate'll be all right, Mum. I'll be good and do all I can to help. We'll be able to visit Kate in hospital, won't we?'

'Oh yes, please, Mummy,' Babs cried eagerly, not realising the seriousness of the situation.

'Fran's eyes filled yet again. 'Kate is very ill,' she said softly. 'But as soon as the doctor thinks it's all right, we'll all go to see her. Meanwhile you can write to her, of course, and draw her some pictures.'

Fran went out into the scullery where Ma had brewed the tea. She carried the tray into the kitchen. 'Come on, Ma, have a cup of tea with us.'

Gran Brown was pleased to see Prue, but doubtful about Luke Hammond's presence. There was something in his dark, bewitching eyes that was just that bit too mysterious, yet he had offered his services gallantly and helped to get Kate to hospital quickly. She felt an atmosphere in the kitchen as they sipped their tea in silence. Fran was hiding something, she could tell, and was bursting with it. Maybe she should be grateful for the visitors' presence in preventing an outburst.

'You have to ring the hospital at two o'clock, I believe you said,' Luke commented. 'Can I take you to the telephone box? You don't have the telephone yourself?'

Fran grunted. 'Heavens, no! And I can't use a telephone. I'll have to see if my neighbour will help me out. He's a policeman and has been very good to me since we came here.'

'I'll phone for you, of course, Mrs Sheldon. There's no need to bother your neighbours. There must be a telephone kiosk nearby.'

'Yes, in the next street. I don't like imposing on you though, Captain Hammond. I'm sure you must be wanting to get back to Sherbrook.'

She endeavoured to sound officious but in truth was grateful for Luke Hammond's help.

'I want to know how Kate fares first, and if there's any way in which I can help further you have only to say.'

'You've been most kind as it is, but you intended to spend your leave with the Maitlands.'

'It's only a short leave now as I'm hoping to return to Sherbrook for Christmas, then it's a three-month trip to the Mediterranean.'

'I meant what I said about staying overnight, Fran,' Prue said. 'Or I could take the two little ones back to Sherbrook with me until things have settled down here?'

Fran answered without hesitation. 'No, you've both been very kind but I can't impose any more. It was nice of you to accompany

Kate to the hospital, Prue, and it's lovely to have you here for a bit, but your family needs you. I'm over the shock now. I've got to prepare myself for when Kate comes home. She'll have to convalesce for quite a while. I must write to Mrs Maitland later on.' She sighed, and looked directly at Luke. 'Perhaps you'd be good enough to thank her from me, for seeing to Kate, and tell her I'll be in touch as soon as we know that Kate is well on the road to recovery.'

'I'm sure she'll want to visit you herself, perhaps when Kate comes out of hospital, but that won't be for at least two weeks, I should think.'

'Mrs Maitland will be busy preparing for Christmas. This couldn't have happened at a worse time.'

Fran busied herself in the scullery, and with Gran's and Prue's help made the meagre Irish stew stretch to feed the visitors and themselves, with plenty of fresh, home-grown vegetables. They had hardly finished eating when Luke reminded Fran that it was almost two o'clock. She felt less strained now after eating the hot food, and there was more colour in her cheeks, but she was in no hurry to contact the hospital. Or was she feeling inadequate because she had been forced to admit that she couldn't use a telephone? Back in the village of Sherbrook there had been no need of such things, and since coming to live in Brimdene she had come to rely on kind neighbours.

'I'd really like to freshen myself up before I go anywhere,' she said. In the bathroom she locked herself in, and while she washed she fought back more tears as she considered the disgrace Kate had brought upon them all. Whether family, friends or neighbours ever found out or not, she would know that Kate had cheapened herself, given her body to the first young man who made demands. Luke's presence here reminded her all too clearly of a certain Christmas party when she had not behaved with as much decorum as she should. She had been disloyal to Henry – and paid a high price. First Lennie, then Henry and Pa, and now Kate in trouble – was there no end to the burdens she must bear? And alone, that was the worst part.

Chapter Seven

The news, when Luke was put through to the hospital ward, was that Kate was back from the operating theatre and was comfortable. She was not allowed to have visitors until the following day. Luke insisted on Ruby accompanying them to the telephone kiosk, and he did his best to show both Fran and Ruby how to use a public call box. Fran was still too on edge to take in what he said, but Ruby quickly picked it up and was able to follow the written directions.

'Just make sure you come with plenty of pennies,' Luke warned, 'as sometimes the phone is out of order. If the operator can't get a reply, she'll tell you to press button B to get your money back before she asks to you try again later. It's quite simple really, and when you've done it once or twice you won't be afraid of it. Then you can teach your mother and sisters.'

Fran was grateful for the trouble Luke was taking to help them, but she was glad when they took their leave. Ruby was sent hotfoot to tell her other grandparents and Aunt Sissy, but Sissy was at work until the next day.

Fran couldn't settle to doing anything, even though there was so much to prepare for Christmas. She knew she had to carry on for the sake of the girls but the burden in her heart was heavy. Everyone was sympathetic and help came from many quarters but Fran was obliged to keep her secret to herself. There was no one she could turn to or confide in.

Kate was frail-looking when Fran visited her the following afternoon. It was Sunday so she went alone while the girls were at Sunday school. The buses had all been full so Fran felt tensed up even before she arrived at Ward 14. Luke had thoughtfully gone out to buy flowers for Fran to take to Kate before he left, but Kate hardly opened her eyes.

'How d'you feel dear?' Fran asked gently, stroking the slim, limp hand.

Kate's eyes flickered and she opened them briefly, but it was as if she couldn't bring herself to look at her mother. 'I'm sorry, Mum,' she whispered huskily, and tears trickled down her cheeks.

'We've weathered a few storms, Katie dear, and we'll get through this one, I dare say. All we want is for you to get well quickly, and come home to us.'

After that there didn't seem much to say. Fran explained that she had brought a clean nightie and some toilet things, but Kate continued to lie still and silent as if she were waiting to die. After a while the sister came on duty and asked Fran to go to the office.

'Your daughter has had a blood transfusion to replace some of what she lost. She might well have died but for the prompt action in getting her here, Mrs Sheldon. You have a lot to thank them for, whoever it was, but Kate is not out of the wood yet.' The sister turned her head to gaze unseeing at papers on her desk and Fran knew that there was more to come. 'Mr Radcliffe will see you himself on Tuesday, but he asked me to tell you that she may never be able to conceive again. She had been quite violently used, Mrs Sheldon. He suspects that internal damage was incurred before the bleeding commenced. She's too ill at the present time to be questioned, so he particularly asked that she be allowed to remain undisturbed for the next few days. She's feeling lonely and hurt. The anaesthetic causes sickness to add to her troubles – but we'll do all in our power to get her well again.'

Fran went home feeling cold and dejected. She knew that Kate's life had hung in the balance, but to hear it from the sister – fear engulfed her. It was her fault, of course; she ought to have brought Kate with the rest of the family to Brimdene. It was too much to expect that Mrs Maitland would keep her eye on Kate, and why should Prue and Sam be made to feel responsible? They had all promised to look after her but she couldn't be watched all the time. Dear Henry, he had done his best to teach the girls honesty and how to behave well. Fran had continued to instruct them in the rights and wrongs of society and she really had thought Kate was old enough to know better. How could she ever hold her head up again?

And to think that Luke Hammond had been the one to give his time to help in matters which, she was sure, were of no consequence to him. He had been kind, Fran had to admit, but once back at sea he would quickly forget her and her troubles in spite of all that he had said in the past. He wouldn't want anything to do with her now that her reputation was scarred. Anger and vexation tore her to pieces, and being obliged to keep the truth to herself did nothing to ease her guilty conscience. She realised she had been a trifle offhand with Prue yesterday, but today she longed for someone in whom she could confide. Instead she returned home. Tea was set out, and the other grandparents had come with Nathan and his family, all eager to hear news of Kate and to sympathise with Fran.

The next week passed uneventfully. Mr Radcliffe saw Fran at last, explaining that Kate would remain weak for some time and must not be upset.

'I have gently tried to persuade her to tell me what happened,' he said, 'for the sake of treating her. But she only says that someone took advantage of her. She will name no names – so I'm afraid there's nothing we can do to bring the young man to justice. I'm presuming it was a *young* man.'

'She was walking out with a boy who is away at college. He could have gone home for a weekend, I suppose. I can only pray that Kate will tell me the truth eventually,' Fran said.

'She's on the mend,' Mr Radcliffe reassured. 'I am confident of that, but only time will tell if permanent damage has been done. It will be some months before she can return to work, though.'

'She won't be returning to her previous employment,' Fran said hastily. 'That's one thing I have decided. She must live with us here in Brimdene.'

'That seems a sensible idea, but that won't be for some considerable time yet.'

Fran didn't feel too happy about her sudden decision. It was as if the words had been put into her mouth, for she hadn't planned to say any such thing. It must be the right decision, though – and she felt it was Henry's influence that had compelled her to make it.

When she told Kate, she remained totally unmoved, showing no sign of pleasure or regret. Although they said she was making progress, she refused to talk to her mother and seemed afraid to look directly at her. Fran took this as a sign of guilt. It created a rift between them and made the situation much more difficult for Fran to handle. Every step she took through the long corridor seemed to be a stamp of disapproval on her own hitherto good character. She was weary of the daily journeys to hospital, and lethargic about the so-called festive season – what did she have to be festive about? She faced the driving rain to go to the bus stop. In seconds she would be soaked to the skin, and shoppers would push and shove to get on the infrequent buses as the late afternoon became dark and dismal.

Suddenly a hand clasped hers round the umbrella handle and raised it higher.

'Here, let me share – the car is just across the road.' Luke's voice was welcome in her moment of self-pity.

'Luke!' she gasped in surprise, her eyes brightening as she gazed up at him. 'I thought you'd gone away?'

'Not yet, tomorrow actually, but I wanted to see you before I left. I would have come in to see Kate but I wasn't sure of what reception I'd get.' He smiled a warm, hopeful smile.

'You should have done. She knows you and you might have been able to cheer her up. They say she's improving, but she won't say much to me.'

They waited to cross the road as an ambulance came rushing round the corner, its bell clanging discordantly.

'How I hate that sound! It makes me feel quite sick,' Fran said.

'Then let's get away from here for a while. I'm sure you know somewhere where we can get a cup of tea?'

'No, Luke, really, I must get home to the children.'

'Your mother is there, and we needn't be long. You look as if you're the one who needs cheering up – and I won't take no for an answer.'

Fran didn't need to direct him to a teashop, he had already seen one on the main street of the suburb where the hospital was situated. It was an 'olde worlde' quaint place with willow-patterned plates, cups and saucers, and the waitress was a middle-aged woman with wrinkled stockings. Her dress, cap and apron had seen better days.

'This isn't quite what you're used to,' Fran said apologetically.

'We can be alone and undisturbed here. I want you to know how pleased I am that Kate is all right. Mrs Maitland would have visited herself, but – ' he shrugged – 'you know how it is, Fran. Christmas and all that.'

Fran smiled. 'Yes, Luke, I know how it is. If she won't come to me, then I shall have to visit her. Kate is my daughter, but being employed by the Maitlands she was in their charge. Surely I have some rights? Don't you think they owe it to me to tell me as much as they know?' Fran clenched her fists across the table as her tone became more aggressive.

Luke covered her hands with his and gently unknotted them.

'They want to give you time. I want to try to give you peace of mind. Forget the Maitlands, forget Kate even – just for half an hour. I want to look at you and hypnotise your worries away. I want to see you smile – just for me ...'

90

Fran pulled her hands away angrily. 'For goodness sake, Luke,' she hissed. 'That's the last thing *I* want. For the past eighteen months I've had nothing but trouble to cope with on my own – I don't know that I can take any more – and now Kate brings this disgrace on me.' She fumbled for a handkerchief. She didn't mean to let herself go but the tears fell unbidden for several seconds. When the waitress brought the tea and toasted teacakes that Luke had ordered, Fran turned her head towards the curtained window and composed herself.

'I ... I'm sorry, Luke. You see, you shouldn't have come here. This isn't your problem.'

'Oh, but it is, and you must let me share it with you, Fran dear. I may not have any family of my own, but no one can ever know just how much I'd like to have someone to share things with. I've thought about you so often, wondered just how you were coping since you were forced to move, but I realised I had to be discreet. I had no address to write to, and it wouldn't have been prudent to send via the Maitlands. That doesn't mean that every waking thought hasn't been tortured with visions of you.'

Fran sniffed and dabbed again at her eyes. 'That's no way to talk. I don't want to hear such things. You're a young man with a different girl in every port,' she said, trying to make light of this embarrassing conversation.

'Oh yes, I admit to being a few years younger than you, and to having a girl in every port – but not a different one.'

Fran looked across at him quizzically, then saw the mischievous twinkle in his eyes. 'You're there in a mist of loveliness on every quayside waiting for me, Fran. It's no use denying it. I'm serious – deadly serious – and now that I've found you I shan't let you go.'

Fran poured the tea solemnly. Luke's presence gave her peace. He was right, he offered her peace of mind. He was outside the family and only he knew the truth of Kate's condition. In-laws, her own brother and his family were all sympathetic, but she couldn't open her heart to any of them, not even dear Sissy. At times she felt like a castaway when Kate wouldn't speak to her.

'Cheer up, Fran,' he urged. 'I can imagine just how desolate you've been feeling over these past few days. Express your fears, and your hopes – I want to be part of them.'

'I have plenty of friends and family,' she said quietly. For a brief moment she had allowed herself to be lured by his persuasive charm, but Luke Hammond had seduced her once before and she wasn't likely to make the same mistake again. She changed her expression

91

to one of cold disdain and sniffed haughtily. 'I've made my life in Brimdene now and live solely for the girls. You've been kind. I don't wish to offend you, Luke, but please, forget me − go away and forget we ever met.'

'How can I when my son, the only thing that is really mine, my flesh and blood, lies in a grave in Sherbrook? One day, when my days in the Navy are over, I want to return there to live − and with you, Lennie's mother, the only woman I have ever loved,' he declared.

'Don't insult my intelligence, Luke,' she snapped impatiently. 'You've travelled across the breadth and length of Great Britain, visited countries all over the world, and haven't given me so much as a mite's consideration. I'm not a fool.'

'If I didn't love you, would I continue to visit the Maitlands for the sole purpose of placing flowers on my son's grave? With an obsession to get a glimpse of you? And in the past torture myself with what might be going on behind the curtains at the old mill house? We were destined for each other, Fran,' he said, leaning towards her.

There was a long pause while Fran fought for control of a situation she seemed in danger of losing.

'I must hurry home to the family. I'll catch the bus, Luke. It would be better. That doesn't mean, though, that I'm not grateful for your support. You might have saved Kate's life − I couldn't have borne another ...'

'Calm down. The last thing I want is to upset or hurry you into anything. But I shan't let go easily, I promise you.'

Fran drank the tea, her mind in utter confusion. As if she didn't have enough on her plate without this man wooing her! She was past all that, and surely there were many women in the world far more sophisticated and attractive than she?

'Perhaps it would be better to wait until after Christmas to see Mrs Maitland,' she said after a while. 'I've decided to keep Kate here in Brimdene, but when she's ready for a job, goodness knows what she'll do. I want to write to these people, the Lamberts, in my parents' old cottage, but until I can get some kind of sense out of Kate I can't go accusing anyone.'

'Give yourself time to think things out, Fran. I know it's a well-worn cliché, but it takes two, you know.'

'Does it? Then perhaps I should refresh your memory, which seems to be equally well worn, Luke Hammond.' She refused to be patronised. 'You took advantage of me all those many years ago. I don't recall that I had much say in the matter, and any disgrace I felt I had to bear alone as well as live with the shame of deceiving the man I married. There was no sharing the experience. The one takes what he wants, the other has to accept the consquences. I was more fortunate than Kate, my wedding was all prepared so my shame was veiled — and luckily I married a kind, thoughtful, good man. You went on your merry way and never gave the matter another thought.'

'Fran, I did — I never ceased to think about you! But what could I do once you were married to Henry? I loved you too much — and still do — to hurt you.' He pushed his empty plate away. 'Besides, my dear,' he added, 'I was not the first.'

Fran's cheeks glowed a dark crimson as she faced him with resentment.

'And *that*,' she said pointedly, 'is not hurting me? How could you be so cruel?'

Luke looked suitably chastened. 'I ... I'm sorry, Fran. That was unforgivable of me.'

'I agree, it was, but for your information and to put the record straight, Henry and I had been engaged for a long time. My employer would not release me and it was only by putting up the banns that we finally made her agree. We were forced to wait — wait beyond human endurance. We saw one another so seldom, and when we did ... As if it's any concern of yours!' Then, with bitter passion, she said: 'You'll never be half the man Henry was.'

During the ensuing silence Fran regretted her condemnation. Her cruel tongue had matched his thoughtlessness.

'I think we had better go,' he said softly but firmly. 'It seems we are both capable of hurting one another. I can only excuse myself by admitting to a feverish jealousy, and I don't intend to apologise for that.'

He clicked his fingers impatiently for the bill, and a few moments later they were walking back towards the hospital. He insisted that he drive her home. She thanked him shortly and ran into the house without inviting him in.

The girls had broken up from school and were excited, so full of chatter and laughter that Fran was obliged to enter into the Christmas spirit, albeit with an aching heart.

Kate improved slowly. She begged to be allowed home in time for Christmas but the surgeon advised against it.

'Another haemorrhage could be fatal,' he warned Fran. 'And,' he added, inclining his head with a sympathetic expression, 'Kate is unhappy. I appreciate that at home with her sisters she might come out of her depression, but it doesn't seem fair to them. I don't want to hurry things, and I must remind you that she will take a long while to recuperate from the fright alone. I'd like to keep her here until the New Year. Perhaps you could come and spend a whole day with her. An unusual request, I know, but I believe there are bridges to be built and I'd like the foundation laid before she leaves here.'

'Naturally I want to know how all this happened, Mr Radcliffe, but I'm not going to reprimand her if that's what you think.'

The senior surgeon was a portly man, every inch the gentleman, with soft grey-blue eyes and an unhurried manner. He laid a convincing hand on Fran's arm. 'I've become very fond of young Katie,' he said. 'There's pain in her eyes. By now, most young girls would have accepted the inevitable − the kind of girl who finds herself in Kate's predicament, that is.'

'Is there a "kind of girl"?' Fran asked.

'Yes, indeed, Mrs Sheldon. But in Kate's case it has become very obvious that this situation arose through no fault of hers, and that the worst hurt is because she believes she has vexed you. I might be quite wrong, of course. Night Sister reports that she cries a lot and when she does sleep she has very disturbing dreams. Now, all I'm suggesting is that after Christmas, when all the revelry is over, you try to find time to spend with Kate to get across your ... well, your forgiveness, perhaps?'

'I'm sorry, Mr Radcliffe,' Fran said in a small voice. 'I wasn't aware that my feelings were so obvious. I'm old-fashioned, and without a father now the girls have to depend on me for their upbringing. I do blame myself for what's happened. If I had paid more heed to the fact that Kate was desperate to come to Brimdene to live, this might have been avoided. I'll do all I can to help Kate, of course.'

The surgeon walked away from the petite, auburn-haired woman, feeling desperately sorry for her. The local GP had given him all the relevant details of the family, and he realised that Mrs Sheldon had borne her crosses stoically. He suspected, though, that she was so determined to bring the girls up the way their father had wished that she was both overprotective and dominant. He didn't tell her that Kate had confided in him and told him everything except the culprit's name. Gently he had explained to Kate that when she was feeling better she must sit down with her mother and tell her the story just as she had told him. But Kate had wept, admitting that she was terrified of what her mother would say and do.

'She can't eat you, child,' he had comforted. 'And when she knows the truth she'll be as sorry for you as we all are. But it's over now, my Katie, and you're going to put the past behind you. Let's hope no one wants to see your appendix scar,' he added conspiratorially, and with a friendly pat he passed on to the next patient.

It was a strange Christmas. To all outward appearances the usual festivities took place. Plenty of good food, mince pies and Christmas pudding, the girls all excited when they found the small silver charms in their portion. Oohs, and aahs at the goodies they found in their stockings and presents, and real excitement that they were going to spend the afternoon and evening with Uncle Nathan and his family. Even Gran Brown was going too, as well as the other grandparents, while Fran walked the three miles to the hospital to spend part of the day with Kate.

Thankfully it was a dry day, and not too cold. Fran set off laden with Kate's gifts and an enormous bunch of flowers. They had arrived by special delivery on Christmas Eve from Luke to Fran with a gold-edged card sending his greetings and begging her forgiveness. She put the card on the fire, once read, then explained the bouquet away by saying they were intended for Kate. Luke need never know.

During that long walk Fran had plenty of time to think. The timing of Luke's reappearance into her life was fortuitous. But for his prompt action Kate might well have bled to death in the ambulance, no matter how efficient the ambulance crew were. He was kind and considerate, handsome, well-mannered – she should be flattered that he paid court to her, a mere humble widow from a different class and background. In a way, deep down she supposed she was flattered by his attention. She had to admit that it was good to have someone to talk to about Kate's problem, but the idea struck her that perhaps he was interested in Kate, not her! The notion grew – was he the man who had taken advantage of Kate, just as he had taken her years before? His concern might be a way of appeasing his conscience, and of course he would have sworn Kate to secrecy. Yes, it would have been so easy for him, visiting the Maitland household with the son of the family – gentry sons made it their sport to seduce young servants. But then her idea was squashed. As she neared the hospital she remembered that Luke had been away at sea for the past eighteen months. She refused to relent, though, and shrugged off the notion that she was quite relieved that Kate's seducer could not have been Luke Hammond – if he had told her the truth.

With so many thoughts swirling round in her brain, Fran reached the hospital sooner than she anticipated. In spite of the parcels she carried, her step had quickened in tune to her ideas. Now she had to convince Kate that she was not an ogre. She accused Kate of not communicating but she guessed that in her turmoil she was equally to blame, so she lifted her head high, put on a happy smile and entered the ward.

Her spirits tumbled. Kate's bed was made up and empty. The blood coursed through her veins and Fran felt dizzy. Then someone touched her arm.

'Hullo, Mrs Sheldon, merry Christmas,' Sister said cheerfully. 'We've moved Kate out on the balcony. We've another patient here a year or so older than Kate. She's made an excellent recovery after her operation and we thought Kate might respond to someone of her own age.' Sister pointed to the double doors where, to Fran's surprise, Kate was coming to greet her.

'Oh, Kate, how lovely to see you walking about! Happy Christmas, darling.' They fell on each other and wept, the barrier of mistrust suddenly crushed. 'Oh, this is silly, isn't it?' Fran mopped up her tears. 'We missed you so much this morning. The girls and Gran all send their love and say, "hurry home".'

'It's been quite exciting here, Mum,' Kate enthused. 'We all had a present, even old Mrs Court who'll be ninety-three on New Year's Day. Come and see. I had a little embroidered picture, which says "The best teacher is Life, the best friend is God", isn't that lovely? I shall keep it for always.'

Kate opened her presents excitedly, while Fran read the picture verse several times over. Such a wise saying. Was this responsible for Kate's change in attitude? What she, Kate's mother, should have been able to achieve, this little picture had done?

'What gorgeous flowers, Mum!' Kate said as she pulled the wrapping off one of the gifts. 'Who sent those? I hope you didn't − ?'

'No, dear.' Fran sighed. 'I'm afraid my pension won't stretch to buying flowers at this time of the year. Captain Hammond sent these. Wasn't that kind? I don't know how you'll thank him, though, as he'll be back at sea by now.'

'He is a very kind man, Mum,' Kate said slowly, and there was some hidden meaning in her words and look which made Fran feel embarrassed. She urged Kate on to open the rest of the presents and cards to hide the faint flush that had coloured her cheeks, and shortly afterwards the nurses brought tea, sandwiches and small fancy cakes as well as slices of rich Christmas cake for visitors and patients to enjoy on this special day.

'The nurses and doctors came round with lanterns singing carols last evening, Mum,' Kate said. 'And tomorrow they're putting on a pantomime. Sister said you could bring the others if you like. There'll be buses, won't there? It's at three o'clock, in the main hall downstairs.'

'The girls will like that. I should think you'll soon be able to come home now. You're looking so much better, Kate.'

Kate's eyes misted over and she dropped her head. 'I want to come home, Mum, of course I do, but I'll think everyone knows — you know?'

'You've had your appendix out so you won't be able to do any heavy work for a while.' Fran made a rare gesture and held Kate's hand firmly in her own. 'I'm your mother, Kate, so naturally I want to know exactly what happened, and I think you'll feel better if you tell me the truth. After all, I shall hve to go and see the Maitlands and the Lamberts ...'

'No! No! It wasn't Maurice, Mum, really, truly it wasn't. I haven't seen him since the summer, he's been away at college.'

'If you don't tell me who it was dear, how can I believe you?'

'It was dark, late, the night I got held up going back to Sherbrook from here.'

'Kate dear, look at me. We'll talk about it when you come home, calmly, rationally, but just set my mind at rest on one thing, please.'

'What's that, Mum?'

'Was it someone at Sherbrook House? Or — um — someone who visits there, maybe?'

'You can't think Captain Hammond would do such a thing! Oh no, Mum, he's so gentle and kind. He acted so quickly, he knew what to do — but he's old enough to be my father. Oh, Mum, whatever would Dad say to all this? I would never bring such shame on you or Dad, you know that, don't you? Please, Mum, *please* ... say you do?' Kate's weeping was heartbreaking. A nurse brought a screen and left Fran and Kate alone in their sorrow — a sorrow at last shared. In hushed tones they talked until the hurt was bearable between them. Fran was horrified at the thought of her Kate being molested and raped almost on the doorstep of Sherbrook House. She chided Kate gently for not telling Mrs Sturmey the truth at once.

'You must have known he might have put you in the family way.'

'I did tell Mrs Maitland eventually. When I realised, I wanted to die, Mum. I thought you'd blame me and honestly there was nothing I could do, nothing.' As she sobbed she remembered scratching

Felix's face with the brooch pin, but she decided against telling anyone that. 'I tried my best to fight him off, but he was too big, too heavy.'

'What made you tell Mrs Maitland then?' Fran asked.

'I went to Dad's grave. I just w – wanted to be n – near him . . . She found me and I was soaked through so she took me home. Mrs Sturmey had already guessed what was wrong with me. I'd been vomiting in the mornings, you see. They gave me some herbal medicine to take to get rid of it, and – well, you know the rest. They all thought it was Maurice, but he's not like that, Mum, honestly he isn't.'

'All men are like that, Kate,' Fran said dispassionately. 'From now on you'll be wary of the types of men around. Give them a hint of opportunity and they'll take what they want, so be on your guard.' Fran sniffed her contempt. 'Still, after this you won't want anything more to do with young men for a while. I don't blame you, Kate. The doctor says you were ill-used, so now you know what men are capable of. You'll have to resign yourself to being a spinster. No man wants a wife who can't give him sons – and it's unlikely you'll be able to bear children.'

'B – but I could still get married, Mum. Maurice and I – '

'I don't want to know, Kate. And don't think Maurice Lambert will have noble ideas of still wanting you. When he knows what's happened – and you'd have to tell him – he'll want nothing more to do with you. No, Kate, you'd best forget him. You'll be staying at home from now on until work can be found for you. But first we want to see you fit and well again. When I go to Sherbrook I'll explain that you've been very ill – they'll understand.'

During the long walk home Fran felt pangs of guilt. Had she been too hard on her daughter? Had she taken advantage of Kate's honesty? Had Kate been truly honest? This college lad, nice though he appeared, wasn't Kate's type. No, all the things she had said had to be said sooner or later. She could not allow Kate to continue the friendship with Maurice Lambert. Henry wouldn't have allowed it and Fran was determined to keep up the standards set by him.

As the January cold, snowy weather came in, and Kate was at last home, she became sick and tired of hearing her mother's words, 'Your father wouldn't approve and that's final.'

One Monday morning when Fran was busy at the wash tub, Kate dusted the kitchen and then sat down by the fire to read the *News Chronicle*. She tired easily and was still seeing the doctor for anaemia but did all she could to help around the house. She took over some of the cooking, which she loved to do, but when her mother and grandmother were doing the family wash she knew better than to intrude into their argy-bargy. It was always over some trivial disagreement, usually involving Uncle Eric, Auntie Annie and May, and Kate was old enough to realise that it was because her mother was tired from overwork and worry.

Kate was eager to be allowed out so that she could post the long letter she was secretly writing to Maurice. Her mother had forbidden her to correspond with him, so she kept silent about the several letters that had been exchanged during her stay in hospital. The young probationer nurse on duty at night had willingly posted patients' mail first thing in the morning when she went off duty. But by now Maurice must be wondering why the letters had stopped, and Kate couldn't understand why she had received nothing at home. Her thoughts were frequently with Maurice. She longed to meet him and explain all that had happened because she knew he would understand.

She turned the paper over and there on the back page the name Felix leapt out at her. She read on to learn that the body of a young man had been found hanging from a branch of a tree in Hyde Park, London. At first they had been unable to identify him except to publish his description, which included a deep, savage scar on his cheek. His friend at college, Maurice Lambert, had then come forward to identify him, saying that the young man had been in trouble at college, as well as with the police for drunken behaviour. His family had disowned him. Unwanted, penniless, a disturbed vagrant, he had finally reached the end of his tether and been driven to commit suicide.

Kate just stared at the printed words in the column. As she read and reread every single word she realised that Maurice must have seen him after the rape incident, as he evidently knew about the scar. How had Felix explained that away? she wondered. Did Maurice know what happened that night or did he have a distorted version from Felix and blame her? It was imperative for Kate to send a letter to Maurice, if only to say how sorry she was for his friend. What Felix had done to her seemed to pale into insignificance now as she visualised him hanging lifeless from a tree. She could never forget what he had done, but he didn't deserve such an end as that.

Later in the afternoon Kate feigned a headache and went upstairs to lie down in the little boxroom, which Fran had lovingly prepared for when Kate came out of hospital. The wallpaper was pale pink with dainty rosebuds all over it, and now Kate sat on the side of her bed and stared blankly at it. She couldn't tell Maurice the true story in a letter lest it got into the wrong hands. She did tell him that she had been forbidden to correspond with him, but that when her mother visited Sherbrook, weather permitting in a week's time, she could meet him mid-morning on the station at Brimdene. In order to post the letter surreptitiously she asked if she might go to meet the younger girls from school to try to get rid of her headache, and Fran agreed. Kate begged Maurice to reply and waited anxiously, but every morning when she asked her mother if there were any letters for her, the answer was always the same: 'Who on earth are you expecting a letter from?'

When a letter had arrived bearing a Sherbrook postmark, Fran knew that somehow Kate had disobeyed her. She was as determined to put a stop to the friendship as Kate was to continue it, so she used it to light the fire in the kitchen grate. Fran watched it blacken and curl, then disintegrate. Only when it was completely destroyed did she feel remorse for her hasty action. She should have confronted Kate with the evidence, but hadn't she had enough to contend with?

Even though there was still no word from Maurice, Kate decided to go to town while her mother was at Sherbrook.

'I'll come with you to the station to see you off,' she told Fran.

'But your interview with Mrs Neale at the hotel isn't until two o'clock,' Fran said.

'I might go to the Labour Exchange and find out if any other jobs are going.'

'But Aunt Sissy has gone to a lot of trouble to fix this interview up, Kate.'

'I shall still go to the hotel, Mum. I'm determined to find a job if I can't go back to the Maitlands. It's pretty obvious they don't want me anyway as they've taken on Maurice's sister — so Aunt Prue said in her Christmas letter.'

'They would know I wouldn't let you return there after what's happened. Mrs Maitland did write quite a nice letter at Christmas. Better to be polite and friendly, I suppose, but I shall speak my mind when I go up to the big house to fetch your wages today.'

'Mum, it wasn't their fault, was it? How were they to know that the train would be delayed that night?'

Fran grunted. 'I wish I could find out whose fault it was,' she said huffily.

'No one knows but me, and I'm not telling you any more than I've told you already,' Kate replied firmly. 'It's over and done with, Mum. It's me that's got to live with the memory, but I want to try to forget.' She buttoned up her warm coat and pulled on her woollen gloves. 'I've realised since I've been home that I quite like cooking, so I might try to find a job in a kitchen somewhere. Come on, Mum, or you'll miss the train.'

At the station Kate bought a platform ticket and waited to see her mother safely in a compartment where it was warm. Soon the whistle blew and the train eased away from the platform. She watched it get smaller and smaller until it turned the bend and disappeared out of sight. She stood still for a moment. It occurred to her that Maurice might already be on the platform. Not having received any reply to her letter, she didn't know whether he had returned to college, but she knew he would make every effort to get here if he could. She had indicated that the reason she needed to see him was most urgent and couldn't be discussed in letters.

There were few people about since it was not yet ten o'clock, so she idled the time away by looking at things on the newsagent's stall. She enquired about the next trains due in. Another half an hour to wait for the Sherbrook one, and from the other direction the London train was not expected for over an hour. As the minutes ticked by she began to feel cold and empty. She hadn't eaten much breakfast so she went into the buffet and bought a large bun and a pot of tea. If Maurice arrived he could share it with her. She longed to see him again. There was so much to talk about, but she couldn't imagine what his reaction would be to her accusations against Felix. And now he was dead and unable to confess to what he had done. Whenever she thought about him she felt sick inside. He had caused her a great deal of pain and distress, but it hadn't warranted killing himself and she managed to feel some compassion for him. She wondered if he had left a letter giving a reason for taking his own life. There had been nothing more about it in the papers, and she was glad that her mother had made no comment about the story.

Kate sat in the buffet for as long as she dared. The Sherbrook train came in but there was no sign of Maurice, so she waited on the platform for the London train. She became very tired of pacing up and down. Eventually she went to the ladies' waiting room where a good fire burned in the hearth. The London train came and went, a later one from Sherbrook, but still no sign of Maurice. By now Kate's spirits had ebbed low. She went to buy a paper and returned to the waiting room to read it, but she couldn't settle. A woman came in to make up the fire for the third time. She looked suspiciously at Kate and grunted 'Ain't you got no place to go, young woman?'

'It isn't any business of yours,' Kate said shortly and with that stood up and went outside. Just one more train – he must be on the next one. But the midday trains arrived without Maurice.

With a heavy heart, aching legs and cold feet, Kate dragged herself away from the station. She mustn't be late for her appointment with Aunt Sissy's employer. Maurice wasn't coming. She must accept the fact that he couldn't make it. The new term must have started, she told herself, but that didn't explain why he hadn't written. A nasty chill crept over her as the thought occurred to her that he might have heard the truth about her illness when he was home at Christmas. While she had been in hospital his letters had been warm, loving and full of concern, especially at the length of time she had to remain there. Usually, Maurice said, after an operation for the removal of one's appendix the patient was allowed home after two weeks. Had there been complications? he wanted to know. In reply she tried to make light of her condition, only assuring him of her love.

Now Kate was forced to admit that her mother could be right. If Maurice had heard a rumour that she may never be able to have children, he might have lost interest. She needed his friendship. There was time enough to divulge the truth, she had thought, but now that Felix had committed suicide, and Maurice had been home to Sherbrook, had she left it too late?

In spite of her dismay Kate's interview went well, but the fact that at last she had secured a job in Brimdene did little to cheer her up. She knew it would please her mother, though, and she was thankful that she arrived home well before Fran. She was preparing the tea by the time she heard her mother's footsteps coming round the path at the side of the house. Hilda and Babs were squabbling as usual, and Ruby was helping Gran butter the bread.

'Whatever's all this commotion?' Fran exclaimed as she closed the back door behind her. She pulled out the hat pin, took off her hat and tossed it onto the sofa wearily. Kate was almost afraid to ask how she got on at the big house.

'Well, Katie, how did your interview go?' Fran asked.

'I can start as soon as the doctor gives me a certificate to say I'm fit. Oh, Mum, he will, won't he? Mrs Neale is so nice and wants to train me for hotel work. I told her I like cooking and she seemed pleased about that.'

Fran smiled. Kate had a job here at Brimdene. She experienced some disappointment when she heard that Kate had to live in. She had looked forward to having the family complete for a while but appreciated that it wasn't safe for young girls to be about at odd hours.

102

Kate didn't seem over-enthusiastic at her good fortune though. Fran supposed it was not hearing from Maurice that was making her downcast and she wished with all her heart she could rescind her hasty action. She knew she ought to own up to what she had done, but she didn't have the courage. If only Kate had been open and honest with her it need never have happened. Kate and Maurice would still be friends. Why was it that mothers and daughters couldn't seem to win one another's confidence? Fran had gone to Sherbrook unaware of the truth. She had been shocked to learn from Prue and Sam the story about Maurice's friend, Felix. By all accounts he had been in the village at the time Kate was raped. Maurice had told his parents all he knew and rumours soon spread so that Prue put two and two together.

The Maitlands had been kind but distant, and Fran was glad that all connections with them had now been severed. They had been reluctant to discuss all that had happened except to offer their sympathy.

Now Fran resolved to put the incident behind her, though she doubted that Kate would ever be able to forget. Kate needed her love and understanding. They must make a new start and at least she had the satisfaction of knowing that Kate had not let her down.

Chapter Eight

As the winter winds and snows were superseded by the bursting of spring, the Sheldons enjoyed happy times as a united family. The second anniversary of Henry's death and that of Fran's father came round and, though the pain strengthened, it became more bearable with the passage of time.

At Easter Gran Brown went to stay with Eric and his family. Fran decided to make the most of this opportunity to repaper her mother's room while the girls visited Sherbrook with Prue, Sam and Marion. The invitation was extended to Fran as well but she was in an industrious frame of mind. It was good to have time and space for herself for a change.

The weather was better than she could have hoped for. With a scarf tied round her head to keep her hair dust-free, and an old worn dress beneath her pinafore, Fran emptied all Ma's drawers and cupboards of their contents. She placed the clothes and linen in tidy piles in the girls' bedroom; then she began the task of tearing off the old wallpaper. It wasn't that dirty, but it wasn't Ma's dirt anyway, she thought, as she scraped and ripped. The previous tenants had chosen dull colours in most of the rooms, but Fran had not redecorated any room except Kate's until now. The room was south-facing, and before long she was flushed from the warmth of the sun and the exertion. Full of enthusiasm, she even began to sing as she worked.

It was strange to have the house all to herself. She was quite alone with her memories, reliving the happy days when she and Henry had first taken over the old mill house. There had been so much work to do to make it habitable, but they shared the renovations and put as much love as hard work into their home. Henry, usually acting the fool, would come home after the day's work smelling of horses, but he still caught her in a bearlike hug, kissing her face and neck in spite of varnish or paste, according to what job she was in the middle of. No amount of protest thwarted his affectionate advances, and tea was forgotten as they made love wherever they happened to find it convenient.

Fran paused and gazed out of the window. In the pit of her stomach she felt an ache, the kind of longing that could not be satiated. Her body throbbed, she felt the sap of desire, and was quite shocked at herself for having such feelings. What was the use of having feelings when there was no man to satisfy her? And, she told herself severely, there was no point in wishing. Henry was gone. Her cheeks bright crimson, Fran put twice as much energy as before into what she was doing, and when she went to bed she fell asleep exhausted.

Each day, loneliness tempted her with sensuous thoughts and desires, but she fought against such dreams as she scrubbed and revarnished the woodwork. Towards the end of the week she was ready to hang the wallpaper. She studied it carefully for the length of the pattern and to make sure she had it the right way up. She managed to find a moment's gratitude to Eric for supplying Ma with some decent wallpaper. It was a soft honeysuckle colour which wouldn't fade too easily, with tiny sprays of flowers all over it. This was the part she liked. It was akin to dressmaking, matching, cutting, placing, and she felt a sense of pride when the first piece was pasted and smoothed into position. By dinnertime she had completed one wall. She was hoping to get it all finished by Friday. Kate had a day off on Saturday and had promised to come home to help her mother. Fran stopped work briefly at midday for a light snack of bread, cheese and pickle. She couldn't spare the time to prepare meals because she was determined to finish everything before Sunday when Eric was bringing Ma home. She looked forward to the girls' returning a few days later. Prue was so generous in having them, but Fran knew it was no hardship to her since she loved children.

She left her plate on the draining board and took her second cup of tea up to Ma's room with her. Yes, she was quite impressed with her handiwork. The paper was going on like a dream. She sipped her tea. She should finish well before —

A loud knock on the front door startled her. Now who on earth could that be? she wondered. The past few weeks, with Kate settled down in her job and at last looking healthier and more content, had brought about a feeling of complacency. Uncertainty now returned. Knowing her luck, Fran thought, it had to be bad news of some kind and she delayed going to the door. Canvassers, someone selling something, she supposed. There wasn't much point in bothering to answer the door – but as she went down the stairs she could see that a man in uniform was standing in the porch. Must be Mr Blake, the policeman who lived next door, who had kindly offered to help during his off-duty period. But he was in uniform so he hadn't come for that. Fran went down the last two stairs as the knocking came again, and this time she realised that it wasn't Mr Blake. The silhouette was familiar, and a strange feeling of excitement leapt inside her. She had to stand for a few seconds before opening the door. Irrational thoughts like dashing to change into some decent clothes spun round in her head – but if she didn't hurry, Luke would go away ...

'I thought you must be out, Fran,' he said, removing his naval cap.

Fran laughed lamely. 'I ... I'm busy papering Ma's room,' she said quickly.

'Does that mean you aren't going to let me in?' In the dim light of the porch his eyes sparkled more than usual.

'Of course you can come in,' she said, a trifle hesitantly, 'but look at the state of me? And the house.'

'I came to see you, Fran, and you look wonderful.' He placed two hands round her waist and gazed at her. 'I like the image of a working woman. My life is full of pomp and ceremony, everyone and everything neat and tidy. The women I'm obliged to meet socially seldom have a hair out of place, with their marcel waves and perms. I like you just the way you are, a hard-working wife and mother.'

'You should have let me know you were coming. The girls are in Sherbrook with the Belmonts.'

His mouth relaxed into a sensuous smile and he inclined his head. He knew! He had plotted ... Fran went very red and became flustered, pushing his hands away and hurrying for no particular reason into the kitchen.

'I thought you'd gone back to sea,' she said, trying to impress him with a hint of indifference.

'The refit isn't finished yet, so I've got a bit longer, and I'm beginning to like Brimdene. I've booked in at Cliff Edge Manor Hotel.'

'Oh, that's nice,' Fran said. 'That happens to be one of the hotels owned by the Neale family. They own most of Brimdene, if it comes to that. Kate's got a job at the Sand Dune Hotel, one of theirs.'

'I'm familiar with the Neale family. The youngest son was a junior officer in the Navy and has served under me. He had a bad accident abroad, so I believe he's involved in the family business now. But

I didn't come here to talk about them. I came to invite you to the theatre with supper afterwards.'

'Oh, but I couldn't, Luke,' Fran said. 'It's very kind of you, but Ma will be returning soon, and I have to get everything straight before the girls come home. There's a lot still to be done.'

'Nothing that can't wait, and I insist. You're looking better than the last time we met. I trust I've been forgiven at last?'

'You presume too much then,' she said. 'I thought you'd come to enquire after Kate.'

'Well, all right, how's Kate?' He was gently mocking her and she found the wicked twinkle in his dark eyes irresistible.

'She's very well,' she said, unable to prevent herself from smiling. 'She's enjoying her work very much. On her day off tomorrow she's coming home to help me finish the room.'

'The past put firmly behind her?'

'As much as it can ever be,' Fran replied with a sigh. 'The future doesn't look too rosy for her personal life.'

Luke surveyed Fran critically. 'You've had a hard time these past two years, Fran. One accident seems to have sparked off a whole string of unfortunate incidents. Have you heard — did you know — that a certain young man committed suicide?'

'I have heard the rumour, but we've no proof that he was connected with Kate's condition. Kate still refuses to discuss the matter and there seemed no point in pursuing it. I'm just thankful that's she's alive.'

'A sensible attitude. I have a nasty feeling that you might have suspected me?'

Fran shrugged this off. 'Of course not,' she said. 'Kate's just a child.'

'I respect women too much to treat them that badly,' he said in a low voice. 'I want to take you out to show you that I respect you, Fran. Please, please say you'll come. I have the tickets here in my pocket. It's one of Ivor Novello's musicals. I know you'll enjoy it, Fran. It's time you got out and about, and I shan't be here for long.'

'But ... but ...' she began.

'There isn't one good reason why you shouldn't come, is there?'

She shook her head. 'You make it sound so easy,' she said simply.

'It is. Just be ready tomorrow evening at seven. I'm so looking forward to it, and I'm sure Kate will understand.'

He strode to the front door purposefully and in the porch turned as he replaced his hat. He touched it politely, his eyes magical as he smiled his farewell.

Fran could hardly breathe. She went into the front room and over the privet hedge watched his sleek saloon car drive away. He had made no attempt to touch her, not even said goodbye, just a smile, a look – yes, it was that expression that rendered her helpless – and she hadn't protested ...

At first she didn't think she could carry on working. Her mind was awash with questions and suppositions. What were the neighbours thinking now? How many had noticed the handsome naval officer arrive? How many had timed his visit? She smoothed down the front of her pinafore as she went back to Ma's room. She had lost some weight. No wonder, with all the worry and work, and over this past week she had not eaten really enough. The thought of supper out in some posh restaurant filled her with both dread and excitement. What could she wear? Gradually, as the minutes slipped by, she managed to return to a level keel and carried on with the papering. Mr Blake came round during the evening and gave her a hand to complete the third wall.

'You've done very well, Mrs Sheldon,' he remarked, admiring the room. 'Hope you've stopped to eat, though?'

'I can get by on very little,' she said with a laugh. 'This job was more important than eating. Captain Hammond is on leave. He called to enquire after Kate, but he has some theatre tickets and wants me to accompany him. D'you think I should go?'

Mr Blake looked down at Fran with a warm smile 'Why ever not? It's time you had some outings, my dear. You work too hard. Now, you've got the chance to get out while Ma and the girls are away, you take it. Go off and enjoy yourself.'

'But whatever will people think?'

'It's your life. Never mind about the gossips.'

Fran felt better for talking to Mr Blake. It was better to be honest. It was sensible for the neighbours to know when she was out and the house left empty, anyway.

Kate arrived next morning soon after nine o'clock. It was another lovely day and she was delighted to see Gran's room nearly finished.

'You've worked hard, Mum,' Kate said. 'It looks lovely. Gran will be pleased. I'm sorry I won't be able to stay as long as I'd planned, though. One of the kitchen girls has gone sick and Mrs Neale wondered if I'd like to help out, so I jumped at the chance. Hope you don't mind Mum?' she asked apologetically.

'Actually I'm going out this evening, Kate. Let's hurry up and see if we can finish this last wall by dinnertime.'

As they worked, Fran told Kate about her evening's outing. Kate appeared surprised but pleased, and together they decided on Fran's outfit.

'It really is time you stopped wearing black, Mum,' Kate said. 'It makes you look so old.'

'Thank you very much,' Fran said. After some thought, she went on: 'I don't know, though, perhaps I ought to've said no. I shan't feel comfortable with someone so ... so ... you know.'

'Captain Hammond is very nice. But wear that pretty dress you made last summer. It's got long sleeves and looks elegant. Navy blue is smart, Mum, and it isn't too dowdy with the sprigs of white flowers on it. You've got that good navy-blue coat that Mrs Maitland passed on.'

Fran was glad of Kate's advice. Working in the centre of town in the hotel, she had become quite knowledgeable about the latest fashions. With Fran's expertise with her needle, they all benefited by having clothes that were exclusive to them and up to date.

They completed the papering in good time, then Kate shared the job of scrubbing the lino.

'I'll leave the window wide open to let it dry while we have dinner, and to let the smell of the paste go off. I must say it looks better than I thought it would.'

'You worry too much, Mum,' Kate scolded good-naturedly. 'I'll help you with the drawers and cupboards, but I can't stay longer than half past three. But after I've gone you're not to do any more — promise?'

'Why ever not?' asked Fran. 'I can carry on for another couple of hours at least.'

'No, Mum. You must have a bath, then a cup of tea while you cool down, then get dressed. You don't want to have to rush and end up looking hot and bothered.'

'I shall be that anyway,' Fran laughed.

'Not if you give yourself plenty of time.'

'Kate, I'm not a young girl going out on a date,' Fran protested.

'Maybe not, but you are going out to the theatre — and that's reason enough to dress up. All our guests wear glittery things and carry evening bags, and wear high heels.'

'Oh, Kate, you are funny. I can't change the way I look, dear. I've had five children, for goodness sake.'

'But you can look stunning, Mum. You've got a lovely face and

109

such blue eyes – and you're *my* mum.' She gave Fran a sudden cuddle and kissed her cheek affectionately. The unexpected gesture brought a lump to Fran's throat, and she was conscious again of the wrong she had done Kate.

'I wish it were you going to the theatre, Kate, ' she said.

'What – with Captain Hammond?'

'No dear, someone nice of your own age, of course.'

Kate sighed and pursed her lips. 'Who'd want *me*?'

'Plenty of young men would love to have a good-looking girl like you on their arm, my dear. Not every man wants to have babies about the place. You might meet someone who's more interested in a career, and as long as they love you for yourself – because you're *you* – that's all that matters.'

Kate went off to the lavatory, leaving Fran a little despondent about her eldest daughter. Maurice Lambert was a hard-working chap with good prospects when he left college. She couldn't have asked for anyone more suitable, and she had come between them. Guilt nagged away at her, and yet Kate didn't seem as upset now. Maybe it hadn't been right – maybe already she had found some new interest ...

On the dot of seven-thirty a light knock sounded on the front door. Fran had carried out Kate's instructions to the letter and had been patiently waiting for the past twenty minutes. Her shoes tapped out a rhythm on the hall lino as she went to let Luke in.

'Ah! I see you're ready, and very smart you look too, if I may be so personal. I must confess I half-expected to be jilted,' he said with a grin.

'That wouldn't have been very fair, would it? I had second and third thoughts, Luke. It's the first time I've been anywhere without at least one of the girls.

'Then it's time you started to live your own life, Fran. At least have time off from your family occasionally to enjoy yourself.'

'The girls are my life, Luke, and provide me with all the enjoyment I need.'

He leaned forward and dropped a teasing kiss just short of her lips.

'The kind of enjoyment I mean has to be shared between a man and a woman,' he said. 'Do you realise that this will be our very first date?' He cupped her chin in his hand as he whispered: 'Let's make it a night to remember.'

Dusk was falling, and some sea mist was hanging low in the town square as Luke parked the car in the forecourt of the theatre. Fran experienced a mixture of excitement and apprehension when she saw so many fashionable people going up the marble stairs leading into the foyer. Luke was not dressed in uniform. His light-brown suit was well cut and styled perfectly over his slim hips and trim waist. He had a confident walk, straight-backed with a military bearing, and Fran felt proud to be his companion. She had dressed up, as Kate called it, as much as she dared. Her dress fitted her neat figure without unnecessary creases; she felt self-conscious about her well-developed bust, but she knew many a woman might envy her. Beneath the navy-blue felt hat, trimmed in the modern style with white ribbon and small wispy feathers, her auburn hair was freshly washed, soft and springy. She didn't like having to wear a hat immediately after washing it, but this gadabout evening had come like a bolt out of the blue. It beat hanging wallpaper and scrubbing floors, she thought as she sat beside her handsome escort and listened to the overture, played by Brimdene's own orchestra.

The show was colourful, the music easy to listen to and the romance of the story enough to touch the hardest of hearts. Fran was quite overwhelmed by it. During the interval Luke excused himself, only to return with a large, beribboned box of chocolates. He smiled down at her protests, and helped her eat some of the sweets until the curtain rose again.

After they had stood to acknowledge the national anthem, they went out into the evening air, which had turned somewhat chill. The mist had rolled away and there was a pleasant, springlike atmosphere in the town in spite of the coolness. Fran wondered where they would be going for supper. Luke ushered her back into the car and drove off towards the cliff. With a screech of brakes he stopped in the car park of his hotel. Fran felt her stomach muscles tighten. She ought to have insisted that he took her straight home afterwards but she was, she realised, entirely at his mercy.

'It's quite late,' she said in a small voice. 'I ought to go straight home.'

He turned to look at her. 'There's no one at home to report to, Fran. This is your night, let's make the most of it.'

'B – but I'm not used to eating in places like this,' she pleaded.

'Then now is the time to start.' He got out of the car and came round to her side to help her out. With his hand supporting her elbow, he took her inside. A huge palm in the centre of the floor was surrounded by plush leatherette seats.

'Just take a seat,' he said. 'I have to go to the reception desk.'

Fran watched as the gentleman behind the counter treated Luke with the utmost respect and then handed over a key. Her nervousness

111

increased. She wasn't sure she could cope with this situation, but Luke smiled reassuringly as he strode back to where she was sitting.

'I expect you'd like to freshen up,' he suggested, and seconds later they were in the lift with other guests going up to the top floor.

The corridors were wide and thickly carpeted so that their shoes made no sound as they walked along. Luke unlocked a door marked 217 and showed Fran inside.

'I believe in home comforts where possible,' he said. 'Not that hotels are in the least like a real home, but this is an improvement on my cabin, where I seldom get any peace.'

'Where is your real home?' Fran asked curiously.

'Mm . . . haven't got one.' Fran thought he seemed less exuberant briefly, then with a smile he said: 'I like to take a suite when I'm in a nice town like Brimdene, especially when I can get one overlooking the sea.' He took off his jacket in the warmth of the room and then walked over to the huge window. 'I can't live too far away from the sea, and this hotel is ideal. The bathroom is through that door if you'd like to freshen up before our supper arrives.'

'We're going to eat up here?'

'Don't look so surprised, Fran. Why not? I've ordered some of their specialities so I hope you have a good appetite. I don't need to enquire whether or not you enjoyed the show, I know you did. Whenever I glanced across at you, your eyes were sparkling and you were engrossed in everything. I'm glad I've been able to give you some pleasure, Fran.'

'The show was splendid,' she said huskily. 'I've never had the time or money for such extravagances. Not since I've been married, anyway. I thought it was a bit late for supper.'

'Not when I can treat you to a real supper. I bet you haven't eaten properly while your family have all been away. You seem to thrive on hard work.'

'There are times when I feel like running away,' she confessed. 'Without a man it's difficult, having to make the decisions — and I don't always make the right ones.' She hurried away into the bathroom. She had nearly dropped her guard and told him about burning Kate's letter. She needed someone to talk to and Luke was evoking her confidence. She recalled how gullible she was in his company, how easily she had succumbed to his charm twenty years ago. She mustn't fall under his spell now. But, as the evening progressed, without her being aware of it, any restraint she had erected between them as a safety barrier was soon broken down.

The topic of conversation was varied. Luke gave her graphic

112

accounts of the countries he had visited from Ceylon to South America, India, Rhodesia and Australia. Fran was soon laughing at the stories he could amuse her with. After a spell of small talk while they ate the fish dish he had ordered, she asked him again about his family. He kept his gaze on his food. She noticed the long, elegant fingers which held the cutlery so delicately. Only small portions went into his mouth, and she found herself comparing him with the men she had been associated with all her life. Working men with rough hands, too hungry after a day in the fields to bother about genteel table manners.

'My family are of little consequence, Fran. They're all in the North Riding of Yorkshire. My father planned to take me into the family iron-ore business, but the sea became my obsession. I'm afraid I broke my parents' hearts by running away to sea at sixteen, leaving the very expensive boarding school that they had thought would tame me.'

'Do you regret it now?'

'No, most definitely not.' His eyes seemed to cloud over for a moment. 'I was the only son, you see. I have three sisters, who aren't much good in the iron-ore trade. I've been disinherited.'

'Oh, Luke, that's terrible!' Fran exclaimed.

'Why? What use is money if your heart is rebelling against family ties and expectations?'

'Isn't that a bit hard on your parents?'

'They wouldn't meet me halfway, so I went ahead and did what I wanted to do — what's in my blood, Fran. Was in my grandfather's blood before me. I didn't mean to hurt them. I believed in my innocent youth that when they saw how keen a sailor I was they would understand, but they disowned me completely. Good friends are often more valuable than family, even though blood is supposed to be thicker than water.'

Fran remained silent, feeling some sympathy for Luke's family.

'Being a mother yourself, I expect your compassion is for them. If I had made a mess of my life I could understand it, but I've reached the height of my career without blemish. If my son did half as well I would be proud of him.'

'But the older generation doesn't think like us, Luke. I feel sorry for them, but I also feel sorry for you. Surely you've missed out on a happy family life? They could have given you so much when you're home from long voyages.'

At the concern in Fran's voice, Luke looked up. His dark, hooded eyes softened with tenderness. This close to him she could see the deep furrows in his brow, the creases that showed white against an otherwise swarthy skin. Each furrow, every crease depicted the kind of life he led away from Yorkshire in hot, passionate countries, and she knew now why he had taken advantage of her all those years ago. He needed a woman's love. He hadn't ever known a mother's care. She felt the atmosphere thicken with emotion. As if on a magic carpet she was flown back to the Hinckleys' household. She recalled the party where several bottles of wine had been consumed. She couldn't remember how Luke Hammond had become involved in a staff party when he was a guest of the family, but she did remember his strong arms which had carried her to her room next to the children's nursery.

'Life has given me compensations,' he said in a low voice. 'The Maitlands, the Hinckleys and others. Families of fellow officers have all made me welcome – but it's not like having a family of one's own.'

Fran drank her coffee slowly. She thought how sad it was that he had nowhere to call his own.

He stood up, pushing the chair back with his legs. He came to her side and as she rose he removed her chair.

'There's more coffee,' he offered, being the perfect host. 'Let's sit on the couch by the window.'

It was totally dark outside now. Luke dimmed the room lights and they sat looking out to sea, sipping their coffee without speaking. A pale crescent moon hung like a lantern in the sky, and the waves lapped gently on the shore below. He took the cups back to the trolley and rang for a waiter to come and remove it. While they waited, Fran went to the bathroom. She looked at herself in the mirror. Flushed, expectant, enjoying these few moments of freedom . . .

Luke was standing close to the huge window when she returned.

'It's been lovely,' she said in a soft voice, 'but I ought to be going now.'

Luke turned slowly – so very slowly. Fran's heart began jumping nervously. You're not a young girl, she reminded herself. But she was a woman. A lonely one – with love to spare only for her children?

Luke took her in his arms gently. She melted in his embrace in spite of some warning which she didn't intend to heed. He stooped to place his mouth over hers and she didn't resist. No longer was he the handsome naval officer for whom she felt sorry. Like the hands of a clock spinning backwards at a fantastic speed, he became the hungry, masculine lover of twenty years ago.

'I love you,' he murmured. 'I really love you, Fran. The only woman I have ever truly loved. My woman, my family, this is what

114

I've longed for and there's no going back. There's no reason at all to feel guilty, Fran. No one can expect you to remain on your own forever. You had a good marriage to Henry — I hope he realised what a lucky man he was to have a woman so utterly capable of making a man happy — but that's in the past now. We must build a future together for ourselves and our children.'

'Luke, I've already got four daughters,' she reminded him.

'And now they'll be my daughters, just as Lennie was my son.'

She knew she ought to argue that point just as she had in the past, but if it pleased Luke to fantasise about her first-born what harm could it do?

'You will marry me, won't you?' he whispered.

Fran turned from him. All the frustration of the past two years had been wiped out this evening. Her feelings of desire made her feel like a whole woman again, but she could not forget the many times she had rejected Henry when fatigue prevented her from being a good wife to him. He had been the capable one, she thought. Virile, untiring, patient in persuasion — he had been the perfect teacher, the perfect partner.

'You're going too fast,' she pleaded quietly. 'Marriage is a big step to take.'

'If you're feeling unfaithful to Henry's memory, then don't. He wouldn't like you to have to share so many burdens alone, Fran. He made you happy, he would be pleased that you found someone else who could look after you and help to keep you young — and I will, I swear before God I'll do everything I can to make life easier for you.'

What a dilemma! How could she refuse? Instead of her having to make important decisions, Luke would be there to advise and give her courage. She should count herself lucky that a man in such a good position wanted her and her family. Most widows of a similar age didn't get a second chance of happiness.

'I can't make that kind of decision without giving the matter a great deal of thought,' she said. 'Whatever will the girls say? And Ma, and my in-laws? Somehow I don't think they'll like it. I can't promise that they'll all accept you without reservations.'

'Then I shall have to persuade them.' He held her shoulders firmly.

'Just as I must persuade you to say what I want to hear.' He kissed her gently, wooing her, until she was returning his kisses with ardour.

Chapter Nine

'Luke and I are going to be married, Ma,' Fran said, doubtful about the timing of such a statement. Would there ever be a right time to tell her mother? She was languishing under a cloud of uncertainty, elevated by a measure of excitement. She wasn't sure of her own reactions, let alone those of her family.

Had she given in because she loved Luke or because it was an easy way out of her troubles? Was her decision made on the rebound?

'I hope you'll give us your blessing, Mrs Brown?' Luke said, standing tall in his naval uniform. 'I'm not taking Fran away from you for ever.'

Ma gazed as if mesmerised from Fran to Luke. Luke placed an arm about her.

'Come and sit down,' he said kindly. 'I'm sorry if this has come as a shock to you. We thought you might have guessed.'

'I knew you were keen on her,' Ma said, disparagingly. 'I'm not blind, but I didn't realise it had gone this far so quickly.'

'It isn't as if we're young, Ma,' Fran excused. Her voice cracked with more uncertainty as she realised the implication of what Luke had just said. Caught up in a whirlwind of romantic adventure, being courted with such flair, she had given little consideration to the future. It wasn't just a decision to become Luke's wife. There was more to it than that. He had talked of appointments abroad. How was that going to affect the girls and Ma? His words 'I'm not taking Fran away from you for ever' brought home the full realisation of what marriage to Luke entailed. She felt her stomach muscles tighten into a knot. To a younger woman there might be some attraction in the lifestyle of a naval officer. Fran felt she was getting out of her depth. They needed to discuss forthcoming plans which involved all the family. Luke had revived sensuous desires in Fran which had lain dormant for too long, desires she thought were dead for ever.

'Fran wanted you to be the first to know,' Luke said. 'Before she tells the girls when they get back from Sherbrook — my girls now,' he added, evidently trying to impress his future mother-in-law.

'I'm sure I don't know what to think, let alone say,' Ma said. 'I hope you know what you're doing, Fran, that's all.' She turned and left the room, leaving Luke and Fran staring after her blankly.

Luke placed an arm round Fran's waist. 'She'll come round, darling,' he consoled. 'It's been a shock to her.'

Fran pulled away. 'I'll get the tea. The girls will be here soon.'

Luke knew better than to press Fran. Her mother's opinion would naturally be important to her. He just hoped she didn't have too much influence over her daughter but already he sensed a stiffness in Fran.

Ma fetched the best china cups and saucers from the cabinet in the front sitting room. She and Fran worked silently together to prepare afternoon tea for all the family except Kate, but including Prue and Marion, who were bringing the girls back on the train.

'I could have gone to fetch them from the station,' Luke said as he watched the procedure with slight misgivings.

'There wouldn't be room for all of us. I told Prue to take a taxi. Ah! Sounds like them now. I'll go and help with the luggage.'

'Want me to come too?' he offered.

'No, it's all right, we'll manage.'

Luke caught Fran before she left the room. 'What's up? You've suddenly changed. Is it your mother's attitude?'

'No!' Fran pushed his hands away and looked up into his eyes. The warmth had vanished from her own, changing them from cornflower blue to the sharpness of steel. 'Your attitude, Luke. I never said I would travel with you and leave the children. You made it sound as if I would.'

'But you'll have to. I have a house in Portsmouth. You surely don't imagine that I'm going to live there and leave you here? No, Fran, it isn't going to be that kind of marriage. I shall probably be given a shore-based job for a couple of years — it'll most likely be in Scotland and you'll be going there with me.'

'I — well, I thought I'd stay here and you'd come home to us when you have leave,' she said. 'I simply cannot part with my girls, Luke.'

'And I simply cannot embark on married life with a ready-made family. The girls have your mother.'

'She's too old to take the responsibility.' Fran turned and went to open the front door. In seconds the house was full of women

117

talking together, until Babs came face to face with a vaguely familiar person.

'Hullo, Copperknob,' Luke said, holding out his hand to her. 'Have you had a lovely holiday back in Sherbrook? That's where we first met — d'you remember? In your garden at the old mill house?'

Babs went all shy and ran to her mother, clutching her tightly.

'It's all right, darling,' Fran said. 'Captain Hammond was very kind when Kate was ill in hospital, wasn't he?' Fran ushered Hilda and Ruby in and they shook hands politely. 'And this is Prue's daughter, Marion; I'm not sure whether you've met or not.'

When the greetings were over, Gran made the tea, and Fran seated everyone round the extended kitchen table.

'Are you going back to Sherbrook tonight?' Luke asked Prue.

'No, they're staying here,' Fran put in sharply. The girls all whooped with delight.

Luke was well aware that this arrangement was a surprise to everyone. He didn't intend to be outdone, and as the children were finishing their meal he looked across at Fran with a smile. 'I think now is as good a time as any, darling,' he said softly but with the hint of a command.

Fran went slightly pink as she stood up. 'I ... I know it'll be a bit of a shock to you, girls,' she began hesitantly.

'Your mother and I are going to be married,' Luke said, taking over the situation.

There was a deathly hush. The girls seemed to shrink in their seats. Babs left her chair and ran to Fran, who had sat down quickly.

'That's marvellous,' Prue said. 'So, congratulations are in order, then?' She reached across and shook Luke by the hand, then went to Fran and kissed her warmly.

'I hope everyone else will be as pleased as you are, Prue,' Luke said. 'Unfortunately I have to return to my ship tomorrow, so it means that I shall have to leave the arrangements to Fran, but I'm sure I can count on you as her closest friend to give her all the help and support she'll need.'

'Of course,' Prue said, but she saw that Fran's eyes were moist.

'I'm sure no one will mind if I take Fran away for this evening,' Luke went on. 'Being my last night we'd like to be together.'

'I must see the girls to bed tonight,' Fran insisted. 'They've been away for over a week.'

'I can see to them,' Prue offered eagerly. 'But first I'll help Gran with the washing-up — or, better still, Marion and Ruby can help me, while Fran sees to the two little ones.'

'We'd better get the case upstairs first,' Fran said pointedly, and Prue took the bait.

Upstairs in the main bedroom Fran collapsed in tears. 'What have I done, Prue? I didn't say I'd leave the girls with Ma to go off wherever he wanted.'

'Now start at the beginning and tell me how all this came about.'

Fran had to tell her story briefly and Prue listened patiently, doing her best to calm her friend down.

'You obviously fell overboard for him, Fran dear. I admire your choice − he's a very nice man − but it sounds to me as if you've rushed into it all without spending enough time thrashing things out.'

'He talked about the girls being his − I naturally thought we would carry on living here and he'd come home when he gets leave.'

Prue raised her eyebrows. 'You've certainly been bitten by the love-bug, Fran dear. A naval captain living here? He'll expect you to join him in naval quarters.'

'He's got a house in Portsmouth which I didn't know about. Now he says he'll be posted to Scotland, and expects me to accompany him. I simply can't leave the girls with Ma. It would be too much for her.'

Prue opened the girls' case and started unpacking. 'I can see why you suddenly decided that we were staying. You'd better have all this out with him before he goes away. Were you really serious about us staying?'

'Please do, Prue,' Fran begged. 'I need someone to talk to − and there's Ma, she hasn't taken too kindly to the news.'

'When you've gone out I'll go and telephone the Maitlands, ask Withers if he'll give Sam a message to say we're staying over. But we'll have to do a bit of borrowing, I'm afraid.'

'The beds have all been remade with clean sheets. My three girls can manage in one bed, you and Marion can have my bed, and I'll go in Kate's room.' Fran wept again. 'Prue, you can't know what it's been like without Henry. So much responsibility, so much worry. When Luke was there when Kate was ill I was grateful for his comfort, and then to turn up out of the blue while I was here alone . . . I'm afraid I just got carried away.'

'I saw him about with the Maitlands, and presumed he'd gone back to sea. There's talk that Mr Nicholas is walking out with a young lady and is likely to be married soon.'

'It must be in the air. I suppose they're getting older and think

119

it's time they settled down. Obviously Luke knew that everyone was away — there aren't any secrets in Sherbrook — so he took the opportunity.'

'I think you're right to remarry, Fran. You aren't old and it isn't right to let the girls dominate your life. After all, they'll all marry one day and you'll be left on your own.'

'That's a long way ahead in the future. I vowed I'd live for them and not let them down for Henry's sake.'

'Remembering Henry as I do, Fran,' Prue said, 'he'd be the last person to stand in your way. Your happiness would have to come first.'

'It all seemed so right before today,' she said miserably.

'You go and get ready and I'll see to everything here. Have a good talk and let Luke know how you feel. It'll be all right, you'll see,' Prue assured her.

Fran kissed the two little girls good night and left the family in Prue's charge. Luke drove to the hotel and immediately ordered dinner to be sent up to his room.

'We may as well make the most of our last evening together,' he said as they went up in the lift.

In the privacy of his suite he gathered Fran in his arms, but she gave him a cold kiss and pushed him away.

'I hope you're not regretting your decision already, Fran?' he asked. 'I'm astounded at your naivety. A serviceman can hardly take a large family around everywhere with him. You must see that, my dear. It wouldn't be good for their education. Schools vary so much from county to county.'

'We should have discussed things more, Luke. It was silly of me to think you'd want my girls.'

'Darling,' he implored, 'I do want your girls — I want what's best for them, and it isn't with us. If your mother can't manage alone, we'll get someone in to help her. Or there's Kate — she could stay at home to look after them all, and I'll pay her the equivalent of wages.'

'No, no, that wouldn't be fair on Kate. She's only eighteen and look what happened when I left her behind at Sherbrook.'

'She met Maurice Lambert and if it hadn't been for that rotten friend of his I dare say he and Kate would be engaged by now. The girls won't consider you when they want to leave the nest.'

They were interrupted by their dinner trolley arriving. Fran wasn't hungry and only toyed with her food.

'Fran, I'm sorry if I've spoilt things between us, but you are rather making a mountain out of a molehill, you know.'

'My girls are my life, Luke. I've devoted my days and nights to those children for Henry's sake, and now you're asking me to desert them.'

Luke dabbed at his mouth with his table napkin. 'Not *asking* you to, Fran, I'm afraid I must insist that you make arrangements for their wellbeing. When the time comes for me to go away to sea for a long stretch, you can return to Brimdene then.'

'I understood you to say that you liked Brimdene?'

'You misconstrued my meaning. I do like Brimdene − because you were here − but I cannot overlook the fact that I'm committed to the Royal Navy.'

'I can't see why we can't all live here together,' Fran said, trying to keep her temper.

'Because we can't,' Luke said adamantly. '*I* can't live without you for weeks on end − until I am obliged to,' he added, 'but maybe this has all been fun and frolic to you. I didn't think you were capable of shallow intentions.'

'That's not fair, Luke,' she cried hotly. 'There was nothing shallow in my thoughts or actions, but I did think you'd have more consideration for my feelings where my children are concerned. Perhaps this has all been a terrible mistake. If you think I was just husband-hunting then I'd better leave.' She stood up abruptly. 'Don't bother coming down with me, I'll call a taxi.'

Luke was on his feet in a flash, and the tension between them was electric.

Later, as Fran lay in Luke's arms relishing the warmth of his affections, her mind was confused about the future. Luke kissed her forehead tenderly.

'Let's talk about this sensibly. Perhaps we could have little Copperknob with us eventually,' he whispered into her hair, diffusing the situation.

'I can't give up my Hilda, Luke, not for you or anyone else − ever. She's not strong, she's like Lennie, she'll always need me. I expect Ruby would be all right with Ma, but Babs − she's so young − and she was Henry's baby ...'

'What about Prue? She's had the girls over Easter − she seems to love children and at least you'd be certain she would look after them well. When she travelled with me the night Kate was taken ill she told me that they adopted Marion.'

Fran murmured in reply. She hated herself for what was happening, angry that she could seem to do nothing to prevent it.

'I'm sure she'd love to have Babs,' Luke continued. 'Children adapt more easily that one would expect. Like animals, as long as they're fed regularly, they're happy.'

'I can't believe my girls will be happy without me,' she sobbed.

'Prue wanted to adopt Babs when Henry died, so she said.'

This was all like a beautiful dream changing dramatically into a nightmare. 'I must go home, Luke,' Fran said. 'They'll be wondering where I am.'

'I'll take you, of course. It's only ten-thirty — quite a respectable hour, but I do have to be up early tomorrow.'

As Fran put on her hat in front of the mirror, Luke pulled out his wallet.

'Here's fifty pounds, Fran.' She looked aghast, as if he might be paying her off. 'There'll be clothes to buy for our honeymoon, extras for things the girls will need and for the wedding — where is it to be?'

'Goodness, I hadn't even thought about *that*,' she said crossly.

He held her fast and looked directly into her eyes. 'Nothing's changed, my sweet. I refuse to let you go now. I'm not a particularly religious man so we can have a quiet civil ceremony if you prefer — but somehow I think you'd like a church wedding. The girls should be there, and as many of your family as you like. Nick Maitland will be my best man and my only other guest will be my sister Elizabeth. We've always kept in touch and I know you'll like each other.'

'What other secrets have you kept from me?' she demanded icily. 'You said you had no home, no family, yet now I learn that you have a house in Portsmouth, parents and sisters.'

'I said that I had no family and home as such. That's what I want more than anything, darling. To know that you're there waiting for me just as I've always dreamed.'

Fran shook her head sadly. 'Oh, what a mess! I never meant to get involved again,' she cried passionately.

'It's happened rather suddenly, I grant you. Time is never on my side, but our dream can be reality if we want it to be. The children won't suffer nearly as much as you imagine and as they grow up they'll be glad to have a step father to turn to sometimes. They'll be concerned for your happiness, Fran.' He went to a small briefcase and took something from it. 'Please wear my ring, darling.' Fran gasped as he opened the small box, revealing a sparkling diamond set in a cluster of sapphires. 'To match your eyes — well, nearly. And now there's no going back,' he said, as he slipped Henry's rings on to the third finger of her right hand, and slipped his engagement ring on the left.

He pressed her fingers to his mouth. 'No longer than three months until we seal this with a wedding ring,' he promised. 'I'll write each week, but you may receive several letters together. Please write to me as often as you can. I'll be as helpful as is humanly possible with any problems you may come up against.'

Fran hadn't the heart to put a stop to this charade. It couldn't, it mustn't happen for the sake of the girls, but neither could she deny herself Luke's love.

Fran thought things might look better next morning, but everyone got up with a gloomy expression.

'You can't marry him, Mum!' Ruby burst out the moment she saw her mother. 'Daddy would hate it — you know he would. It's horrible — I hate him, and I hate you too.' As always Ruby let forth great wails of dissent, and Babs clung to Fran wherever she went. It was as if she knew what her fate was to be.

After breakfast Fran insisted that the girls went out into the garden to play while she and Prue sat down to talk.

'Well, what have you decided?' Prue asked.

'*He's* decided,' Fran said slowly, 'that I can take Hilda with me and you can have Babs, but I can't do it, Prue.'

'And what about your mother and Ruby?'

'They've always been quite close. Ruby's twelve now and it isn't as if Kate's far away. There's Sissy, too — though how I'm going to tell Henry's family, I just don't know.'

'You've just said you can't do it, but you seem to have made all the arrangements' Prue perceived.

'Oh, Prue, I hardly slept a wink. My mind was in such a turmoil.'

'Answer me one thing, Fran dear — do you love Luke Hammond, enough to marry him?'

'Oh yes! I don't have any doubts on that score. But it isn't fair to make me choose between him and my children.'

Prue sighed, and placed a comforting hand over Fran's. 'This is one time when I agree with him. It's your life. It was your life that was ruined by the accident. You've been a good mother to the girls, and no one dare say otherwise. Surely now you can grab some happiness while you've got the chance. He might not be ashore for as long as he thinks, and then you can come home again. It won't be the end of the world, Fran. And you know you don't need an answer to whether Sam and I will give Babs a good home or not. We'll love to have her.'

Fran looked at Prue through bloodshot eyes. Yes, she thought, but what would Babs think about it? Her baby! How could she bear to part with any one of them?

Prue and Marion went home later that day. The girls had all quarrelled a great deal, and Fran was glad to see the back of her visitors even though she valued Prue's opinion. But wasn't Prue biased? She had always coveted Babs, so it was to her own advantage to be on Luke's side. Kate was all right at the hotel, doing well in fact, and Fran was proud of her for picking herself up and getting on with her work. But Ma was already seventy-three. Was it fair to give her the responsibility of Ruby? Ruby was the one who was never going to forgive her.

'Stop worrying, Fran,' Ma said as they prepared dinner together. 'I admit it all seems a bit hasty, but Luke appears to be a kind man and I reckon he thinks it's time he settled down. He won't always be in the Navy, will he? I dare say he never intended to fall for a woman with four daughters. You're the one who has to make the choice. 'Tis your life, and if he can offer you the kind of life you want then you must follow your heart.'

Fran couldn't bear to see the uncertainty in her mother's eyes even though she was the one who, having recovered from the initial shock, was now accepting the inevitable. Fran felt guilty. Surely her mother of all people should be attributing blame? It wasn't fair to leave her in this house, which was still strange even after two years. If she had been able to leave her in the shepherd's cottage in Sherbrook it would have been a different matter. Fran was confused, sure that behind the pleasant accord her mother must be feeling aggrieved at what was taking place.

When the meal was over and her mother went upstairs for her afternoon nap, Fran stood on the landing feeling claustrophobic.

'I must get out for a bit, Ma,' she said suddenly. 'I've got a headache coming on and a breath of sea air might blow it away.'

Ma's brow puckered in a frown, but her warm smile reassured her daughter that she understood, and Fran set off to catch the bus into town.

The day was overcast, but still people crowded on to the bus, and when she reached the gardens leading down to the sea there was no shortage of folk admiring the beautiful tulips and late daffodils and narcissi in decorative beds and borders. Nothing looked beautiful to Fran. Her footsteps took her out to the promenade and she walked along, the bracing air fanning her cheeks, while she argued with herself as she fought against the fateful choice she had to make.

She walked briskly until she was midway between the two piers, and there were fewer people. She went to sit in one of the shelters, and took out her brother Eric's letter to read again. He was very good at accusing, she thought defiantly, but his life had been an easy one.

The blue-eyed boy, he usually managed to sway anyone to his way of thinking if he tried hard enough, but he hadn't succeeded in getting Ma on his side this time. Dear Ma! Fran knew she didn't deserve her blessing. She hadn't always been as thoughtful and patient as she should have been, and now she was casting her responsibilities on old shoulders. She tried to picture Ruby and Ma together. Ruby was wilful and stubborn, but she was also kind and caring and if anyone would look after her gran it was Ruby.

Fran realised why Luke didn't want the children, of course. Their presence would affect their marriage, and since they were not his offspring it was understandable he might feel they were in the way. Just thinking about the controlled passion that existed between them brought a glow to her cheeks and a pain in the pit of her stomach. She had thought of no one but the children since Henry's death, resulting in emotional frustration as well as physical. Surely no one had the right to deny her this new-found happiness? She ought to be feeling deliriously happy. Most women would envy her, especially widows who, like her, had found it difficult to make ends meet, not to mention coping with the loneliness. It was as if fortune was smiling on her for once. It wasn't as if Luke was a complete stranger either – far from it. Time and distance seemed to have strengthened his affection for her. If she was truly honest, she had never quite put him out of her thoughts even in nearly twenty years. It was like a daydream come true. An age-old fantasy of the kitchen maid falling in love with the elegant master of the house, only in this case it was the nanny and here she was realising the idle fancy. She ought to be counting her blessings.

But it was the price she had to pay for her new way of life that troubled her conscience. The loss of her children, splitting the family, each of the girls somewhere different. Hilda would be with her, but she would miss Babs just as Babs was going to pine for Hilda. How was Babs going to like being taken over by Prue and Sam? They'd be good to her, she didn't doubt that, but Babs was hers, hers and Henry's. A funny little thing who showed her affection in a variety of ways. She was demonstrative, needing to be cuddled and kissed. She had accepted Luke and was ever ready to sit on his knee and allow him to fondle her. No wonder he wanted to take her as part of the deal. Part of the deal? What was she thinking about? This was marriage – for better or worse, richer or poorer, in sickness and in health, to love, honour and obey.

The sea stretched out to the far horizon. Waves rolling into the shore with an occasional white horse, before they lapped at the water's edge and disappeared. Luke loved the sea, just as much

125

as Henry had loved his horses. The sea brought a calm to Fran's troubled breast, and she listened for some distant voice to advise her, but there was no answer to her agonised plea. Was it so wrong to want to change her life style? To want more than working, keeping house, thinking for so many people, sewing to make ends meet, and no one to share the burdens of everyday complications?

Destiny had offered her an escape route, a means to freedom. Chances like this came but once in a lifetime, and Luke had made the decision for her. Who was she to disobey?

Chapter Ten

Fran had cause to be proud of her girls. Once they got over the shock of her decision to marry Luke Hammond, they viewed the event with mounting excitement. During the weeks leading up to the June wedding day Fran was fraught with changing emotions, but she worked all her doubts into the dresses she made for the girls. Long, lonely hours of toil while with every stitch she tried to qualify her decision. Ma, bless her, uttered not one word of reproach, yet Eric made loud noises of disapproval. As an act of protest he decided not to accept the invitation to come to the wedding. Fran was sure that Annie and May were disappointed to miss such an occasion.

The morning started with an overcast sky, but by midday, when the bridal party stood ready and waiting in the front sitting room, the sun broke through with the promise of a warm day.

Ruby, Hilda and Babs looked enchanting in dainty voile dresses decorated with satin ribbons and bows. They travelled to the church in one car with Gran Brown and Kate, who acted as Fran's bridesmaid. She wore an ankle-length dress. Her hair was hidden by a large-brimmed straw hat and she appeared three inches taller in her high-heeled patent-leather shoes.

Fran, looking elegant in a midnight-blue silk dress and jacket with grey accessories, tightened her grip on the ivory-covered prayer book she carried. A white ribbon bookmark with a spray of pink rosebuds hung from it. Nathan, who was giving her away, noticed that she was trembling. He took her gloved hand in his and squeezed affectionately.

'I know you're having doubts, Fran dear,' he said gently. 'Don't. Henry would give you his blessing, be sure of that.'

'Not to the price I'm paying for my selfishness,' she said softly. 'I've done everything to try to make Luke change his mind about taking the girls to Scotland with us, but he'll only agree to taking Hilda. The others will never forgive me, will they?'

'You're feeling guilty, but I dare say that Luke's decision is best for the girls. It won't be for ever, Fran. You deserve a holiday, a break from the past. You know we'll be here for Ruby and Ma, should they need us. Kate will be on hand, too, as well as Sissy. Babs will be fine with your friends in Sherbrook. For her it will be like going home again and she'll meet up with her old friends. You worry too much. None of us are indispensable.' Nathan lifted Fran's quivering chin and wiped away a stray tear with his finger. 'Come on now. Head up, walk tall with a big smile to greet Luke, who's a very lucky man.'

The parish church in Brimdene was only a five-minute drive away. Soon Fran was walking down the aisle on Nathan's arm. All her fears and doubt vanished as Luke turned to admire his bride − the woman of his dreams.

Fran's expression lifted as Luke smiled lovingly at her. Two handsome naval officers were standing side by side below the altar, one of whom was to be her husband. How could she have doubts when happiness beckoned invitingly? Happiness because she knew how fortunate she was to have a second chance in life. The chance to make Luke happy, and in return have someone with whom to share the responsibility of her family.

In a soft, barely audible whisper Fran made her vows solemnly before God, promising to love, honour and obey her husband. Luke responded with his vows in a clear, polished and confident voice. The ceremony lasted only half an hour and after signing the register they emerged in the sunshine to pose for the photographer.

The rest of the day passed so swiftly that Fran had to search her mind afterwards to recall certain incidents. The girls throwing confetti, everyone's amusement when Babs asked for another piece of wedding cake, and after the small reception the worst part of saying goodbye. Not just goodbye for the three-day honeymoon but − for how long? Her darling Babs was going home to Sherbrook without her. Fran felt a tightness in her chest when the moment of parting came.

The sea crossing to the Isle of Wight was calm, and it was growing dusk as a taxi took the newlyweds to their hotel. Luke had made most of the arrangements and Fran could find no fault with anything.

'Would you like a meal sent up?' Luke asked her as the porter delivered the suitcases to their room.

'No thanks, I couldn't eat a thing.'

The porter left hurriedly and Luke gave his wife a wicked kind of smile. 'And all I want to eat is you, my darling.' With no more than a couple of long strides he spanned the distance between them and gathered her in his arms. 'How I've managed to restrain myself all day I can't imagine,' he said, laughing down at her. 'Was everything the way you wanted it, Fran?' he asked, suddenly serious.

'It was a very happy day, Luke,' she said. 'Thank you for everything. I hope it all came up to your expectations too?'

'All I've ever wanted was you, and now you're mine — really mine. I'm a very lucky man.' His mouth touched hers with the briefest of kisses. 'Let's unpack in the morning.'

Fran went to the bathroom, where she looked at herself in the mirror. Flushed, expectant, she knew the moment of reckoning had come. For over twenty years she had kept a memory locked inside her heart, never exposing it to anyone lest it should fade. Was it all a young girl's dream? Had almost twenty years of marital bliss with Henry devalued that night of passionate embraces?

Fran didn't hear the bathroom door open without so much as a creak, but suddenly she was looking at two faces in the mirror. Luke rested his cheek against hers, then his moist lips found the sensitive spot in her neck and the memory quickly changed to reality.

'You've kept me waiting too long, Mrs Hammond,' he said playfully. 'You cruelly denied me before I went to sea, now you'll have to forgive my impatience.'

In spite of all the thoughts that were taunting her, Fran melted in Luke's arms. His body was firm and strong, protective too. Luke demanded, Fran gave. He turned her round to face him.

'My dream fulfilled at last,' he whispered breathlessly, then he picked her up and carried her to the large bed. His lips forced hers apart, his tongue curling around hers, hot and passionate with a thirst as yet unsatiated.

Every pulse in Fran's body was racing as he helped her to undress. Her new shimmering nightgown was unnecessary. She could hardly wait while he took off his clothes and then he was teasing, exploring, exciting her to breathtaking heights. The past drifted into oblivion, everyone else forgotten as she felt a sweet breeze waft over the lower half of her body. He was astride her, eager yet holding himself in check as he took his fill of the beauty of her cornflower-blue eyes. 'We shall always be good together, my darling,' he whispered.

Fran was conscious of the rise and fall of her breasts, fuller now than they had been twenty years ago. Luke's lips travelled down from her throat, briefly caressing each breast in turn, causing her the wildest sensations. There was satisfaction for him in just gazing

129

at her beautiful white skin and he moaned with delight as he buried his face in the soft valley of her bosom. Fran wrapped her arms around his bronzed torso, drawing him ever closer. They were both in their prime, eager for each other ...

Clouds scudding across the sky passed unnoticed as Luke and Fran explored quaint villages and old churches and admired Osborne House and Carisbrooke Castle. They were staying in Shanklin, one of the island's most popular resorts, and after dinner in the evening of the second day they strolled through the lovely Chine where a cascade of water flowed beneath an ivy-clad stone bridge to the sea. Life here was unhurried, uncomplicated. With their common love of the sea they could bask in the summer sun by day and allow their feelings for each other full rein during the hours of darkness.

Last-minute shopping brought their three-day idyll to a close. As they stood on the deck of the ferry returning to the mainland, Fran shivered with the cold realisation of the heartache she had brought upon herself. No matter how much she loved her husband and wanted to please him, she couldn't rid herself of the heavy burden of guilt at splitting up her girls.

But Luke saw to it that she didn't have time for recriminations. No sooner were they back in Brimdene than the family were waving them off on the train to London, where they boarded the night train to Edinburgh.

Nine-year-old Hilda showed no signs of dismay at having left her sisters behind, The majestic *Flying Scotsman* standing at the platform at King's Cross station hissed impatiently as passengers climbed aboard, and Hilda ran along the corridor enthusiastically to find their compartment. Fran did her best to appear light-hearted but she was coming down to earth with a bump. Once they were on their way it seemed to Fran as if the metal chattering on metal was sending out a message for her ears alone. 'You're left them behind, you've left them behind ... clackety-clack ... clackety-clack ...' Fran's head began to ache and she felt she wanted to run, to place her hands over her ears to shut out the condemnation. She thought she was a strong woman, had grown stronger since being left a widow, and yet she had fallen under Luke's spell almost gratefully. Had she only considered the plus side? Was having a handsome husband to pay all the bills more important than having the girls under her wing?

The night journey seemed never ending even though the bunks were relatively comfortable. Hilda was quickly asleep and Fran could tell by Luke's even breathing that he was too. But sleep only came in fits and starts for Fran, and as dawn came up she went to the washroom at the end of the corridor. On the way back to their compartment she paused, the pretty sky attracting her attention. An orange glow on the eastern horizon touched the fluffy balls of white cloud, turning them into pale pink snowflakes floating in a turquoise-coloured heaven. She clung to the handrail as she stood at the window looking out. Looking out to a new future, which appeared bright at this moment. The scenery that sped past was unfamiliar to her, yet it was green countryside similar to her native Dorset. For Luke's sake she must be happy. They wouldn't live in Scotland for ever. Eventually Luke would return to the sea for a long period, and then she would go home to Brimdene and her house full of women.

Smoke-blackened buildings, tall church spires and a distant castle on a hill were their first sight of Edinburgh.

'How's your head now?' Luke asked Fran with concern.

'Still throbs a bit, but the Aspro helped.'

'Getting out in the crisp morning air will make you feel more human. You're not used to travelling such long distances. We'll have a break now for breakfast – a proper one, not just tea and toast.'

'I couldn't have eaten anything else on the journey,' Fran said. 'And Hilda looks rather pale.'

'We'll find a nice restaurant and have scrambled eggs and some coffee.'

'What's the matter with the station buffet?' Fran asked.

'Too crowded, and it'll be nice to get away from the smell of engines. Our connecting train to Dunfermline doesn't leave Edinburgh until mid-morning so we've plenty of time.'

'When are we going to get to our new house?' Hilda whined.

'Not much longer, Hilda,' Luke said. 'It's a cottage, similar to the old mill house at Sherbrook. There's a lake nearby – well, the Scots call lakes lochs – and we'll be sheltered from the winds by the Cleish Hills.'

'I wish we were going to a town like Brimdene.' Although Hilda had slept for most of the long journey north it was evident that she was travel-weary.

'Your mother prefers the country, Hilda,' Luke said shortly. 'Dunfermline is only about five miles away and there's a school bus every day.'

Hilda didn't appear to be impressed by the mention of school, but after they had walked to the restaurant in Princes Street, and enjoyed their breakfast, she perked up considerably.

Luke left Fran and Hilda window-shopping while he went to a telephone kiosk and made a call.

'The car is waiting at Dunfermline station,' he said, as he rejoined them. 'I had it transported earlier in the week so I needed to check that it had arrived safely. Hope it hasn't got too battered about.'

Fran loved everything about Princes Street, the different tartans colourful in the shops, and the friendly atmosphere.

'We'll be able to come here sometimes, darling,' Luke assured her. 'We can drive in for dinner or go to a show.'

Fran shot Luke a doubtful glance. He replied by giving her an affectionate squeeze. 'I know,' he murmured softly, 'we have to think about Hilda. I have thought, and arranged that the woman who will be our housekeeper will also act as Hilda's minder. She lives in the same village of Craiglee, but as she's a widow she'll be free to stay overnight any time we need her to.'

'But I couldn't leave Hilda with a complete stranger.'

Luke laughed. 'I didn't say we were going to paint the town every night, or even tomorrow or the next day. I shall be more than content to be at the cottage with you. When you get to know Mrs Logan you'll find she's most trustworthy.'

'But how d'you know?' Fran asked. 'You haven't seen the cottage yet, have you?'

'No. But I know my sister Elizabeth wouldn't have employed anyone she wasn't completely confident about. The Royal Navy made most of the arrangements. They have certain properties on their list for naval personnel, and Elizabeth came up one weekend about a month ago to check everything out. Mrs Logan comes highly recommended, so I'm sure you've no need to worry.'

'That was kind of your sister,' Fran said. 'I wish I'd had time to get to know her better, Luke, but it was nice that she could attend the wedding. It's a shame you don't even correspond with your parents, though.'

'Elizabeth and I are very close, even though we may not see one another for months or even years. There's only ten months' difference in our ages. We were more like twins in many ways. My other sisters are younger.'

'Tell me about them, Luke?'

'Oh,' he sighed, 'not much to tell really. Cecilia comes next, she's about thirty now, I suppose, and Dorinda is the youngest, she's twenty-eight. They're both married with families. Boys mostly, who'll go into the family business.'

'And you were the only boy?'

'There were two more after Elizabeth, but both died in infancy.

That's why there's a large gap between Elizabeth and Cecilia.'

'It does seem a shame that as the eldest of the family, and only son, you've distanced yourself from them all.'

Luke shrugged. 'The sea is my life and always will be until I'm forced to retire. Being the eldest and only boy my parents gave me the best education, sending me away to boarding school, so it wasn't surprising that I grew away from them all and made my own decision about my career. I didn't feel the foundry was the place for me. I do realise how disappointed my father must have been, and if I hadn't run away to sea he would have compelled me to go into the business.'

He sounded bitter, Fran thought.

'I think we'd better go back to the station,' he said, indicating that he didn't wish to discuss his family any further. Fran had heard enough to understand what it must have been like for him, an only boy with three younger sisters. She didn't blame him for the decision he had made. He was something of a rebel, and he had obviously wounded his parents deeply. Being a parent herself she could sympathise with them. On the other hand, after all these years she felt that they should have forgiven him. He had proved himself and they ought to be proud of him.

The steam train puffed its way out of the station and was soon passing over the magnificent cantilever bridge that spanned the Firth of Forth.

'The Forth Bridge is one of the great wonders of the world,' Luke explained as he took Fran and Hilda to the window to look out. 'A great engineering achievement. Here's a penny each for you to throw out for luck, as it's your first time across.'

'This will be something to write and tell your sisters about,' Fran said, and immediately became engulfed in remorse that the others were not able to share these new experiences.

They returned to their seats and very quickly reached their destination on the other side of the water, the neat little town of Dunfermline. Then came the task of collecting their many trunks and cases, which a porter took to Luke's car. The five-mile journey was the climax now to so many hours of travelling. Hills rose from green pastures where sheep and cattle grazed undisturbed, and nestling in the valley was the Craiglee Loch, blue from the reflection of an azure sky. The village consisted of a few isolated whitewashed cottages dotted among rocky hillocks.

'This is the main street, if you can call it that,' Luke said. 'There's a post office and general stores where you can get most of the supplies you'll need. The local kirk — '

'What's *that*?' Hilda demanded.

'Church, and attached to it is a local infant's school, but you're past that, aren't you? So you'll go by bus into Dunfermline every day. I expect you'll soon get used to it and make friends with the other children.'

Hilda remained thoughtful after that, and Fran too, as Luke drove beyond the so-called main street, past the cluster of cottages, and down a steep hill where he turned left and up an incline until a handsome stone house came into view. Fran gasped with pleasure. It was larger than she had imagined. Several windows on the upper floor were curtained with dainty lace, and on the lower floor the front door was reached by a flight of steps running down the side of the house. Even before Luke had switched off the car engine, the front door opened and a thin little woman ran down the steps.

'Hullo there,' she called cheerily. 'You'll be Captain and Mrs Hammond. I'm Jenny Logan. I'm pleased to meet you.'

Luke got out of the car and went to shake hands with the housekeeper, and then he introduced Fran and Hilda. Jenny Logan was well past sixty, Fran thought, but the warmth and friendliness of her welcome made her seem much younger.

First Fran just had to inspect her new home, and it was the view from each window that took precedence. Below street level was the basement floor housing the kitchen and living rooms, which at the back of the house looked out over green pastures and a stream that led into the loch half a mile away. It was past noon and the sun was high, its reflection glistening on the distant water. Fran was enchanted.

'This house was owned by a wealthy landowner many years ago,' Jenny said. 'Not many houses here run to three floors and two bathrooms. By town standards it's regarded as a cottage, but most in the area are very tiny compared with this. You have other children, I understand, so there's plenty of room for them to come to stay for their holidays. It's been well modernised, but they had to conform to keeping the original character of the house. I hope you like it, Mrs Hammond, and I hope you'll be happy here in our little community.'

'It's quite lovely,' Fran said. 'I'm sure we'll be very happy here.' She looked at Luke, wondering whether he was responsible for telling Jenny Logan about the other girls. She felt her spirits lift at once at the suggestion that they might come for their school holidays.

'I'll serve dinner as soon as you're ready,' Jenny said. 'And then I'll start the unpacking while you're eating.'

They freshened up in the basement cloakroom, and then sat at the long oak refectory table in front of the dining-room window. Luke placed a hand over Fran's. 'Happy, darling?' he whispered.

'Couldn't be happier,' she answered, her blue eyes shining contentedly. 'It's all so fresh and the air so bracing. The house is much larger than you led me to believe.'

'I wanted to surprise you. From the information passed on to me it seemed ideal. On the next floor there's a large sitting room where we can entertain. The smaller one can connect up to it by opening the folding doors, but we can enjoy long winter evenings cosily there together. Then there's a smaller room at the front next to my study which you could use for your sewing room. It can double up as a spare bedroom since it has a sofa bed in it. On the top floor we have four good-sized bedrooms and a bathroom. I know you can't wait to investigate everywhere properly when Jenny Logan has gone home.' He mouthed a kiss. 'I'll get rid of her as quickly as I can,' he whispered.

'How do you know so much detail about the house if you haven't seen it before?'

'I told you; Elizabeth. She came to inspect it, made a plan of the house, the rooms and everything in the rooms. I didn't want you to get here and not have everything you might need. Elizabeth did a good job − and in finding Jenny Logan. How often she comes and the hours she works will be our joint decision.' He leaned across and held her chin gently. 'Just make sure you're never too tired for me when I come home.'

'By what you've told me about your work I'll never know when to expect you.'

His dark eyes smouldered as he gazed into hers. 'That's the whole idea, darling. The element of surprise. Never let me come home to find you wallpapering, as you were in Brimdene. That life style is over for you now. I want you to have time to enjoy our married life.'

The light went out of Fran's eyes. Could she possibly cope with this new life of grandeur? Without Ma and the girls to work for, how ever was she going to occupy her time? She was grateful that at that moment Jenny's footsteps could be heard coming from the stone-floored kitchen with Hilda assisting her.

'Now you sit yourself down with your mummy and daddy. I haven't prepared anything heavy, Mrs Hammond,' Jenny said, half apologetically. 'But in my experience travelling lessens the appetite, so I've cooked some potatoes to go with a cold platter and a green salad.'

'It looks delicious, Jenny,' Luke said. 'Kind of you to take so much trouble. So many hours' travelling has made us all tired. I think you can leave whenever you're ready.'

Jenny looked surprised. 'But the clearing, and washing-up?'

'Um, well, yes ... after you've done that, of course.' Luke smiled at the housekeeper in his own charming way. 'We can help ourselves to anything else we might need. It'll be an early night, I think. Time to explore tomorrow.'

'I'll leave you to eat in peace then,' Jenny said. 'I'll start on the unpacking.'

When she had left the room, Fran said: 'I could have done that, Luke. And the washing-up. I hope I won't be banned from my own kitchen.'

'Not at all. Jenny will want at least one day off a week, and part of Sundays, but you must arrange all that with her. Just put yourself in Mrs Maitland's shoes now. You're the lady of the house.'

'Are you really my daddy?' Hilda chipped in.

'I'm officially your step father,' Luke said. 'It is a kind of adopted Daddy. I would consider it a great honour if you would call me daddy, even though I can't hope to take the place of your own father. It'll sound nice and homely, don't you think?'

Hilda looked at Fran, and Fran averted her gaze. It was small details like this that she felt she couldn't handle. Luke was very good at answering Hilda's awkward questions, so she decided it was best left to him.

'My real daddy's been gone a long time, so I don't expect he'd mind if you take his place.'

'Eat your dinner and stop chattering, Hilda,' Fran said. 'We'll have a rest afterwards and then explore the garden.'

Hilda ate quite well for her, but Fran's appetite had vanished.

'You'll have to do better than that, Mrs Hammond,' Luke said, after Hilda had left the room to go and find Jenny Logan.

'I'm just not hungry, Luke,' Fran excused. 'We've had so little exercise, and the long, tiring journey is beginning to catch up with me. I shall feel better after a good night's sleep.'

'Sounds as if you're warning me off.'

'Don't be silly. But we do have to come down to earth sometime.'

'You wouldn't let me make love to you at Brimdene because you were embarrassed with your mother and the girls under the same roof. I can't promise that I can always be so accommodating. This is still our honeymoon, you know.'

'Give me time, Luke – please?'

Luke stood up and helped Fran to her feet. He held her in the circle of his arms, placing his mouth over hers until she relaxed and he knew that he was drawing the doubts away from the forefront of her mind. When her body became supple he relaxed his hold. Just the hint of arousing a response in her satisfied him for the moment. Didn't he have a lifetime to indulge himself with his lovely wife? He must be the happiest sailor in the world, he thought. At last the woman of his dreams was really his, to make him happy for the rest of his days.

Chapter Eleven

There were just about six weeks left of the school term, and Fran felt it was of little value to send Hilda to school for that short period of time, but Luke insisted that it would help Hilda to adjust. Each morning they got up early so that Hilda was in the village to catch the eight-thirty school bus into Dunfermline. Fran went with her the first day, but after that Hilda went with the other children from Craiglee and the surrounding villages.

Luke was on leave for a further three weeks, and the weather was fine and warm for most of that time. Once Hilda had left for school and Jenny Logan had arrived to look after the house, Fran and Luke were free to explore their new habitat. At first there was a slight tension between them. Luke wanted to make the most of every minute they were alone together, while Fran worried about Hilda and needed constant reassurance that she was all right. She worried, too, about the family back in Brimdene. Her mother's letters, instead of helping her to settle, had the opposite effect and made her homesick, even though Ma assured her that they were all fine.

Luke drove them into Edinburgh so that Fran could see the castle and visit the shops. He did everything he could to keep her mind occupied. On the way home they picked Hilda up from school as they passed through Dunfermline.

Instead of sitting in the car to wait near the gate, Luke got out and helped Fran from the passenger seat.

'We can't go in,' she said hesitantly. 'We'd best wait here.'

'We're going in to see the head teacher,' Luke said. 'Just to put our minds at rest that Hilda is quite happy here.'

Fran looked up at her husband with a new understanding. What a kind man, she thought. He was doing this for her, recognising her concern for Hilda. It was so good to have a strong man, a masterful man to take her arm and guide her along, demanding attention.

138

They were shown into the head mistress's study almost at once, and invited to sit and take tea, which Luke politely refused.

'It's a big step to bring our daughter from the south to the north,' Luke said. 'She's quite a delicate child and we felt we needed to know, without her knowledge, of course, how she has settled in.'

Fran listened with nothing but admiration. The middle-aged head mistress took off her glasses and looked at her visitors with favourable esteem.

'How sensible of you to come to see me, Captain Hammond – Mrs Hammond. Hilda seems a bright child, and is enjoying her school work. I'd say that mebbe she's a wee bit behind the other girls of her age, but it's early days yet. I'm sure it's nothing serious, and if necessary when we make an end-of-term assessment we'll give her special coaching in order that she catches up before it's time for her to take the scholarship. Naturally she was a wee bit cautious to begin with, but already she's making friends with her classmates.'

'We'll help in any way we can, Miss McGregor. I shall be away at sea periodically so my wife will be able to give her extra tuition if you can advise her.'

'I've tried to help her as much as I can in the past,' Fran put in. 'She's lost quite a lot of schooling due to illness, especially in the winter, so I shall be very grateful if you can allow her to bring work home.'

'That shouldn't be necessary for the rest of this term, Mrs Hammond. We'll take time to make a proper valuation of her capabilities and tell you our findings on the end-of-term report.'

Luke carried the interview to its conclusion in his usual charming manner, and then they went to sit in the car to wait until the school bell rang and the children, aged between eight and eleven, poured out. When Hilda appeared she was surrounded by other girls of her own age and seemed reluctant to make for the school bus.

'She looks contented enough to me,' Luke observed. 'This change could be the making of her. She's evidently the sociable type and has quickly made friends.'

'It depends on the Scottish winter,' Fran said. 'It just might be too much for her.'

Fran caught the impatient sigh Luke gave as he got out of the car and called Hilda. She guessed that like everyone else he considered she pampered Hilda too much, but he didn't know – no one knew – the worry she'd had in bringing Hilda up. Like Lennie she was frail, fell victim easily to coughs, colds and winter chills, and no one was going to tell Fran how to rear her own children.

On the drive home Hilda sang them a new song she had learned at school, and was full of all the activities she was enjoying with her new friends, so that any tension between Fran and Luke quickly vanished.

At the weekend, Hilda's first week at school over, they drove to Loch Lomond for a picnic and then travelled farther north to stay overnight in a small crofter's cottage on the shore of the loch in Glen Dochart. They enjoyed a leisurely two days, driving in a circular route to return to Craiglee by late Sunday afternoon. Luke saw the colour back in Fran's cheeks, and he thought Hilda had never looked better. The Scottish air was suiting them, and they appeared to be enjoying the new adventure. Fran was more at peace with herself, he thought, though he knew she watched eagerly for the postman to come each weekday.

As soon as Hilda had left for school the following morning, and Jenny had begun her work, Luke suggested a long walk over the hills. At first Fran seemed reluctant. There had been no word from Prue, and she was worried that Babs might be pining for her. She knew it was no use talking to Luke about it. He was being considerate about Hilda but she couldn't expect him to worry over the other girls the way she did. When the postman had passed by, Luke managed to persuade her.

'It's going to be a very hot day according to the paper so we shan't need coats or anything,' he said.

They walked across hillsides where sheep grazed in the morning sunshine, rested on boulders before going on while Luke related amusing stories of his life in the Navy to lift Fran's spirits. At midday they found an isolated spot among some rocks to sit and eat the sandwiches Jenny had prepared, and afterwards they spread out the day's papers to read together.

'I don't like the look of the news from Germany,' Luke said with a worried frown.

'You don't think there's going to be trouble, do you?' Fran asked.

'Who can say? This Adolf Hitler sounds like a maniac, bent on persecuting the Jewish people. Hundreds are being taken from their homes and put in concentration camps. I don't care for the sound of it, Fran.'

'There isn't going to be another war, is there? Oh, Luke, I couldn't bear it! The last one was bad enough.'

'We mustn't look on the black side, darling — but, just in case there is, we mustn't waste a minute, must we?'

He snatched the pages of newspaper she was holding and pulled her into his arms.

140

'Not here, Luke!' she protested.

'I can't wait any longer, and why not out here? Not a soul about except for the sheep, and I'm sure they'll be discreet and leave us alone.'

They had left the beaten track to rest on a lonely hillside overlooking a small loch.

'These huge boulders of rock will protect us from the breeze, and keep us out of sight of stray walkers,' Luke said, as his mouth explored hers, silencing her protests. The grass was dry and soft beneath them as he gently undressed her, fear of war forgotten in such peaceful surroundings. Her porcelain-white skin was sensitive to his touch, her breasts cool beneath his lips. Tender hands smoothed her rounded belly, and long fingers teased in the silky hair between her thighs. She moaned with ecstasy, arched herself in an urgent need to mate with him. Their heavy sighs and measured heartbeats melded together as the rhythm increased until an explosive climax united them as one.

'My God!' Luke panted. 'You devastate me — how can I go away and leave you even for a day?'

Fran coiled her arms round Luke's neck and drew him down again so that their cheeks rested gently against one another.

'Don't speak of leaving — not yet,' she said. 'I'm sorry if I've rejected you, but I'm not completely here, if you know what I mean.'

'I do understand, and the parting will get easier as time passes. Just remember that I shall be back, wanting you just the way you are today. Say you love me, Fran. I want to hear the words as well as enjoy the action.'

'You know I love you, Luke. What woman in her right mind would even consider ... doing ... what I've done ...' She sat up suddenly, sobs of anguish escaping unchecked.

Luke wrapped her in his arms, lovingly protective. 'Darling, forgive me,' he begged. 'Have I been utterly selfish? Your girls are the one thing that comes between us — they make me feel inadequate. However perfect our union is, I don't feel that I can compete with them.'

'Luke,' Fran said. 'There's no question of competition. I'm the mother of four girls and nothing can change that. I can't help my feelings for them and I can't rid myself of the terrible guilt. They shouldn't, they mustn't come between us. But why — oh, why can't they come here to live with us? We could be happy all together. They'd be company for me when you're away at sea, and you'd learn to love them. It would give them a chance to learn to love you.

141

At least during their schooldays. They'll leave home soon enough. Please, Luke, I can't bear the pain of rejecting them.'

'So now you know the pain I had to endure when you rejected me,' he said savagely. 'You've never tried to understand what hell my life was. First I was rejected by my own parents, spurned and made to feel like an outcast. You were the one good thing that ever happened to me, Fran. But you went off with another man.'

'Luke, I was practically married. If only you'd never invited yourself to that wretched party. The pain you experienced you brought on yourself. You knew the situation — but no, you became obsessed with the notion that you wanted me. I wasn't even aware of it. We shouldn't be compatible — we're from different backgrounds. How am I ever going to feel at ease with the other officers' wives?'

She had tried to sit up but he kept her securely on her back, his body almost covering her nakedness.

'But we are compatible, Fran darling. You know that, and whatever differences we have, our love will prove to be strong enough to surmount them. Let not the sun go down upon thy wrath — rather let the sun go down every night on our union.' He kissed her again, ingeniously inducing her lips to respond to his desire. 'It's inhibiting enough having Hilda with us, let alone four of them.'

'There would only be three. Babs should be here for company for Hilda, and Ruby would keep her eye out for both of them. Kate wouldn't want to leave her job now, and she could watch out for Ma. It would be all right, Luke, really it would.'

'No, Fran. Don't build up a dream that can never be reality. You'll only torture yourself. They're better off as things are. Too much change in children's lives can ruin them. It's much wiser to let them remain in familiar surroundings and school. They've already had one major change in moving to Brimdene.' He kissed her again with passionate aggression. 'This is my dream, and I'm going to hold on to it. As to fitting in with my life style, of course you will. I shall always be at your side to carry you through any awkward moments, but the other women will love you — just as I do. Just take care, though, that you don't let any other officer fall in love with you. I'd kill to keep what I own.'

'Now you're being ridiculous, Luke. Don't talk such utter nonsense. You sound so possessive.'

He growled, and caught a fold of her neck in his teeth, biting playfully as his hands roamed over her pliable body. Fran lay replete, with her eyes closed against the glare of the sun, while Luke caressed, knowing that he would always be the winner of this contest. But he

142

was also clever enough to know that in order to retain Fran's love he must share her concern for her girls. He sighed, knowing he must forgo any further pleasures to make sure they were back in the village in time to meet Hilda off the school bus.

They sat on the stone wall that fronted the shop and post office, Luke with his arm casually round Fran's shoulder. Neighbours passed the time of day as they went in and out of the shop.

'I'm sure people will think it strange for a couple of our age to be behaving like this,' she said, feeling that they were drawing attention to themselves.

'Behaving like what?' Luke asked. 'They know that I've most likely been away at sea for weeks or even months. Some chaps think separation keeps the sparkle in a marriage. The waiting, wanting − and then the satisfaction.'

'We may have only just got married but we're not in our twenties, for goodness sake.'

'No one knows that we've only just got married. That's our secret, my darling. People will look at us and see how we feel about each other, and envy us.'

Fran stood up as the bus came chugging round the bend in the narrow road. She supposed Luke was right. What did it matter to anyone in this vicinity that she had been a widow until recently?

As always the boys were first off the bus, and then some little girls who lived nearby; then a pause − where was Hilda? Fran went closer to the open door and saw a young teacher who came from the next village helping Hilda along.

'What's the matter?' Fran asked with considerable concern. 'What's happened?'

Miss Murray helped Hilda down the steps until Luke stepped forward and lifted her the rest of the way. Her leg was stiff with white bandages, and at once she began to cry and reached out for Fran.

'It isn't very serious, Mrs Sheldon,' Miss Murray began.

'Hammond,' Luke put in shortly.

What an unnecessary interruption, Fran thought, glancing back to Miss Murray with impatience.

'Oh, I do beg your pardon,' the embarrassed young woman said, flushing as her gaze met Luke's. 'I didn't realise − '

'Please, Miss Murray, what's happened to Hilda?'

'She fell in the playground. She's grazed her knee rather badly. We cleaned her up and as it happened the school nurse was in the building so she attended to Hilda. She put some healing cream on it and bandaged it up.' Miss Murray smiled at Hilda. 'Now, come

143

along, Hilda, you've been so brave all day. You'll be all right, and we don't let a little thing like a fall interfere with our school work, do we?'

Hilda, with dirty wet streaks running down her cheeks, opened her large brown eyes and stared at the teacher. 'No, Miss Murray,' she replied softly, but with a hint of defiance.

'Perhaps we should let the doctor look at it,' Fran said, her blue eyes ice-cold. 'She may have got dirt, glass or anything in it.'

Luke placed a hand on Fran's shoulder. 'Thank you very much for looking after Hilda, Miss Murray,' he said. 'We'll see how it is in the morning. Better not to disturb the dressing for today.'

Miss Murray's face was still scarlet, and her eyes burned with obvious admiration for the handsome man. 'That's what the nurse advised,' she said breathlessly. As the bus driver revved his engine, she added: 'I'm sure you'll be all right, Hilda. See you tomorrow, dear.'

'Not if I have anything to do with it,' Fran muttered crossly as the bus drew away.

'Fran dear,' Luke said quietly, 'don't jump to conclusions so easily. It's probably nothing. I don't always have a ship's doctor on board so as captain I have to deal with quite a few minor ailments. Let's wait and see how things are in the morning.'

'You may be used to tough sailors, but you don't know anything about children,' Fran snapped.

'No,' he responded softly, after a lengthy pause. 'I never got the chance, did I? I was denied caring for my own son.'

'He wasn't *your* son,' Fran hissed. She reached out and took Hilda's hand, but the child made a great display of her stiff leg. Luke swung her up in his arms and hurried along the narrow road to the track which led to their home. No one spoke, but there was a tight spring of tension between them.

'Oh, deary me,' Jenny said when they got in. 'What have you been up to, lassie?'

'Fallen in the school yard,' Fran said shortly. 'That's the trouble with a mixed school. Boys are always so rough. At home the girls went to a proper girls' school.'

Fran helped Hilda to sit on the couch in the sitting room and Jenny went away to prepare afternoon tea.

'It wasn't the boys who pushed me, Mummy,' Hilda explained, now less tearful. 'We were playing a game and I just fell. It wasn't anyone's fault.'

'Well, you just rest there, dear,' Fran said. 'What would you like for your tea?'

144

'She'll have the same as the rest of us, and she'll sit at the table,' Luke said. 'It will only get stiffer by keeping it immobile. I doubt very much that such a large bandage is really necessary.'

Fran shot him an angry frown, which was met by a look of exasperation.

'Let's do a puzzle, Hilda, to help us forget,' Luke said brightly, and he went away to fetch some of Hilda's things. Fran followed him up to Hilda's bedroom.

'You're deliberately undermining my authority,' Fran said, her cheeks glowing red with impatience.

'You look delightful when you're angry, darling, but we're not going to embark on a slanging match after such a perfect day. You know as well as I do that you're making a mountain out of a molehill just as you usually do where Hilda's concerned. Children fall and hurt themselves all the time. The average mother would do nothing except tend her children if they all pampered their offspring like you do Hilda.'

'I do not pamper her!' Fran shouted. 'You just don't care.'

'I care a great deal more than you realise. I want to see Hilda grow up to be independent of you, Fran. You won't always be able to run to her aid. She can stand on her own feet much better than you give her credit for and she's a devious little madam, she knows she can use you for her own ends.'

'Just as you use me for your own ends.'

Luke grabbed Fran's wrist tightly. 'And what is that supposed to mean?'

'Let go,' she pleaded in a softer tone. 'You're hurting me.'

'And you're hurting me by your insinuations. How do I use you, for goodness sake?'

'Didn't you use me for your own pleasure that first time we met?' She inclined her head as she was forced to look upwards into his demanding glare. 'Haven't you used me ever since to satisfy your own guilt? Lennie was not your son, so stop saying that he was. And don't you use me just to go to bed with?'

Luke flung her hand away from him and Fran burst into tears. Hot, angry, frustrated tears. Tears that no man could understand, let alone Luke Hammond.

Luke picked up the few items he wanted for Hilda, started for the door and then turned back. 'If you're not in a warm bath in five minutes I shall come and dump you in one. You're over- reacting, Fran. A bath will soothe away your troubles. I can appreciate that you're homesick, but you made the sacrifice – don't plead martyrdom as well.' He stalked off with

145

determined footsteps, and Fran threw herself down on Hilda's bed and wept.

She felt angry with herself for allowing such a minor incident to blow up out of all proportion, but the truth was she felt guilty on so many counts. Guilty that she had allowed Luke to come between her and the family. Guilty that she had split the girls up. Guilty that she had not insisted that they have the girls with them wherever they went. And, most of all, today – guilty at allowing Luke to make love to her out there on the hills. In fact, she had to admit, if only to herself, that she felt guilty at the way she responded so readily to Luke's demands. She wished she could say that in times of passion she thought only of Henry, but she loved Luke with a different kind of love. The physical side of marriage had become less important to her after bearing five children. She and Henry had enjoyed intimate times but left to her those occasions would have become even less frequent. There was always work and worry, and she had been too tired really to enjoy the mating times. Now Luke saw to it that she had little of importance to do except keep him happy. And, to her chagrin, making him happy made her happy too.

The fact that Hilda was hurt at school while she and Luke were indulging their new marital status pricked her conscience with a degree of shame and remorse. Luke was right, she did coddle Hilda, perhaps over-zealously. She couldn't excuse it as salving her conscience in the present circumstances, for even Henry had gently chided her over the same thing. She felt the need to cherish Hilda more than the others. Fran didn't care what other people said, Hilda was more delicate, and so much like Lennie.

A tender touch on her arm interrupted the bout of self-criticism. 'I've run the bath, darling,' Luke said. 'Have a good long soak. I've asked Jenny to delay tea for an hour to give you time.' He pulled her to her feet and held her close. 'Forgive me, darling, I know it's time you need. We'll make up later.' Luke kissed her cheek lightly and guided her to the bathroom. 'I'll keep Hilda company.'

As Fran removed her clothes and stepped into the cloud of steam she thought of the moments of sheer bliss enjoyed earlier. This, after all, was still their honeymoon, and Luke on leave for just another ten days. She felt herself shiver with apprehension. With Hilda away at school, and Luke absent from home, how on earth was she going to fill her time? She must raise the subject with Luke before he returned to duty. Maybe she could dispense with Jenny Logan's services? She could run the house by herself.

Soothed and much calmer, Fran went downstairs to the sitting room, where Luke was beside Hilda on the couch fitting pieces

146

of a jigsaw puzzle to make a picture of a farmyard scene. Their dark heads were almost touching, and at the sound of her footsteps they both looked up simultaneously. Fran stared, shocked by the similarity in their looks. Dark eyes, dark hair, and an expression of − she couldn't put it into words − a mixture of self-satisfaction, triumph or curiosity? Hilda was exactly like Lennie in looks, which was why Fran adored her so much − and for the first time a flash of real doubt entered her mind.

'Feeling better, dear?' Luke asked softly. 'Less tense, I'm sure. A nice cup of tea and all will be well.' He stood up, and smiled right into her blue eyes as if he could read her troubled thoughts. 'I'll go and have a wash and shave while you keep Hilda company for fifteen minutes.'

Everything organised for her − isn't that just what she had longed for?

'Daddy's so good at finding the right pieces,' Hilda said.

Fran experienced a stab of pain at the easy way Hilda referred to Luke as Daddy, but she knew she should be getting used to it. Luke hadn't forced the issue, she remembered. Hilda herself had suggested it.

'We've nearly finished this puzzle,' Hilda continued. 'Daddy said that he's taking you into Edinburgh tomorrow to do some shopping and he'll buy me another one to do. A bigger, more difficult one to last me while he's away.'

'I don't know about that,' Fran said quickly. 'We'll have to see how your leg is, won't we?'

'It's nothing, really. Daddy says I'm too grown up to stay home just because I fell over. I cried only a little bit at school, otherwise the boys would have called me cry-baby. And if I don't go to school tomorrow they'll laugh at me. Besides, I want Daddy to buy me that new puzzle.'

Jenny came to announce that tea was ready so they went downstairs to the dining room. Fran noticed that Hilda's leg wasn't so stiff that she couldn't manage the stairs quite easily now.

Across the table Luke's gaze met Fran's. A moment of indecision, a warm smile from Luke − and any animosity vanished.

They were up a little earlier next morning after a good night's sleep. Undisturbed sleep, after a time of apologies, followed by cuddles and gentle kisses, but no further demands made by Luke. Fran almost wished he had been aggressively passionate; instead he had cradled her in his arms and lulled her to sleep.

147

By the time Fran emerged from the bathroom, Hilda was lying on her bed while Luke removed the bandages on her leg.

'Come and inspect this, Fran,' Luke called. 'It's very clean-looking, and with a new dry dressing each day it shouldn't fester.'

'Mm,' Fran agreed, 'it doesn't look too angry. Will you rebandage it or shall I?'

'Hilda? Your choice,' Luke said.

'Daddy can do it while you see to breakfast. Are my sandwiches done?'

'I'll see to it now,' Fran said. She went downstairs to the kitchen, where Jenny had just arrived.

'Morning, Mrs Hammond. Another good day by the feel of it. Quite a haze over the hills − heat haze, I shouldn't wonder. How's the lassie this morning?'

'Oh, she's fine, Jenny, thanks. My husband is rebandaging her leg. She seems keen to go to school, so we're going to Edinburgh. Must make the most of the time my husband is home on leave. It goes all too quickly.'

'Ah. Morning, Jenny.' Luke came striding into the kitchen. 'Mrs Hammond has told you we're going into Edinburgh today? I'd really like to take her out to dinner there − how are you fixed today?'

'Nothing so important that I can't be free when Hilda comes home from school, sir,' Jenny said, with an understanding smile.

After breakfast, Fran paused in their bedroom to look out over the landscape. The meadows were white with sheep this morning, and the sun glistened on the ribbon of water as the stream chortled its way through the valley. So much like Sherbrook, Fran thought, yet vastly different with craggy hillocks and boulders, an altogether more rugged scene. She remembered the rising river back home. Here the house was situated on high ground so that there was no fear of flooding. So much had happened in the past two years that the bad memories were less frightening, but she could still call them to mind and a chill ran through her.

She heard a car engine running so she hurried to complete her toilet, and within the hour she was sitting beside Luke, starting out on the day's adventure. The road was quietly pleasant to Dunfermline and then they were on the ferry, crossing the wide stretch of water to enter the capital city.

Luke was a good companion and an expert guide. They visited places of interest, had coffee in a plush restaurant, and then shopped in the elegant stores, Luke insisting that they buy presents for the girls and Ma. They sat in the gardens while Fran wrote on picture postcards to include in the parcel. She hadn't had much opportunity to write long letters yet, but she knew that a surprise parcel would please them, especially Babs. Her heart ached with longing for them all, and writing to them brought a lump to her throat as she penned several kisses to each one.

After the parcel had been posted they reclined on the grass in the gardens and listened to the band of the Scots Guards. Fran took off her shoes and sat up, hugging her knees. The music was too nosiy to allow any conversation and she was grateful for a time during which she could allow her thoughts free rein. Tomorrow she could expect to receive her weekly letter from her mother. She wished one would come every day, but she knew Ma didn't have the time. Here, life went at a slower pace, and with no washing, cooking, or cleaning to do, she had all the time in the world to express her feelings on paper, even if her long screeds usually ended up in the kitchen fire. She had to rethink each and every sentence. To Ruby and Ma she compiled a long list of do's and don'ts, hoping that they were remembering to turn the gas off at night and change the bed linen and their clothes regularly. To Kate, her instructions were to visit Ma and Ruby at every opportunity. And to Babs she wrote saying how much she loved her, and how sorry she was that she couldn't have her in Scotland with them. That letter always went into the fire, usually several attempts, before she could compose what she considered was a happy, lively letter that wouldn't make her baby unhappy.

Fran prayed that her second marriage would strengthen, so that she could influence Luke in bringing them all together again. The thought of returning to Brimdene for the long summer holidays kept her going, yet at the back of her mind lurked a dreadful feeling that it wasn't going to happen. How could it, when Luke was going to be working from the Rosyth dockyard? The ship of which he was now captain was undergoing major repairs and refurbishment, so his hours would initially be similar to those of a bank clerk. As the weeks and months went by, the ship would be taken out for trials, and instead of preparing to return south, Fran knew she was expected to remain in Craiglee like a dutiful wife, ready to greet her husband with open arms on his return, just like other naval women. She hesitantly suggested that perhaps Ruby and Babs could visit them in Scotland with Kate, while Ma was having a holiday with Eric and Annie, but Luke quickly reminded her that Kate, being in the hotel trade, would not be able to take her holiday during the season. He considered it unwise to allow Ruby and Babs to make such a long journey on their own.

'There'll be other times, darling,' he consoled. 'I may be away for a longer period, and then if it coincides with school holidays

149

you and Hilda can go down to Brimdene.' It didn't take Fran long to realise that either Luke wasn't telling, or he really didn't know how long he was likely to be at sea at any given time and her hopes of going home diminished rapidly.

Chapter Twelve

Hilda had begun to make friends with girls of her own age. Fran was left on her own. At first the other naval wives invited her for afternoon tea, or coffee, or to help with some project for the needy. Luke had cleverly used that last visit to Edinburgh to attend a dinner for officers and their wives. Fran had protested that she wasn't suitably dressed for such an occasion but it had turned out to be a casual affair and she had enjoyed meeting the other women, while Luke had become acquainted with some of the men he would be working with. Various invitations had followed, and before Luke's leave was over he gave a small cocktail party for some of his colleagues and their wives. Fran had blossomed, organising the affair with Jenny Logan, whose niece helped with the preparations as well as being waitress for the evening. Hilda proudly wore the dress she had worn at her mother's wedding and was quite the sophisticated daughter of Captain and Mrs Luke Hammond.

By the time the long school holidays had arrived, though, Fran noticed that no further invitations were forthcoming. Luke had assured her that naval wives always stuck together while their husbands were away at sea, but it was Hilda who enjoyed the most exciting social life.

When Fran came out of the post office one morning, she collided with a woman she had met on several occasions. Hilda frequently visited their house for tea with the daughter, Alice.

'Not a very nice morning, is it?' Fran greeted, after they had apologised for literally bumping into each other.

The woman looked sternly into Fran's face, shrugging indifferently as she said: 'Can't expect anything else up here in Scotland.' Then Alice's mother turned and hurried into the post office.

Fran felt the rebuff keenly. She couldn't believe that she had offended the woman in any way and they had always seemed on the best of terms. Maybe Luke was her husband's superior officer. There was, she knew, some professional ranking jealousy, more among the wives than the men. Fran walked home perplexed, then decided that maybe the woman wasn't feeling too good that day and dismissed the incident from her mind.

On another occasion, when Fran and Hilda were approaching the bus stop on their way in to Dunfermline, Alice and her mother, who were already waiting there, suddenly turned back towards their house.

'Oh, can we wait for Alice?' Hilda begged. The bus could already be heard in the distance, rumbling along the lonely country road.

'Better not, dear, there isn't another one for ages. If Alice and her mother don't get a move on they'll miss it. They either changed their minds or had forgotten something.'

Fran and Hilda boarded the bus and it started off with no sign of Alice and her mother. Fran experienced a feeling of unease. No, she thought, she was imagining things. Alice's mother couldn't possibly have missed the bus on purpose because she and Hilda approached. All the same, it did look as if they had turned back as soon as they saw them.

Walking along the narrow streets of Dunfermline they met one or two other officers' wives and their children. Not many of them lived as far out as Craiglee. Some lived in Dunfermline, but most as near to the dockyard as possible. The girls exchanged greetings, but the women all seemed in a mighty hurry today. Fran felt as if she were being sent to Coventry – but why? What had she done? Did they know, could they tell that she had come from a less affluent background than most of them?

That evening, when the rain had begun to pour down in torrents, and Hilda was in her room playing with her dolls, Fran went down to the kitchen to help Jenny pot the jam she was making.

'I can manage, Mrs Hammond. It's a messy old job.'

'Oh no, not you as well, Jenny. I made plenty of jam at home in the country. I can't get used to having nothing to do except sew, and I don't feel like that this evening. I get the feeling that everyone's sending me to Coventry. Perhaps you can tell me why?'

Jenny turned the gas up until the jam in the large preserving pan boiled and spat angrily. She went on stirring briskly, not wanting to face Fran.

'There is something,' Fran said, now indignant. 'Jenny, please, for goodness sake, what have I done?'

'Well, ma'am,' Jenny said hesitantly, 'it's a story that's going about, but I dare say there's little truth in it.' She sniffed haughtily as if she didn't intend to reveal anything further.

'Go on, Jenny. It's better that I know what people are saying about me.'

Jenny turned the gas lower, balanced the long-handled wooden spoon across the top of the pan, and looked straight at Fran. 'I don't really like to say . . .' she began.

'Please, go on, Jenny,' Fran said.

'There's always gossip in a small village, ma'am, and especially among servicemen's wives. Some of the women have been asking me about you . . . and your other children, ma'am.'

'My other children? I'm sure by now everyone knows that we have three other daughters back home.'

'But they aren't — Hilda isn't — the captain's children?'

'No.' Fran paused. So, in spite of Luke's reticence, it hadn't taken long for the truth somehow to come out. 'I'm a widow. Was a widow, until I married Captain Hammond. I would have thought that was fairly obvious as Hilda's name is Sheldon.'

'It's just that the women feel it was wrong of you to leave the others behind when you came north. If you could bring Hilda, couldn't her sisters have come too?'

Fran felt her lips stiffen and her cheeks pale as she bit into the side of her mouth.

'It wasn't up to me,' she managed to say in a low voice, and then she fled to the seclusion of her bedroom.

Fran's guilt exploded into hurt, angry tears. Now Luke must let the girls come to them. Surely he wouldn't want himself and his wife criticised for the neglect of their children, even if they weren't actually his? But they were his, Fran thought angrily. They were his stepdaughters, and when he married her he became responsible for them too. How was she ever going to hold her head up again? Shame was something she had seldom felt before. People had admired her and Henry for the way they lived and conducted themselves. And more recently they respected Fran for being able to manage on her pension, the girls always looking well turned out and their home kept clean and comfortable. Whatever would Henry have said? Brother Eric too, and Henry's parents? They would all share her shame and feel so vexed — thank goodness she was many miles away from them.

It was no use indulging in self-pitying tears, though. She splashed her face with cold water and went back to the kitchen.

'I'm so sorry, Ma'am, I didn't mean to upset you,' Jenny said kindly. 'Folk are quick to condemn without knowing all the facts. I can see now that it has been a terrible wrench for you to leave your family.' She placed a hand on Fran's arm and led her into the dining room. 'Look,' she said softly, 'I've taken the liberty of making a pot of tea. I'm sure it will help. I've finished potting the jam and it looks good. Setting just right.'

Fran sat down heavily in the chair Jenny pulled out for her. 'This is the price one has to pay for marrying a man in the Royal Navy,' she said dismally.

'I don't know all the facts, Mrs Hammond, but I do know you care about your girls. You've spent hours making new dresses for them, and you write regularly.'

'I hoped Hilda and I would be going home for the long school holidays, but my husband is uncertain about his movements, and it's only right that I should be here when he comes home.'

Jenny sniffed disapprovingly as she poured the tea. Fran couldn't help wondering how Mrs Maitland would have handled this situation, but no one in her employ would have dared to question or criticise anything she did.

'Of course,' Jenny said, 'especially as you haven't been married that long.'

'Sit down and have a cup of tea with me, Jenny,' Fran said. 'My husband doesn't like our affairs discussed publicly, which is only natural, but I need to talk to someone as I miss the girls so much — so very much ...' Her voice broke as sobs persisted.

'Tell me more about them,' Jenny said. 'It might help — and bring them closer to you. I was hoping they'd be coming to stay with you for a holiday. That's what servicemen's children usually do for the longest holidays.'

'Katie, my eldest girl, works in a hotel in Brimdene. She has to live in as she wants to make a career of the hotel trade. She's good at her job, loves cooking and in her last letter she says that her employer is going to pay for her to go to night school in the autumn to learn hotel management and book-keeping. And on another evening she's going to cookery classes.'

'My word, she must be keen! Most young girls are off out with boys at the first opportunity,' Jenny said.

'Not my Katie,' Fran said, remembering and hating herself for not responding to Kate's needs much earlier than she had done. 'I suppose everything happened so quickly really.'

It was a relief to talk to someone, even though Fran knew Luke would be angry at how much she had divulged. That night she lay awake for several hours, her heart aching, her body burning up

154

with an anguish that seemed to tear limb from limb. Not because she had talked to Jenny Logan — Fran knew that she could trust her to be discreet — but her guilt was out in the open now. Her unshared guilt had been bad enough, but to think that women had been discussing the situation behind her back, learning as much as they could, it seemed, from Hilda, an innocent child. Fran was at a loss to know how to react. Luke would insist that she carry on as if nothing had happened, but Fran was capable of sending everyone else to Coventry just as they had her.

By the time Hilda returned to school for the autumn term, Fran had succeeded in building a barrier around herself. She noticed that the attitude of her neighbours changed. The women wanted to acknowledge her, but Fran merely nodded and passed by. She suspected that Jenny Logan had loyally defended her and endeavoured to put down the rumours, but, as always, Fran had her pride.

Early September, and Luke miraculously reappeared. He had been away for almost the whole of August, and Fran felt annoyed that she had been obliged to remain in Scotland when there had been no earthly reason that she couldn't have gone home to Brimdene — except that she didn't have sufficient money to make the decision herself. Luke was generous up to a point, insisting on certain standards in their comfortable life style to keep up appearances with fellow officers and their families. He saw to all the domestic financial arrangements, allowing Fran an ample allowance so that she could keep herself well dressed, but Fran quickly realised that he kept her on a tight purse string when he was away.

As always Luke's charm and sensuality swept her off her feet when he returned. She quickly forgot the unpleasantness she had encountered during his absence as he demonstrated his need for her. For several days he drew her firmly into his aura so that they loved and laughed in complete harmony. Then came the anticlimax as Luke tried to adapt to being on dry land again. He relived his month away by relating stories of some of his adventures, but he was restless, and was soon eager to attend social functions.

'We'll go to the dinner dance at the officers' mess at the weekend,' he suggested one evening as they sat in the small cosy sitting room.

Fran was thoughtful. She sat sewing the hem on a dress for Babs. 'Do we have to?' she asked.

'We do have to mix, darling. It's important to be seen to socialise. I thought you'd got over any shyness.'

'It's not that, Luke.' She stitched on, then looked up at her

155

husband. 'I know you don't like people knowing that we've only recently got married, but Hilda has been talking to her friends.'

Luke's expression became serious. 'What's she been saying?'

'I don't know, but enough so that the women showed their dislike of me. It was almost as if they were sending me to Coventry.'

'You must be imagining things, Fran.'

'I don't think so. I mentioned it to Jenny and she was aware of the rumour which was circulating, that I had chosen to bring Hilda here with me but left the other girls behind.'

Luke stood up and paced the room. 'I knew I should have stuck to my guns and insisted that we start our married life on our own like any normal couple.'

'But we aren't a normal couple, Luke. I was a widow, with daughters who are my responsibility − and yours, if you wanted me to give up my independence to marry you.'

'You didn't need much persuading, as I recall.'

'You didn't give me much time to think about all that getting married again entailed.'

'So now you regret it?' His dark eyes flashed angrily.

'Luke,' Fran pleaded softly. 'You know I don't regret it. I don't like being parted from the girls. What woman − what mother − would? But I still can't see the reasoning behind leaving them down south when we've got room for them here. It isn't as if they'd get in your way. You aren't at home that much.'

'But when I am I want you to myself. I considered we had resolved such matters amicably and sensibly. Ruby is a capable girl and is company for your mother. I would have preferred that Babs had come with us. She's younger and would have adapted better than Hilda.'

'Hilda has settled down extremely well, though how she'll fare during a bad winter I don't know.'

'Hilda is old enough to be able to talk too much. You must make her understand that what goes on in this house is our business and must not be discussed outside.'

'She has always understood that. All my children know better than to talk too much outside the home, but children will be children. You can't expect her to forget that she's got other sisters.' She inclined her head with a wry smile. 'Even if you would prefer to dismiss them as if they don't exist.'

'You won't let me forget. For heaven's sake, I'm only home for a few days.' He ran his fingers through his hair in agitation. It sprang back into the mass of waves that helped to make him so attractive.

156

'We'll definitely go to the dinner dance,' he said. 'We have nothing to reproach ourselves with, so we can go with a clear conscience. We've done what we consider to be best for the girls, and it's no one else's business.'

'Wouldn't it be more sensible to reconsider and let the girls come here?'

'No! Definitely not, Fran, and don't get ideas about returning to Brimdene. Your home is with me.'

'But you aren't here all the time. I'm not used to having so much time on my hands. It's all such a — waste.'

'Waste!' Luke repeated with contempt. 'Is that how you see our marriage — a waste?'

Fran put aside her sewing and stood up to face him. 'You know I didn't mean it like that, Luke,' she said softly. 'I appreciate that you consider my happiness, but you can't know the unhappiness I've had to endure when you're away and I have time to think. Whatever would Henry say to the girls being separated like they are? It's so unjust, so unfair of me to have put my happiness before theirs.' Her chin quivered slightly but she fought off the emotion, which Luke would see as weakness. 'I find it very hard to live with myself,' she said.

She made for the door, but Luke was quick to grasp her arm and encircle her with a fierce embrace. 'You've been very brave. I do understand what it must be like. More so than you realise. Haven't I been separated from my family for far too many years?'

'But you made that choice. And you were sixteen when you ran away to sea.'

'Only a couple or so years older than Ruby. I hated the Navy at first. I hated the sea for luring me away from the security of a loving family. Maybe I'd have returned, with enough persuasion, but being totally rejected there was little choice but to stick it out. There was the matter of pride too, which became more important as the years went by.'

'We all suffer from too much pride,' Fran said. 'Maybe your parents would accept you willingly now. It often only takes one person to make the first move.'

'They rejected me, they must make that first move,' Luke said defiantly. 'The sea is my life now.'

'Does Elizabeth talk about you at home? Do they know you and she have always corresponded?'

'As far as I know my name is never mentioned. My being the only son, you'd have thought they'd have forgiven me and tried to understand, but it's too late now.' He sighed deeply, and Fran

157

saw that he cared about the situation much more than he let on. 'Twenty-four years, to be exact. The longer the separation, the harder it is to be reconciled.' He bent and kissed her with some aggression. 'That's all in the past. It's our future that matters now, and we will go to the weekend event.'

'I don't want to go, Luke,' Fran said. 'I can't pretend that everything's all right when it's far from that.'

'You'll have me there to protect you. Just be your lovely smiling self. No other woman holds a candle to you – they're only jealous, after all.'

With his usual expertise Luke managed to quell all Fran's fears.

Blizzards, snow and ice heralded the beginning of a winter unlike anything Fran had ever experienced in the south of the country. Luke came home at intervals but for only short periods and when Hilda went down with a cold, Fran was glad to keep her home from school for company. Together they prepared for Christmas. Fran was ever hopeful that Luke would relent and please her by suggesting they all went to spend Christmas in Brimdene. Hilda painted pictures of the snowy scene on cards for all her sisters and grandparents, while her mother sewed and embroidered to make pretty garments for Kate, Ruby and Babs.

Luke arrived home on the day before Christmas Eve and Fran had to hide her disappointment. Ma had written to say that Kate would have to work over the Christmas holiday. Ruby's letter was full of the plans for her and Gran to spend the time with Gran and Grandad Sheldon, Uncle Nathan and his family. Babs, in her childish writing, expressed her excitement and hopes of all the presents that Father Christmas was expected to bring. Fran felt as if her heart had frozen solid. Wasn't it *her* duty to fill stockings and make the festive season as jolly for them all as possible? She sat in the kirk beside Luke and Hilda on Christmas Eve, which was a Sunday, and felt numb. Nothing could punish her more than not being part of a complete family at Christmastime. But they never could be a complete family again. Sometimes she visualised returning to Sherbrook, imagining that Henry and her father would be there, but with their deaths everything had changed. She found no enjoyment or solace in her devotions. Singing carols and watching the children act out the nativity play gave her no pleasure. She felt sick and empty inside.

Fran was almost relieved when Luke returned to his naval duties after she had experienced her first Scottish New Year. There was much to look back on with some measure of enjoyment. The pipe band, tartan skirts twirling in precision folk dancing, and the ceremonial serving of the haggis. She had to admit that Luke had done everything he could to make her happy, and Hilda had enjoyed a succession of parties before the new school term began. But the weather worsened. Snowdrifts reached window ledges, and the depth of it on the roads made going out an impossibility so that Hilda had to be coached at home by Fran. The postman was unable to deliver mail, and Fran knew it was hopeless to expect her letters to get any further than the post office, so she wrote to Ma and the girls in diary form, saving the pages for several weeks until at last the thaw came.

She was overjoyed when a batch of mail eventually reached Craiglee from all the family. It brought them all together during the time she spent reading and re-reading the news from home.

Kate had begun night school courses in catering and hotel management. She assured her mother that she was well, and so were the rest of the family, apart from the usual coughs and colds. Uncle Sam and Aunt Prue had brought Marion and Babs to Brimdene for the day before the younger girls returned to school. Gran was looking after the house very well with Ruby's help. Aunt Sissy visited them often and supervised things. Ruby was doing well at school and was nearly always top of the class in every subject. Fran felt the hint of guilt as she remembered how she had persistently grumbled at Ruby. As she stood, letter in hand, gazing out of the back windows at the distant, snow-capped hills, she could see Ruby clearly, kneeling in front of the old mill-house range, her small fingers black as she black-leaded the stove doors. Henry's voice came clear and gently reproaching, 'She's only ten, love.' Now Ruby was heading for her teens. A difficult time for most girls, and Fran wasn't there to see her through it. But she had to admit, as she read Kate's letter again, they seemed to be managing very well without her at the helm. She couldn't help wondering, though, whether they were conspiring together to make sure that Fran had nothing to worry about. Was everything really as serene as they made out? Another year had to pass before she could look forward to returning south again. Luke had made it clear that during his two-year service in Scotland she was to remain in Craiglee.

Before Luke came home again, Hilda caught a cold. Fran kept her home from school for much longer than was necessary, so that at the end of the next term her report was far from satisfactory. Luke's homecoming after several weeks at sea coincided with the arrival of the report, accompanied by a letter to Fran from the headmistress. Fran hurriedly folded the letter and tried to stuff it back into the envelope.

'Something I should see?' Luke asked. They were in the bedroom, still in night attire.

'Only a letter with Hilda's report,' Fran mumbled, as she sat on the side of the bed, pulling her knickers on. Luke had just come from the bathroom. Now he came to Fran's side of the bed and took her knickers away from her.

'I've only just got home after being starved for weeks,' he said softly.

They played tug of war with Fran's underwear for a few seconds.

'Jenny will be back in a minute,' Fran protested.

'She's gone shopping and won't be back for the next couple of hours.'

'Oh, Luke, how could you? It's not nice her knowing what we're doing.'

Luke smiled knowingly. 'So you know what to expect then?' He bent and kissed Fran's forehead. 'Jenny will be discreet. You should know that by now. She's worked for naval people before, you know.' He pushed Fran back across the bed, lifting her nightgown above her head while he teased, forcing her to roll in a ball. Luke was naked, having removed the loose-fitting robe he had been wearing, and just the feel of his virility next to her body roused Fran's womanly instincts. He looked almost out of place in the chilly climes of Scotland after spending some weeks in the Mediterranean. His body was healthily tanned from head to toe, an exciting image of masculine perfection.

Fran entwined her arms around his neck, momentarily forgetting the school report. Following the period of separation she was receptive to his kisses, and his intimate caresses stirred her to an impatient longing for the ladder of ecstasy they soared together. She surprised herself at the desperation she experienced in wanting to feel his power thrusting inside her. She was conscious of how much Luke adored her as he controlled his passion, pleasing her with gentle words while she begged to be satisfied.

'Now, Luke, now – I can't wait,' she implored.

He drew away, just enough to make her gasp and clutch at his buttocks with her hands, urging him to match her rhythm. She knew that she had the power to make him lose control as she wrapped her legs around him. He was sweating as he endeavoured to reach far into her secret lair. They climaxed together, holding the union, wanting it to last for ever . . .

*

160

After a few days of such passionate activity they came back to earth, and Fran was obliged to share her concern with Luke over Hilda's report.

'Maybe it's the teacher's fault,' Fran said, hardly able to bear to look at the low marks for most subjects. 'She's much more capable than this report says.'

Luke took the sheet of paper from Fran and paced the room as he studied it. He went to sit in the window seat of the small sitting room in the morning sun and re-read it. Then Fran realised that he was surveying her with a troubled expression.

'I'm afraid, Fran darling,' he said slowly, 'you have no one but yourself to blame for this. I don't wish to be cruel or hurt your feelings, but by the look of Hilda's attendances you've been keeping her away from school far too often. Last term she was hardly at school at all, so what else can you expect?'

'Of course she went to school,' Fran replied tersely. 'Except when there was no school bus on account of the weather. And she did have a bad cold and cough through January and February.'

'Here in the north people can cope with bad weather. The roads are always cleared, the school bus is rarely cancelled, so don't make excuses. You know perfectly well, my dear, that you keep Hilda home to satisfy your whims.'

'I do not!' Fran snapped angrily. 'She's a delicate child and I do have to protect her.'

'From what? Attending school is subject to law, thank goodness. She won't thank you in years to come when she can't get a job because she's not had the education. She's a bright child, but she needs both the company of other children and the tuition of qualified teachers.'

'We've always managed before. I know enough to help her when they let me have the proper books, but the ones Miss Murray sent were for a younger child.'

'Nonsense, Fran. I'm afraid you leave me no alternative but to send her to a boarding school. That way she'll be on the spot, and the weather can't be an excuse to be absent so frequently.'

Fran stared at Luke in horror. The shock of his suggestion was such that she was stunned to silence.

Luke observed that he had dealt his wife a cruel blow. He had been considering this move for some weeks now. Not because he didn't want Hilda living with them, although he had to admit it did curtail their life style somewhat, but he recognised that she was capable of better things if she wasn't so strongly influenced by Fran. Smothered would be more apt, he thought as he recalled, with wounded pride, some of the snide remarks overheard from colleagues since their arrival in Scotland. It was evidence of how the other women gossiped, and there was the danger of Hilda talking too much to the other children. He hadn't been able to hide the fact that he had only recently married a widow with a daughter, but no one need have known that Fran had three other daughters if it hadn't been for Hilda's chatter. He quite liked the child and found her a challenge, though he was sure he would have preferred having the youngest one, Babs.

'I hope you're not serious,' Fran said in a low, hurt tone.

'I'm afraid I am, darling,' Luke said, lifting his voice slightly to ease the tension. 'I've been thinking about it for some time. Most of the senior officers send their children to a very good school in Aberdeen.'

'If Hilda goes to Aberdeen, then I go too,' Fran said.

'Don't be ridiculous, Fran. Aberdeen is a charming town, rather like Brimdene in many ways. Sea air like Hilda is used to, and an all-girls school, which I think you'd prefer.'

'Hilda stays here with me, or we'll go home to Brimdene.'

Luke noted that Fran's cheeks were quite pink. He had expected a confrontation of sorts but he wasn't prepared for that statement.

He stood up, deciding that the battle may as well commence now as later. It was Jenny Logan's day off and the day was young.

'And how will you do that, my dear? The train fare is rather expensive, which is why you've had to remain here. It costs too much to travel back and forth often.'

'I haven't said I wanted to go often,' Fran argued. 'But we could have gone for the summer holiday. It isn't being fair to the girls. I haven't seen them for nearly a year now. It's no wonder Hilda can't settle in her new school.'

'You won't let her settle,' Luke said, raising his voice. 'And there's always a chance that my next appointment will be abroad. India is on the cards, and then you'll be expected to join me there.'

'Never!' Five hundred miles was distance enough; Fran couldn't begin to comprehend three thousand and more. She felt her muscles tighten throughout her body. Luke was planning a strategy she didn't like, hadn't even considered, and one that she was adamantly going to refuse to accept. 'I don't ever intend to go overseas,' she said.

Luke spanned the distance between them. He towered over her, tall, masterly, humiliating her.

'I think you'll have to do whatever I think is best,' he said.

'You can go wherever you like,' Fran said, 'but I know what's best for me.'

'I'm your husband. I vowed to love, honour and keep you, and you vowed to obey me. I won't ever let you forget that. Too many years have been wasted. You made your own happiness while I had nothing except exile.'

'Don't be so melodramatic, Luke,' Fran shouted at the top of her voice. 'You chose your way of life, and you enjoyed all the travelling, so don't try to tell me otherwise. You just saw middle age looming, and you took advantage of me when I was in a vulnerable state. I was just beginning to get on top of things when Kate got into trouble.'

'You were glad of me then,' he reminded her. 'Glad of my support and glad to have some of the responsibility taken from your shoulders. Well, now I'm taking more of the responsibility still. I agreed to bring Hilda north but you're making a fool of the girl. You must let her go, Fran. She's ten years old, and it's time she pulled her socks up at school. She'll be better away from you where she can concentrate on her studies. I've already got the prospectus and when you're calmer you can see it. In fact I shall show Hilda before I let you see it. Her reaction can decide whether she goes to Aberdeen or not.'

'No, Luke, please – *please* – don't do this to me, Luke.' Fran buried her face in her hands and wept bitterly.

'Don't think you can soften me up with tears,' Luke said savagely. 'I'm doing it for Hilda's sake. You're far too emotional about her, so you may as well get used to the idea.'

'I ... I'll leave you, Luke. As soon as you go back to your ship I shall fetch Hilda, and we'll walk, if need be, back to Brimdene.'

Luke tossed his head back defiantly. 'Don't talk such utter rubbish,' he said. 'You don't know how well off you are with me. Do I keep you short of anything? Do you go hungry or have to wear worn-out clothing – you, or any of your girls? Aren't you well provided for? And your mother – who pays the rent on that house? If you leave me, my dear, who's going to pay it then? You can't live off your mother's old-age pension and you aren't a widow any longer.'

Fran was reduced to silent penitence for a second, then she ground her teeth. 'I think I hate you,' she said. 'I've always hated you.'

Her crimson, tear-stained cheeks did not evoke any pity from Luke. He inclined his head, a slow smile widening his sensuous mouth, his eyes alight with desire. 'Oh, yes?' He stepped forward

163

just as she raised her fists to beat on his chest. He caught her wrists and twisted her round so that she fell away from him. He held her up awkwardly, laughing down at her, taunting her. 'You don't hate this, though, do you?' He lowered her to the floor and sat astride her, still holding her wrists tightly.

'No, Luke, for God's sake. This issue is too important to make fun of.'

'I'm not making fun, darling. I'm deadly serious. I married you to have this to look forward to. At every opportunity. What do you think fills my thoughts when I'm away? I told you once and now I'll remind you — a quayside with the vision of you waiting for me. Now you're my wife that vision has changed slightly. I carry a vivid picture in my mind of the most beautiful woman lying beneath me, panting, begging for more, her bosom heaving with anticipation, just as it is now.' He let go of her wrists and placed both hands over her breasts, squeezing gently. Fran gulped, shutting her eyes tightly, trying to turn over, hitting him for all she was worth. They fought, they rolled across the sitting-room carpet, pushing a chair out of the way as they struggled frantically. Fran quickly ran out of breath as Luke stretched beside her, his hands firmly holding hers above her shoulders. His fingers entwined in hers, and one long powerful leg lay over one of hers.

'This is silly, Luke,' she managed to say. 'Let me get up, please?'

She could hardly bear to look up into his eyes, but no response from him forced her to. His dark, satanic eyes glinted in the sunlight — and Fran knew she would have to submit. But she didn't give in easily; she fought against him as she tried to escape his clutches, while at the same time she voiced all her malice.

'You're the most despicable man I've ever met,' she said as he tore away her underwear. Her dress was pushed up over her face. 'And forcing yourself on me doesn't change anything — I shall still leave you,' she yelled. She tried to bring one knee up to make contact with his groin but this only seemed to increase his feverish enthusiasm, and he laughed as he bent his head and kissed her intimately. Her struggling diminished. God, she thought, he knows every weak, sensitive spot. Even though she tore at his hair, her body reacted spontaneously, arching up to derive the maximum amount of pleasure from his exploring mouth. But still she refused to give in completely. Even when their bodies were as one she drew her knees up and pounded on the floor with her feet in protest. And as she pounded, the force of her actions lifted her bottom off the floor, tightening their coition until wanton craving had to be satiated. Violent in nature, the climax of their lust resulted in Fran sobbing as if her heart had been broken.

Luke was unable to pacify her. When he did finally release her she got up and rushed upstairs to the bathroom. She wanted to soak away all contact with this demon of a man she had married. She had known he was his own man, that he took rather than persuaded, but there was a better side when he was considerate and loving. Love or lust? That was a question she simply couldn't answer.

Chapter Thirteen

To Fran's surprise, when Hilda was told about the boarding school she was delighted. Her ready acceptance of going away for weeks at a stretch wounded Fran deeply. Hilda was the one she had felt would always stand by her whatever happened. Now she had to admit that Luke had come between them. Hilda idolised her stepfather as much, it seemed to Fran, as Ruby had adored Henry. But Fran could not forgive Luke for what he had done, and she made this quite clear to him by her belligerent attitude.

As the weather got better, Luke took Hilda on long hillside walks while Fran chose to remain at home sewing. She put all her aggression into the tacking stitches along seams of a dress for Babs. Somehow this year she would get home to see the other girls, she vowed. Her heart ached with longing for the family to be reunited, even though her mother assured her that everything was all right. Prue's letters confirmed much the same, but Babs's own letters became less frequent. 'She's only young,' Prue wrote, 'and although very good at her school work, placed in the top ten after the examinations, she finds writing letters take up too much playing time. Everywhere Sam goes, Babs follows.' When Kate wrote, she was full of all her activities at work and in her night school studies. She sounded happy, and that should have pleased Fran, but doubts lingered as to what any of them were keeping from her.

Ruby wrote more than any of the others: neatly written pages of news, always ending with a declaration of her love for her mother and Hilda. This brought pain and only added to Fran's guilt. Ruby had felt the parting more acutely than the others. In spite of her waywardness she was the most sensitive of them all. She mourned the loss of her father and grandfather, and was not ashamed to show that grief. Nor was she ashamed to show her contempt of the man who had taken her mother away. Her letters always began

166

the same: 'Dearest Mummy and Hilda'. Fran knew that Luke must notice that he was not included, but he never commented. Dear Ruby, for all the impatience Fran had shown her at home, was now the one who brought the most love through her letters in return. Fran regretted her resentment of her middle daughter now. She wished she could turn the clock back. Wished with all her heart she had taken heed of Ruby's outburst when she had announced her intention of marrying Luke. 'Mummy, you can't marry him. Daddy would hate it!' But Fran had married Luke Hammond – in haste – and was reaping her reward. Was Henry looking down on her and frowning, wreaking his revenge? And well he might, Fran thought. Their children, who had meant everything to Henry, were all living apart. Fran disliked herself intensely, and Luke even more for being the reason she had acted so hastily.

The rift between them grew wider as the weeks passed, and after Easter, when Luke drove them to Aberdeen to leave Hilda at her new school, Fran felt nothing but cold antagonism towards him.

Aberdeen was everything Luke had said it would be. A pleasant seaside town with bracing air, surrounded by beautiful countryside. Apparently ignoring Fran's resentment, Luke had booked them in at a hotel near the school for a week.

'We can visit Hilda at Melville House at the weekend, and you'll see for yourself how well she's settled in,' he told Fran.

Fran knew that Luke expected her to weep and wail as the time for parting drew near. Maybe he wanted another battle. Surely he didn't imagine that her frosty silences meant that she had given in? She hardly spoke to him and gave little response to any suggestions he made. To the school authorities she appeared the submissive little wife, letting Luke do all the talking. But inside she was desperately unhappy, and angry too. She might have won Luke round if Hilda had resisted. Fran could hardly believe that her favourite had actually become wild with excitement at going away to school. While Luke was signing documents and paying what Fran considered were exorbitant fees, she helped Hilda unpack her clothes and personal belongings in a small dormitory.

'Now you will write each week, won't you, darling?' she said.

'Of course, Mummy. It's one of the rules. Didn't you read the prospectus properly? Our letters have to be read by the matron before we can post them.' She ran to look out of the window. 'Isn't it beautiful here? Aren't I lucky? I shall make lots of new friends, too. It would have been nice if Babs could have come as well, but she'd only keep crying for you, I expect.'

Fran and Luke were invited to stay to tea before having to say

167

goodbye to Hilda. She wrapped her arms round Fran's neck as she kissed her, but with excitement rather than any other emotion. Then Hilda threw herself into Luke's arms.

'Thank you so much for letting me come here, Daddy,' she said, planting a big kiss on his cheek. 'You will come to see me and take me out to tea if your ship comes to Aberdeen, won't you?'

Luke assured her that he would. He laughed with her, patted her bottom and then shook hands with the headmistress before accompanying Fran outside.

'I'm sure you have nothing at all to worry about, darling,' he said, placing his arm round Fran's shoulder. Fran didn't answer. She was biting her lip to control her anguish, while at the same time she felt too angry for words. Why did she allow this man to rule her life? To possess her the way he did? Why hadn't she stood up to him and refused to allow Hilda to be separated from her? Why on earth had she married him in the first place? Bitter contempt ate away inside her. She longed to lash out at Luke but she had learned that he revelled in that kind of action, and it was likely to end in the way he chose to resolve any differences. So she remained cool outwardly and seemingly indifferent.

At the small hotel, overlooking a sandy bay where white-edged waves washed in from the North Sea, they changed for dinner, hardly exchanging a word. During the meal Fran listened impassively as Luke tried to discuss world events – events that were gloomy with rumour that Germany was re-arming. Troubles in Austria, Greece, Italy and Spain all contributed to the dark clouds that were accumulating in Europe. Fran couldn't be bothered with such matters, which did not appear to concern her or her family. It was all happening somewhere else, too far away to be of any interest to her. Luke, having travelled abroad extensively, obviously was deeply disturbed by the news and soon became engrossed in conversation with a middle-aged couple seated at the next table. When Fran had finished eating she put aside the crisp white table napkin and excused herself.

'It's been a tiring day,' she said. 'I hope you'll excuse me.'

Luke stood up briefly, but was evidently keen to resume his conversation, for which Fran was profoundly grateful. She went to their room. After taking deep breaths of sea air she closed the window and prepared for bed, thinking and worrying about Hilda. Her head ached, so she took two Aspros, and once she lay down in the darkened room, her hair unpinned and plaited, she was soon fast asleep.

The chill of early morning made Fran shiver as she woke. She was surprised that she had slept so soundly all night, and had not heard Luke come to bed. Immediately he responded to her movement by placing his arm across her waist. Fran wriggled farther away out of his reach in the outsized bed. She pushed her feet free of the sheets on the other side, and slid noiselessly to the floor. With slippers and dressing gown on she went along to the bathroom at the end of the passageway. Her headache had gone. Before returning to the bedroom she stood at the landing window and looked out on the peaceful scene. A promenade empty of people. Blue skies as far as the eye could see, and the sun rising in the east to greet a new spring day. Fran knew that she ought to be content, and feel privileged to be seeing sea and landscapes that until now had been but pictures in books and magazines. She felt less fractious, but she was determined to remain aloof towards Luke.

She tiptoed back to the bedroom and stood against the closed door as she surveyed her husband. He looked so devilishly appealing in sleep. She wondered whether he was feigning sleep and would jump to catch her at any moment, but his breathing was even. His eyes were hidden by smooth lids fringed with long black lashes. An elegantly straight nose and a jawline set firm, with the hint of self-satisfaction in his expression. Why had he chosen her of all the women in the world? During this first year of marriage she had enjoyed the delights of conjugal bliss. Learned that Luke Hammond was determined and masterful. Thoughtful, kind and lovingly considerate too when it suited him. She could appreciate that he wanted them to share a private existence when he was home on leave, but he was away more than he was home. What was she supposed to do with herself when he returned to his ship? She couldn't bear to imagine life without Hilda now. It was all right for him. He lived with a group of men who sailed the seas to exotic places. He said that he thought of no one but Fran while he was away, but she doubted the truth in that. In Far Eastern countries she knew there were brothels where a man's lust could be indulged. It filled her with disgust. To choose a life in the services seemed an unnatural way of life to her. She couldn't believe that Luke could remain celibate for long. He was too virile, too intensely potent. He might be in his prime but he hadn't survived all these years without using women. He certainly did not lack experience.

Luke stirred, and opened his eyes lazily. Fran moved away from the door.

'Come back to bed.'

'I'd rather get up,' she replied.

169

As she sat at the dressing-table mirror, she kept a watchful eye on her husband, hoping he would go to sleep again. She unplaited her long hair and began to brush it vigorously. Luke yawned and stretched, then pulled himself higher in the bed. He wore only pyjama trousers in bed and Fran felt a twinge of admiration at the glimpse of his bronzed torso. She knew he was watching her so she avoided eye contact through the mirror.

'How long do you propose to keep up this cold war?' His voice was low, and gravelly seductive.

'I don't know what you mean,' Fran said after a few seconds.

'Oh yes you do, and you're making a martyr of yourself again. Fran, I do understand how you feel. After all you've been through, this must seem like the last straw, but you didn't realise just how you were suffocating Hilda.'

'You're suffocating me!' Fran retorted crossly.

'With love perhaps — to make up for all the years I longed for you and couldn't have you. I didn't expect to find life easy being married to you. You've had one married life which was happy, or so you say. I realise that it is hard for you to adapt, but I consider we've have a good first year. You evidently like being married but you want all your own way, and married to me that's not the way it'll be. A serviceman's life is difficult enough and what he needs most of all is an understanding wife.'

'And you tell me that it's me who likes my own way? You're the selfish one. You've given no consideration at all to my feelings. Just get Hilda out of the way so that you can indulge yourself in my bed.'

'I have no wish to go to bed with a woman who is so obviously hostile.' Luke got out of bed and walked slowly towards the dressing table, his hands on his hips. 'I could force myself on you. I daresay you'd like me to do just that so that you could show your righteous indignation and hurl abuse at me. No, Fran. I'll show you the respect a wife deserves. You are, after all, only hurting yourself. I know that it's hard for you to admit that Hilda was actually excited about coming to Aberdeen, but she needs her freedom.'

'She's only just ten years old.' Fran felt a shiver go through her, like a ghost walking over her grave. Henry's words so often haunted her. He had pleaded on Ruby's behalf, now she was doing the same over Hilda. Only the situation was much, much worse, she thought with despair.

'And by the time I get a new commission she'll have taken the scholarship. Who knows what results a different environment and new methods may bring forth? Above all she needs lots of encouragement, as well as discipline, and she'll get that at Melville House. I would have done the same for Babs, had it been she who came north with us.'

Fran paused, her cheeks tight with unspent passion. Realisation hit hard. Luke Hammond had planned this from the moment he agreed to bring Hilda to Scotland.

'You may as well get used to the idea, Fran. I've paid advance fees for her to stay at Melville House until they break up for the summer holiday in 1935. That will be the time for you to return south. That can be your goal, so you may as well get used to the idea.'

'And if Hilda is ill? Or begs to leave Melville House?' Fran tried to retain her scorn, but her voice betrayed her pain.

'We'll cross that bridge if we come to it. According to the matron and headmistress, you can expect Hilda to show signs of homesickness during the first couple of weeks. It'll be up to you to reassure her. I shall be back at sea.'

Luke picked up his towel and toilet bag and went along to the bathroom. Fran could hardly believe his cruelty. No hope of seeing the girls until next year? Now she had been parted from each one of them. How could she bear it? What was she going to do with her time? One thing was certain – she would not be waiting like a dutiful wife to indulge her unfeeling husband the moment he returned home.

Pride helped Fran through. She knew that Jenny Logan was watching her every move, so she kept herself busy at her sewing machine and started knitting as well. But nothing would entice her to join the officers' wives' club. She wrote frequently to her mother and the girls, trying to sound cheerful, but there seemed hardly any news now that Hilda was not in Craiglee. Inwardly she hoped that Hilda would become homesick, and perhaps make such a fuss that the school would be glad to have her removed, but Hilda hardly had time to write a weekly letter. When a batch of letters arrived from Luke saying that he was well, but busy and unable to tell her his whereabouts, he commented on the delightful letters he had received from Hilda.

Fran felt desolate. She was torn between taking a train to Aberdeen one weekend, or taking out some of her own meagre savings to travel south, but she knew that once she set foot back on Dorset soil she would never return to Scotland again. She began to make plans for the Whitsun holiday, short though it would be. Then Hilda wrote saying that she had been invited to spend the bank-holiday weekend with one of her school

171

chums. She hoped Fran wouldn't mind if she didn't come home after all.

Fran couldn't believe it. She roamed the house, alternately weeping and declaring to the walls her contempt for Luke. Jenny Logan was away visiting relatives on the Isle of Skye for a week. Fran experienced the worst loneliness of her life. She managed to rid herself of some of the despondency by scrubbing floors that were already clean. She turned out cupboards and drawers. Luke was meticulous in his personal habits, his belongings always kept in neat and tidy order. She found a bundle of letters under a pile of civilian shirts. After cleaning out the empty drawer, Fran was overcome by curiosity. The postmark was foreign, from some remote part of Asia, she thought. Prying wasn't something she was in the habit of but she untied the bundle and looked at the date on the first envelope. It was 1921. She peeped inside, then drew out the single sheet of paper. The writing was small and in a foreign language, but the signature was clear enough: Sarita.

Fran became even more curious. Here were hidden secrets of Luke's past. She felt mildly jealous of the woman who had written regularly to Luke from the other side of the world and whom he thought so highly of that he had kept her letters for thirteen years. She looked at each letter in turn. Half-way through the bundle she came across a thicker package which contained photographs. The image of the young, virile Luke Hammond leapt out at her. He was standing, naked except for a pair of swimming trunks, at the water's edge of a palm-fringed, sandy beach, and encircled in his right arm was a petite and very beautiful girl. Fran could tell that the girl was probably a native of Asia. Fran's mind whirled round with all kinds of notions, not least the vision of Luke making love to this gorgeous creature. She wished she could read the messages, but then decided that it was probably best that she couldn't, for the language of love was clearly evident from the poses isn the photographs. Luke sitting on the sand with the girl lying across his thighs, laughing up into his face. The two of them kneeling in the shallow water, facing each other, their lips just touching in a light kiss. A wooden fishing boat with Luke and the girl lying intimately together. Fran could almost feel the kiss of the breeze, the heat of the sun and the magnetism of Luke's desire. Was this then the reason that he had never married previously? Was Sarita his mistress whom he visited when calling at some foreign port? Where was she now? Why did he never receive letters from abroad? The last envelope was dated 1930, the year before he had returned to Sherbrook.

Fran felt a tightness growing in her chest. Had he used this poor girl for his physical needs and, when he had discovered that Fran had become widowed, rejected her? Or was Sarita still his mistress? Did he keep her in reserve for when he was away from home, but forbade her to correspond with him any more? Fran felt numb with inquisitiveness. She couldn't identify her emotions. Was she jealous? A little bit, yes, she had to admit. Hurt, too, that Luke had not mentioned Sarita, whoever she was.

After a long time Fran tied up the letters just as she had found them and returned them to the bottom of the drawer. If she was experiencing the pain of rejection, wasn't that her own stupid fault? When she calmed a little she realised that she should be thankful that such letters were not delivered through their letterbox regularly.

Fran was very glad to see Jenny back, she was good company.

'So you've been here by yourself all week?' Jenny asked in astonishment.

'Yes, but it was only a week, thank goodness.'

'Ooh, deary me,' Jenny sympathised. 'I would'na gone if I'd known.'

'Then it's as well you didn't know, Jenny,' Fran said. 'You look after us so well, you deserved your holiday and I'm glad you enjoyed it.'

'I wouldn't have if I'd known that neither Captain Hammond nor young Hilda weren't coming home.'

'I didn't really expect my husband to come home yet. It does get lonely when he's away.' Fran sighed. 'A man can't really understand what it's like to not have your children round you.'

'This past year has gone by quickly though, and the second year won't be as difficult as the first. The time will rush by, you'll see.'

'It would if Hilda were still here, but counting days with nothing much to do is quite foreign to me, Jenny.'

'Have you no' thought about doing some charity work, Mrs Hammond? There are some wives who either don't have children, or their children are away at school like Hilda, and there's plenty needs doing for the poor folk in Glasgow. You'd be a real boon to some wi' your ability with your needle.'

'Glasgow?' Fran echoed in surprise. 'That's too far away, surely?'

'We-ell, yes, mebbe it is, but a few of the wives do give up some of their spare time to help with charitable organisations. You could ask the vicar. He'd know where help is most needed, I'm sure.'

Fran wondered afterwards whether Jenny had spoken to the vicar

173

on her behalf, for a few days later the Reverend Jimmy Kyle called to see her about teatime.

Jenny fussed about, serving tea in the sitting room upstairs promptly at four o'clock, while the rather shabbily dressed, elderly vicar enquired abut the health of Fran and her family.

'It must be quiet for you around these parts with your man away at sea, and your young wee girlie up in Aberdeen, especially after moving from the south of England,' he said.

'I'm used to living in the country, but I've always had so many family members with me,' Fran said. She was wary of giving too much away about her private affairs. 'The days are long, though,' she admitted.

'My dear wife is crippled with arthritis now and finds it most frustrating that she can't do the parish work she once did. There's an orphanage just outside Dunfermline where she goes to help three days a week. She used to play the piano and help teach the talented children, but she can't do that any longer.'

'And I'm afraid I can't offer my services there, vicar, as I can't play or read music.'

'But you have other talents, my dear Mrs Hammond. The little garments you made for the Christmas bazaar were quite unique.'

'I do like sewing, but that wouldn't be much help to orphan children.'

'On the contrary, dear lady, there's always a great need for clothes for the poor unfortunate children who have been abandoned. We get plenty of cloth given to us from the mills but it isn't easy to find someone willing to give up their time, or indeed with the necessary competence to use it wisely.'

Fran laughed nervously, remembering Jenny's suggestion. 'I'm not a professional seamstress,' she said, 'and I'm not sure that my husband would approve.'

'I think the men understand that time hangs heavily while they're at sea. Of course we wouldn't hold you to any commitment when he returns home. Your assistance would please my wife enormously and be greatly valued. Perhaps you would care to come to the Manse for tea tomorrow afternoon to discuss the matter?'

Fran didn't have a valid excuse for refusing the invitation, and the longer she stayed in the company of Mrs Kyle the following day, the better she liked her. Fran was overwhelmed with pity at the sight of the poor woman's disability. Her hands were crooked and difficult to use, yet she had baked a cake and managed to pour tea without spilling it. Fran felt that such a painful condition should be etched in her face, yet Mrs Kyle had a radiance about her that was breathtaking. Her features were almost flawless. She had soft, blue, sparkling eyes set wide above high cheekbones, and skin of a delicate peach colour. Her lower lip was full and sensuous, but she didn't need to part her lips to smile, because her generous zest for life shone from her face. They were soon chatting like old friends, and Fran found consolation from the experiences of the older woman.

'We have children in the orphanage of a wide age range,' Mrs Kyle explained. 'From babies through to twelve years old. At twelve they go to a hostel to prepare them for work. Mostly the girls go into service, though it's getting more and more difficult to place them these days. If you want to, and we know you love children, you can assist in looking after the children in a general way, but sewing would be a marvellous help, and at the same time you could have a group of the older girls to teach.'

'I'd like that,' Fran said eagerly. 'Before I went into service as a nanny I helped in our village school. That was a long time ago, though. As I said, I'm not a professional needlewoman, Mrs Kyle, but Lady Hinckley paid for me to have a course of lessons which gave me a good start. Since then, with four daughters, I've had plenty of practice.'

Fran's spirits lifted from her very first week at the orphanage. Life was worth living again, her days full, and her letters to her own family were hastily composed ones filled with news of the children who had been rejected for one reason or another, usually because they were illegitimate. At first she went three mornings a week, but soon she was so engrossed in the work of caring for the tiny mites who had been separated from their mothers at birth that she decided to stay in the afternoons to sew and help the older girls to learn to make clothes for themselves. In some of the children she saw reflections of her own girls, and in the dark-haired boys of about ten years her vision of Lennie was refreshed. Her somewhat saintly memory of Lennie gradually faded, and in its place she remembered him as the teasing, mischievous boy he sometimes was. The boys endeared themselves to Fran and she to them, but she was also good at controlling the girls. Her methods of strict discipline earned her their respect, and on occasion a wayward girl or boy who appeared to be unmanageable reacted favourably to Fran's persuasion. There were times when she felt guilty at harsh words spoken in the heat of the moment to Ruby or Kate in the past. Now she could couple her experience with the compassion she knew these children needed. And she had all the time required to give of herself to them.

She wrote to Luke, telling him what she was doing to keep herself

175

occupied, but after several weeks, when a batch of letters arrived from him, it was apparent that her news had not yet caught up with him. At the sight of his handwriting she felt a pang of jealousy. Did he still write to the Asian girl, Sarita? Were they letters of love as hers were in spite of the rift? What if he was spending time with this girl during his long absence? There was no means of checking his whereabouts. She might never know whether he was living a Jekyll and Hyde existence.

The weather grew warmer, the days long and bright, which matched Fran's cheerfulness. Her thoughts were always with her family, and she longed to see both Hilda and Luke again. The weeks had passed quickly, just as Jenny had said they would, and she was quite surprised when she turned the calendar over to the first of June. She was working so hard now that she looked forward to the quiet peacefulness of Sundays, and on the first Sunday in June, after going to morning service at the kirk, she set off alone to walk over the hills to the lock.

The sky was azure blue with smudges of white cloud. Sheep grazed contentedly, and birds sang as they rested on trees and boulders after flying on the currents of warm air high in the sky. Fran's mind drifted back over the year. It was time for stock-taking. Three years now since Henry and her father had perished in the flash tide. The pain was easing but the memories vivid as if it had happened yesterday. Would Henry think she had been disloyal to his memory? Her brief courtship and marriage to Luke had been another flash tide. She had been swept away on a current of emotion, and yes, there had been many moments of regret, but now, oh, how she longed to lie in his arms again to be comforted.

The yearning to see Luke again, to be made to feel a desirable woman, was marred by the thought that another whole year had to pass before she could be reunited with her family. She glanced at the gold fob-watch pinned to the front of her dress, which Luke had given her as a wedding gift. It was nearly four o'clock. She decided it was time to walk back, have a cup of tea, and then write to the girls. She stood up and stretched. Voices from far away floated across the loch. Some children were playing near the water's edge and she could see one or two fishermen trying their luck. It was almost too lovely a scene to leave. There was such peace here, but it was a peace impaired by the painful guilt that tormented her.

Already in her mind she was penning the words she was about to write to Kate as she picked her way across the craggy hillside. The sun was at its highest now, and bore through the clothes on her back as she skirted the burn in the valley. She met one or two families out for their Sunday afternoon walk, and as she drew near to home she felt she was being watched. She stopped to look up, and saw a tall figure standing in their garden. Her heart leapt, pulsating hard against the wall of her chest. It couldn't be – was it? Yes, there was no mistaking Luke's upright stance. She waved excitedly and began to run, all past differences forgotten, as well as the Asian girl, Sarita. Luke vaulted the low stone wall and hurried towards Fran. The distance between them was greater than either of them imagined. They were impatient to bridge the gap, and at last Fran fell into Luke's embrace, unable to speak from lack of breath.

Luke held her close to him, his hand caressing her back, his lips nuzzling in the folds of her neck. She regained some breath and pulled away to gaze up at him. 'It's so good to see you, Luke,' she whispered.

'My darling, you can't know how I've longed for this moment. You look as perfect as ever – more radiant than I dared hope.' With arms entwined about each other they walked along the length of the stone wall to the track at the side of the house. They went in through the front gate and round to the back door, which Fran found unlocked. 'How long have you been here?' she asked, her blue eyes alight with affection. Dear God, she thought, would he ever know just how much she loved him in spite of everything?

'About half an hour, and from the bedroom window I saw you out there on the hill.'

Over tea they chatted amicably, yet Fran felt that this time it was Luke who was in a reticent mood. He asked about the girls and Fran's mother. She begged to know where he had been and how long he expected to be at home. He didn't reply at once but kept stirring his tea. Then she noticed some sign of strain in his furrowed brow.

'I'm home on compassionate leave, Fran,' he said.

'Compassionate leave?' she questioned, all kinds of ridiculous thoughts crowding into her brain. Her mother – or Ruby? Kate? Babs? No, he had enquired about them all.

'My father has had an accident at the foundry. It's bad. You won't have heard from Elizabeth because she's helping Mother look after him. She contacted me and I was able to transfer ship in the Indian Ocean to get home quickly. I'm afraid we have to pack up and drive to Middlesbrough tomorrow as my parents have requested that I visit.'

'Oh, Luke, I'm so sorry,' Fran said. 'To think it takes something like this to get you all together again.'

'It's my mother who wants to see me. I doubt very much that my father will acknowledge or ever forgive me, Fran.'

Fran did everything to support Luke, and by midnight their cases were packed, ready for the long journey the next day.

If Fran expected a passionate reunion she was disappointed. But, in spite of the anxiety she knew Luke felt, once they were lying together in the big bed he could not resist showing his feelings with tender caresses. His kisses were long and ardent, demonstrating his love until his desperate need of Fran took precedence over concern for his father. Their coming together was a unique experience of gentle satisfaction, healing the wound that had remained festering for too long.

Chapter Fourteen

'How long will the journey take?' Fran asked, as she spread butter lavishly on a crusty roll. They had stopped for mid-morning refreshment in the delightful town of Berwick-on-Tweed. They had spoken very little thus far, but now she could tell that Luke was readjusting to land and his features looked less strained.

'Something between five and six hours. It's well over a hundred and fifty miles, I reckon. We'll have a proper meal when we reach Newcastle. We can freshen up, too, before we make the last lap to Middlesbrough. We'll find a hotel not too far away from the family home.'

'Won't they expect you to stay with them?'

Luke grunted. 'I doubt it. I can't imagine what kind of reception we'll get. I expect it'll be best if you leave most of the talking to me, darling. I wouldn't have put you through this ordeal, but it's important to me that my parents meet my wife at last.'

'How long is it since you saw them?'

'Many years. During my earliest days in the Navy I did go home to spend my leaves there. Stupidly I thought they needed to see that I was all right, but my father made it quite clear that I was an embarrassment to him.'

'But surely your mother didn't reject you, Luke?'

Luke's chin trembled slightly. 'I think I broke her heart,' he said at length.

'You know I'll be with you and support you, whatever happens,' Fran declared loyally. 'Did Elizabeth tell you just what your father's injuries are?'

'It sounded as if he may have damaged his spine. As soon as I docked I telephoned Elizabeth. She's the businesswoman of the family. She manages the firm's accounts department, but she lives in a delightful cottage of her own away from the foundry. I know

179

she would want us to stay with her, but after so long I feel I can't impose. I need to tread warily. There were faults on both sides, I dare say, but if I'm to − well − to become on better terms with my parents and sisters, I must be discreet.'

'I can't imagine why you should need to be discreet, Luke,' Fran said, finishing her coffee as she gazed across at Luke affectionately. 'I'm sure your parents, especially your mother, and your sisters will welcome you with open arms.'

Luke's dark eyes glinted in the sunlight, which streamed through the curtained window where they were sitting. A smile fleetingly passed across his face, the kind of smile Fran had never seen before, and she was suspicious of it. The foreign letters came back to torment her. The girl called Sarita. Was it the Navy that had come betwen Luke and his parents? Or was it the Asian girl? A shiver of mistrust swept over Fran as she stood up. She wished there wasn't this feeling of secrecy about Luke Hammond. But that enigmatic smile confirmed that there was an area in his life which she knew nothing about.

As the day became warmer, the temperature inside the car rose to unbearable heights even with the windows down. Fran didn't care for the smell of engine fumes which blew in on them, and she was relieved when at last they reached the cathedral city of Newcastle-upon-Tyne, 'capital' of Tyneside. Luke seemed to know exactly where he was heading, and they parked on the forecourt of the Railway Inn. They had an excellent meal, before continuing towards Middlesbrough.

Pleasant countryside seemed to open up the coal-mining city's dark sky, but, after a further hour's travelling, as they came to the border between Durham and North Yorkshire, the heavily industrialised Teesside became even more of a reality to Fran. There was evidence of blast furnaces, foundries and mills. Tall chimneys emitted thick, dirty smoke which clung round the high, blackened brick buildings.

'The foundry is just south of the river. My father has the ideal site close to transportation, but Hammond House is nearer the east coast. Elizabeth lives just outside Skelton in a tiny village.'

Fran felt that she was growing nearer to Luke's past, but she also felt tension increasing.

She wasn't prepared for the narrow country lane or the ornate iron gates that led to Hammond House. A low iron fence bordered grassy meadows in the grounds, where sheep grazed and a horse cantered excitedly at the sound of the car's engine. The wheels crunched on the gravel drive as Luke brought the car to a standstill below a flight of stone steps. The huge oak door appeared forbidding. Fran gasped.

'This is your home? Where you spent your childhood?' she asked, with a hint of disbelief.

Luke managed to laugh. 'I suppose it does seem rather grand, even to me now, after all these years. It's old, probably some might say ugly, large, cold and unfriendly – so be warned.'

'You sound bitter, Luke.' Fran placed a hand on his arm and he covered it with his own. 'Maybe the years have brought warmth to the house,' she said. 'I'm sure you'll find it more welcoming than you imagine. Think of the pleasure you're going to give your parents.'

Luke leaned across and kissed her lips. 'What would I do without you?' he said.

Voices distracted Fran from replying, and they saw a woman coming down the steps to greet them. She pushed her head in the window.

'You must be Fran,' she said. Then, with a wry twist to her mouth, she glanced across at Luke. 'Well, well, brother dear, who ever thought you'd grace us with your presence after all these years?'

'How did you know I was coming?' Luke asked.

'Elizabeth didn't want Mother having a heart attack with shock. She'd had shock enough with Father's accident.'

'How is he? Oh, by the way, darling, this is Dorinda, my youngest sister.'

Fran smiled at Dorinda, but received only a frosty look in return.

'He's just about holding his own. You might not have got here in time, but I suppose that wouldn't have mattered to the old man. He hasn't changed his mind, if that's what you're hoping for. He gets more crotchety with each year. Still, Mother will be delighted to see her darling son.'

Another figure appeared at the front door.

'For goodness sake, don't stay out there. Dorrie, we all want to share him,' the woman called.

Luke opened his door and got out. Before he could get round to Fran's side, Dorinda had opened the door and was helping Fran to her feet.

'Stiff, I expect, if you've travelled from Scotland,' Dorinda said. 'Golly, aren't you tiny?'

Fran smiled. 'You all seem to be taller than average. I'm very pleased to meet you, but I wish it were in happier circumstances.'

181

'Can't imagine why Luke hasn't brought you home long before this.'

Fran just caught the exchange of vindictive looks between brother and sister, and she feared that this visit might not be as pleasant as she hoped.

With an arm around Fran, Luke guided her up the steps after Dorinda. The woman waiting at the top was more attractive than Dorinda, maybe because she seemed less hostile. She held her arms out to her brother and they kissed with some measure of affection.

'Cecilia, this is my wife, Fran.'

'It's really good to meet you at last. We never ever thought Luke would marry and now we hear that he's been hiding you away for all these years.'

Fran began to repudiate this statement, but was suddenly aware of Luke's fingers jerking a warning against hers.

'I'm sorry to hear ... about your father,' she said falteringly. She went quite hot, and was glad that at that moment a frail, elderly woman came through the hall.

'Let me see you both.' There was no doubting that this was Luke's mother. She came with arms outstretched and tears running down her narrow face. She fell on Luke, sobbing unashamedly. 'He wouldn't let me ever send for you, my dear, dear boy,' she said. 'I can hardly take it in that so many years have gone by. And now our days are numbered. We're both growing old, and it looks as if Father may be taken from us. I'm glad Elizabeth could contact you in time, Luke. It wouldn't be right not to see his only son before he dies.'

'I came as soon as I could, Mother, but I was in the Indian Ocean. Have you told Father that I was coming? I wouldn't want to upset him.'

'Oh, you'll do that all right,' Dorinda said sharply. 'He's still the supreme head of the family, in spite of anything Liz may have told you, and don't expect him to rush to change his will.'

'That will do, Dorinda.' Mrs Hammond turned quickly to her youngest daughter. 'We're all a little overwrought with worry.' She smiled gently at Fran. 'So you're the woman who has brought happiness into my son's life? I might have known you'd be pretty — and a redhead. He always did have an eye for something special.'

'Fran is very special to me, Mother,' Luke said, drawing Fran close to him. Then he raised his eyebrows at his mother. 'And we have come a long way. We're tired and dying for a cup of tea.'

'I'm so sorry — of course. Why on earth are we standing out

182

here? Well, it's probably warmer out than in. This old house keeps out the sun, you see, my dear.' She took Fran's hand and tucked it through her arm as she led the way into the dim, musty smelling hallway.

After the glare of the June sun, Fran found it difficult to see inside, but she welcomed the coolness. Taken into the drawing room, she fell in love with the comfort of the house.

Luke did not follow at once and Fran suspected that he was having a confrontation with his younger sister.

The Adam fireplace looked well used and the grate was laid ready with paper and sticks. A tall Chinese vase containing branches of mauve and white lilac stood by the side of the hearth, and a bowl of sweet-smelling roses in a variety of shades stood in the centre of an occasional table. The room was cold, yet warm in atmosphere. Mrs Hammond sat in her chair between hearth and table as Luke joined them.

'I can't do much these days,' she said, half apologetically, 'but the girls will make sure you're comfortable.'

'We're going to stay in the Founder's Arms, Mother,' Luke said gently. 'We don't want to put anyone out − and it happens to be our wedding anniversary next weekend, so I thought it was about time Fran had a special celebration break.'

The door opened softly and Cecilia came in carrying a tray. Fran glanced to the doorway and saw that Dorinda was hovering uncertainly.

'And how many years is that?' Mrs Hammond asked.

'More than we care to admit to − eh, darling?' Luke's expression was one of daring as he glanced at Fran. They were sitting side by side on a long sofa and he took Fran's hand in his and squeezed.

'Elizabeth tells me that you have four daughters. What ages are they?'

Fran felt her muscles tighten in her cheeks as Luke answered quickly. 'From seven to nineteen, Mother.'

'So you've been married this past twenty years or more and we never knew.'

Fran couldn't believe what she was hearing. Luke was playing a game of charades, which was evidently why he had said he would do all the talking. It seemed as if he anticipated his mother's questions and had the answers ready on the tip of his lying tongue. For what reason? The girl Sarita laughed up at Fran from her memory of the photos. Just what had Luke been up to? Then Fran recalled Dorinda's sarcasm about their father and his will. Was that the real reason for this sudden decision to visit? Could Luke really be capable of such scheming? The conversation drifted on above her head as suppositions and accusations muddled her weary brain. She was glad of a good strong cup of tea, but declined to eat anything.

'Perhaps you're being sensible,' her mother-in-law said kindly. 'We shouldn't spoil our appetites before supper.'

Supper! How on earth could they keep up this pretence? Was Luke planning to stay here for the rest of the day? Fran felt sure she would forget herself and tell the truth. She simply wasn't used to deceiving anyone. What reason could Luke have for deceiving his family? Could it be that he had been disinherited because of Sarita? As she sat quietly observing the Hammond family, she came to the conclusion that this must be the answer. Luke Hammond had certainly not been celibate during the past twenty years and now Fran began to wonder if in fact he had been married while overseas? Bigamy, a family of dark-skinned children, all began to agitate in Fran's mind and she longed to get away.

When the tea tray had been removed, Cecilia suggested that Luke and Fran should go upstairs to see James Hammond.

'Perhaps you'd prefer to go on your own as you haven't seen him for so long,' Fran said to Luke as he stood up. 'It might not be good to have too much excitement in his condition.'

'No, we don't want him killed off just yet, do we, Luke?' Dorinda said. She had been sitting on the wide window seat as if she didn't want to be a part of this family reunion. 'He doesn't say very much, but it's my opinion that he's quite capable of knowing what's going on, and hearing everything.' She went to the door. 'My boys will be in from school shortly, so I must prepare their tea.' She left the room, and in her wake Fran sensed a venomous sting in the air.

'That's one sister who isn't pleased to see me,' Luke said, trying to laugh it off.

'Well, you can't blame her, Luke,' Cecilia said as she led the way upstairs. 'You know Dorrie. She has the foundry earmarked for her two boys.'

'You have sons as well,' Luke said.

'Dorrie was married before me, even if I am two years older than she. Her boys are the eldest so she thinks they're entitled to the family business as you have no sons.'

They had reached the large square landing. There was a faint smell of disinfectant, and Fran guessed which the sickroom was by the heavy brocade curtain that hung across one door. She felt nauseous. She didn't want to be part of this at all, and by the anguish in Luke's face she guessed he was dreading this meeting with his father.

Cecilia drew back the curtain and opened the door softly. Luke followed her in. As Fran hesitated, a nurse in starched blue and white came forward and ushered her in quickly.

'I shall be just outside, should you need me,' she said.

For a brief moment Fran thought she could smell death in the room. An involuntary shiver swept over her body. She tried to avoid looking at the bed, but suddenly Luke was drawing her forward to greet his father.

'A surprise for you, Father,' Cecilia said. 'Luke's come home, with his wife.'

'Hullo, Father,' Luke said. 'We were so sorry to hear about your accident.'

'Bet you were,' came the mumbled reply from the bed.

Fran looked at the white-faced figure lying flat in the bed. She had prepared herself to meet a man near to his end but James Hammond's eyes were bright and alert. He stared hard at his son and Fran saw that a moistness came into his eyes. Eyes that had faded with time, she suspected, but they had once been as magnetic as his son's. He still had a shock of dark-brown hair and a wiry moustache. As devilishly handsome once as Luke is now, Fran thought. Luke went closer to the bedside and took the hand lying outside the covers. The word 'foundry' had presented a picture of heavy metal, black dust and gnarled hands, but, to Fran's amazement, James Hammond's hands were like a gentleman's hands. Long, tapering fingers with well-manicured nails, as if they had never wielded the tools of a rough, tough, working life.

'Let me see the woman,' a shaky voice demanded.

Luke urged Fran nearer, and all her anger subsided. The old man's eyes were seeping tears, but she doubted that he even realised. There was strength in the features even if his condition caused a general weakness.

'I'm so sorry to have to meet you when you're not feeling well,' Fran said, gently clasping his hand.

'You can kiss me,' the old man said. 'I shan't bite.'

Fran placed her lips against his cheek and kept them there for a moment. She felt her warmth transfer to his cold face, and he tightened his grip on her hand.

'Why has it taken you so long to come?' he asked, in a quivering voice.

'Luke has to travel about,' Fran answered.

'And where are the children?'

'Because of my job, Father, we feel it's best that they remain at school in the south while I'm away at sea.'

185

James looked at his son with pitying scrutiny. Then he closed his eyes, and his face screwed up as if he was in pain.

'Shouldn't he have something for the pain?' Luke asked Ceclia.

'Yes, I expect it's time for his medicine. It might be best if we leave him now.'

They walked downstairs in solemn procession. Dorinda was nowhere to be seen, and Luke's mother was dozing in her chair.

'You haven't asked about his injuries,' Fran whispered to Luke.

'I told you, it's a spinal injury.'

'What was he doing, then? How did the accident happen?'

'Poking his nose in the most dangerous part of the foundry, by all accounts.'

'You heard that from Elizabeth?'

'Why the inquisition?' Luke hissed impatiently.

Footsteps in the hall echoed loudly, and in a few moments two young boys of about seven and eight entered the room.

Mrs Hammond came to life again. 'Ah, my grandsons. Come along, Howard and Jamie. Come and meet your Uncle Luke and Auntie Fran.'

The boys were very much alike, with mousy hair and hazel eyes. They were still wearing school uniform and making an effort to be on their best behaviour. Fran was certain that boyish giggles were being suppressed.

'Hullo,' she greeted brightly. 'How was school today? What was it – football, games or boring old geography?'

The younger boy, Jamie took a step closer and smiled. 'History today, but I enjoy it. English isn't bad, but I hate arithmetic.'

'Not too good at sums?' Luke said with a smile.

'No, sir. Well, I'm not bad, I supposed. At least I'm not at the bottom of the class.'

'Not quite,' his elder brother put in.

'And how was your school day, Howard dear?' his grandmother enquired.

'Quite good, Gran. I came top in last week's tests so now I can join the science group.'

Fran was quick to hear the distant screech of car brakes outside in the drive, and a few moments later the door was flung open and Elizabeth rushed in.

'Oh,' she said, breathlessly, 'you got here before me. I'm sorry Luke, I got held up at the bank.' Elizabeth kissed her brother and then hugged Fran warmly as she kissed her too. 'How are you both? Looking very well, I see.'

186

'We seem to have managed without you very well,' Luke said in a low voice as Mrs Hammond took the two boys outside.

'I'm sorry, Luke,' Elizabeth said again. 'I'm afraid I couldn't help it. How did it go?'

'Cecilia and Mother were pleased to see me, but Dorinda is ready to fight me all the way.'

'More important, how did Father react? How does he seem to you?'

'Better, I think, than you led me to believe. He managed to say a few words, and he didn't order me out of the house, but it's obvious that he's in considerable pain.'

'By tomorrow we shall know the results of the X-rays. They kept him in hospital for the first, critical week, and I really doubted whether you could possibly arrive here in time, but then he rallied. He's made every effort to survive.'

Luke and Elizabeth were talking in subdued tones. Fran felt as if they had forgotten that she was there, so she moved away to the window. The two boys, now wearing clothes suitable for playing in, were kicking a ball out in the meadow. The whole scene appeared somewhat bizarre to Fran. She had never expected to meet Luke's family, and it seemed odd to her that out of the blue his mother had requested a visit. Not so unlikely, she told herself, when the head of the household had been involved in an accident that could have resulted in his death. Fran was glad that he was recovering, and pleased that Luke had made the effort to see him, but she was suspicious of an ulterior motive.

This was confirmed at supper. Fran was tired after the long tedious journey, and would much have preferred to go to the hotel and return the next day when they were fresher. Now she struggled to eat the roast beef on her plate. She was pressed to take larger helpings of home-grown vegetables than she wanted and found it difficult to push them down.

Cecilia's husband, Alex, was a pleasant-mannered man who said little and seemed subservient to his wife. Their three small children were introduced briefly before supper: Edna, aged six, Teddy, four, and an eighteen-month-old baby boy, Derek. A young nanny whisked them away to the nursery before the supper gong sounded.

Dorinda's husband, Giles, was late arriving. He was shorter than Alex, stocky and round-faced with plump red cheeks, and something of an exhibitionist, Fran decided, as he took his place at the table next to her. He constantly nudged her elbow and made silly remarks while slurping his soup, and ate the main course as if he were afraid

187

someone might remove it if he didn't hurry. Fran learned that he was a wages clerk at one of the many coal mines in the area. Alex worked in the ship-building industry. Fran silently thought how uncharacteristic of their jobs they were. She could well have imagined the burly Giles with blackened face and miner's lamp, heaving a truckload of coal along a tunnel down a mine, while Alex was a much more likely candidate for a white-collar office job.

The women contributed little to the conversation during the lengthy meal, but the men all appeared to converse easily, and Luke was in his element, recounting sea stories. They adjourned to the drawing room for coffee. Luke's mother was eager to hear about the girls while Luke and Elizabeth chatted secretly in a corner.

'Suppose when you heard father was about to snuff it you thought Luke ought to reinstate himself in the family circle?'

Fran had been enjoying a quiet conversation with Mrs Hammond and was surprised at the animosity in Dorinda's voice. She had long legs, long face, long everything, Fran thought, as she glanced up at her sister-in-law.

'Why should you think this visit has anything to do with me?' Fran said shortly. 'I was most surprised when Luke came home unexpectedly and announced that we were to come to Middlesbrough.'

'I bet,' Dorinda said. 'We expected him to return like the prodigal son when retirement from the Navy was approaching, but we didn't think he'd make his reappearance so obvious just when Dad was critically ill.'

'That's enough, Dorrie,' Elizabeth said. 'It has nothing to do with Fran. I felt it was right that Luke should know the situation. Besides, Mother wanted to see Luke. He is her only son, after all.'

'Yes, a disinherited one, remember. He hasn't cared one jot for Mother all these years. Don't you think it strange that he should come home now? We aren't stupid, Liz. Pity you couldn't conjure up a son yourself, Luke. That way you might be successful in wheedling your way into Father's affections.'

Luke dug his hands into his pockets. Fran saw a frown crease his brow and to her surprise he said: 'Actually, we had a son soon after we were married. Sadly he died of consumption at the age of ten.'

Fran opened her mouth in surprise. She wasn't aware of gasping, but she heard an intake of breath from the rest of the company. There was a thick silence.

'Fran has never quite got over it, although she is devoted to the four girls.' He put a tight grip on Fran's arm. 'Now I think we'll go to our hotel. Good night, Mother. Will it be all right if we call again tomorrow?'

Mrs Hammond, clearly shocked, stood up. She clung to Fran, kissing her and offering her sympathy, which brought fresh tears to Fran's eyes. Tears of anger as well as sorrow. Then Luke's mother wept on her son's shoulder as Elizabeth accosted Dorinda.

'I hope you're satisfied. You always were a vindictive little horror. Luke and Fran have as much right as you in this house, and don't you forget it.'

'I'm sorry, Fran. I ... I didn't know ...' Dorinda tossed her head then in defiance. 'It still doesn't alter the fact, though, that Father disinherited Luke when he ran away to sea.'

Fran thought that Luke was about to strike his youngest sister, but he resisted the temptation. He tugged at Fran's arm, and they went outside to the car.

He opened the door for Fran, but she paused before sitting inside.

'You've got some explaining to do,' she said, tight-lipped.

'Not now, for heaven's sake, Fran,' he said between his teeth.

Elizabeth had come after them. ''Bye for now, Fran. It's just a question of time. They'll come round to accepting Luke again, you'll see.'

'I'm not sure I know what's going on,' Fran said, 'but I don't think I approve.'

'Hammond House is where Luke belongs. He's the only son and when he retires from the Navy he should come into the business. It's what I've always wanted and what I shall go on working towards, regardless of what the others may think or say. Mother naturally wants Luke to have his inheritance in due course.'

'I don't wish to be party to any scheming, Elizabeth.'

Luke drew his sister away from the car and they stood aside talking in low voices so that Fran could not hear. Fran watched, noticing how alike they were. Elizabeth was almost as tall as Luke, and both were bright and alert like their father. Luke kissed Elizabeth and she waved again to Fran as they drove away.

Fran decided to let the tension ease before saying anything. The hotel seemed quite a distance away from Hammond House, but at last they left behind the riverside traffic and came to the coast. The air was clear and sweeter-smelling.

'It's not a large place, just a small family-run hotel. It's comfortable and serves excellent food,' Luke said.

'And how long are we to stay here? Until you're sure of your birthright?'

'Don't be sarcastic, Fran. You don't understand.'

'I understand that you've tricked me as well as your parents. I can see a lot more clearly now, and I do believe you've used me from the very beginning to get back in their favour.'

'Come along, I don't intend to sit here and argue things out. We must sign in.'

He fetched the cases from the boot of the car and Fran reluctantly followed him into the reception. She stood aloof from him. She could hardly believe that she was in this situation. She had vowed she hated him when he took Hilda away from her, but now to discover that he had planned to use her from the start was shocking. A young pageboy took them up in the lift to the first floor, where they were shown into a room overlooking the sea. It reminded Fran of the hotel Luke had stayed in when he visited her in Brimdene. What a fool she had been to fall for his scheming plans! Luke tipped the young boy and then closed the door firmly.

'All right,' he said angrily. 'So you think you've found me out in some dastardly plot. Is it wrong of me to want to get to know my family again?'

'For the wrong reasons, yes, Luke, it is. I thought you were genuine in wanting to make it up with your parents, but not for one moment did I believe it was to make monetary gain. Have you no pride? Creeping and crawling to your father so that he'll put you back in his will? It's the most despicable thing I've ever heard of, and then to use me − and my dead son − for your own ends. To pretend that the girls are yours? What else have you stooped to for your selfish greed? Yours and Elizabeth's, I suppose.'

'Leave Liz out of this. At least she gave me hope and love during my early days at sea.'

'And then Sarita came into your life,' Fran flung at him. 'Now where does *she* fit in? Is she your other wife? Mother of your children, perhaps? Is that why your father disowned you − because you married a foreign girl?'

Luke was stunned. He turned quite pale and his cheeks looked drawn. It was as if his tongue had cramp. He just stood and stared at Fran, unnerving her. Then he slowly walked towards her, clenching his fists into a tight ball as he did so.

'You've been prying,' he accused. 'How else would you know anything about Sarita?'

'You took my Hilda away, so I was left in Craiglee alone when Jenny had her holiday. I couldn't bear it without Hilda − and you. But you wouldn't know what it's like for a woman to be separated

190

from the children she bore. I had to occupy my time as best I could so I cleared out drawers and cupboards. Husbands and wives shouldn't have secrets, Luke. Henry and I never had any – and I thought we didn't either. Yes, I found the bundle of letters by accident, and I had to satisfy my curiosity. Snapshots of you and a beautiful girl – and you maintain that it was the image of me you carried everywhere with you.'

'I never claimed to be celibate.'

Fran was sick of hearing those words. 'But you never told me you had loved another woman that much before?'

'How can you know how much I loved Sarita?' He glared at Fran with contempt, then covered his face with his hands as if he couldn't bear the truth.

'Are we within the law, Luke?' Fran asked, almost afraid of what she might hear. 'For goodness sake, you've used me enough, I must know everything now.'

Luke went to look out of the window. He turned and stared at Fran unseeing. He paced the room in agitation. Fran felt afraid of him, yet she knew she mustn't show it.

'If we're not legally married, Luke, then I want to go to Aberdeen, fetch Hilda, pack up everything in Craiglee and go home to my family.'

Luke came out of his trance. 'What are you saying? Darling – do you think so badly of me that you think I'd coerce you into a bigamous marriage? For what purpose?'

'To gain your inheritance, of course. You're a liar and a cheat!' Fran shouted.

Luke shook his head solemnly. 'No, not that, Fran. I admit to this little scheme to regain my position in the family, but nothing more.'

'Then you might have had the decency to tell me. I could have repudiated everything you were saying. I've always been honest and straight. If this is how the wealthy live, then I'm glad I came from a poor, working-class background. I hope they turn you away and I pray that I may never have to face your parents again.'

'Please don't desert me now, Fran. My parents are getting on, Dad already into his seventies. It isn't so much the money as that I'm getting older too and I don't want the rift to go to the grave with them. I know the other girls see me as a fortune hunter. But there's room in the foundry for all the male heirs, for goodness sake, and I can't stay in the navy for ever.' He arched his back and flexed his muscles.

He'd never seem old, Fran thought. Right now he was tired, and possible a little relieved that the awkward moment of meeting his family again was over.

He turned to her after more pacing, and placed his hands on her shoulders. 'I should have told you about Sarita.' He ran his hand through his tousled hair. He looked so unhappy. 'We met when I was in my early twenties. She adored me, waited at the dockside for me whenever we returned to Asia. In her I saw you. Oh, I know you're nothing like each other in looks, but she loved me passionately, gave herself to me just as you did that Christmas at Lady Hinckley's. She said she was expecting our baby. I thought it was a trick to get money from me. When I went away I did give her some money and then gave little further thought to her, much to my chagrin. My thoughts were truly only of you and Lennie.'

'And you expect me to believe that?' Fran said in a high-pitched voice.

Luke shrugged. 'It is the truth,' he said. 'Then one day when I went back to Asia she wasn't there. I made enquiries, only to be told by the barman on the quay that she died giving birth to my baby. Only then did I realise that I had loved her quite deeply. It was you that prevented me from recognising that love. Then, when I returned to Sherbrook one day, I heard that Lennie had died, and I felt I had lost everything. I needed you desperately then, Fran, but you had a husband.'

'It sounds to me as if you're making it up as you go along, Luke,' Fran said bitterly. 'Sailors aren't renowned for acknowledging their foreign mistresses once they've left them behind on the quayside, and I don't imagine for one minute that you're any different. It was only your own guilty conscience that made you believe Sarita was any more special than the others.'

Luke bit his lip emotionally and turned away from her. 'I suppose I can't expect you to see any good in me. I'm fond of children, Fran, and I would love to have had a family similar to yours. But, as time went by, the Royal Navy and my commitment to king and country became all-important. It was my way of life, and women and children couldn't really have a place in it.'

'Other men marry, have children and remain loyal to them, even when they're away at sea for long stretches.'

'That's what the women think, my dear. Few men can do without a woman for long, which is why there are established brothels in dockside areas.'

'Don't be so disgusting,' Fran spat out.

'I'm afraid you've lived a sheltered life, Fran. Probably the most daring thing you've ever done in your life was to go to bed with me when you were under the influence of too much wine.'

'And haven't I lived to regret *that* incident? We all have to pay for our mistakes, Luke, especially when they're made with evil intent, just as you and Elizabeth are doing now.'

'You're a hard woman, Fran.' He glared at her. The words were spoken as if he really meant them, and yet was hurt by having uttered them.

She turned away and wept. Henry had seldom needed to say such words; just one look from him had been enough to subdue her.

Luke took his time before taking her in his arms to console her. 'You really are and have been the only woman I've ever wanted, darling,' he whispered. 'I do love you, and I want us both to be a part of the Hammond family.'

'I wish I could believe you, Luke,' she said. 'But everything you do seems to have an ulterior motive. Why on earth couldn't you have told your parents the truth? That we weren't married until a year ago. How can I pretend that the accident never happened to Henry and my father? I'm not used to being secretive over such important matters. I just hate deception.'

'But you deceived Henry,' Luke reminded her. 'Why didn't you tell him that you slept with another man before you made your vows in church?'

'It ... it would have upset everything,' she said miserably. 'Don't you think I've suffered torment over that? And haven't I been punished enough for my sins? Losing my son, and then Henry – all the people I loved most in the world.'

'And what of our love, Fran?'

'I believed we had made a new beginning. I really tried to love and obey you, Luke,' she said tearfully. 'Your deception is deliberate. In just one year you've taken me from my children, sent Hilda away to school, and now you've lied about us to your parents. How can I love a man who has no conscience? You can't really love me or you wouldn't use me so shamefully. I ... I wish I never had to lay eyes on you again!'

'But we made vows in a church, and there's no way out. I need you more than ever now. You promised to be my wife, and I vowed to be as good a father to your children as I know how. Don't I pay for the rented house in Brimdene? Who sends money to Prue and Sam for Babs, and who's paying for Hilda's education?'

'We were happy as we were in Brimdene. It was a struggle, there's no denying, but at least we had each other. My in-laws were good to us then; now they can barely bring themselves to acknowledge me.'

'Don't you think you owed yourself a little happiness?'

'Where's the happiness?' she questioned.

'Come on, Fran. You know you've enjoyed the marital relationship.'

'And that's the answer to everything? Well, not any more, Luke. I'll sleep in the chair.'

'And I say you will not,' he said decisively.

Fran was afraid to carry her rejection any further. She went to the bathroom at the end of the corridor and then undressed in silence, hoping against hope that Luke would be the one to sleep in the large armchair.

He slid into bed beside her, turned his back on her and soon his even breathing told her that he was asleep.

Fran did her best to lie still even though she was unable to sleep. Dawn was poking its nose in the opening between the curtains before, from heartache and weariness, she too fell asleep.

Chapter Fifteen

A light knock on the door roused Fran, although she had been coming out of a deep slumber gradually for some time. Before she could answer, the door opened and a young girl came in carrying a tray.

'Morning, ma'am. I'm sorry you weren't feeling too well after your journey from Scotland. Captain Hammond requested that we bring you a breakfast tray for eleven o'clock.'

Fran sat up and looked at the girl through bleary vision.

'Thank you, that's very kind,' she said softly.

'Your husband said not to hurry, he'll be back midday.'

The tray was set down close to the bed and the girl left. Fran looked around her at the emptiness of the hotel bedroom. She felt desolate, and lonely for Luke. She despised him for the way he behaved, for the way he had used her so calculatingly. And yet ... and yet ... she knew she couldn't do without him.

She took the breakfast tray to the small table near the window. A cool breeze wafted through the open window and she was glad of the clean, fresh air. Far away on the horizon, where sea met sky, a mist hung. It promised to be another warm, sunny day, she thought. She sipped the hot tea slowly, letting it warm her right through. Feeling revived, she ate the scrambled eggs that had been kept hot underneath a cover on the tray. She was glad of the chance to be alone to think things out. Her conscience told her that she ought to go to Luke's family and explain exactly how they had first met – but what did that matter after all these years? At least she felt she owed them an explanation of how she had been widowed and then married Luke a year ago. She couldn't really believe that it would make any difference to the way they thought of Luke. His mother was just so happy to see him again that Fran was convinced she would never turn him away, whatever he had done. Perhaps it didn't really matter what his sisters thought, but it did matter what his father made of the prodigal son's return. At present, though, James Hammond wasn't in a stable condition, and it was best not to add to his worries. Fran had steeled herself for the shock of seeing a sick, dying man, but he was far from that, she considered. She had felt that she could trust Elizabeth, but now she wondered if this whole episode had been magnified in order to get Luke back into family favour.

It was a disturbing thought that Luke, now over forty years old, had to confront his upcoming retirement from the Royal Navy. Fran had never thought to enquire how many more years he had to serve. What he would do when that event occurred had certainly never entered her head. Now she could see more clearly his reason for wanting to be married. He would need a wife to satisfy his needs as well as run his home. He had a house in Portsmouth, rented out to other officers and their families when he had no use for it, so why then did he seek to reinstate himself within his family circle in the north?

The more Fran thoughts about the situation, the more she realised that, being the eldest, and the only son, he must feel piqued that he had been disinherited. She had to admit that as far as she knew he had not done anything that bad to discredit the family name or honour. Most parents would be proud of a son who had fought for his country during the Great War, and risen by his own merits in the ranks of the senior service. She supposed it all came down to money in the end. Did money matter so much to him? He was reasonably generous in every respect to her and her family, as he had reminded her. When he came out of the Navy he would need to find a job. Was he hankering after going into the family business as Elizabeth had suggested? Deep down, Fran knew that she could never be mean enough to divulge the details of her past to Luke's parents. She just wished there was no need for the deception. Something at some time was sure to leak out. She only hoped it wouldn't come from her.

After she had eaten she took a long warm bath and felt refreshed. She put on a pale-blue silk dress with slim-fitting sleeves. The V neck had a deep cleavage and was elegantly finished with a wide picot-edged frill of the same material, exactly meeting the shoulder seams. From the dropped waist, unpressed pleats hung gracefully down to the mid-calf hemline. For the first time in her married life Fran was able to spend time and money on her own clothes. She had enjoyed making this dress in readiness for when Luke came home on leave. But she had packed mostly dark clothes in view of the reason for the hasty visit to Middlesbrough. Now, believing that James Hammond was not in a critical condition any longer, she felt she could wear a lighter-coloured dress. Surveying herself in the mirror, she knew she looked elegant with navy-blue accessories, including high-heeled T-bar shoes, and that her appearance would impress Luke.

When she had finished brushing and styling her hair, she tidied the room and went to look out of the window. The sun was high and glaring down. She longed to go out and walk by the sea, but it was well past noon, and the maid had said that Luke would be back before midday.

Soon she saw him coming along the sea road at the top of the cliffs. He was wearing grey flannels, white shirt and a sports jacket in dog-tooth check. His dark hair was blown free by the wind. Her heart seemed to skip in time to his brisk tread as he hurried towards the hotel. He glanced up as he crossed the road towards the entrance to the hotel. Even from this distance she could see his solemn expression change to one of pleasure as he spotted her, lifted his hand and waved. How could they be at odds on such a lovely day, and in such a pleasant seaside resort as Saltburn-by-the-Sea?

Fran remained at the window until the door opened and Luke came in. He came straight towards her, hands outstretched.

'Darling, you look lovely,' he said, holding her at arm's length. 'A new dress – especially for me?'

Fran felt herself colouring slightly. 'I've had plenty of time to sew,' she said softly.

'You made it? It's splendid – I thought you were going to tell me it had set me back several guineas.' He laughed as he pulled her towards him and planted his mouth very firmly over hers.

If she had wanted to continue feeling angry towards him, it would have been useless. His dark eyes melted her heart, and before she knew it she was returning his passionate kisses.

'I wish I'd got back before you'd dressed,' he whispered. 'But we have a luncheon appointment with Elizabeth. I hope you don't mind?'

'Why should I?' She looked up at him, unable to disguise her admiration. 'I wish you had woken me earlier. I'd have loved a walk by the sea to chase away – well – you know.'

'I'm sorry I gave you cause to be angry, Fran dear. I realise how things must look to you, but to be reunited with my family is important to me. You may think I should be content with my lovely wife and family of girls, and believe me, I am. But if anything happened to either of my parents, and I hadn't made the effort to be reconciled, I should find it hard to live with myself.'

197

'But is deceit really necessary, Luke? Do we have to tell lies? Surely they'll understand about us meeting after I was widowed?'

'Father never cared about me as a son − only that I would marry and produce a son and heir for him. Fate has been unkind to me in that Lennie died. But it might make all the difference to Father if he knows I had a son, once.'

'But you didn't, Luke. Lennie was Henry's son and you'll never persuade me otherwise.'

'There's no way of knowing. I feel it in my gut that he was mine, and I shall go on believing that. All I beg of you is that you won't tell Father that you've been married before. What harm can it do to allow those years to fade out of our lives? If we really love one another it shouldn't be difficult to imagine that we've been together for a lifetime.'

'You asking me to forget Henry? That's impossible, Luke.'

'Of course not, but for the sake of my parents and sisters, let them think that there hasn't been anyone else in our lives. No Henry, no Sarita.'

Fran sighed. 'You are asking a great deal of me, Luke,' she said.

'I know, darling, and I'm truly sorry. Please do it for me? Elizabeth knows everything and understands. She wants us to do it this way and she'll always be supportive.'

'You must do what you feel is necessary but I shall prefer to remain silent. I'm not a good liar and no good will come of making up stories for gain.'

'I can't agree that it is for gain, Fran,' Luke said solemnly. 'It's to make my elderly parents happy. Merely a white lie to save any further hurt.'

'Put like that you make me appear selfish, but I've always been honest, so I shall leave the talking to you. Now, what time do we have to meet Elizabeth, and where?'

'At her cottage at one o'clock.' Luke looked at his pocket watch. 'It's time we left − are you ready?'

Fran was relieved that they were on better terms. She hated deception and lies, but she hated animosity between them even more.

They took the road south, and then turned inland to travel through rural countryside. The scenery was more like Dorset, Fran thought. Fresh fields, cows and sheep grazing, picturesque villages and hamlets. Luke stopped outside an ivy-covered cottage beside the village green. Elizabeth appeared at the door immediately and came to open the neat garden gate.

'Welcome to Purbeck Cottage,' she said, kissing Fran warmly.

'Purback Cottage?' Fran repeated in surprise at the familiar name.

'Yes, I fell in love with your part of the world, Fran. The family think I just wanted to get as far south as possible for some clean air. Naturally I enthused about Dorset and the Purbecks when I returned home, so I decided to name my cottage as a constant reminder of that area.'

'It's certainly very much like a Dorset cottage,' Fran agreed. 'I'm glad you enjoyed your visit south.'

'It was a real pleasure, especially as at last Luke took the plunge and got married. Come along in – we have a lot to discuss.'

Elizabeth talked non-stop until they were seated at the table in the living room. A vase of sweet peas of varying shades of pink and mauve, with some white ones, placed in the centre of the table, gave off a gentle perfume, reminding Fran of the splendid flowers Henry had grown and been so proud of at the old mill house. Here, in a country cottage again, much smaller than the house in Craiglee, she couldn't help feeling nostalgic for Sherbrook.

'Father seemed much brighter this morning,' Elizabeth said. 'I always go to visit before I go into work.' She put an extra slice of boiled ham on Fran's plate. 'Do have plenty,' she said, 'and we must eat up the cauliflower cheese. It isn't nice kept, is it?'

'Your father seems to have turned the danger point,' Fran said.

'I expect you're thinking that I sent for Luke needlessly, but honestly, Fran, Father was in a very poor condition after the fall. Some machinery failed to function and Father being Father had to go to investigate, probably cursing the men because they couldn't get it to work. The doctors believe he may have had some kind of blackout going up so high at his age. A metal bucket swung round, hitting him in the back, which caused him to fall several feet on to a concrete floor. Fortunately there was a pile of sacking on the floor, and this broke his fall. We were afraid he'd broken his back, and at his age that would have been the end of him, but you know Father, Luke. He'll never give up as long as he can draw breath.'

'Any news from the hospital about the X-rays?' Luke asked.

'I telephoned Dr Ackroyd and he was going to chase things up before he visited Father this morning. You're going to see him, aren't you? Mother is expecting you to dine with us tonight at Hammond House.'

'I think Fran finds such a large family altogether something of a strain, don't you, darling?'

'If your mother is expecting us we'd best not disappoint her,' Fran said. 'I am quite used to large family gatherings, Luke.'

'Take no notice of the girls and their sniping,' Elizabeth said. 'They're only jealous that Luke has returned to the fold, but why shouldn't he? It's a shame you don't have any sons – that would really have pleased Father. Dorinda has got her boys' future all mapped out to take over the business. Maybe they won't want to after they've completed their posh education. Foundry work is heavy and dirty and I can't see any of them really wanting to actually work there. Times are changing, and there's so much opportunity for youngsters these days in much more exciting careers.'

Fran didn't feel that it was quite fair of Luke, wanting to return to the business when he had chosen to go to sea against his parents' wishes. She could see both sides of the argument. She appreciated how his sisters felt. She just hoped that once Luke was reconciled with his father they could return north to Craiglee and get on with their lives.

After the very nice meal Elizabeth had prepared, they sat and talked for over an hour. Then Elizabeth said she must return to the works. Luke drove on a circular route to Hammond House. Everywhere seemed quiet. The boys were are school, the younger ones and Cecilia were out walking in the park, and Mrs Hammond was resting.

A maid showed them in to the sitting room and shortly afterwards Dorinda joined them.

'I'm sure you'll be pleased to know that father shows signs of improvement.' Her voice was cold, and she eyed Fran contemptuously. 'Can't think why he should be so pleased to see you after all these years. Mother too, though heaven knows the shock is enough to kill the pair of them. Still, I suppose that's your intention.'

'Dorinda, dear,' Luke said patiently, 'I haven't come here to antagonise you, or upset our parents. I'm glad that Elizabeth sent for me, and as we're living in Scotland at present, the journey here was much shorter than if I'd had to travel up from Portsmouth. We shall only be here for the rest of this week. Surely you can make an effort to be amicable for that short time – at least to my wife.'

'Suppose it was her idea to come home, cap in hand? Trying out your charm on Father to see what you can get out of him, eh?'

'Fran had no say in coming here. By the way you're behaving I imagine that she'll be jolly pleased to leave and never return.'

'My place is beside Luke,' Fran said in a strong voice. 'I can understand why he needed to see his parents again, but I do assure you, Dorinda, that neither he nor I have any ulterior motive. Luke has a good rank, and is well provided for when he retires from the

Navy. Not everyone sees things from a mercenary point of view as you seem to do.'

Fran was quite surprised at her own eloquent speech, and she knew Luke was impressed when she felt his hand smooth across her back.

'It's time to let bygones be bygones, Dorinda,' Luke said. 'I've never had anything from Father and I don't expect anything. But I am his eldest child, his only son.'

'And it's rotten luck for you that you don't have a son of your own,' Dorinda flung at him.

Fran felt Luke flinch. By the venom in Dorinda's eyes, Fran was afraid that somehow this younger sister of Luke's had learned the truth.

'We came to see Father. I think the less said the better,' Luke said in a quiet tone.

'Go on up,' Dorinda said haughtily. 'He can't leave a business or money to a ghost.'

She flounced away, her head held high in defiance.

'Take no notice,' Luke said softly in Fran's ear. 'I never thought she'd behave so badly or I wouldn't have brought you with me.'

'We must put up a united front − although I'm still not happy about deceiving your parents, Luke. If you're not bothered about an inheritance, why can't we tell them the truth?'

'It's too late now, Fran. We must stick to the same story. Father will certainly never want to see me again if he discovers we've misled him.'

'If only you had discussed this with me on the way here, Luke,' Fran said heatedly. 'There was no need for any animosity at all.'

'You wouldn't have understood, darling. You don't fully understand now.'

'I understand that you're using my Lennie to gain favour with your father − and that's unforgiveable.'

'But you can't deny me − can you?'

'Your charm won't always get you out of trouble, Luke. I'll stand by you this time, but don't ever try to deceive me again.'

'So you're back?' James Hammond greeted his son.

'Yes, Father. I only have a week's leave,' Luke said.

'Stupid woman, insisting that I should sleep all day and all night too,'

'Probably for your own good, Father,' Luke said. 'Sleep is the best healer.'

'What would you know, boy? You're a sea captain, not a doctor.'

201

'I have to have a certain kowledge about a number of things. Anyway, how are you today?'

'No better for staying in this confounded bed,' James Hammond complained. He looked directly at Fran. 'Well, lass, and what d'you make of your husband's family?'

Fran smiled and went to take the old man's hand. 'I've hardly had time to get to know everyone yet,' she said. 'We're here to visit you. It must be irksome having to remain on your back, but it'll be worth it if it means you can resume your life again in due course.'

'And what would a pretty young woman like you know about such things, I wonder?' He screwed his eyes up and surveyed Fran as if he could see into her very soul. She was sure that reflected in his haunting eyes she could see a mischievous twinkle.

'Life teaches us what we need to know,' she replied gently.

'And it's taught you a thing or two, I can tell,' he said with a wicked grin. Like father, like son, Fran thought. There was no mistaking whose son Luke was. James Hammond must have been a bit of a devil in his younger days, she reckoned.

'Well, now that you're here, sit down and make yourselves comfortable. Have you had dinner?'

'With Elizabeth, Father.'

'Ah, yes, my Lizzie. Good girl. Wish she'd married and given me a grandson — but it wouldn't bear the name of Hammond, any more'n any of the other scheming wenches' offspring do.' He turned his head to one side and looked at Luke. The mischief was gone and in its place Fran saw a moistness in the old man's eyes. 'Pity you didn't have a son, Luke.' He looked across at Fran. 'You can't be too old to bear your husband another child, surely?'

Fran nearly chocked. 'I — I — my youngest is seven now, and I've borne five children. Isn't that enough for any woman?'

'My Emma had seven altogether, my dear.' James Hammond's voice was softer now as he recalled his youthful years. 'Beautiful, she was, and blossomed when the first boys were born. Twins, you see — died within the week. Poor Emma never got over that.' He sighed deeply. 'Then Luke came along, and another boy within the year, but he died too — of convulsion at a year old.' There was a deep sigh and Luke's father caught his breath in what was almost a sob. 'Nothing but damned girls after that,' he added aggressively to hide his emotion. 'Every man should have a son to carry on the family name. When Luke's gone the name will die out.' He glanced at Luke, but Fran could see no love there and she felt for her husband. 'Tell me about your son, me dear, if you will.'

Fran had to turn away. Her heart was full with compassion for her father-in-law and renewed sorrow for her own first-born. Guilt pressed painfully side by side with pity.

'Lennie had consumption and died when he was ten years old,' she said. Then, as if she could not bear to speak of him, she got up and went to the window.

'Fran has never been able to come to terms with our son's death,' Luke said.

Fran glared at Luke, and saw fear in his expression. She burst into tears and rushed from the room.

Back at the hotel that evening, after a meal eaten with the Hammond family under obvious restraint, Luke took Fran in his arms.

'I'm sorry that today was so difficult for you.'

'Sorry? Oh, Luke, no good can ever come of this cheating. For God's sake tell your father the truth. I can't go on with this charade. Lennie belonged to Henry and me, and you know that. You're not only deceiving your father but yourself as well. You haven't worried about your family all these years — why now?'

Luke ground his teeth in bitter agitation. 'Because this is where I belong. Don't they owe me something for turning their backs on me? Father goes on about wanting sons, but he disowned me for joining the Navy. It isn't too late, surely, to put my experience and knowledge of foreign countries into the business, and be the son he always wanted?'

'But you chose your way of life, and you can't expect them to understand why, Luke,' Fran said.

Luke paced the floor. 'We'll try for a baby,' he suddenly said. 'That would really please Father.'

'Luke!' Fran laughed him to scorn. 'You can't be serious. At my age? I don't want all that work again.'

'Father will make it worth your while, Fran. A baby of our own would draw us closer together, darling.'

'No, Luke! For goodness sake, think what you're saying. I'm forty-five years old. A child would look on us as old parents by the time it was ten or twelve. Whatever would people think? It was you who made me split up my girls and desert them — what else will you demand of me? No, Luke! I'm definitely not having any more children. I probably can't anyway.'

He came towards her with a glint in his eye. Fran backed away.

'There's no harm in trying,' he said. A struggle ensued. Fran kept her shrieks of protest in check lest other guests or the proprietors heard what was going on. Her lovely new dress was almost ripped off her back and thrown to the floor. Luke pushed her back across the bed as he pulled off her stockings, and although she fought desperately her underwear was quickly discarded. He was like a savage – wild, relentless in his passion. There were no caresses, no tender words of love, not even a kiss, only a cruel bite into her shoulder as she tried to get up. She slapped his face, but this only served to strengthen his intent. He was inside her easily as he forced her legs apart, and the weight of him seemed unbearable. She wanted to reason with him. Had they kept themselves in check during this year of marriage? For the most part no, and yet she had not conceived. Why did he think that this brutal attack could result in conception just because he wanted it to? He was selfish – a greedy, selfish animal. After his lusting he collapsed on top of Fran, crying with relief.

'Oh, my darling, I know it's going to work, I just know it.'

Fran turned her head away, bit into her handkerchief and wept bitterly.

'Fran, darling, can you ever forgive me? I hate myself for what I've done to you.' He was stalking the floor, still naked, while Fran sneaked in between the sheets and pulled them tightly round her. 'I know you think I'm cruel, but you don't know how hard it is for me when I come home. I just want to make love to you all the time. You mean everything to me, Fran, *everything*,' he pleaded desperately. 'I promise that if you do conceive, I'll do all in my power to make it easy for you. It could happen, Fran. Some of the men go on giving their wives babies until well into their fifties. Being abstemious while we're away at sea makes our sperm grow strong, darling.'

'Then why hasn't it happened during this past year?' Fran flung over her shoulder. 'Why don't you wake up to reality, Luke? I'm almost past child-bearing age. A woman's body is not an object to be used just any way a man wants to satisfy his lust. Babies should be conceived in love and with tenderness, not in that barbaric way.'

Luke sat on the side of the bed and caressed her cheek with his hand.

'Darling, I do love you, and it wasn't lust – not in that sense. Desperation perhaps. Life at sea has never compensated me for not having a loving family to return to. Maybe I'm growing older and wiser now. I feel the need of my parents. You've been put to the test throughout your marriage to Henry. You've had to undergo the most dreadful tragedies. But you had your mother to lean on, and your in-laws.'

'And thanks to you I now have no one. Now, when my mother and I need each other most of all, I'm at one end of the country and she at the other. I must have been crazy to allow you to talk me into this situation.'

'It was love, Fran dear. Despite your contempt for me at this moment, you know you love me – have always loved me – and our son was proof of it.'

'*No*! You took advantage of me then and you've done so ever since we met again. Why couldn't you have kept out of my life?'

'I offered you security and affection. Alone with your problems in Brimdene you'd have grown old before your time, darling. Now you've become even more beautiful to me. You're fulfilled again and with another baby of our own you could blossom into a new phase of motherhood.'

'Oh, you and your clever words,' she shouted, as she beat her fists into her pillow. 'I want to go home to my own people.'

'Thy people shall be my people, and my people shall be thine,' Luke quoted quietly.

Luke seemed well pleased with the outcome of his visit. His parents made him promise to write when he could and visit again at the earliest opportunity. But when he rejoined his ship it was to make a voyage to the Americas which was to last six months, perhaps longer. He went away in good spirits, telling Fran to take good care of herself in readiness for the new life that he felt sure was growing inside her.

Fran was amused at his boyish enthusiasm. She managed to put aside the memory of his brutal attack on her, excusing his behaviour as eagerness to please his father. She busied herself at the orphanage, and the summer passed pleasantly enough for her. Hilda came home for the whole of August. Fran could hardly believe the change in her daughter, who seemed far too sophisticated for a Sheldon girl. It was heartening to read her school report, and Fran was forced to admit that Luke had been right in giving Hilda the chance of better schooling. She had caught up with her classmates and was placed fourth in the exam results.

Fran's heart ached with longing, though, when she read letters from the other girls and Ma. Kate wrote that she had been given her week's holiday immediately after Whitsun, and Uncle Eric had come to take Gran Brown back to Stockclere for a week, so that Kate and Ruby could go to stay with Aunt Prue, Uncle Sam, Marion and Babs. Fran looked out over the mists of time, and wished she was back with them all. When she replied to their letters she hid her heartache, even though tears flowed freely, but said how much she and Hilda were looking forward to their return south when Luke was reappointed in a year's time.

Hilda went with her mother to the orphanage three times a week during her summer holidays. She showed an ability to care for the younger children, especially babies of under a year old. Fran was quite surprised, as Hilda's place in the family was the second youngest. She and Babs had been the two little ones, sometimes protected, sometimes bullied, often tormented by Ruby and even by Kate before she had gone into service.

When they weren't at the orphanage they visited Edinburgh and Glasgow and enjoyed bus rides up into the mountains on hot sunny days, but all too soon they were checking school uniform and packing Hilda's case ready for her return to Aberdeen. Luke had given strict instructions that when Fran took Hilda back to school she was to remain in Aberdeen, in the same hotel they had stayed in before, for as long as she needed before making the return trip to Craiglee. But Fran was fortunate in obtaining a lift by car back to Dunfermline with the parents of another girl. They assured her that she need not make the journey again: they would bring Hilda back and forth while Luke was away at sea.

A batch of letters arrived from Luke after several weeks. Only in the first two did he mention the hope that Fran was expecting his baby. The rest of his letters contained little but details of his visit to the Americas, and it was evident to Fran that he was thoroughly enjoying himself. Dear Luke, she thought wistfully. A man of his time. Totally devoted to whatever took his fancy at any given moment. He was much too fascinated by foreign countries to worry any further about his wife's condition. Fran doubted that he would really want to have the extra responsibility of a child of his own. The thought intrigued him, and when he was with the family it seemed important, but once he sailed the high seas, domestic matters were quickly forgotten.

Perhaps not as easily as Fran thought. When the first shades of autumn appeared, followed by early snowfalls on the surrounding hills and mountains, she received a letter from Luke, telling her that they were making their way back to Britain, and he was looking forward to being with her for Christmas. Secretly, Fran had hoped he might not return until some time in the new year. She had been syphoning off a small amount of cash each week from the allowance Luke made her, saving it up for a surreptitious visit down south for the festive season. Her hopes were dashed. Instead, Luke informed her that they had been invited to spend Christmas and New Year with his family at Hammond House. Her hard-saved money had to be spent on presents for his sisters' children. Luke was bringing gifts from exotic South American countries for the senior members of the family, but he thought she would know best what to buy for the children.

Fran dreaded the visit. She hated having to be on her guard. More pretence, more lies, renewed hope that she would produce more offspring. Just this one last time, she told herself, and by next year she could revert to being her old self, back among her own kith and kin. Once they were settled back in Portsmouth, the journey would be too long for them to visit Hammond House again.

Luke arrived in Craiglee three days before Christmas. To Fran's surprise all the plans had been made, and because of the icy weather they were to travel by train to Middlesbrough on Christmas Eve.

Any disappointment Fran had experienced was quickly forgotten once she was cradled in Luke's arms. He was full of energy, warmth and love. Apologetic, too, for the way he had behaved previously.

'Of course it would please me if you were to have my baby,' he said, 'but we must be patient. Above all, I want it to be conceived in love.'

Fran responded as she usually did so that Luke's homecoming was a memorable one, and as dawn broke with him sleeping contentedly beside her, she smiled to herself, satisfied with the knowledge that she would not, could not conceive, however much he willed it to happen.

Chapter Sixteen

Hilda was excited to be going to Hammond House. Luke drove as far as Edinburgh, where he left the car at a garage for servicing. Although it was bitterly cold, the train journey was pleasant enough and when they arrived at Middlesbrough they took a taxi to Hammond House.

It was late afternoon, the daylight fading, but the large, old house looked inviting with coloured lights strung out in the entrance hall. A tall Christmas tree, festooned with gaudy baubles and plenty of sparkling tinsel, could be seen standing majestically in the huge bay window of the sitting room. Hilda skipped up to the heavy oak front door in happy anticipation.

'Come along in, my dears,' Emma Hammond greeted them, kissing Fran's cold cheeks. Then she lifted her thin, bony hands to frame Luke's face. 'There's log fires in all the bedrooms, and it's lovely to think we're going to be a complete family at last.' She turned to look with admiration at Hilda, who was wearing a mid-blue coat and hat which Fran had made herself. 'So this is Hilda – how d'you do, my dear child.'

Hilda seemed a little in awe of both the size of the hall and the graciousness of Luke's mother. Coats were taken off and a servant took the cases up to their room. In the dim light of the back of the hall, Fran noticed a solitary figure leaning heavily on a stick. She knew that James Hammond was now up and about but she hadn't realised what a tall man he was. She went up to him and he hugged her to him, his rough tweed jacket smelling of tobacco. 'How are you?' she asked.

James refused to let Fran go. She had said like father, like son, before, but now that he was standing tall and looking a better colour, she could only remain in his embrace and observe him with deep admiration. Now this man, she thought, I could really fall in love with. What was she thinking of? Admitting that her marriage to Luke was a failure? Not in the marital bed, that was for sure. But in some ways she felt that she and Luke were miles apart. Luke had returned home full of energy, warmth and love, so what made this older edition so much more attractive? There was strength in his grasp and warmth emanated from his body. And in his dark, brooding eyes she saw every emotion she longed for. A certain wickedness, a definite twinkle, and a fondness for the feel of a woman.

She placed her hands on his arms. 'It's lovely to see you up and about, Mr Hammond,' she said in a low, husky voice. 'I didn't realise that you're as tall as your son.'

James gave her an affectionate cuddle. 'But much better looking, Fran, my dear, and I'd rather you called me James, if you will.' He placed his lips gently over hers. 'I just know we're going to be friends.' Fran began to feel uneasy at being held so long in his grip, so she asked again, 'How do you feel, Mr Hammond?'

'Not as agile as I'd like to be,' he said slowly. 'Not quite back to my old self, but getting there, and all the better for seeing you again.' His hand slid down her back and he gave her a light tap on her bottom. 'Don't forget, it's James. It's also Christmas, a time for behaving a little less formally.' He glanced up, indicating that she should follow his gaze. She laughed aloud when she saw the huge bunch of mistletoe hanging immediately above them.

'I wondered what you were up to,' she said.

James held her head steady with one hand as he planted his mouth over hers. 'Getting old I may be,' he said mischievously, 'but never too old to kiss a pretty woman.'

Luke hurried forward and claimed his wife then, to kiss her in his own special, intimate way. All Fran's fears melted away. This was how she remembered Christmases in the past. A family — a large, happy family — and even if the faces of those around her were somewhat different on this occasion, she knew she was being accepted into the Hammond tribe.

They went up to their bedroom, a large, airy room overlooking the gardens at the back of the house, with Hilda in a smaller room next door. They even had their own bathroom along the corridor, and when they had freshened up they went downstairs for afternoon tea.

With the rest of the family they sat round the magnificient sitting room in cosy armchairs, with small occasional tables beside each person. Hilda was being carefully assessed by Dorinda's two young boys, who had been allowed to join them, but Cecilia's two youngest children were having tea in the nursery with their nanny. Edna, Cecilia's daughter of six, had already made a friend of Hilda. Fran thought Edna probably reminded Hilda of Babs, being roughly the same age.

The room glowed with warmth and festive goodwill. A pile of presents lay stacked beneath the Christmas tree and the children eyed them hopefully. Luke had brought their contributions downstairs to add to the rest.

Before they had finished their tea, the door opened and Elizabeth joined them. There were greetings all round.

'This is Hilda,' Luke's mother said. 'Isn't it nice that at least one of Luke's children has been able to join us?'

'Hullo, Aunt Elizabeth.'

The familiarity in the child's voice brought the room to an embarrassed hush.

'Oh, I supposed you've met before when Elizabeth visited Dorset?' Emma Hammond asked innocently.

'Yes, of course,' Hilda replied pertly. 'When Mummy and Daddy got married in Brimdene.'

A deathly silence, a few embarrassed smiles, a cough from Luke as if he hoped he could erase what Hilda had just said.

'I . . . I don't think I quite understand,' Emma Hammond said shakily.

Dorinda stood up. 'I think I do,' she said, tossing her head defiantly.

'No, you don't,' Elizabeth interrupted, 'so sit down and get on with your tea.'

Dorinda's cheeks turned crimson. 'Don't speak to me like that, Liz. I'm not a child. Indeed I'm *not*! You've been covering up for Luke this past couple of years, trying to get him back on good terms with Dad.'

She stared hard at Fran, who suddenly felt as if every drop of blood had drained from her cheeks. A few minutes ago she had been enjoying herself. Now her beloved Hilda had ruined everything. She and Luke had been so convinced that everything was going to be all right that they had overlooked the fact of Hilda's knowledge. Out of the mouth of babes, she thought.

'So you're the sly, scheming one,' Dorinda accused. 'Let's have the truth. How long have you known Luke? How many children has he got, I wonder? All you're after is his inheritance, I suppose!'

'No! *No*, that isn't so,' Luke said. 'None of this is Fran's doing.' He laughed lamely. 'Can't see what you're making a fuss about, Dorrie. Fran and I met years ago – 1912, to be exact – but

210

circumstances prevented us from getting married then. We did have a son, and he died when he was ten. Fran married someone else. The girls aren't mine. Fran's husband was killed in a dreadful accident in 1931. I waited until a respectable amount of time had passed and then I asked her to marry me. The rest you know.'

'Take the children to the nursery,' a voice thundered from the largest armchair near the fireplace.

Cecilia seemed relieved to get up and leave the room, hustling the children before her, Hilda included.

James Hammond stood up and faced Luke, who by now was also on his feet.

'I ought to turn you out this instant,' he said. 'You're a liar and a cheat!'

'Oh no, James, don't say such things!' Emma whined.

'And as for you, Lizzie,' James said, 'I find it hard to believe such scheming of you. I know you've always kept in touch with Luke, and I was glad that you did. It was right that Luke had one member of the family to turn to. But he made his own destiny. He chose to leave his family and join the Royal Navy — nothing changes that.' James's gaze fell on Fran and she stared him out. She had nothing to be ashamed of, but she did intend to remain loyal to Luke, even though she didn't agree with what he had done.

'You are a guest in my house,' James said to Fran. 'I find it hard to believe that you knew you were marrying a cheat. Perhaps we ought to hear the truth about your past from you?'

'It's as Luke said. We did meet in 1912 when I was in service as nanny to Lady Hinckley's children. There's no need to go into the sordid details. There is one detail on which Luke and I disagree and that is who the father of my son was. Luke is obsessed with the idea that it was he, but I'm sure it was my husband, Henry Sheldon, who fathered all my children. I'm afraid, Mr Hammond, Luke has not sired any grandsons for you, and I'm sure I'm past the age of child-bearing.'

'There you are, father,' Dorinda said. 'I told you they were a scheming pair. I could tell it the minute I laid eyes on her.'

'Then you aren't a very good judge of character, my dear,' James yelled angrily at his younger daughter. 'If you aren't very careful, there's not one of you will benefit from my death.'

Dorinda burst into a flood of tears and hurried from the room.

'Well, that's got rid of her,' James said without pity.

'Poor Dorrie,' Emma Hammond said. 'I'd best go to her. Oh, what a dreadful start to Christmas, and I was so looking forward to being a family again.'

211

'Go to her if you must,' James shouted.

As the door closed behind his wife, James sat down again and motioned that the others should do so too.

'I'm sorry, Father,' Luke said humbly. 'I didn't mean to spoil Christmas for everyone.'

'It isn't going to spoil anything. And what's the point of being sorry, I'd like to know? Once you've lied and cheated, no amount of being sorry will retract your mistake, my boy.' The sparkle had gone out of his eyes now as he gazed into the fire. The only sound came from a spitting log. 'I'm disappointed in you, Luke, and you, Elizabeth. So, Luke, you married a widow woman with daughters. How many?'

'Four,' Fran said quietly.

'Are you wealthy? Is that why my son married you?'

'I had nothing but the widow's pension when Luke asked me to marry him'

'So he cheated you too, eh?'

'No, I'm sure he didn't. What could he possibly gain by marrying a penniless widow?' Fran asked.

'He's very good at scheming, Fran, my dear. I dare say he and Elizabeth thought that once he got you to Scotland he'd somehow manage to worm his way into his home. Yes, Luke, this is your home and nothing can change that. I can't deny a mother her son, but don't expect any medals from me for what you've done. You thought you'd get the best life out of being in the Navy and still be able to claim an inheritance when I'm dead and gone. You cheated the girls out of their pocket money many a time and I know you for what you are. I hoped the service had knocked some sense of fair play into you. Your mother spoilt you and now she can see what a fool she made of you.'

'Doesn't the fact that I've reached the rank of captain in the Navy mean anything to you?' Luke said heatedly.

His father eyed him suspiciously. 'If you earned your rank, Luke Hammond, then yes, I am proud of my son. But you and I know there are things about you which I'd rather not know.'

'What happened in the past is over and done with.'

Fran noticed that Luke's face was stained dark red with guilt down the sides. She wondered what else there was in the family cupboard that ought to be aired.

'You thought to use Fran's son to get your birthright,' James went on. 'You thought that you could use the boy's death to gain our sympathy. And to think you aided and abetted him, Elizabeth. I'm thoroughly ashamed of you both.'

'It wasn't like that, Father,' Elizabeth said. 'Mother wanted to see Luke again, and surely, when you had your accident, it was right to send for him?'

'Oh yes, Liz, you've done well in bringing us all together again.' James got to his feet and lit his pipe thoughtfully. 'You've done me a good service, for in Fran here I see the daughter I could have been proud of. I'm sorry she had to marry a scoundrel like our Luke, but I reckon she's a match for him any day. One day, my dear,' he said to Fran, 'I'd like to know a great deal more about your past life, but it's Christmas Eve. We must consider the children and bury our differences for the next few days. I can't say I'm not shocked. A man never thinks his own children will practise deceit on him, but I did think there was something not quite above board by Fran's attitude. Remember this, Luke. Fran's eyes tell all.' He drew on his pipe, keeping his gaze fixed firmly on his son until Luke was obliged to turn away. 'Now, let's get the children in for a song before they go to bed, and then we'll get ready for supper.'

'Father, please let me explain,' Luke pleaded. 'There is one thing I want you to know before you judge me too harshly. I admit I hated the Royal Navy within three weeks of joining. I would have come home then, but you told Liz you never wanted to see me again. I also had my pride, so I was obliged to go through the hell that all boys go through in the services, bullied, tormented, abused. But my time at boarding school stood me in good stead, and for that I thank you. If I don't sign on again for further service in the navy I shall need to work, and I'd like to put something back into your firm, perhaps in an administrative capacity. I've travelled the world, can speak a smattering of a few languages besides French and German fluently, which should be helpful in trading abroad. I could even help Liz.'

'I see, you've got it all worked out so that you and she can bleed me of my profits. Why should I trust you now? Either of you? Don't blame me for having to live a hellish kind of life.' He screwed his eyes up cannily as he scrutinised his son. 'All you had to do, my boy, was come home and tell me then what you've told me now. Was I such an ogre that you couldn't talk to me?'

'Yes, Father, you were − and you haven't changed that much either.' The contemptuous tone in Luke's voice indicated that he assumed he had lost everything now, so there was no point in hiding his feelings.

Fran felt some compassion for him. How would Henry have reacted if Lennie had wanted to go to sea? For a brief moment Fran felt glad that Lennie had died before he had to face the forces

213

of evil in the world. Probably Luke had been forced to live by his wits, and that was an ugly thought for a boy of sixteen.

'If you'd stayed at home you'd have ended up a wimp, I dare say, in a house full of women,' James said. 'At least you learned one of life's hardest lessons, Luke: how to be a man. And yes, I am proud of you for standing on your own two feet and getting to the top in your career. Don't tell me, though, that you didn't come to love the service in the end. Being the shrewd man you are you'd have got out long before this if you'd hated it that much.'

'I said I'd have got out during the first few weeks, Father. But I stuck it out, and yes, the sea is my life now. But there comes a time in a man's life when he looks back and acknowledges his mistakes. I realise what pain I caused both you and Mother. I needed to see you all again. Most of all I wanted you to meet Fran.'

'So you finally got the woman you wanted?'

Luke placed his arm round Fran's shoulder as he sat on the arm of her chair. 'She's made me very happy. She was worth waiting for.'

Fran watched the old man's expression. She knew that if he had voiced his thoughts he might ironically have called it 'a moving story', but was he convinced that Luke was truly contrite?

'Why the need for secrecy that Fran has been married before, and that the children are hers, not yours?' James asked quietly.

'I ... I suppose it was silly, but – ' Luke shrugged – 'I felt embarrassed that I've only just got around to getting married at my age.'

'You mean you thought I'd look on you more kindly if you'd had a son. I might at that, Luke Hammond, but deceit is something I will not tolerate. You and Elizabeth have conspired to hoodwink me. Don't blame the young lassie for being truthful – remember the truth will out eventually. Now, the air is cleared, let's get on with Christmas. It's a time for children, games and presents and I want my grandchildren round me – who knows for maybe the last time?'

He suddenly looked rather older than when he had kissed Fran underneath the mistletoe. Fran wanted to go after him as he left the room, planting his stick on the carpet very purposefully with each tread. But she was the outsider.

Immediately the door had closed behind him, Luke and Elizabeth accosted each other irritably.

'We weren't very clever, were we, Luke?' Elizabeth said.

'That's all Dorrie needed to get what she wants.' Luke turned to Fran. 'Couldn't you have warned Hilda not to let on she had met Elizabeth?'

'I had no reason to keep secrets, Luke. It's no use blaming Hilda. It might have been better if you'd let me go home to my family and you'd spent Christmas with yours. I refuse to collaborate in anything underhand. You knew I was against it from the start. What could you possibly hope to gain? What have you got to lose by telling the truth?'

'More than you think, Fran dear, more than you think,' Luke said.

'Money? Is that what this is all about? A family business? I imagine you've lost all hope of that now. For goodness sake hold your head high and earn what you get in life. I don't want anyone else's money or pity.'

'You've had a better life since you married me,' Luke said.

'If you think money is more important than people. All the money and high living in the world can't make up for being separated from my girls. This kind of Christmas is all a farce as far as I'm concerned. Where d'you think my heart really is, Luke Hammond?' The stressful situation was too much for Fran. She burst into tears and hurried from the room, straight into the arms of James Hammond who was hovering outside the door.

She wasn't aware of how she got into the small, cosy room her father-in-law used as his study, but she was grateful for his comforting support.

'Come now, my dear,' he crooned. 'We don't want a pretty face spoilt with tears, especially at Christmas.' He allowed Fran to weep as he patted her head gently.

'I'm so very sorry,' she said at length.

'Why? What have you got to be sorry about?' James laughed mockingly. 'I know my family. Any family, if it comes to that, where there's a bit o' brass to gain. Have no fear, Fran. I haven't lost my senses yet. I know, too, that you had no part in this deception. I saw that much in your eyes when we spoke of your son way back when you visited me after the accident. Your tears then puzzled me. I can understand any mother weeping for her lost children even after ten years, but I saw some other hurt in your eyes, my dear. Maybe Luke hasn't come up to your expectations in this marriage?'

'Oh, it isn't that,' Fran said. 'Luke has been kind and helpful in the past, but the children aren't his, so how can he understand how much I miss them?'

'He insisted that you came to Scotland with him, I believe?'

'Well, yes.' Admitting that was admitting to her own weakness. 'He did rather sweep me off my feet just when I was beginning to come to terms with all that had happened. I should have thought

215

things through more thoroughly. I can see that now, but Luke has a way with him, and it was good to have a man to lean on after such a struggle. I never should have agreed to leave my girls.'

The sound of children running through the hall interrupted her train of thought.

'I can understand the private grief you experience every time you hear the sound of these children,' James said softly. 'I want to get to know my new daughter-in-law much better.' He leaned across from his leather armchair and took both her hands in his. 'Not now, not here, but later, when the weather improves, we'll meet again. Just the two of us, and we'll learn about each other – through honesty.'

'But I . . . I'm an outsider – James.'

'That's the first hurdle bridged. Now we can be friends.' He had a warm, understanding smile which won her heart just as Luke's charm had in the past. 'I want to try to understand my son,' he said. 'No, I don't mean pry, but I reckon that if he's loved one woman for over twenty years and tried to trick his own father in order to gain wealth for her – then there must be things his pretty wife can tell me about him.'

Fran could have told her father-in-law about Luke's bitterness at being disinherited. She doubted, though, that such a disclosure would help Luke now. And wasn't James Hammond the type of man who would know of his son's bitterness? Luke didn't exactly hide it. She could also have said that Luke didn't want wealth for her, only for himself and his future.

'I've only lived with Luke for eighteen months,' she said. 'And for much of that time he's been away at sea so I'm still learning about him myself. It's a big step to take to marry a woman with four daughters.'

'A cruel step to take her from them,' James put in. 'How often do you see them?'

Tears spilled from Fran's eyes again as she shook her head solemnly.

'I haven't seen them since we married. Luke would have allowed me to bring the youngest one, Babs, to Scotland with us, but I insisted on keeping Hilda with me. She was born just before I lost my Lennie, so she's very dear to me, and delicate too. I refused to be parted from her. Kate is the eldest, now twenty years old. She's working in a hotel. My mother lives in Brimdene with Ruby, who's thirteen, and my baby lives with some very dear friends in Sherbrook, she's seven now. Luke has been very generous. He pays the rent on the house in Brimdene as well as sending Hilda to a good private school.'

'But he makes sure you don't have enough ready cash to go hurrying back south?' James shook his head sadly. 'I'm truly sorry, Fran. Luke is a selfish bastard. I'm ashamed to own him as my son.'

Fran looked at James with a shocked expression. She had hated Luke in the past for the misery he had caused her. But wasn't forgiveness easy lying close to him between sheets of marital bliss? Now, for the first time she realised just how all this looked to an outsider. She couldn't understand why James Hammond was speaking so confidentially to her, or being so understanding. She just knew that here was a man who was just, and possessed qualities lacking in his son.

'It won't be for much longer,' she said, as if excusing Luke's mean behaviour. 'Luke will get a new appointment next summer, and then we'll move back to Portsmouth. Naturally I can't wait to see the girls again, and Ma.' Fran sighed. 'I must confess I'd been saving hard in case Luke didn't get home for Christmas. I was determined to go down to Brimdene if he didn't.'

'Luke is very clever at managing his own destiny, my dear. He didn't visit me out of sympathy, or loyalty, or trying to make amends. He wants what he thinks is his right. Selfishness never earns respect or wealth.'

There was a knock on the door and Dorinda put her head inside.

'Come along, Dad. You wanted the children to sing some carols before they go to bed.'

James stood up and took Fran's hand. 'We're coming,' he said. 'And remember, Dorrie, no more back-biting. I'm still quite capable of managing my own business and signing my own will. At least let's show Fran here that we can be a happy family and behave with some dignity. She's missing her own children, so let's try to make up for that.'

With his hand at Fran's waist reassuringly, James led her back into the sitting room, where Cecilia was already seated at the piano. Fran placed her hands on Hilda's shoulders as they stood round the piano with the Hammond family, but her thoughts were elsewhere. It was a scene she had participated in for as long as she could remember, and now James Hammond's strong bass voice reminded her of Henry's. She didn't try to check the tears that streamed down her cheeks as she did her best to join in the singing of favourite carols.

There were emotional goodbyes when James Hammond drove Luke, Fran and Hilda to the station on 2 January 1935.

James kissed Hilda affectionately, offering a few words of advice about her school work. Then he shook hands with Luke.

'This will be a Christmas to remember, Luke,' he said. 'I wish I could say it's brought me pleasure, but I can't pretend to be anything but vexed at your secret plotting to get back in my good books. But I'm growing tired of schemes and deals, and it's time we buried the hatchet. The one good thing is that for once you've made a sensible choice in marrying Fran. I hope her honesty will influence you for the better. It's time you realised that a man gets the best out of life by treating other people well. Be good to Fran and her family. They're our family too now, and I shall be watching developments.' His ageing eyes were still keen, and could, Fran observed, cause a reaction in Luke.

'All I want is for us to be a united family again, Father,' Luke said. 'I shall go away much happier knowing that Fran has you to turn to in an emergency. I wish Dorrie and Cecilia would accept her more kindly, though.'

'You can't blame them for the way they feel. I did hope that I'd have the joy of seeing a Hammond boy come into the family, but it seems it's not to be.'

Luke glanced at Fran and there was the immediate glow of intimacy as he said: 'There's still time, isn't there, darling?'

Fran responded with a wistful smile. How could she disillusion him? She had tried to explain that it could no longer be, but he refused to accept it. He looked young, and so hopeful for the future. She knew that the bond created during that first union over twenty years ago could never be broken entirely. Their relationship would hang precariously by many a fraying thread, but the deep-rooted need of each other would always weave a cord of reparation. Was it really love?

James turned to take Fran in his embrace.

'And you, my dear, take care.' Fran felt the rustle of paper rather than heard it as something was pressed into her gloved hand. 'Use it to go south, Fran dear, at the first opportunity. And let me know if your mother or girls need anything,' James whispered.

Fran broke away as tears threatened. She opened her bag to find her handkerchief, and managed to hastily conceal the paper money inside, out of Luke's sight, which she knew was what James intended.

'Keep in touch, my dear,' James said. 'I hope you don't think too badly of me and my family?'

'You've been most kind,' Fran said. 'Now it's back to work in

218

the orphanage and preparing Hilda for school. And Luke – who knows where he's going next?'

'To the China seas most likely, for several months. Trouble is brewing in various areas of the world. I could be sent anywhere.'

It seemed a sombre note to leave on, but news worldwide was causing concern, and Fran felt a renewed drawing towards Luke as the ugly thought of war crossed her mind.

At the earliest opportunity Fran investigated her bag and found that Luke's father had given her two white, crisp five-pound notes. She was amazed at his generosity, having hardly ever had in her possession so much wealth. She wished he hadn't tempted her with it, though. It would be so easy to take herself off, away from Scotland, to visit the family. But after the reunion would come another parting, and she knew that she wouldn't be able to tear herself away ever again. So she decided to put it in her Post Office account when Luke had gone away, and then send a handsome sum of money by postal order to Ma to use in any way she chose.

In the privacy of their bedroom back at Craiglee, Fran waited, expectantly for the accusations to come. She was certain that Luke would blame her for Hilda's indiscretion. She was ready to defend both herself and Hilda. She would not be party to any more deceit. Luke had to understand that children were normally open and honest. But the matter was not mentioned. Luke had only one thing on his mind and that was to give her a baby before he returned to his ship. Fran tried to tell him that he must not be too optimistic, but he was about to go away for a long time so she did all she could to satisfy his desires, which gave her a measure of enjoyment too. She was genuinely sad when he left, and even more sorrowful when Hilda returned to school in Aberdeen.

Work at the orphanage was her saviour. Here were children who needed a mother's love, and she was able to give them that as well as using her talents as a needlewoman, and teaching it to some of the older girls. They made clothes and began a patchwork quilt, involving helpers and girls alike.

For a few weeks into the new year there was no communication from either Luke or his family. Fran began to think that the money had been the final pay-off, that James and Emma Hammond were heartily glad to see the back of them.

Then a registered letter arrived, which contained letters from each of Luke's parents, and tucked inside James's was another five-pound note.

'I want you to use this to come and visit us one weekend, Fran dear,' James wrote. 'I've booked a room for you at a small private hotel called the Hawthorne, as I think it best if my wife and daughters don't know of your visit. I'd like to show you over the foundry, so that you can see the family business for yourself.'

Fran read and re-read the letter. It was true that the weekends dragged. She went to the kirk, talked briefly with her neighbours, and occasionally went to tea with Jenny or the vicar and his wife, but on the whole she spent the time writing letters to the family. Right until the last moment she couldn't decide whether to go to Middlesbrough or not, but it seemed churlish not to accept the invitation when James had gone to the trouble of booking a room for her.

As the train steamed out of Edinburgh's Waverley station she experienced some misgivings. Supposing Hilda had an accident or came home unexpectedly? But as the train chugged its way over frosted lines and icy points, she felt in her bones that she was doing the right thing. If James wanted to see her, then for Luke's sake she should honour his request. She just hoped that he wouldn't harp on about having a Hammond heir. She was certain that she was in the 'change'. It was almost a disappointment to know that she was not capable of conceiving again. It meant that she was no longer young, and seeing the tiny abandoned babies at the orphanage made her broody and secretly wish she could please Luke by having his child.

On arrival at Middlesbrough, Fran had to take a taxi to the hotel because she was unfamiliar with the town. The Hawthorne was a small but clean and tidy hotel. After settling in she went down to the lounge for afternoon tea. To her surprise James Hammond was already there waiting for her.

'How did you know I'd come?' she asked, responding to the intimate smile with which he greeted her.

'Ah, I know women,' he said, as he pulled her towards him and kissed her. 'If it was any other woman, Fran, my dear, I'd say you came to see what I had to offer, but not you. You came for Luke's sake, and that I both admire and respect.'

Fran felt indignant. She opened her purse. 'I came,' she said, 'to return this, James. I don't want your money.'

James bent her hand, containing a five-pound note, in his. 'I didn't mean that. I was teasing you, Fran. If I was a few years younger I'd give young Luke a challenge. Don't look so shocked. I'm no saint, any more than my son is.' He chuckled as he indicated one of the wicker armchairs to Fran. She noticed that he sat heavily, putting most of his weight on his stick. 'I dare say I could even find

220

a Hammond heir if I wanted to renew old acquaintances. But that's a young man's foolish dreams. I don't get such urges any longer.' He leaned across and patted Fran's knee. 'I'm sorry, my dear, I don't wish to embarrass you, but I am very envious of Luke. He's a lucky man and he doesn't deserve you.'

'You flatter me,' Fran said. 'But I'm sure you didn't want me to come all this way just to tell me that. Why the secrecy?'

At that moment a waitress brought a tray of freshly brewed tea, warm teacakes hidden beneath a domed silver cover, and a variety of home-made preserves. Fran was desperately in need of refreshment, and felt revived even after the first sip of tea.

'Women gossip too much for my liking. Besides, away from the rest of the family we can talk honestly, I hope. I want you to tell me all about your background and family, Fran. I want to know why a nice woman like you should fall in love with a scoundrel like my son.'

'You know you don't really believe that of Luke,' Fran said. 'We all have our faults. Lack of family life has contributed to Luke's, I'm sure you'll agree.'

'So you're blaming me?' James pursed his lips and shook his head sadly. 'There are things you don't know about us, and that's what I want to put straight, Fran. Maybe it was being the only boy, the apple of his mother's eye, but Luke was always something of a rebel. We thought a boarding school where he could be with lads of his own age would help him to mature. It did that all right. He got involved in several petty pranks. Now I reckon he won't have told you that?'

'No,' Fran said, 'he hasn't. But it was all so long ago. Why should he?'

'Perhaps the last one wasn't so petty, certainly not for the unfortunate young woman he got into trouble. It cost me a lot of money to get him out of that one. Well, like I said, I'm no saint, but I had to reprimand him, and to hurt him over money was the only way he understood. I stopped his allowance. I hoped that would make him toe the line – settle down to hard work and study. Instead he ran off and joined the crew of a cargo vessel.'

'He was always eager to go to sea, though, wasn't he?'

'Oh yes. He didn't get that from the Hammond side, mind you. Emma's father and grandfather were all seafaring men, so I suppose to a certain extent it was in his blood. He was brought up on sea stories.' James sighed. 'Emma was heartbroken when she heard the news, as you can guess. When Luke came home after several weeks at sea, I offered to pay for further education, but the cheeky bastard

221

gave me an ultimatum, if you please. A place in the running of the foundry – of which he knew nothing – or he'd join the Royal Navy.' James drank his tea thoughtfully. 'What would you have done, Fran? I had to call his bluff. He had to be brought down off his high horse, and I reckoned the Navy were the best people to do it.'

'It must have been a hard decision to make. And a cruel one for your wife.'

'She never forgave me – which is why now, after all these years, I'm glad he's wormed his way back into the family home.' James leaned towards Fran. 'Can he be trusted, though? Or is the selfish greed still there?'

'That,' Fran said softly, 'you'll have to judge for yourself, James.'

'He wants to run the business himself. He wants to be cock of the walk. He's still a young man, strong and virile, and he doesn't see why my grandsons should inherit the position in Hammond's he thinks is his. He'll need something to do when he retires from the Navy. Trouble is with Luke he wants everything his own way.'

'But surely his knowledge and capabilities would be advantageous in the business?'

'I may not have many more years left, Fran dear. The accident shook me up. I'm lucky to be alive, lucky to be able to get to the foundry at all.'

'I thought you'd made a good recovery.'

'Ye-es, as far as we can tell, but I worry as to who will succeed me when I do pass on. The name of Hammond has been well thought of among tradesmen hereabouts for over a century. Emma's no good at business. A woman's place is in the home.' He chuckled. 'Except where Liz is concerned. She's good, much to everyone's surprise, but the men won't take a woman boss. If I let her succeed me, she'll take Luke on board, and my grandsons will lose out.'

'Surely that depends on how you leave everything in your will. But really, James, this is a ridiculous conversation. You're good for a few years yet. If you want the young boys to be taken into the business, then it's up to you, and there's plenty of time to have them trained for it.'

'But they won't be Hammonds, will they? Elizabeth and Luke both are, but they have no offspring.'

Fran smiled. 'You could persuade your married daughters to include the name Hammond with their surnames, couldn't you?'

James screwed his eyes up as he surveyed his daughter-in-law. 'Would that any of my children had your canny perceptions, my dear. What did you say you did before you got married – a nanny? You were capable of something more mind-stretching than that.'

'You know as well as I that girls have always been the domestics in life. A nanny was considered quite something, you know.'

'Don't I just know it? They've cost me a pretty penny over the years. Some were made for the job, others were too soft, while many were the opposite. You fit into the first category. You obviously love children, so why can't I dream an old man's dream of having a grandson on the Hammond side?'

Fran sighed. 'Because, James, as I told you, I'm past the age of child-bearing. I'll be forty-six this year. It wouldn't be fair to the child even if I could suddenly become fertile again. But you can't alter nature. I've tried to tell Luke, but he refuses to accept it. I felt certain that you would understand. What's so special anyway in having a grandson who bears the name Hammond? Your grandsons are your grandsons whatever their name.'

'And I felt sure that you would understand how important it is to me to have the name carry on after me.'

'Perhaps you should have taken Luke back when he wanted to come into the business?' Fran suggested hesitantly. 'Maybe he should have married the girl he got into trouble. Did she have a boy?'

'No.' James laughed. 'Twin girls, would you believe? Family moved to Ireland to live down their shame at my expense. Luke had to be made to pay for that, Fran. A man must be master in his own household.'

Fran listened patiently as James unburdened himself. It seemed as if everything had been said by the time they had finished their tea, but James was eager to see Fran again that evening after dinner.

'I suppose I'm being thoroughly selfish,' he said, as he again joined Fran in the seclusion of the hotel's lounge. There were few visitors at this time of year, just one or two commercial travellers, who went to their room immediately after their evening meal. James ordered a whisky for himself and a Maderia for Fran. It warmed her, and she experienced a cosiness in the atmosphere. They chatted about many things and soon she found herself telling her father-in-law how she and Luke had first met.

'Go on,' he urged. 'These are the things I want to know – not out of idle curiosity, Fran, but to help me understand and know about Luke's life in the years we lost track of him.'

'He had a charm that few women could resist, James,' Fran explained. 'I suppose you could call our first meeting an illicit night of love. It would never have happened if I hadn't been given such a rousing send-off by the Hinckleys. It was Christmas, and everyone was pretty merry even before we started celebrating my departure. Luke had no right to go below stairs, let alone take me to the nursery and – '

'He forced himself on you? He raped you?'

Fran shook her head. 'Goodness, no! I can't accuse him of that. It ... well, it just happened, as these things do. We were young, only human, after all – and I was about to get married. Henry and I had been through a frustrating time as Lady Hinckley refused to allow me to leave. Luke wasn't the first, you see. Henry and I resorted to hoping that I would get pregnant, that way I would have to be released. But I wasn't aware of being in the family way when we got married that Boxing Day, and I'm almost positive that Lennie was Henry's son, not Luke's. Luke just turned up out of the blue after Lennie died, with this obsession that Lennie was his son.'

'Did he try blackmail? Did he threaten to tell your husband about your liaison?'

'No, he never did that, nor did I ever think he would, strange though it may seem. He went back to sea, of course, and I seldom thought about him. The memory quickly faded once I was a busy housewife and mother. I didn't even know that he knew the Maitland family in Sherbrook, until he appeared in the churchyard after Lennie died.'

'I suspect he did genuinely love you then as he does now, Fran. There was another woman, though, who seems to have been important to him.'

'Yes, I know. An Asian girl called Sarita?'

'He told you about her?'

'No. I only found out quite recently when I tidied some cupboards and drawers. I accidentally found a bundle of letters and a picture. A very beautiful girl. She was expecting his baby, I understand, and died in childbirth.'

'He was genuinely fond of this girl, according to Liz. In fact he tried to get me to arrange for her to come to England and have her baby here. Perhaps I should have done, but we would have found it difficult to accept a foreigner. I suppose life has been unkind to Luke in some ways.' James grasped Fran's arm. 'I do love my son, Fran,' he said earnestly. 'I only wish I could trust him, but I don't entirely, especially now, having discovered his plotting with Liz to get back in my favour. They're jealous of the two younger girls being married and with children. I know their little game. They mean to get the business for themselves before the grandsons are old enough to be taken into it.'

'Is it really so important, James? Human life is more important than money and goods. Henry and I never had much. He worked hard for small wages, but we had a good family life. It all ended so suddenly.' Her chin quivered as the memory of that horrific freak tide came into her thoughts. 'That nightmare still haunts me,' she said.

Gently, and without causing too many tears, James extracted the full story from Fran, of Henry's death by drowning, and her father's too. She doubted that he could possibly understand the trauma of uprooting to move away to a town, living simply to make the pennies stretch for the necessities of life, or the added worry of leaving Kate behind with the Maitlands, and the reason for her leaving Sherbrook in disgrace.

So much of the past had been bottled up in Fran's thoughts with no one to share it with. It was a relief to pour it all out to James, who appeared to be sympathetic to the reasons she had for marrying Luke. In some ways, too, it helped to hear that James was doubtful of Luke's intentions.

'I'm sure he loves you,' he said. 'But he also may have used you, and your son, Lennie, to try to win favour with me. So far, nothing he's done convinces me that he is truly repentant for the past. I doubt that he'll be competent enough to take over the foundry from me. He may work towards its success while I'm alive, but then what? A business in ruins while he squanders the profits?'

During Sunday morning, while the family were at church, James fetched Fran from the hotel and took her to the foundry, where machinery lay silent as if it too was resting on the Sabbath.

The name HAMMOND was blazoned on the front of the building across a huge brick archway over the main gates. It was all much larger and more prominent than Fran had envisaged, and as she toured the works, with James pointing out blast furnaces and moulds as they went along, she was much impressed by all that she saw. She learned how the castings were made in the foundry where pig iron was melted down with coke in something called a cupola. It was similar to a small blast furnace where hot gas was allowed to escape from the top.

'Cast iron is stronger than pig iron, you see,' James explained. 'The castings are brittle, though, compared with steel, so it's mostly used for lamp-posts, domestic boilers and cookers, and cylinder blocks for motor cars. It's useful for gas mains and sewage and water pipes, too. It's a thriving industry, as you can see.'

225

'I can now understand your concern for the future of the business,' Fran said to James as they went into his office. 'You must be proud of your achievements in supplying work for such a large number of men. They and their families depend on Hammond's for their livelihood.'

'Indeed they do and it would be a shame if it were allowed to run down or be sold off for monetary gain. I hope the name Hammond will long be seen as visitors enter the approaches to Middlesbrough.'

'I'm sure it will, James, and I feel equally sure that Luke must be proud of the family business. All your children will be. They'll never let it be sold, or run down, for the sake of their children. I'm sorry I can't oblige you with a grandson, James, but you already have four. Whether you allow Luke to enter the foundry is your decision and yours alone. I'm sure your wife would love to see him take your place eventually.'

'With you at his side, Fran?'

Fran looked at James quizzically. 'I'll support him as his wife, of course,' she answered.

'When he's got what he wants he might not want you,' James warned.

'I thought you were of the opinion that he truly loves me?'

'I am, my dear. But whether his love of worldly goods and money exceeds his love of you, I cannot say. His love for you has not prevented him from hurting you in most painful ways. Taking you from your children, for instance, sending Hilda to boarding school, almost as if he were paying you back for being sent away to school himself.'

'I suspect he knew that if Hilda went to Aberdeen I was not so likely to up and return south while he was away. I know Luke now. I know he schemes for his own ends. He's different in every way from Henry, and I have to admit that if I could have afforded to I probably would have left him. The trouble is,' she added with a gentle smile, 'he has a hold over me. There's something magnetic about him. I want and need my children — I feel the same way about Luke.'

Chapter Seventeen

On the train journey returning to Craiglee, Fran had plenty of time to reflect on her visit to Middlesbrough. She had talked far more intimately to James Hammond than to anyone over the past two years. They were like kindred spirits with similar attitudes and standards. They both loved Luke, yet neither could be sure of his intentions.

Fran cared nothing for the foundry. The thought of living permanently this far north depressed her, but, as James had said, Luke wasn't due for retirement from the Royal Navy yet, and when he was, her girls would probably be grown up and making their own lives. That thought depressed her too. She couldn't forgive herself for deserting them. She wished that she could turn the clock back and carry on with their upbringing as Henry would have wanted. But there was no going back. Her destiny now was with Luke. As Ma would say, she had made her bed so she must lie on it. She wondered what life would be like if Luke was at home all the time. His homecomings were an adventure that kept the freshness in their marriage.

She caught sight of her own image in the carriage window, dirty and sooted though it was. A middle-aged woman. Back in Brimdene she knew that she had begun to look old before her time. Now she was able to dress fashionably. Her hands were white, her fingers long and slender. No more the roughened, chapped skin from her years of washing and cleaning for the family. She supposed people thought she had married Luke to make good her escape from the life of drudgery. Well, hadn't she? No! Nothing, not all the clothes from the best shops in Edinburgh, nor the freedom from scrubbing floors, could make up for being parted from Ma and the girls. Still, it wouldn't be too long now before she could begin to pack up her belongings in Craiglee. In fact, spring was only just around the corner even if there was still snow on the mountains. Down south it would already be warming up. Lambing time was about to start, with Easter only a few weeks away. It wasn't too soon to start thinking about preparing to go home.

Fran experienced mixed feelings. She was a woman of the world now. A few years ago, when Henry and her father had been alive, she had never given travel a single thought. She smiled a secret little smile. Going to Brimdene on the train from Sherbrook was the big adventure then.

Her thoughts raced ahead of time, to hot, sunny days sitting on the beach while Hilda, Babs and Ruby played on the sand. How exciting the reunion would be! She felt love and longing swelling in her breast. But her home wouldn't be in Brimdene, it was to be in Portsmouth with Luke. Brochures were already arriving from grammar schools in that area. Luke was determined to be Hilda's mentor. He organised everything, even when he was miles away.

When Fran reached Edinburgh she went into a café for a meal, and then did some shopping. Everywhere was fairly quiet, it being Monday morning, so she was able to browse and take her time.

It was quite late in the afternoon when she let herself into the house in Craiglee. She was desperate for a cup of tea so she put the kettle on even before she took her hat and coat off. She had enjoyed her long weekend away. Without Luke and Hilda the weekends were the worst and she hoped James might invite her again. She wondered how he explained away his absence from home, and why he was so keen not to let the family know of their meeting. She didn't mind. In a ridiculously childish way she felt that it made her special to him. She thought he was genuinely fond of her but, knowing his son as she did, now that she was home with time to consider the matter she wondered if James had some ulterior motive in seeking her company. What could he possibly want from her, though? Then she smiled. A grandson, a male heir to carry on the name after Luke, and she wished with all her heart that she could oblige him.

After the first sip of tea, Fran went into the sitting room and found the mail lying on the side table where Jenny always left letters if Fran was out. There were two from Luke, but she didn't open them immediately. Instead she noticed a telegram propped up against the vase of daffodils Jenny had picked. Fran's heart jumped. Was it to say that Luke was coming home unexpectedly? Was he ill or injured? Or could it be Ma or one of the girls? With unsteady fingers she tore open the yellow envelope, and drew out the single sheet of off-white paper. The printed message read: 'Epidemic of scarlet fever. Hilda only mildly ill. School in quarantine.'

228

Fran put her fingers to her lips. Her Hilda – scarlet fever! She read and re-read the message, her first motherly instinct to go to Aberdeen at once, no matter what the consequences. Hilda was ill and needed her. Surely quarantine didn't affect Fran? She heard the back door open and close. Jenny hurried in with a worried expression.

'Mrs Hammond, I've been so anxious. I didn't know what to do when the telegram came. I do hope it isn't bad news? I thought I'd best come to you in case there's anything I can do.'

'Hilda has scarlet fever, Jenny. Oh, dear, what am I going to do? The school is in quarantine. How long for, do you suppose?'

'Mm . . . we-ell, I dare say it'll be a month at the least, but more likely to be six weeks.'

'Will she have to go in hospital?'

'Not if the school has a good sanatorium. They may keep the girls there to contain the disease. Don't worry, Mrs Hammond. She'll be well looked after.'

'If only I'd been here,' Fran said.

'It wouldn'a made any difference, Mrs Hammond,' Jenny consoled her. 'There's nothing anyone can do. Let's hope and pray that she doesn'a have it badly. Have you eaten today? Is there anything I can get you?'

'No, Jenny. I'm being silly. It was a shock seeing that telegram. I thought it might have been my mother or one of the other girls who was ill. You're right. If I'd been here there was nothing I could do. I'll write, of course, to Hilda and the school. I must think of things to make up a parcel for her. She'll need something to occupy her time when she begins to feel better.'

'Scarlet fever isn't considered to be so serious these days. If she was fit and healthy to begin with she'll likely have it mildly.'

'That's what the telegram says, but Hilda's never been strong.'

Jenny stayed until she felt that Fran had recovered from the shock, then she left. Fran sat down to write to Hilda, and by the time she went to bed she had written several letters, including one to James Hammond and her new in-laws. She wished they lived closer and that one day her sisters-in-law would accept her as a friend – that was what she needed in times of stress.

Fran kept herself busy during the next few days, writing to Hilda and buying books and puzzles to send so that she would have plenty to keep her amused as she convalesced. When she wrote to the family in Brimdene and her friends in Sherbrook, she begged them all to write to Hilda so that links with home and family were sustained.

Fran watched for a letter from Luke's parents, but each day she was disappointed. She was so thankful to be able to go to the orphanage, where she could forget her worries over Hilda and her loneliness.

When she reached the house late one afternoon, as she put her key into the front-door lock she heard footsteps coming from the side of the house. Luke? Always her first thought. Next she wondered if they had sent Hilda home to complete her convalescence. Instead the slow tapping of a stick on the path made her hold her breath, and then with relief she smiled a welcome to James Hammond.

'James!' she exclaimed. 'You're the last person I expected to see.'

'Fran, my dear, dear girl.' James held her close for some seconds before he allowed her to open the door.

They went inside, and Fran's questions followed quickly with some curiosity.

'How did you travel? Why didn't you let me know you were coming?'

'Because, my dear, you don't have the telephone, and I've come by cargo vessel. Happened to be one owned by an old friend, and as he was coming to Leith, I begged a lift.'

Fran busied herself making tea and warming some scones she had made the day before.

'I don't have too much in the larder, James,' she said. 'Living almost entirely alone means that I only buy small quantities.'

'I had a meal near the station before catching the train here. We were sorry to hear about young Hilda. How is she now, getting better?'

'Yes, she wrote saying that they're all doing lessons in the mornings now. She won't be able to travel home for Easter, but she's looking forward to a long weekend at Whitsun maybe. I'm counting the days, of course, and that'll be the last holiday before we can pack up and start for the south again.'

'You know, Fran, I've been thinking, and wondering why Luke hasn't had the telephone connected for you. It's mighty thoughtless of him to leave you here on your own with no contact with your folks. So I'll be staying a few days, if that's all right with you, and I'll see that it's installed as soon as possible.'

'That isn't really necessary, James,' Fran said with a smile. 'For just a few months it would hardly be worth it.'

'Well, I think it would, so I'm going to do it anyway. At least I can ring you up to see that you're well, and if there's an emergency you'll be able to get in touch with me immediately.'

'But I can't use the telephone, James.' She laughed weakly. 'To tell the truth, I'm a bit scared of such contraptions.'

'Then all the more reason to have it in your own home so that you can get acquainted with it. A mixed blessing, I'll grant you that, but I'm surprised Luke didn't think of it when you first came here.'

'He'd be thinking of the enormous bills he'd have to pay, I expect,' Fran said with a smile. 'If I'd had it when we first came here I'd have been ringing Brimdene or Sherbrook every day.' Her expression changed to one of sombre reasoning. 'It's a kind thought, James, but to be able to talk to my girls now at this late stage would only make the time seem longer until I actually see them. No, I think it's best to let things remain as they are.'

'I'm going to get it fixed, my dear. I want to know that you can call on me any time, and I can get in touch with you. If you'd had the telephone, you see, I'd have been able to ring you early this morning and tell you that I was on my way.' He went closer to the window and looked out over the valley. 'This is a lovely spot. I'd no idea Luke had such good taste when it came to setting up house. Ideal for a newly married couple, but not so good for a wife being left on her own for weeks and months at a stretch.'

'I haven't minded for most of the time. When Hilda first went to Aberdeen it was lonely. I have to admit that if I could have afforded to I would have left Luke then, but I love the country, and since I went to work at the orphanage I've managed to fill my days satisfactorily.'

'But you can't wait for summer to come.' James looked at his daughter-in-law with admiration. 'I wish Luke had brought you to see us when you first came here. Such silly nonsense, trying to make me believe you and he had been married for twenty years or so. As if he would have been able to keep a secret that long. I had ways of knowing where he went during his leaves from duty.'

Fran set the table, and they sat opposite one another, going back once again over the past. Here, where they were on neutral ground, it was easy for them to be honest, even more so than when Fran had visited Middlesbrough by herself.

'I want to see as much of you as I can before you return to Brimdene,' James said.

'Why don't you bring Mrs Hammond to stay for a few days' holiday?' Fran suggested.

James was thoughtful. 'Emma doesn't take kindly to travelling, Fran. With the girls living at Hammond House, and their husbands and children, she's much more tied up with them than with me. Oh, I know I have the works to supervise.' He laughed with an edge of scorn. 'If I hadn't, I reckon I'd have spent many hours looking for a mistress.'

'James! You mustn't say things like that.'

'She never got over losing Luke to the sea. Nor forgiven me for disinheriting him. We've grown apart, Fran — sadly. We should be able to spend time together enjoying our old age.'

'But you're not old yet.'

'Emma will be seventy next birthday, and I was seventy-two just before my accident.'

'But you wouldn't like to give up working at the foundry — or at least managing it, would you?'

'No. I'd like to rest up more than I can, but there's only a few of the old workers left who I can trust to put in a good day's work. Now, if Luke had come into the business, by now he would be taking over completely from me.' James shook his head. 'It's too late now. He'd be all right to organise things, but the men wouldn't take kindly to a boss who hadn't worked his way up the same as they. What am I going to do, Fran?'

'What about Dorinda's husband, or Cecilia's?'

James threw back his head and laughed. 'Don't you let my girls hear you say that. They'd fight then over who should be the boss, and to tell you the truth, although they're nice enough fellows, neither of them has the guts to take over from me — and the men wouldn't wear that either.'

'I don't know what else to suggest, then, James. You'll just have to keep going until your grandsons are old enough to learn the business thoroughly.'

'But that'll be years yet, and I doubt that I have that much time left, Fran.'

'Let's see, Howard is eight, and Jamie seven. Howard needs another eight years at school — but what are you worrying about, James? Aren't you forgetting Elizabeth?'

'No, my dear, I'm not forgetting my Lizzie. She's keen and she's an expert with the book-keeping, the wages and the like.'

'There you are then. Make sure that she can take over from you when the time comes.'

'I know you mean well, Fran. I respect your advice — you've a great deal of commonsense, and few in business have that. A good head for business usually means a love of money. Small matters get overlooked in the quest for profits. In my foundry I know each and every one of my workers, their families, what kind of homes they live in — and if they suddenly have money to burn, I ask the question, Where did it come from?'

'But surely Elizabeth has the workers' welfare at heart, too?'

'She does – but in a womanly manner. The men need a strong man at the top.'

'James, there must be someone you can trust enough to be manager, under Elizabeth?'

'Yes, my present manager is reliable and trustworthy, but he's like me – getting on in years. That fall made me realise – and too late – that I should have persuaded Luke to come into the business many years ago. Don't tell him that, though. Seeing h'm again – and his lovely wife – helped me to recover, as well as seeing things differently. I was pompous enough to believe that I would go on for ever.'

'Maybe Luke would come out of the Navy now if he realises that you feel like this.'

James shook his head vigorously. '*No*! Oh, no! He and Lizzie between them tried to deceive me – did deceive me, in fact. But for young Hilda I'd have gone on believing that your son was Luke's too. And I was prepared to overlook Luke's past, and would have given him shares in the foundry because of the tragedy of losing his only son. But he has no son, which brings us back to the same old question – who is going to take over after me?'

'Oh, James, I wish I could help you, but I can't, I'm afraid.'

James sat opposite Fran and stared directly at her. 'Forgive me, my dear. I shouldn't be asking such personal questions, but is it really impossible for you to have more children?'

Fran laughed. 'Yes, James, I'm afraid I think it is. And if I could conceive again, how would that help you?'

'I'd have a real Hammond to leave the works to. I'd make certain that suitable men were put in charge for the next twenty years under Lizzie's supervision. I'd die a happy man knowing that there was a Hammond boy to follow in my footsteps.'

Fran didn't know how to tell an old man that he was dreaming impossible dreams. Luke was the genuine Hammond heir. Fran could understand now how much his running away to sea had grieved his father.

As the days went by she came to understand a greal deal more about James Hammond, the man. His fiery temper when things didn't go his way. The Post Office came in for some flak when they didn't come as arranged to install the telephone, and Fran reckoned all Craiglee heard about it. But he was also good company. He talked at length about the old days and the Hammond ancestors. He also listened with interest to all that Fran would divulge about her family, and when the time came for him to depart she felt genuinely sad. She

233

went with him to Leith docks to see him off with the promise that they would meet again as soon as was convenient.

'I shall be telephoning you quite often, Fran, my dear. I understand what you mean about not getting in touch with your family in the south, though.'

'If I give Ruby and Kate the number,' she said happily, 'they'll be ringing up every few minutes. I'm really grateful to you, James, for being so thoughtful, though, and I promise I'll use it.'

'You take care now, d'you hear?' James said as he kissed her goodbye. 'And you just ring me when I'm at the works. You can talk to Lizzie if I'm not there. She'll like that.' He pressed crisp notes into Fran's hand. 'Buy yourself something pretty for when Luke comes home. It isn't to be for quite a while, though, did you say?'

Fran sighed. 'Several months. China is a great way off and the news everywhere, especially from Europe, isn't good, is it?'

'It's this damned man Hitler and his Nazis. Germany is increasing armaments all the time. Churchill has been warning since last year that we're not up to full strength in our defences. War might be good for business, but that's all. Luke has fought in one war, I wouldn't like to see him involved in another one. Maybe it's just as well I don't have adult grandsons after all.'

Fran watched the cargo vessel chug its way out into the Firth of Forth until it was a black dot in the distance. It was a nice morning so she walked into Edinburgh, had coffee and then sat in the gardens on Princes Street to listen to a military band. Then she went to the post office. She put one of the five-pound notes in a registered envelope which she addressed to Kate, asking her to buy Easter eggs and something special for each member of the family for next weekend.

Fran didn't mind that she would be alone for Easter. Extra help was needed at the orphanage, there were flowers to arrange in the kirk, and she had plenty of sewing to do in readiness for the summer.

During the month of May the country celebrated the king's silver jubilee. Fran cut out all the photographs from the daily papers so that Hilda could add them to her scrapbook. She bought several newspapers so that she had extra pictures to send to Ruby and Babs. London enjoyed a day of pageantry. Everyone was interested in the two young princesses, Elizabeth and Margaret Rose, granddaughters of King George V and Queen Mary, but it was a small dog trotting in front of the royal carriage that became the centre of attraction. It eventually hid beneath the carriage. Soldiers tried to corner it with their swords, and policemen made a brave effort with their truncheons. It became known among the crowds as the Jubilee Dog.

When Hilda came home for the Whitsun weekend Fran was amazed to see her looking so well. Her cheeks were quite rosy. She had filled out as well as grown, and her hair shone black and glossy.

Fran hadn't made any plans to do anything special. Instead they began to pack cases and trunks ready to go home to Brimdene in August.

Hilda returned to school in Aberdeen for the last term. If Fran was excited about going home it seemed that Hilda was reluctant to say goodbye to her friends. She even hesitantly suggested that she might be allowed to go to a grammar school in Scotland, where some of her chums would be going.

'It would be much too far away to keep journeying to and fro,' Fran said in horror. 'Besides, surely you want to see Kate, Babs and Ruby?'

'Ye-es,' Hilda replied indifferently. 'But they aren't the same as my friends.'

'No,' Fran said sternly. 'They're your sisters, and if you aren't anxious to go home, then I most certainly am.'

In her own private thoughts Fran decided that if there was going to be another war she must be with the rest of her family. But she did her best to forget thoughts of war as the summer arrived, and she was able to tick off the days on the calendar. Luke seemed happy to give Fran instructions on getting to Portsmouth and taking up residence in his house at Southsea.

James frequently telephoned, usually admonishing Fran for not ringing him.

'If you won't come to see us, then I'm coming to see you,' he said one day. 'Or I can see you'll be going off to your own people and we shan't get to say goodbye even.'

He arrived by car one evening. Fran had made up the spare bed and was genuinely delighted to see him.

'I've decided to take more holidays,' James said as he greeted her. 'So you'd best keep a bed aired for me when you get to Portsmouth. The LNER now has a steam train which travels at 108 miles per hour on the journey from London to Newcastle.'

'You know you'll be welcome any time, James. I hope, though, you won't mind if this week I carry on with my work at the orphanage. We're short-staffed at present and soon I shan't be here to care for the babies.'

'You're going to miss them all — and they'll miss you, I fancy,' James said.

'We see such sad cases: children whose mothers have died and the fathers can't cope. Lots of unwanted babies — I'd just love to give them all a home,' she said earnestly.

'You can always start up a home down south. I suppose there's as many unwanted babies there as anywhere else.'

'Don't.' Fran laughed. 'You're giving me ideas.'

'Your love of children is very obvious, my dear. I'd help you. Now, that's a good idea — why not the Hammond Orphanage?'

'If you have money you don't know what to do with, James, we need every penny we can get at our orphanage.'

'Mm. Who owns and finances it now?'

'The actual house, which is old, large, cold and always in need of repair, was donated to the Church of Scotland for use as an orphanage. We have to rely on voluntary helpers to run it, and money from the kirk and any charitable organisations that will contribute.' Fran looked at her father-in-law and smiled. 'Now I'm feeling guilty, James,' she said. 'All those notes you've been giving me I've been sending to my family, but I realise that there's a greater need here.'

'But you give of your time, Fran. Money can't supply love — and I believe that's what you're giving to these poor unfortunate children.' He stroked his chin thoughtfully. 'I want to come in to the orphanage tomorrow with you. Will anyone object?'

'I shouldn't think so. We only get the dignitaries occasionally when their consciences prick. Since it's Jubilee Year we've had extra money, parcels of clothing and an abundance of goodies. It's all very nice, but we don't want everything at once. We need a steady income, genuine helpers who will be permanent, and enough food to feed them all.'

Fran was surprised that James appeared to be so interested the next day when they reached the orphanage. Fran was able to get on with her work feeding the babies, bathing and changing them, while Mrs Muir, a war widow from the Great War, escorted James round the large mansion house, explaining in great detail the history of the orphanage.

Fran was feeding her special charge when Mrs Muir brought James to find her.

'I never need look long for Fran,' Mrs Muir said in her strong Scottish accent. 'She loves the wee ones. She's many a talent, has our Fran. Beautiful needlework she does, and the older girls listen and learn from her, but if there's a wee, newborn baby in, then no one but Fran is allowed to care for him.'

236

'Meet young Gordon,' Fran said, lifting the top of the shawl to reveal a shock of black, curly hair. 'Only four days old. Isn't he gorgeous?'

'He is indeed, if you like tiny babies,' James said with a mischievous twinkle. 'Not really my department.'

'Such a sad case,' Mrs Muir put in. 'Young wee lassie not really old enough to be wed. No' illegitimate is young Gordon here. Ach, no! They came from Herefordshire originally. The father was a young stable boy who took the lassie of the big house off to Gretna Green to marry. Family were against it, d'you ken. He managed to get a job here in Glasgow, but the wages weren't enough to feed both of them properly and she died giving birth. The young man was so heartbroken he hanged himsel' from the nearest tree. If ever a child was born of love it was this one. Poor wee laddie. And to think the girl's family don't want anything to do wi' him.'

'Will you be able to place him in a good home?' James asked.

'Mebbe, in time, but Fran won't let him go easily.'

'He's so much like my Lennie,' Fran said wistfully. 'I just wish I was young enough to adopt him. I suppose I'll be gone before a home can be found, but I sincerely hope it'll be a good one. My heart bleeds for all these children.'

'You can't take on the worries of the world, Fran, my dear.' James sounded genuinely sorry. He stayed a while longer, but Fran got the impression that he wasn't happy in such surroundings. 'I'll take a walk now and then go back to the house for a rest.'

'Don't overdo it, James,' Fran warned, and turned her attention back to the sleepy babe in her arms.

Before she left that evening she went to look at Gordon in his crib. Memories tumbled painfully, and happily too, in her brain as she relived the early days of her marriage to Henry. The excitement they had shared when Lennie was born, a tiny wee mite with similar black hair and pale skin. What was Gordon's destiny? Lennie may have lived to be only ten years old, but he had been born of loving, caring parents who had done their best for him. Fran was filled with despair for the parents of this orphan. They had defied their family code of honour. Run away to the notorious blacksmith's shop in Gretna Green to get married as honourably as they knew how. How could fate be so cruel? To take a young mother's life?

Fran wept tears of anguish for them both as she laid her finger on the child's cheek. She felt the same way over all the babes who were brought in unwanted and unloved. But at least Gordon had been wanted, and had been conceived in love. Fran placed her fingers to her lips and then on the baby's delicate rosebud mouth before she tore herself away.

It had taken her nearly two years to become accustomed to a new way of life. Now she was finding it difficult to imagine herself anywhere else, and yet her heart yearned to see her own daughters and Ma again. She was glad of the walk home, which gave her time to recover.

Jenny had prepared supper, which was all set out and ready when she got in. James was sitting outside on the garden wall, gazing out over the valley of meadows where the sheep with their young grazed in peaceful contentment. The hills and mountains were green now, and somewhere up there roamed the local red deer, only seen occasionally.

Fran washed and changed. Then she went to the dining room and called James from the window. He came in slowly and Fran was afraid that he felt unwell.

'Are you all right, James?' she asked with concern.

James nodded and sat down in the huge carver chair heavily. He ate slowly, hardly speaking at all. Fran gabbled on about nothing in particular until, receiving no response, she too fell into an awkward silence. What had she done, she wondered? Suddenly she felt nervous in James's company, whereas before she had always felt so much at ease. When she offered him some hot blackcurrant-and-apple pie, he raised his hand and dabbed at his mouth with the crisp, white table napkin.

'You don't seem hungry tonight,' Fran ventured. 'Was it not to your liking?'

'The food was fine, my dear. I've something on my mind, that's all.'

'Can you share it? Or is it to do with business?'

'Business – in a way. I expect you'll tell me that I'm a foolish old man, and I dare say you'd be right.'

Fran leaned on the table, looking expectantly at her father-in-law. 'It must be something serious, James, or is it that you're tired? Maybe coming all this way by car was too much for you.'

'Now you sound like Emma and the girls.' He sat back in the chair and toyed with his elegant silver watch chain. 'Seeing you with that babe today, knowing the circumstances, and something that you said, gave me strange stirrings – and an idea, Fran.'

'Whatever d'you mean?' Fran sighed. 'Oh, dear, James, I do hope you aren't expecting too much of me. I have explained that I can no longer conceive. I'm simply too old and that's the end of it.' She hadn't realised just how obsessed James had become about a grandson. The mere mention of a baby and he embarked on his favourite subject.

'I appreciate what you're telling me, Fran. I understand, really, and I'm not being totally unbalanced about it. You lost your son and it must have been a great tragedy for you. I know how it was when we lost our boys. It may seem like an old man's whim to worry about the future of the family name, but my life has been spent making the Hammond foundry well respected. It's not the immediate future that bothers me. If I'm spared to continue for a few more years I'll see that Lizzie is accepted as the new boss with an under-manager. But what will happen in twenty years' time? There'll be no more Hammonds to take over. Oh, I know what you're going to say – I do have grandsons, and yes, I could insist that they add the name Hammond to theirs, but it just wouldn't be the same.'

'What's in a name, James? The foundry will still be Hammond's, no matter who runs it.'

'I've been conjuring up a – scheme. Just between you and me, my dear. You obviously love that small boy. You said you'd like to adopt him – so how about it? Take him back south as your own son?'

'*James*!' Fran shrieked. 'You must be out of your mind! I ... I ...'

James laughed. Fran was relieved to see the laughter lines back at the corners of his eyes. What a joke! What a silly notion to come up with! But he was looking solemn again, and by his expression she realised that he didn't intend it as a joke.

'Money will buy almost anything, Fran,' he went on. 'I know it can't be the same as having your own son. Even I can't make him a genuine Hammond, but under your care he'll grow up just the way a Hammond boy should. He's not illegitimate, remember, and it almost seems to me he came as an answer to a prayer.'

Fran dropped her head in her hands. How could she tell this dear old man that he was being ridiculous?

'James, you're just letting this obsession of yours get out of hand. They wouldn't let me adopt a baby at my age. Think of the child's future. By the time he's fourteen I shall be sixty. It wouldn't be fair.'

'There's little that's fair in life, Fran, as you well know. No one would ever need to know – not even Luke. He was home at Christmas. We're nearly into August. Babies often come a month early. The birth certificate can be a brief one. I'll deal with all the formalities. All you have to do is to bring the boy up to be a Hammond. Yours and Luke's son – my grandson.'

'James, I can't ... I *won't*. It wouldn't be right.'

'Luke tried to deceive me, so did Lizzie, and the other girls will always quarrel over who has what. This way I shall have settled the matter to my liking. And you won't have to say goodbye to that baby. Just seeing you sitting there feeding him, loving him — Fran dear, he can be yours. In twenty years' time he can be well trained in the foundry.'

'But supposing he doesn't want to do that kind of work? You can't impose your will on others, James. You should know that from losing Luke.' Fran knew that she was being unkind, but someone had to make James see that his idea was preposterous.

'That's hurtful, Fran. I thought you were more sensitive to my feelings than that — but I'll put it down to the shock of my suggestion. The idea was there at the back of *your* mind or you wouldn't have mentioned adoption. You're so honest and straight. You'd never think of plotting and planning your destiny. Sometimes an opportunity comes along that enables us to steer our lives along a certain course. I believe this is one of those opportunities. Now, aren't I going to get a cup of tea?'

Fran got up and hurried away to the kitchen. She looked out over the country scene in soulful dismay while she waited for the kettle to boil. When it did, she scalded her hand and tipped tea over the stove with her unsteady fingers.

'He wouldn't be mine, and he wouldn't be Luke's,' she said irritably as she placed the teapot on the iron stand. 'Moreover, he wouldn't be your grandson, James.'

'Let's sleep on it, my dear. Don't be angry, please. Think of the good you'd be doing, apart from pleasing me. Giving a home to a poor wee orphan child. You said yourself he was like Lennie to look at.'

'And he might grow up to be quite different.'

'I know you'll bring him up to be God-fearing and trustworthy. Luke tried to cheat me, remember, so where's the harm in beating him at his own game? He need never know the truth, but I shall honour your decision about that. Adoptions are legalised under the strictest conditions of confidence, as you must know, but money will always talk, my dear. I shall pay for absolute secrecy, and the orphanage will benefit greatly.'

'James Hammond, you're doing your best to bribe me, I do believe,' Fran said.

'I can't force you to make a decision one way or the other. There isn't much time. You travel south in less than two weeks' time.'

Fran ran her hands over her cheeks, pausing, feeling the blood hot beneath her fingers.

'But what could I tell Luke?' she asked in despair. 'I'd have told him if I'd been expecting his baby. It's what he wanted more than anything else in the world.'

'Gets better and better, Fran. You thought you were at that certain age when you couldn't conceive again. You won't be the first woman to confuse pregnancy with the change. It does happen. Might easily to you as you aren't yet fifty.'

'You're too knowledgeable for your own good,' Fran flung at her father-in-law crossly. This was getting out of hand. She must put a stop to it at once before he actually persuaded her to go through with his devious little scheme. Not such a little scheme. It was a mighty big one, and not impossible at that.

Chapter Eighteen

Two weeks later Fran and Hilda waved goodbye to James Hammond from the London-bound train as it puffed and complained its way out of Waverley station in Edinburgh.

Fran looked down on the plush seat of the first-class compartment which James had insisted upon. It held a brand-new wicker basket covered with a snow-white shawl. The baby bonnet revealed nothing of the infant's jet-black hair.

Hilda sat beside the basket proudly. 'Oh, Mummy, isn't it lovely to have a new baby? He's so beautiful – and to think you didn't even tell me.'

'Your step-grandfather thought it was best that you concentrate on your school work, especially as these last examinations were so important.'

'I wish we didn't have to go to Portsmouth first. I do want to show him off to the others.'

'Mr Hammond thought it was foolish to take all our luggage to Brimdene and then have to move it all again when we go to Portsmouth. I'm just as anxious as you to see the family after all this time. Two whole years – it's been a lifetime.'

Fran sat back and closed her eyes. Gordon James Hammond slept on, blissfully unaware of life's new adventure, and Fran herself was hardly aware of the enormity of what James had convinced her was a grand gesture towards protecting the helpless baby.

If Luke was a schemer, his father was even more adept at secret intrigue. He had put the plan in operation, demanding that no one knew except those in authority. The babe would take the name Hammond and that was all anyone needed to know. A sizeable amount of money changed hands. Legal papers were rushed through the local magistrates' court to satisfy the Adoption of Children Act 1926, though no one questioned the rights of James

Hammond. The child's future and wellbeing were assured, and Gordon might as easily have been physically borne by Fran as by his unfortunate young parents, neither of whom could return to claim the child at a later date. Fran signed the legal agreement. James Hammond put himself in loco parentis, which meant that he undertook to pay for the education of Gordon, agreeing to accept all duties and liabilities of the child, since his son, Luke Hammond was mostly away at sea.

Fran had been swept along on James's tide of enthusiasm. Like father, like son, she thought, and not for the first time.

She felt quite weary now. There had been hasty letters to write to her family. She informed them that she had thought the symptoms she had been experiencing were due to her age, so it had come as something of a revelation to herself that she was about to produce another child. But the arrival of Gordon James made her feel young again.

James had remained at Craiglee with her. Advising her, telling her how to break the news to family and friends, even to Luke, while he passed on the joyous tidings to his own family. Elizabeth had telephoned and wanted to visit but he had put his daughter off. Better, he told Fran, that this was just between the two of them. He had thought of everything, seeing that Jenny was handsomely rewarded for her diligent care of Fran during her time in Scotland, and supervising the removal of their personal belongings, which he had arranged to have picked up and delivered by a carrier within the week to the house in Portsmouth. Fran had the barest of necessities to carry herself. James had done everything to make it easy for her, yet she still worried that someone would find out.

'So what?' James had said with a raucous laugh. 'The adoption is legal enough. I shall be generous in acknowledging you for giving me a grandson, Fran, my dear. A Hammond boy at last.'

'But he isn't, James. Not truthfully. We're deceiving everyone. I never thought myself capable of deceiving my own husband.'

'Luke will be so overjoyed at the prospects for himself and his son that he won't question anything. The legal documents as to my claim on Gordon will be in the hands of my solicitor. A clause will be inserted in my will for the boy's future — education and so on — which any grandfather is likely to make.'

'Don't be too generous, James,' Fran had said. 'Or Luke and the rest of the family will be suspicious. At least let Luke and me bring Gordon up as our own, or I can't be party to the deception.'

James had reassured Fran on all counts, but now that she was actually on her way home at last she had grave misgivings as to what she had done.

The baby quirked. It was almost time for his feed, which she had brought in a flask. After two years of so-called luxury living she was back to changing nappies and feeding. Above all, she had a baby boy to love and cherish. James was right — it was of no consequence to anyone else.

The taxi pulled up outside a terraced house in Southsea, a suburb of Portsmouth. The street was long and straight, tree-lined, with a wide pavement. Fran, cradling the tiny babe in her arms, sat still for a few moments as she viewed her new abode with mixed feelings. The iron railings and tall gate were newly painted, shiny black, as was the guttering and pipe-work, but the sash window frames were sparkling white, giving the house a distinctive appearance in an otherwise somewhat dreary residential area. Dreary-looking perhaps to Fran, but prestigious.

Luke had informed her a month ago that the last tenants had vacated the property in good time, so that repairs and redecoration could be carried out before she and Hilda arrived. He hoped he would be joining them by the end of August or the beginning of September. Fran took a deep breath. By now, she hoped, he would have received her letter informing him that he was the father of a son.

The taxi driver carried the suitcases and bags to the front door. He rang the bell, and almost immediately it was opened by a young woman in maid's uniform. She bobbed a curtsey as Fran walked up the steps to the front door.

'Evening, Ma'am. You must be very tired after a long day's travelling down from Scotland.'

'Yes, we are rather weary,' Fran said, and held the bundle out to the girl. 'Take the baby for a moment while I pay the driver.'

'I can have him, I can have him,' Hilda cried, but Fran had already passed the baby to the maid.

A few minutes later Fran stood in a large square hall with deep red carpeting. She took off her hat and gloves and placed them on the oak hall stand, looking at herself in the mirror. She looked like Fran Hammond, but she didn't feel at all like herself. Another house, a new home, different surroundings — if only she could have gone home to Brimdene, better still to Sherbrook, where memories of her past still beckoned. The third move in four years. How many more times? She'd had enough of adventure, she just wanted to go home. But this is your home, her conscience said loud and clear, and Fran felt a lump come into her throat as the dull ache of longing returned to punish her.

Movement behind her made her turn quickly, and to her astonishment she came face to face with strange people.

Now she knew why she didn't feel like herself. These, she supposed, were her appointed servants, but hadn't she been raised to be one of them?

A middle-aged man stepped forward and politely lowered his balding head in acknowledgement. 'Rudgwick, Ma'am, and this is my wife, Edie. We've always managed for Captain Hammond, and we're very pleased to welcome his wife and the new baby.'

Fran shook hands with them both, and then with the young woman who had answered the door. 'This is Betty, the housemaid, and — ' Rudgwick paused where a young girl in a blue uniform dress with starched white apron stood, holding the baby — 'this is Nanny, Miss Norma Marlow.'

Fran was hesitant as she said: 'This is my daughter Hilda. It's getting rather late, but it's nice of you to be here to meet us. I expect you're anxious to get to bed, and we certainly are. A warm milky drink would be nice to help us settle for the night.'

'I've taken the liberty of laying up trays, Ma'am, which you may care to have brought up to your rooms,' Edie Rudgwick said. 'But first, I think you should come into the drawing room.'

Fran looked nonplussed. Not trouble already, she hoped. She really was too tired for confrontations of any sort.

Edie opened the varnished door. There was a distinct smell of fresh varnish, paint and wallpaper paste pervading the whole house, Fran thought, but then a lovely sweet scent wafted out of the large drawing room to greet her. The huge bay window was a blaze of colour with flowers of every shade and variety.

'We managed to find enough vases,' Edie said hesitantly. 'Your husband arranged by cable to have them specially delivered on the day of your expected arrival.'

Tears filled Fran's eyes. Until she married Luke she had never been used to lavish presents and flowers. It was all done for show, of course, but the thought touched her deeply.

'And this letter arrived for you yesterday, Ma'am.'

Fran felt her heart jump with anticipation, even a little fear. She knew that Luke would be delighted about the baby, but he might be put out that he hadn't been told earlier.

'These are quite beautiful,' Fran managed to say for the benefit of the staff. 'Thank you for arranging them so well.' She ran a hand across her weary brow. 'Now I think we all ought to get to bed. Nanny, perhaps you'd carry the baby upstairs. I'll come to see to him at once. And Hilda, you can bring up your own small case and get ready for bed too.'

'Oh, can't I see over the house, Mummy, please?' Hilda begged.

'Tomorrow, after a good night's sleep. We'll explore it together.'

The suitcases and bags were taken upstairs to the bedrooms that Edie had prepared.

'The nursery is at the back of the house, with Nanny's room adjoining,' she explained. 'I thought Miss Hilda would perhaps like the middle room. And the master bedroom en suite occupies the front of the house. If anything is not to your liking, Ma'am, we shall be pleased to change things tomorrow.'

Fran assured the housekeeper that everything was in order. She was amazed at the way things had been organised. Luke could not have known about the baby in time to employ a nanny. Fran wasn't sure that she required the services of a nanny. She was quite capable of looking after Gordon herself. It would give her something to do when Hilda went to the grammar school in the autumn term.

Hilda had followed Nanny to the nursery and Fran was guided there by their voices.

'I'll see to the baby,' Fran said. 'Top and tail will do tonight, a bath in the morning.'

'I was just undressing him, Ma'am. That is why I'm here. I'm sure you must be travel sick.' Fran's expression evidently showed the doubt at the back of her mind. 'I can be putting the baby down while you have your supper,' Nanny suggested. 'My references came back from Middlesbrough today. I have them in my room if you wish to see them, but I am properly trained, Ma'am.'

'Of course, Nanny.' Fran smiled. 'I didn't mean to imply that your ability is in question.'

Middlesbrough! So all this was James's doing. The old rascal hadn't said a word.

Edie was coming up the stairs carrying a large tray. 'I've put the young lady's in her room,' she said. 'Just a few sandwiches in case you feel like something to eat.'

Fran was glad to kick her shoes off and sit down in the easy chair in the huge bay window. She decided she couldn't put off opening Luke's letter any longer. It was warm and loving. Didn't he know she could give him a son? He was full of gratitude and effusive in his praise of her, making her feel thoroughly guilty. He hoped she would like the Rudgwicks, who were to engage any additional staff they considered necessary for number 10 Kingswood Grove, but he thought the employment of a nanny was best left to her. But employ one she must, he insisted, as he didn't want her to be overworked. What he really meant, she knew, was that he didn't want the baby or anyone else to intrude into their private lives when he came home on leave. He seemed to be very clever in arranging his homecomings to coincide with term times, she had noticed. Fran didn't mind one bit. It meant that she was free to visit the family in Brimdene at the earliest opportunity.

When the telephone rang early next morning, Fran picked up the extension on her bedside table.

'Are you feeling tired after your long journey?' James asked.

'It seemed a long day, James,' Fran said. 'But I've had a good night's sleep. Haven't heard a thing — thanks to the nanny you engaged.'

James laughed. 'The least I could do in the circumstances.'

'You could have told me,' Fran said.

'Not in front of the lassie, my dear. I dealt through a well-known agency. The girls are very well trained and this one has worked for Royal Navy officers before, so she should be all right, according to her references.'

Fran told her father-in-law about Luke's letter and the flowers. 'He's thrilled to bits about Gordon,' she said happily.

'And so he should be. If you need anything or run into problems before Luke gets home, don't hesitate to get in touch, Fran.'

She still doubted the wisdom of what she had agreed to, but she knew that she had made James very happy, and Luke too. From the tone of his letter she questioned whether she would ever be able to tell her husband the truth, but she knew that he had a right to know.

It was a sunny summer morning. After breakfast the housekeeper showed her all over the house, which was both appealing and impressive.

The Rudgwicks lived in the basement flat, which they insisted Fran should view so that she could see for herself that they were clean and respectable people. Betty had a gabled attic room right at the top of the house. It reminded Fran of the Hinckleys' house, and the Maitlands' in Sherbrook, where Kate's bedroom had been right up in the roof. Fran wished with all her heart that she could have Kate, Ruby and Babs join her here in Southsea. Now that she had provided her father-in-law with a Hammond heir, and her husband with the son he longed for, maybe she could use her powers of persuasion in getting Luke to let the family live all together again. There was plenty of room here for everyone, even a room for Ma. But did she really have any persuasive influence? She was the one whom others influenced! She had fallen victim all too easily to Luke's charm, and once she had agreed to become his wife she had been carried along with whatever he chose to do. And now, submitting to James's crazy plan of adopting young Gordon. Luke and James both seemed able to sway her to their way of thinking without undue pressure.

When she looked in on the sleeping babe, though, she had few doubts that she had done the right thing. He was adorable; his dark-blue eyes, which she felt certain would soon change to brown, seemed to look right into her very soul. He had a lusty cry and strong limbs, as well as a healthy appetite. Nanny Marlow was already quite possessive about her new charge.

Although Fran was anxious to visit Brimdene at the first opportunity, she remained in Southsea for the rest of that week in order to unpack and generally settle down. Then she gave Nanny a week off, with the excuse that there was not sufficient accommodation for her to go with them to Brimdene.

'I'll have enough nursemaids in my other daughters when I get there,' she explained. 'We'll be going to Sherbrook, too, to visit old friends from when I lived there.'

'Are you sure you can manage on the trains, Ma'am?' Nanny said. 'I could travel with you and stay with an aunt in the New Forest. Then meet you again at Brimdene station to come home.'

'Home'! Would this ever seem like home? Fran wondered. In time, when she was used to the streets, the shops and parks, and when Luke returned, she supposed she would fall into her new life style with few problems. She recalled with some pain her arrival in Craiglee. It was inevitable that those first few months were fraught with misery and guilt. At least here she was within easy reach of her family again.

Fran agreed to Nanny's proposal readily. James Hammond had been crafty in choosing a nanny who had relations living not too far away from Brimdene. Fran had no doubts as to the depth of his inquiry into the girl's qualifications and background, which made her ideal for the post.

The station at Brimdene was packed with holiday visitors so that Fran had to strain in her search for familiar faces. Then a tall girl rushed into her arms and hugged her, nearly knocking her off her feet.

'Mummy! Oh, Mummy, how lovely to see you,' Ruby cried. She refused to let go as she kissed her mother not once but several times. She didn't seem to care about Hilda or the new baby, she just clung to Fran as if she never intended to let her go ever again. Tears ran down their faces as mother and daughter, who had so often been at odds before, tried to make up for the lost two years. 'Let me help with the luggage,' Ruby said, brushing away the wetness from her cheeks. 'Gran can't wait to see you again. Oh, Mummy, it's been *such* a long, long time,' she said with passionate emotion.

'Look,' Hilda interrupted excitedly as she put her arms round Ruby and kissed her sister, 'we've got a new brother. His name is Gordon James. And this is Nanny.'

Ruby glanced at Nanny, who smiled reassuringly, and then went to peep inside the shawl.

'Kate couldn't get off, I suppose,' Fran said.

'No, but she's cycling up from town this afternoon, just for her two hours off.'

'My, you've grown, Ruby. Had your hair cut, I see,' Fran said.

Ruby looked quickly at her mother, apprehension in her eyes, as she recognised the voice of authority she had almost forgotten.

'Gran thought it was best because she couldn't do it the way you always did. Aunt Sissy tried, but it looked awful and the plaits came undone.'

Fran laughed, and Ruby's expression relaxed again.

'How is Gran? She's all right? And the other grandparents, Uncle Nathan and his family? Has Uncle Eric been down lately?' Suddenly Fran wanted to know everything, and the platform was empty by the time she remembered that they must go in search of a taxi.

Nanny held on to the baby until they were all settled inside the large, shiny, black car; then she passed him to Fran, and in minutes they were on their way. Fran was at last reunited with two of her girls, her stomach cold with the ache of strangeness, warm with longing.

While she paid the taxi driver the two girls rushed into the house, Hilda carrying the baby, to show off the new arrival, and then Fran saw Ma. She looked pale and small, as if she had shrunk. Her pale-blue eyes quickly filled with moisture as they fell on each other's necks and wept unashamedly. What have I done to her? Fran rebuked herself. Leaving an old lady of seventy-five to manage a house as well as a young, wayward girl like Ruby.

'And to think you've had another baby,' Ma wept. 'At your age!'

She turned away from Fran and went to look at the crying infant lying on the couch where Hilda had lain him.

'And if I know anything about babies,' Fran said brusquely, 'he wants changing and feeding.'

249

It helped to diffuse the situation as everyone gathered round, admiring Gordon James Hammond.

'I'll see to the dinner, Ma,' Fran said, when the bottle was heated up. 'You sit quietly to give him his bottle, and get to know your new grandson.'

Fran went from room to room, reacquainting herself with everything that had once been the centre of her life. A great gnawing in the pit of her stomach made her feel quite sick, and she was glad to have a few moments alone in her bedroom, where she had spent lonely nights weeping for Henry and Lennie. Tossing, turning, trying to rid herself of the anger aimed at God for His injustice. Now she could hear angry words from God accusing her of deserting her family. She had run away from her responsibilities with a man who said he loved her, but who had not treated her with the love and respect she had known from Henry. But Luke and Henry were two vastly different people.

She looked about the room, recognising her belongings which she had not been able to take with her: the dressing-table set comprising an engraved glass tray with matching trinkets; the ring stand that Henry had given her when they had married on Boxing Day in 1912 – twenty-three years ago come Christmas. Suddenly there was a great roar in her ears and she was back in Sherbrook running for dear life, shouting at Ruby to get in the house before the wall of water swallowed them up. Little knowing that her father, his sheep, and her husband were being carried away downriver to their deaths. Fran placed her head in her hands, and wept as if her heart was breaking all over again. She was seated on the edge of the bed when Ruby found her.

'Don't cry, Mum,' she said softly, placing her arms round Fran's shoulders. 'You're home now. We're all together again.'

Fran wiped her eyes, sniffed, and stood up abruptly. 'It's been such a long time, dear,' she said. 'Seeing you and Ma, being back in my own bedroom – where did you get the cot, for heaven's sake?'

'Gran and Grandad Sheldon's got new neighbours. Their youngest little boy is nearly four, so he's ready to go into a proper bed. Uncle Nathan said the least he could do was to buy a cot for your new baby, and we're all to go to tea on Thursday when Kate's off for the day.'

'D'you mean to Uncle Nathan's, or to Gran and Grandad Sheldon's house?'

'Gran and Grandad Sheldon's for a big family party. They're all excited about the new baby.'

'And are you pleased, Ruby?'

Ruby looked away to avoid her mother's gaze. 'Yes, 'course. But I didn't think you'd ever want another baby. I thought you'd had enough of all of us.'

Fran sat down again, and it was a few moments before she could compose herself. She drew Ruby close, both hands round her waist affectionately. 'Things are different now,' she said solemnly. 'We don't understand why things have to change – but sometimes they do even when we don't want them to. It was a very sad day for us when that nasty storm took Grandad Brown and your father away from us all. But we just had to make the best of things. It was hard for me to manage on just the pension, dear. I didn't plan to marry again, but Luke has been very kind. You've had lots of things you wouldn't have been able to have otherwise. And although I went away for a while, I still thought about you every day. I still love you just the same. I didn't go away because I'd had enough of you. You must never ever think that, Ruby. Once I'd decided to marry Luke I was committed, as his wife, to go wherever the Royal Navy sent him. Now, tell me how Babs is. Have you seen her lately?'

'They're coming tomorrow. We see them once a month. Auntie Prue thought you'd want to go to Sherbrook, too?'

'Of course I do. We'll be seeing a lot of each other from now on. Portsmouth isn't nearly as far away as Scotland. You must let Hilda tell you all about her school, and about Luke's family in Middlesbrough.'

'I don't really want to know. I'm just glad you're back. I wish you could stay here all the time.'

Fran pushed Ruby aside gently, and they went downstairs. Fran found that Ruby had everything ready for dinner. Young, new potatoes from the garden, peas and carrots which Nathan had planted, and a lovely piece of boiled ham, with a treacle sponge pudding to follow.

It didn't take Fran long to realise that the family had managed very well without her. Although she looked for signs of neglect around the home, she could find no evidence of it. The pantry was spotless, the chimney had been swept, curtains and paintwork washed and carpets beaten. On enquiring who did what, she learned that Ma and Ruby did most of it. When they knew Fran was returning, Aunt Sissy organised a working party, and with Kate's help they had spring-cleaned the whole house from top to bottom during the Whitsun holiday. Now they refused to let Fran do anything. Didn't she have a new baby to care for? She mustn't spoil her lovely hands now that she no longer had to slave away to keep house.

251

They ate their meal in comparative silence. Ruby and Hilda, having argued over some trivial matter, had nothing more to say to each other. Although Fran asked lots of questions, wanting to know how Ruby was doing at school and how all the neighbours were, as well as the family, the conversation seemed strained. Fran watched the minutes ticking by, longing for Kate to arrive. When she did, she came into the house breathless and quite flustered.

'Oh, Mum, how lovely that you're home at last!' She kissed and hugged her mother. 'I couldn't make my pedals go round fast enough. It was such hard work cycling up that hill.'

'Let me look at you, our Katie.' Fran said, holding her at arm's length. 'You look different, older – oh, dear, you're all growing up so fast. Ah, it's the hair, you've got it in a bun.'

'D'you like it? It's nice and neat for work.'

'And how is work, dear?'

'We're busy this month, of course. I help in the kitchen when anyone's away.'

'And what about your studies? D'you still enjoy cooking?'

'I love it. I love everything about hotel work, Mum. One day I'm going to have a hotel of my very own.'

'Such grand ideas, Kate. You just be careful you're not heading for a fall, my girl. Anyway, at twenty you'll be thinking about getting married soon, I expect.'

Kate's eyes misted with memories. Then she laughed. 'Not me, Mum. I don't want to tie myself down for a long time yet.'

Fran knew by the look in Kate's eyes that she had briefly thought of Maurice. She felt a knot in her stomach at the reminder of her guilt in confiscating Maurice's letter. She didn't like to ask whether Kate ever saw him when she went to Sherbrook to Aunt Prue's to see Babs. It was an episode in their lives that Fran preferred to try to forget, but her shame would go with her through the rest of her life. She had confided in James Hammond about the whole horrid affair, and he had shown sympathy, saying that it was a parent's lot to have to contend with such events within the family circle.

'You did what you thought was right at the time,' he said. 'Best to put the matter out of your mind, as young people soon get on with the business of living.' But Fran knew that Kate would never forget how ill-used she had been by Maurice's friend Felix. She wasn't likely to forgive Maurice either for deserting her just when she needed a true friend, and no one was to blame for that but Fran herself.

Kate's two hours off was quickly spent, and by the end of the day Fran felt weary. Emotionally weary – perhaps a little hurt that

252

they didn't really seem to be at ease with her. There was tomorrow to look forward to, she thought. At least Babs would be overjoyed to see her.

Gordon James was fretful, and Fran was up several times during the night. She had just managed to get off to sleep when Ruby brought her a cup of tea in bed.

'Oh, Ruby, and I'd only just dropped off again.' Ruby left the room hurriedly.

Later Fran heard Ruby and Hilda arguing about who should feed Gordon, and it was as if she had never been away, except that no matter how hard she tried to fit in she felt like a stranger. They waited on her, fetched and carried when she was seeing to Gordon, and even Ma appeared to be reluctant to chat about things the way they had always done before. Fran watched the clock eagerly, and was at the window when the bus passed the end of the road. She ran out of the front door and waited by the gate until Prue appeared hand in hand with the little girl with bright copper curls. Fran waved. Prue waved back, but Babs sidled closer to Prue's skirt. No, that was only in Fran's imagination. Babs had never been the shy one. Marion was coming behind, carrying the bag. Babs's belongings, Fran supposed. From now on things would be like the old days — a house full of women, she thought wryly.

Fran opened the gate and walked the remaining few paces to meet her youngest daughter.

'Darling,' she breathed with emotion, as she clasped the child to her bosom. 'Oh, my baby, my Babs!'

Fran could not believe it. Babs fought to get out of her embrace.

'You can't have forgotten me,' Fran said, trying to make light of it.

'Hullo, Fran dear,' Prue said, as the two women kissed a warm greeting. 'Give her time, Fran,' she whispered. 'Two years is a long time to a child.'

When Fran tried to take Bab's hand she pulled away and hung on more tightly to Prue's.

'Shall we go in and see our new baby?' Fran tried, but two large brown eyes surveyed her with disdain. 'You've got a new brother, called Gordon. Have you missed me, darling? I've missed you dreadfully. But now I'm home and we'll all be together again. Won't that be nice?'

But Babs didn't think anything was nice. And very soon Fran began to feel even more wretched. When the time came for Prue to catch the train in the late afternoon, Babs refused to be left behind.

253

'I'm coming home on the train with you,' she shouted to Prue.
'I want to go to Uncle Sam. I want to sleep in my own bed.'

'Let Marion stay as well?' Fran suggested. Ruby and Marion had
spent most of the day pushing Gordon about in the pram, largely
disregarding Fran and Hilda. Babs had hardly moved from Prue's
side and looked at her sister Hilda as if she couldn't understand
her at all.

'No, no!' Babs screamed. 'We'll all go home together.'

Prue looked at Fran apologetically, but Fran's expression was one
of anger. Prue and Sam had deliberately set out to help Babs forget
her. Prue had always wanted Babs, and now she had brainwashed
her into not knowing her own family.

'Aren't you pleased that Hilda and I have come home from Scotland? I've written to you all every week,' Fran said, on the verge of
frustrated tears. 'You knew I was coming home again, dear.' She
knew she had said the wrong thing as soon as she had spoken.

'You went away,' Babs accused. 'Auntie Prue is my mummy
now, and Uncle Sam is my dad.' She looked up at Prue with
pleading. 'Let's go home now.'

Ruby and Hilda tried to reason with her but she yelled and
became hysterical.

'I'm sorry, Fran, really I am,' Prue said. 'Perhaps we'd better
take things step by step. It isn't any good to upset her any more
for today. When are you coming to Sherbrook?'

'I think I'd better come tomorrow,' Fran said shortly. If Prue
and Sam thought they'd got Babs for good, they had another think
coming.

But when the house was quiet again, Fran realised that she
couldn't retrace her steps.

'You must be thankful that Prue and Sam have been so good to
Babs,' Ma said softly, feeling helpless in the situation and knowing
how deeply wounded Fran felt. 'We can't go back, Fran dear. In
the circumstances it was best that she went with them. Sherbrook
was familiar, after all, and I couldn't have managed Babs. Not at
my age.'

'Have you had any trouble with Ruby, Ma? Be honest now, don't
try to hide things from me.'

'Bless you, no. She's been a good girl. She's settled down. She
missed her father most of all of them, you know. And you and she
never got on because you're both alike, Fran. She's done well at
school − well, you've seen her reports.'

'I wish I could go to the school to see the teachers myself. Maybe
I can come again in school termtime.'

'You don't need to fret about Ruby. Miss Baker came along to see me. They knew I couldn't get to the school, and although Sissy offered to go, Miss Baker sent me a letter to say she was coming here. She's very nice, and they're so pleased with Ruby that they want her to stay on until next summer. She'll be all right when it comes to getting work, Fran. Henry would be proud of her.'

Fran dabbed at her eyes. 'He wouldn't be proud of me, though, would he, for leaving them, splitting them all up? Babs looked at me as if she hated me.'

'Well, two years is a long time to a child. She was a mite of six when you went away and she's only eight now. Give them all time, Fran.'

'What difference will time make, Ma? We can never be back all together again. We can't bring Pa and Henry back any more than I can pretend I didn't marry Luke. Everything has changed,' she said dismally.

'That's right enough, Fran, but you can plan for the future, and you've got this young son of yours now, to take Lennie's place.'

'No one can ever do that, Ma.'

Fran's mind and heart were in turmoil, and when she visited Sherbrook the following day her spirits drooped still lower. It was no use thinking that she should never have left Sherbrook four years ago; there had been no choice. The only choice she'd had was in marrying Luke. Now she doubted that she had made the right decision. Her family had grown away from her — or was it she who had grown away from them?

She stood at the graveside of lost loved ones and wept bitterly. This wasn't how she had imagined her homecoming. She had been greeted cordially, no one could deny that, but things were not the way she wanted them to be. Sam and Prue looked at her pityingly, and she knew she couldn't blame them for Babs's rejection of her. A child of that age needed constant love and security, and Babs had found that with the Belmonts. At least Henry would have been pleased for his Babe. But Fran knew that he wouldn't condone what she had done in splitting up the family. The other girls were old enough to fend for themselves under supervision. Kate was a young woman now, and had proved herself to be capable in her work and in watching out for Ma and Ruby.

After visiting Henry's family later in the week, Fran found herself wanting to run way. It wasn't anything they said, but she felt that they found her new baby an embarrassment. They looked upon him as an affront to Henry's memory, she supposed. She was relieved when the visit was over and she could leave.

During the journey back to Southsea, Hilda chatted to Nanny, who had met them at the station, while Fran tucked herself into a corner of the compartment, trying to sort out her emotions as the train carried her along the track. A new track. A new beginning, for now she must come to terms with the fact that she, having deserted her family, her house full of women, was no longer important to them. She wasn't really needed. Their lives had continued much the same as before, whereas hers had changed dramatically. She thought of the hours of longing and weeping into the night during the past two years of separation. She had no way of knowing how they had coped emotionally in her absence. Even Ruby, who had written so lovingly while Fran and Hilda were in Scotland, appeared to be relieved to see the back of them. Fran had begun to feel as if she were in the way.

It was a bitter pill to swallow, after yearning to be home for so long.

Chapter Nineteen

In spite of several visits throughout the month of August, during which the family bond was restored to some degree, Fran realised that things could never be the same again.

Gordon grew, and gained weight. Smiled his first smile, which pleased the girls when they visited Southsea with Aunt Sissy. They loved the house and gardens, and admired Hilda's new school uniform, ready for her first term at a girls' grammar school. And even Babs seemed happier and more approachable when she visited with Sam and Prue during Sam's holiday from work.

'It's all a question of time, Fran, my dear,' Sam said wisely. 'It isn't that we haven't talked about you coming home, because we have, but if Luke doesn't intend that you should all live together again, then it was unkind to build up Babs's hopes, wasn't it?'

'The old times are past,' Fran said, with trembling chin. 'I must look to the future, and do the best I can to make it up to them all.'

''Tis a worry — what kind of future will this maniac Hitler let them have, I wonder?'

'You sound as worried as Luke sounds in his letters,' Fran said. 'There won't be a war, will there, Sam? The last one was bad enough. Didn't we learn anything from that?'

'There'll always be wars and rumours of wars — and when you get a man who is obsessed with ridding his country of Jewish people by such violent means, there's bound to be trouble. I'm trying to think rationally, Fran, but the news doesn't give us much hope.'

Fran tried not to dwell on the rumours. Luke would be in the thick of things if there should be a war, and she would have to protect her girls as well as Ma and the new little life entrusted to her care.

When Luke arrived home at the end of September he was so overjoyed with Gordon that he refused to be drawn into any warmongering.

'Don't spoil my leave, darling,' Luke breathed impatiently as he gathered Fran in his arms. 'I hear enough about Hitler and Germany while I'm at sea. All I want to do now is to love you, my dearest, dearest Fran.'

He had arrived mid-morning, and after he had been introduced to his new son, Nanny had taken Gordon to be walked in the park, leaving Fran and Luke free to do the first thing that was always on Luke's mind. At the sight of her handsome husband, elegant in naval uniform, Fran never failed to feel the tiniest bit shy, but in his own inimitable way Luke swept her off her feet, literally.

The bedroom door was locked, and with an almost indecent haste to rid themselves of clothes, Fran lay in Luke's bronzed arms where she felt that nothing in the world mattered. This moment was sacred, intimacies shared as they explored each other as if they were young lovers all over again.

'Was it an easy birth?' Luke whispered into her hair. 'Is it all right to carry on as before? Will I hurt you? My darling, to think you went through all that pain and discomfort for me, and without letting me share it with you, even in thought.'

'Luke ...' Fran panicked. She must tell him the truth now, rather then let him go on thinking that Gordon was their own child. But his tender, loving, warm, sensuous mouth, drawing every emotion from within her, soon made her forget about the adoption. They were crazy with desire. Hearts beating in complete harmony, their bodies eager to ride the crest of the wave, waves that eventually exploded in unison ...

The need to express their love seemed insatiable. After a bath together, drying each other with loving caresses, it seemed the most natural thing in the world to begin all over again.

Luke's only interruption came when Nanny went off duty and Fran had to look after Gordon. Luke remained at Fran's side no matter how menial the task, and even offered to give the baby his bottle. The more Fran saw Luke tending to his son, the harder it was even to consider telling him the truth. She couldn't bear to hurt him, and she knew it would.

As the days and weeks passed, Luke, working from Portsmouth docks, was at home much more frequently than ever before. A new contentment drew them together as a family. Although she was estranged from her girls, even from Hilda, who had made new friends at her school now and was hardly at home, Fran at last felt that her life had taken a turn for the better. Any previous animosity or mistrust between her and Luke vanished as Gordon James became the idol of their lives.

One night as they settled down together between the sheets, Luke asked Fran how the girls had reacted to her homecoming and the new baby.

'I've been so wrapped up in my son,' he said, 'but I don't want you to think I haven't thought about them.'

'Babs had forgotten me, Luke,' she said softly. 'Can you imagine that? She actually rejected me.'

'I'm sure it's only temporary, and it's probably just your imagination, Fran,' Luke said gently, kissing her forehead. 'You've never been able to forgive me for taking you away from them, and you're haunted by your own guilt.'

'I don't blame *you*, Luke,' she said. 'I didn't *have* to marry you. I could have made a stand and refused to leave Brimdene.' She sobbed while she entwined her slender fingers in the tangle of hair on his chest. 'I think you take after your father. You both have an irresistible charm. I should have been stronger − I thought I was − but not where you're concerned.'

'What's my father got to do with anything?'

'I've become very fond of him, Luke. He came up to Craiglee − would you believe on a cargo vessel?'

'And he disinherited me because I went away to sea?' Luke laughed. 'Maybe we aren't so unalike after all. I'm glad you've been getting on so well. It was something to look forward to − letters from my parents, and the very last one from Mother was full of the new baby. They really are pleased, Fran. It might make all the difference to my place within the family.'

Fran remained quiet for several minutes. She had her opportunity now to be totally honest, but somehow the right words just refused to come. Instead she murmured: 'Money isn't everything. Position and status don't count for much. It's human relationships that matter. Caring for each other, being kind and understanding is what makes for a happy life.'

'And you've made me happier than I could ever describe, my darling. Remember that I told you the girls would all grow up and leave home, make their own lives? Now, when that happens it won't be so hard for you. You'll have Gordon − we'll have Gordon. I know he can't ever take Lennie's place, but he's so dark, so good, so perfect in every way that he must keep your memories of Lennie very much alive.' He lifted her chin, forcing her to look at him. 'You don't regret marrying me, do you, Fran?'

She shook her head. 'Of course not. It's just taken me a while to adjust. I wasn't bred for your kind of life, for one thing.'

It was because Lennie was so frequently in Fran's thoughts that at times her guilt cast a great shadow over her happiness. But as time passed she delighted in the baby boy, and her love for both husband and son grew stronger.

Preparations were made for Christmas and New Year. The house at Southsea was large enough to have Ma and the girls to stay for several days, but Babs refused to leave Prue, Sam and Marion.

'Don't fret about it,' Luke consoled. 'When she's older, just try keeping her away. She'll see things very differently as she matures.'

Apart from that one disappointment, the festive season was thoroughly enjoyed by everyone. After Ma and the girls had returned to Brimdene, Luke, Fran, Nanny and Gordon set off for Middlesbrough to celebrate the New Year at Hammond House. It was only a four-day visit because Luke was due to take up his duties aboard ship, but it was long enough for James Hammond to see for himself that his adopted grandson was well and established within his son's household.

'My worries are over, thanks to you, Fran, my dear,' he said as they walked alone in the frost-covered garden after breakfast one morning. 'I can never tell you how truly grateful I am that you agreed to our little deception.' He chuckled mischievously. 'And Luke doesn't know?' He shook his head as if he could hardly believe his luck. 'There's no point in spoiling the fun now, is there?'

'I should have told him at once, James,' Fran said. 'I wanted to, but he was so pleased about Gordon that I just didn't have the heart. The longer I've left it, the harder it has become.'

'Having the boy has helped your relationship with Luke?'

'We're extremely happy,' Fran said with a beaming smile. 'The girls are coming round slowly, all except Babs, and Luke assures me she will, given time. It was so hard to feel the barrier between us all. I hated it, but most of all I hated myself.'

'And that was punishment enough.' James Hammond tucked his arm reassuringly through his daughter-in-law's arm. 'Let it go now, Fran. The girls have had their own space to develop, which they'd do anyway in their own good time. Now be a good and trusty friend to them whenever they need you. Be a real mother to young Gordon. Bear in mind what his young parents had to sacrifice to have him – he'll always be very special to you and me, because we know the truth of it. This is a new phase in your life, and you're still young enough to make the most of all the opportunities that come your way. Officers in the services have a good life. Enjoy every damned minute of it. You deserve some good times.' He squeezed her hand affectionately.

There was a sombre beginning to 1938 when the government announced that all schoolchildren must be fitted with gas masks. Trouble in Europe was increasing all the time and Luke feared that at any moment he might be sent out on the high seas. But he had had two good years spent mostly at home. During their annual visit to Middlesbrough for New Year, Fran, Luke and little Gordon, now a bonny toddler, entered into the party spirit at Hammond House, and tried not to think too much about what might or might not happen in the near future. They were all together as a big happy family, too busy enjoying themselves to notice that James was not his usual masterful self.

When Elizabeth Hammond telephoned Luke at the end of January to tell him that their father had been rushed into hospital in a critical condition, Fran suggested to Luke that perhaps James had been under the weather.

'I didn't notice it at the time,' she said thoughtfully. 'But on reflection, James was quieter than he normally is. He didn't suggest our early-morning walks, and he took a longer rest during the afternoons.'

'But, darling, it was freezing cold, and he is an old man.'

'All the more reason to notice changes. And now that I come to think of it, his complexion was quite grey, and sometimes he was irritable with the children.'

'I think we hardly see him often enough to compare.'

'That's the trouble, Luke. When you're with someone constantly, as Elizabeth and the rest of the family are, you aren't aware of anyone gradually changing, but *we* should have been more observant. D'you think we should go to Middlesbrough – or me at any rate?'

'You're panicking, Fran,' Luke said. 'I know you and father seem to have a special relationship, but it may be nothing more than some kind of spasm. Maybe the excitement of Christmas and New Year, seeing young Gordon, which obviously gave him so much pleasure, was a bit too much for him. Let's just wait and see. I'll telephone tomorrow evening when I get in and we'll see how he is then.'

But time ran out for James. At 6.30 the following morning the telephone rang while Luke was in the bathroom. Fran answered it and at first thought no one was there. Then a tearful Elizabeth spoke.

'Oh, Fra-an ... It – it's Dad. He's gone.'

'Gone?' Fran replied.

'Ye-es, he died at four o'clock this morning. An embolism, the doctor said, probably relating back to when he had that fall at the foundry.'

'Elizabeth!' Fran gasped. 'I'm so sorry – oh, my dear, so *very* sorry. Luke's in the bathroom. Shall I get him to ring you back? It sounds as if he and Gordon are having a high old time. Just give him five or ten minutes.'

Fran dashed upstairs to the bathroom and banged on the door. Shrieks of laughter were coming from inside. Fran guessed that Gordon was probably by now pasted with shaving soap, and it would be all over everywhere as Luke and his young son enjoyed their usual early-morning frivolity.

Fran banged again. 'Luke! *Luke*! Open the door.'

He did and promptly dabbed his shaving brush on Fran's nose.

'What's the rush? I'm not late,' he said.

'Oh, Luke,' Fran said with a trembling voice. 'Elizabeth has just telephoned. It's bad news, I'm afraid.' Fran wiped the soap from her nose. 'Your – your father. He's ... dead.'

They stood facing each other as if the world had suddenly stopped turning. It was Luke's complexion that was ashen now, and Fran burst into tears as the full realisation hit her. Gordon was still eager to continue his game, but Fran ushered him away, calling to Nanny to take her charge down to breakfast.

'We'll see you in a moment, darling,' Fran said. 'Be a good boy and eat up your breakfast.'

'Father's dead?' Luke echoed. 'Are you sure? Is that what Lizzie actually said? Poor Mother. I shall have to go to her now. But first, I must speak to Liz.'

'I told her you'd telephone back in five minutes. I did call, but you were making such a racket with Gordon.'

Luke was sombre as he dried his face on the towel. 'Wouldn't have made any difference, Fran,' he said as if in a trance. 'If he's dead, he's dead.'

'Hurry up, darling,' Fran said. 'Elizabeth was in such a state. It's you she wants to speak to.'

Later, when Luke put the receiver back in its cradle and turned from the phone, Fran saw a steely look in his eyes. She couldn't identify her husband's reaction to the news, except that it had come as a shock to both of them.

'We must go, of course,' he said solemnly, and the expression changed to one of concern for his mother and sisters.

It was a cold February morning when they boarded the northbound train. Luke, smartly dressed in his heavy naval greatcoat, and Fran, dressed warmly in a thick, black, woollen coat with astrakhan collar and cuffs, both looked strained. They left Gordon behind with Nanny.

'I hate leaving Gordon,' Fran said with moist eyes. 'But it's much too cold, and such a long journey for a small child.'

'It's too sad an occasion for him,' Luke said. They were sitting opposite one another in a first-class compartment. 'He'll be fine with Nanny.'

'James did want to see him grow up. It's such a tragedy that he has passed away so suddenly, and without warning.'

'As you said, my dear, the warnings were probably there, but we didn't see them. Perhaps it's as well. At least he had his family round him for the New Year, which he always enjoyed.'

'And thankfully you were reconciled with them all.'

'Thanks largely to you, I'm sure.' Luke smiled warmly. 'It's good of you to come with me, Fran.'

'Why wouldn't I? I'm your wife.'

'You've been through so much of this kind of thing. It hardly seems fair, darling.'

'I suppose that's the penalty for growing older. We do have to face these unpleasant tasks. No one likes funerals – they're so depressing.'

'That's why we couldn't possibly bring Gordon. It was hard enough for your girls. Being in the same village they couldn't escape – but even you must agree, Fran, they don't seem to have been affected by it too much.'

Fran watched the bleak countryside weaving past as the train clacketty-clacked over the rails.

'Only time will tell whether or not my deserting them has affected them,' she said with a great sigh. 'With the worrying news from Germany, and Europe in general, I feel anxious for all the family. For Ma, in particular. At nearly seventy-eight she shouldn't have to keep house. If there is another war – oh, God forbid ...'

'We'll cross that bridge when we come to it, Fran. You worry too much. For all your concern over the girls, they haven't come to any harm during these past few years. Kate's working in the kitchen of the hotel, which is what she wanted to do. She's a fine young woman.'

'Yes, she looks well and happy, but never speaks of boyfriends. I'm concerned that her experience with Felix has put her off men for good.'

'I doubt that. She probably wouldn't tell you even if she did have boyfriends. And Ruby seems all right even if she still doesn't like me. You must be proud of the way she's turned out.'

'It doesn't seem possible that she'll be seventeen this year. Henry would be pleased that she did so well at school. It's a relief that she was able to train as a telephonist at the Brimdene telephone exchange. She's the fashion-conscious one. I don't think Henry would be pleased about her cutting her long hair short, though.' Fran had to admit, although only to herself, that Ruby's fair hair, waved and curled, suited her, and probably contributed to the number of boyfriends she obviously attracted.

Hilda had learned self-confidence at the private schools she had attended. She wasn't top academically, but she conversed like a much older girl, and she liked to show off in front of Ruby, which usually ended in conflict when they were together.

Whenever Fran looked at her youngest daughter, though, she was filled with remorse. The fact that Babs felt secure with the Belmonts was small comfort. She had grown into a pretty girl of eleven, who was bright at school and evidently happy in Sherbrook with Sam and Prue. As Luke said, the changes did not seem to have done the girls any real harm. But now uncertain times loomed ahead.

Of late, Fran and Luke had not had time for serious discussion about the family. Gordon was a sturdy little boy. The experience and competence of Norma Marlow enabled Luke and Fran to enjoy a happy social life in the company of other officers and their wives. Fran, like Hilda, had become much more sophisticated and self-confident. She had never dreamed that her marriage to Luke would have become so satisfactory in every way.

He leaned across and placed his hand over hers. 'Didn't I tell you that your girls would grow up and leave the nest eventually? I may have been wrong to force the issue. Perhaps it would have been kinder to wait until they were past school age – I was selfish – but that's all in the past now. You're your own woman, Fran. You've changed so much – you're quite a hit with everyone at social events. And Father adored you.'

Fran dropped her gaze into her lap. She hated the sound of the past tense. She had grown to love James Hammond – why else would she have done what she did? She felt the knot in her stomach tighten. Here, where they were alone, was an opportunity to tell her husband the truth. Life had gone rushing past, giving her time to push the secret into the dark crevices of her brain.

'I owe you so much, Fran, dear,' Luke was saying gently. 'You helped to bind the Hammonds together as a family again. And you've given me the most precious thing I've ever possessed. I really had given up all hope of having a son of my own. And by the woman I love most in the world.'

There was a long silence before Fran said softly: 'You did give Sarita a baby, though. You must have loved her very much.'

'I – I'm afraid I have to admit that I used Sarita. When we were together I imagined that she was you. She merely filled a physical need, Fran.'

'But what became of the child?'

'Her family refused to let me have access to it.'

'Was it a boy or a girl?'

'They wouldn't even tell me that.' Luke gazed out of the window. 'I can hardly believe that at last I have the things most dear to me.'

Fran was surprised to see an almost excited anticipation about Luke's expression. Was it because of Gordon? Or was there an even stronger motive for his eagerness to reach Middlesbrough?

He drew his long, elegant hands round his carefully shaved chin in a gesture of impatience. Then he looked directly at Fran again, his mood warm and brown.

'I lost Sarita and my child in Asia. I came home to discover that I'd lost Lennie too. I felt at times as if I were useless as a man. How could life be so cruel? I had position and financial security, but no family of my own.'

Fran smiled in a meaningless fashion. How could she ever tell Luke the truth about Gordon? She thought that, like his father, he needed a son to carry on the Hammond name, but there was a disturbing thought in the back of her mind that all Luke needed a son for was to inherit some of his father's wealth. Had James been astute enough to realise that fact fully? Fran turned things over and over in her mind, wanting the train journey to end, yet afraid of what was about to be revealed. Suppose James mentioned their little plot in his will? That would surely upset the apple-cart, and Dorinda and Cecilia would have every right to contest any future James had earmarked for Gordon. If Luke found out the truth he would have every right to dissolve his marriage to her and refuse to have anything more to do with Gordon James. It was a sobering thought, which troubled her for the rest of the journey.

265

All Middlesbrough turned out to bid a last farewell to James Hammond, founder and owner of the vast ironworks, which provided work for many men in the area. In solemn procession they walked behind the funeral cortege, caps in hand, despite the inclement weather. After the church service, followed by interment in the cheerless churchyard, the men returned to the foundry, where they were given refreshment and drink before going to their homes. Work would be resumed the following day.

The family, cold and emotionally numb, were thankful when at last they were behind the closed doors of Hammond House to eat and drink while they talked affectionately of James Hammond, husband and father. Fran sat in the background watching and wondering why, once people fortified themselves with food and wine, they became a different species. Dorinda and her husband flitted from one person to the next, while Cecilia and her husband cosseted Emma Hammond. Elizabeth and Luke were in earnest conversation until different members of the far-reaching Hammond family interrupted. Fran felt the tension grow. No one in her family had either possessions or money to be divided between would-be beneficiaries, so this was yet another new experience for her.

The tension grew until a thick silence fell, and then a middle-aged man entered the room and bowed slightly.

'Good afternoon, everyone. I wonder if I might ask the immediate members of the family to join me in the small sitting room? Mrs Hammond senior — Mrs Emma Hammond, that is.' He offered his arm to Luke's mother, who looked rather dazed as if she wasn't really aware of what was happening. 'Mr and Mrs Luke Hammond,' the solicitor intoned, 'also Miss Elizabeth Hammond, and daughters Dorinda and Cecilia and their respective husbands.'

'Not me,' Fran whispered frantically to Luke. 'I'm not family. I'll stay here.'

'You will be required, Mrs Hammond,' Mr Hindle said, glancing over his shoulder.

Fran had viewed the tension as coming from the others; now she felt it within herself. She took Luke's arm and they followed the solicitor and Luke's mother to the back of the house. The room had a dark atmosphere and looked horribly formal with a long oak table placed in the centre, covered with papers and legal-looking documents. Fran pressed her lips together. James was a wily old devil. What tricks was he going to play on them all? Without realising, she tightened her fingers on Luke's arm. He reacted by placing his other hand over hers, and looked down at her with concern.

266

A few moments later they were seated in various armchairs spread round the room. A huge fire burned in the grate, yet a chill cut across Fran's back and she shivered involuntarily. Luke let go of her hands and sat forward in his chair almost eagerly. Fran noticed Dorinda watching him and she felt a renewed urgency to escape. She wasn't a Hammond. She had no right to be here.

With solemn expression Mr Hindle untied the bundle of legal documents on the table and opened it out flat. He coughed, and Fran thought it was like watching a film at the cinema.

'This is the last will and testament of James Montague Hammond ...'

The solicitor's voice droned on monotonously as to James's state of mind when he signed the will, but at last he began the bequests.

'To Emma, my dear wife, I leave Hammond House and an annuity of one hundred and fifty pounds for the rest of her life, as well as 10 per cent of the profits from the foundry.'

Luke leaned forward even more prominently. Fran was somewhat bewildered by the legal jargon, but she understood that Elizabeth now owned a row of cottages in Middlesbrough and would inherit Hammond House after her mother's death. It would then pass to the youngest grandson, Gordon James Hammond. A stifled gasp rippled round the room. All eyes turned towards Fran, and Luke sat back in his chair as if he might be trying to hide from embarrassment.

Subsidiary companies that James owned were left between Dorinda, Cecilia and his only granddaughter, Edna. A small percentage of shares in the foundry were left in trust for the four other grandsons with the proviso that at twenty-one they had served their apprenticeship and continued to work in the foundry.

Seventy-five per cent of the shares in the foundry were left in for Gordon James Hammond if he too worked his way up in the foundry and showed capabilities towards running the ironworks. It took several seconds for this to sink in. Fran dared not look round the company, for she guessed there would be tight lips and long faces.

'Lastly, to Mrs Frances Hammond, a very dear and special friend and daughter-in-law, who has given me the Hammond heir, I leave ...'

The sum of money was incomprehensible to Fran. She buried her face in her hands as she silently cried, Oh no, James, how could you? How could you do this to me?

Fran sensed the fidgety movements of everyone present. But the eminent solicitor had not yet finished.

'This last bequest is to be passed down to her four daughters in the event of her death. She has suffered greatly at the hands of my son, Luke Hammond, who needlessly lured her away from her girls at a time when they needed her. He also tried to trick me into believing that Fran's children were his offspring in order to gain favour with me. But for young Hilda I might never have learned the truth. Luke chose to desert the family home. I choose to leave all that I have worked a lifetime for to those who have proved themselves to be honest and loyal to me. In order that Luke never again forgets his heritage, I leave a token from the foundry. A brass plate, the last moulding I have cast myself of the family name, HAMMOND, which he may care to display on his front door.'

The air was thick, and then suddenly Dorinda burst out laughing. Her hysterical screams filled the room and no one seemed to know how to react, until Luke stood up. With one long stride he crossed to where Dorinda was seated, lifted his hand and struck her across her left cheek. Giles, Dorinda's husband, counter-reacted by punching Luke straight in the face. Blood gushed from Luke's nose. Elizabeth placed herself between the two men, and Cecilia's husband, Alex, remonstrated, while the stunned Mr Hindle cried in astonishment: 'Gentlemen, *please*!'

Fran caught Luke's sleeve. 'Come to the cloakroom, Luke,' she said. 'Don't make a mess on the carpet.'

'Never mind the carpet,' Mr Hindle said impatiently. 'This is disgusting behaviour from a naval officer. An apology must be made.'

'Do stop it! All of you!' Emma Hammond shrieked in a quivering voice.

Elizabeth rushed to her mother's side and tried to comfort her while the others heatedly disputed the contents of the will.

Fran led Luke away, and in the downstairs cloakroom blotted the blood up with anything she could lay her hands on.

'Get me a brandy,' Luke growled angrily. 'Stop fussing, Fran. It isn't the first time I've had a bloody nose and I don't suppose it'll be the last.'

'I sincerely hope it is,' Fran said. 'You're a grown man, for heaven's sake, not a schoolboy. You're much too old to get involved in brawls.'

'I am not that old!' Luke replied savagely.

'Darling, calm down, you'll give yourself a heart attack,' Fran said.

'It's all right for you.' Luke turned on her aggressively. 'You seem to have come out of this better than anyone. All that money — '

'But it's ours — yours as well as mine, Luke.'

'Didn't hear you properly? I get nothing but a blasted brass plate. As if I should be grateful for being a Hammond.'

'Isn't that why you wanted a son so badly?'

Luke didn't answer but tipped his head back, keeping the wet towel over the bridge of his nose.

Elizabeth came to see how they were getting on. 'It'll soon stop bleeding, Luke,' she said. 'Come on back and sit down. We all need a drink.'

'I suppose you were in on all this?' Luke demanded of his sister.

'Luke, you know Father. He was a law unto himself. Mr Hindle has just told us that he tried to dissuade Father from leaving you out — from playing that mean trick on you — but he was adamant that Gordon was the main beneficiary. It's for his future, Luke, for the future of Hammond's.'

'And to hell with the rest of us except Fran?'

Elizabeth took her brother's arm and led him back to the room where the family were in earnest conversation.

The solicitor called them to order, asking them to be patient while he concluded the business by reading details of certain clauses as to where money and property went in the case of the grandsons not fulfilling their obligations, or predeceasing their parents.

Emma Hammond needed smelling-salts and was escorted to her bedroom by Cecilia, while the others argued passionately.

'Those are the wishes of your father,' Mr Hindle said dryly. 'Of course, there are avenues open to any of you who wish to contest, but it would be a costly business, and I strongly advise against it.'

Luke paced the floor angrily, not defending Fran when the others issued spiteful accusations against her. Even Elizabeth had turned sour.

'I knew father was besotted with you, Fran, but I never thought you'd wangle so much out of him,' she said.

'I did not *wangle* anything out of anyone,' Fran said. 'I didn't — I don't want the money, so go ahead and contest the will.'

'We all know that would be a waste of money,' Alex said. 'The old man did what he wanted to do — set you all against one another — and you're showing yourselves in your true colours.'

'And what have you got to be so damned patronising about?' Luke demanded. 'What did you manage to wheedle out of the old man while he was alive?'

'Nothing!' Cecilia came to her husband's rescue. Alex was a mild-mannered man, seldom ruffled, always pleasant. The furore

269

had sickened him and now, finding himself the butt of Luke's anger, he left the room, pulling his wife behind him.

'I hope you're satisfied.' Dorinda accosted Fran. 'You certainly knew how to play up to a man – just like you did to Luke, I suppose. All this nonsense about deserting your girls – you didn't need much persuading, did you? Well – did you?'

'When I agreed to marry Luke,' Fran said calmly, 'I didn't realise that he meant me to leave the girls to accompany him to Scotland. I know now that I should have stuck to my guns. I should have remained in Brimdene. Then I would not have met any of you, or your father. I don't want anyone else's wealth. I've been hard-working all my life and earned my bread and butter. If this is how wealthy people quarrel among themselves, then I want no part of it – and you're welcome to James's money. When I get it I'll divide it between you – have the lot for all I care.'

'Oh no you don't!' Luke said. 'Father wanted you to have it – and I can see that he wanted an heir so badly that he was besotted with you because you gave him one.'

'You've been away, Luke,' Dorinda said. 'How can you be sure that Gordon is your son?'

Fran felt the colour drain from her cheeks, then flush dark red. Luke stared at her, but eventually said: 'That's a pretty low thing to insinuate, Dorrie. Of course Gordon is our son, and it pleased father that at last he had a Hammond heir.'

Mr Hindle packed up his briefcase. 'Mrs Hammond, I wonder if I might have a word with you before I leave?'

'Can't it be said in front of all of us?' Luke said.

'Um, er – it is just a small private matter. Something that concerns only Mrs Hammond and her legacy.'

'Come on,' Dorinda snapped. 'Let's go and leave them to it. It becomes more obvious by the minute that Fran wormed her way into Father's affections to get what she could – not for Luke but for herself. Funny when you think about it. Luke marries her to help him reinstate himself within the family – to get money, of course. Instead, his wife and son get it all. Rough justice, if you ask me.'

She laughed sardonically and led the way to the large front sitting room, leaving Fran feeling very vulnerable alone with Mr Hindle. He smiled and indicated that she should sit down while he made sure that the door was firmly closed and locked.

'I'm sure it's nothing that my husband shouldn't hear –' Fran began.

'On the contrary, my dear, this must be for your ears alone.

Perhaps you hadn't realised that I had some dealing with the legal matter of the adoption of your son, Gordon James?'

'No. I left it all to James. It was done in rather a rush, which I regretted afterwards.'

'I'm sure you don't now, Mrs Hammond.' Mr Hindle inclined his head with a rare smile. 'James assured me that it was exactly the right thing to do. He was very proud of his grandson, and he knew that Gordon made up in part for much of your unhappy past.'

'He is growing into a fine boy,' Fran said. 'But inheriting into this family is going to make life hard for him in the future. I should have told Luke at the outset, but he's become so passionately fond of Gordon that I haven't had the heart.'

'It'll probably be best if you never tell him. This is why I had to see you alone. James Hammond asked me to keep the adoption papers in my safe, which I have done, but at his death he wanted you to have them. Keep them in a safe place or, better still, deposit them at the bank wherever you live.'

'That's something I hadn't given any thought to. Gordon has a brief birth certificate and we assumed that would be sufficient.'

'It will be for most legal purposes, but someone should have the rights of the case for — shall we say — posterity?'

'I hope Gordon never finds out his true identity. It would be a dreadful shock to him.'

'There's no reason why he should, Mrs Hammond. His parents came from a different part of the country, and you live down south. In years to come, when Gordon comes north to work in the foundry, there should never be any query as to his parentage. I've prepared a copy of the will for each member of the family, and a copy for you separately as there is just one other matter James asked me to divulge in private to you.' He watched the expression on Fran's face. 'James had the notion that you may at some time in the future wish to leave your husband.'

'Leave Luke?' Fran exclaimed. 'Why should he have that idea?'

'Maybe there was a conversation between you — some hint that you were not happy, perhaps?'

Fran lowered her gaze and tried to recall some of the many intimate conversations she'd had with her father-in-law. She was weary of the day's events. The day which should have been solemn, leaving happy memories of James Hammond; instead it had ended in disharmony. She wished James had consulted her about his intentions. He could easily have done during their walks and quiet moments together. Then she remembered. She had told him once that she would have left Luke if she could have afforded to. That was all so long ago.

271

'There was a time when we first went to Scotland,' she admitted. 'I don't suppose I was really serious, though. Evidently James thought I was.'

'He knew the extent of family discord his will would evoke. He probably guessed that Luke might turn against you, so he thought, if he left a substantial sum to you, it would leave you in a position to live independently of your husband, should you wish to – and you'll have sufficient to keep yourself, Gordon and your girls in reasonable comfort for the rest of your life.'

'It's most generous of James. But,' Fran sighed, 'I do wish he hadn't left any money to me. It should, by right, be Luke's, and I'm pleased to say that since Luke came home we have lived most harmoniously. Gordon has made all the difference to us. My own girls – well, they don't need me now in quite the way I assumed they would.'

Mr Hindle smiled again, this time with a hint of sympathy. 'A lesson perhaps that we are all dispensable.'

'I suppose a mother does not like having to admit that,' Fran said. She put the papers the solicitor handed her away in her bag. 'I'm quite overwhelmed by what has happened today. I must contact you in the near future when the shock of James's death has lessened a little, and perhaps you would draw up some kind of agreement that half of the money is to be transferred to Luke, or at least put into a joint account.'

Mr Hindle shook his head. 'I'm not at liberty to do that. The money is yours and yours alone – to secure a financial future for yourself and your girls, mainly. Mr Hammond senior foresaw your generous intentions, and made a clause to the effect that it must remain under the jurisdiction of the trustee.'

'But if it's my money, why can't I use it any way I want?'

'Because much of it is in securities, only to be released by agreement with the trustee – who happens to be me and, in the event of my death, my partner and his son. You can draw substantial amounts at any time which, of course, you may share with your husband. But Mr James Hammond was well aware of his son's – I don't like to use the word greed, but ... Believe me, Mrs Hammond, your father-in-law was most particular in every detail of his wishes, and there is no way round it.'

Fran bade the solicitor goodbye and went in search of Luke. The sitting room was empty. Upstairs in their room she found him lying on his back on the bed, hands clasped behind his head.

'Well,' he said sarcastically, 'what was all that about?'

'Just to explain how I can withdraw money. It seems to be very

272

much tied up. I wanted him to transfer it to a joint account, but it's mostly securities or something, and held in trust.'

'In other words, if you wanted to share it with me you can't?'

'Something like that. Oh, Luke, it's all so horrible! So mercenary,' Fran said, flinging her bag on the chair. 'I don't want your father's money.'

'Then why did he think you did?'

'I suppose it was his way of saying thank you for Gordon.'

'But he's left him better off than anyone else. Why you as well?'

Fran sat down heavily in the chair on top of her bag. She retrieved it and put it away at the bottom of the wardrobe, remembering the secret that was hidden inside.

'When are we going home?' she asked.

'Got what you came for so now we can leave the others to it, I suppose,' Luke said unkindly.

'That's not fair, Luke. I never knew about the money or how your father was going to share his wealth. I liked him as a man. We understood each other and we got on well together.'

Suddenly Luke got off the bed and gripped Fran's arm. 'They tell me he was always going off to Craiglee to stay with you. They also say that you came to Middlesbrough and stayed in a hotel with him? Now, tell me that isn't true? Tell me who Gordon's father really is?' His eyes narrowed, his grip tightened and he looked at Fran as if he despised her.

'What on earth are you suggesting?' she said. 'Luke! You're as bad as the rest of the family – cold, calculating, scheming –'

'And some might well think those things of you, Fran. My father was not renowned for his generosity or liberality towards others – women in particular.'

'Then you didn't know him very well. He saw you all for what you were. He was kind, very kind to those in need. He was caring, too, in his own way. We had things in common: the loss of our children. He understood my grief, my concern for my girls. He was far more understanding than you've ever been. I thought you were changing, Luke – had changed – since Gordon was born.'

'So you went to my father's bed in order to satisfy an old man's lust? To satisfy an old man's whim of having a Hammond heir? Strange that he should be successful where I failed.'

Luke twisted Fran's arm behind her back and forced her body against his. She could feel his strength – a strength of rage in his belief that she had committed adultery, and that his father had tricked him. She gave no thought to the consequences as fear made her shriek: 'All right – so I'll tell you the truth. You failed because my time for child-bearing has long been over. I have been faithful to you, Luke Hammond, but you bring out the very worst in everyone. You can believe what you like of me and your father. We were friends – real friends – with trust in one another, which is more than can be said for the rest of your family. James didn't trust any of you except your mother. But there was never any question of us having an affair, or of me knowing what he had left to anyone. I didn't even know that he had property and money, and I certainly didn't want any of it. But you won't believe that because you were so desperate to get what you considered was your birthright.'

'So why the secrecy in meeting in a hotel? And if you couldn't have children, where did Gordon come from? Answer me, damn you, answer me!'

'Stop it, Luke. stop it! I'm trying to tell you the truth.'

'That Father went off with some whore to have a child for us to bring up as his grandson and heir? God, Fran – have you stooped that low?'

'Your father visited me at Craiglee. He became interested in the orphanage and just before Hilda and I were due to go to Southsea this baby came to us. I got very attached to him, knowing the facts of his parentage and the tragedy surrounding his birth, but it was James who suggested that we adopt him.'

'We?'

'James dealt with all the legal matters, but the actual adoption is in my name. Gordon is my legal son. Our son, and I meant to tell you, but you were so overboard, so obsessed with the fact that he was our baby. He made you so happy, how could I refute it, Luke?'

Luke's face was dark with disbelief. Ugly with thoughts of revenge. Fran went to get her bag to show him proof, but Luke wasn't interested.

'The wicked old devil,' he said. 'He was far more cunning than me. And you deceived me. Between you, you connived and schemed against *me* – your own husband!'

'It wasn't like that, Luke. If you'll just calm down we can talk about this sensibly. James didn't want anyone else to know. There still isn't any reason for your family to know.'

Luke ran his hand over his head in fierce frustration. He beat one fist into the other palm and then he turned on Fran once more.

'And you hadn't better ever tell anyone. What a fool this makes me! What a complete idiot – to think I actually believed that you had borne me a son. God! I could ... I could ...'

'Kill me? Oh, Luke, sometimes you behave worse than any of my girls. If anything should ever happen to me, everyone will know the truth then.'

Luke sat down in the nearest chair and sobbed.

Fran looked on helplessly, realising that he had lost face, that his pride was hurt. That once more Luke Hammond had not got one over on his father. And what hurt most of all was that his wife had reaped the rewards of his furtive efforts.

The atmosphere at Hammond House was too explosive for them to remain. After a visit to Mr Hindle's office, where Luke received confirmation of the adoption and was satisfied that all had been executed legally, they travelled down to York and then caught the night train to King's Cross.

When they reached Southsea the following day, Luke packed his belongings and went back to his ship. He refused to see Gordon and said no more than was important to Fran.

Fran took to her bed, exhausted from all the recent events and lack of sleep, and with a monstrous headache.

She had lost face with her girls, Luke had lost face by his father's cunning, and now they had lost faith in each other.

Chapter Twenty

Fran found it difficult to believe that James's family had behaved so badly after his sudden death. She wished with all her heart that he had not left her such a vast sum of money. Just when the family appeared united he had created a bigger rift than ever before, and she felt responsible. She couldn't imagine what the outcome might be, but she disliked the idea of Luke being away at sea, especially in the shadow of impending war, and not on speaking terms with her. She tried to write to him, but after several unsuccessful attempts gave up the idea. James had every right to share his wealth any way he wanted to, but with her help he had cheated his family. It made the blood rush to her cheeks even to think of it. She experienced a measure of guilt that he had found in her a willing ally to his scheming. What was it about the Hammond men that they could persuade her so easily to do their bidding? She spent many unhappy hours sitting miserably in the armchair in her bedroom thinking by bygone days. Tears were ever ready to fall steadily down her cheeks. She was unable to share her burden with anyone, and yet she desperately needed to talk to someone.

'What would you do, Henry? Pa?' Instead of looking ahead at all that her fortune could provide, Fran found herself looking back at the mistakes she had made. She couldn't seem to find answers to her problems, and although there were times when she wished she had never set eyes on Luke Hammond and his wretched family, she still loved and missed him. Even more so since they had enjoyed an especially happy relationship over the past two years, both together and with Luke's family. She supposed she had enjoyed a sense of false security once Luke had accepted Gordon as his own, never anticipating James's death. How stupid she had been! Her own commonsense should have warned her that James would not live for ever.

Fran found it incredible that James obviously did not want Luke in the foundry after his death. No one could question that it was Luke's birthright, but for some reason James could not forgive his son for running away to sea. She despised herself now for being party to a mean conspiracy. She wished there was some way she could make it up to Luke, but he knew that his father would have done everything to protect Fran's interest. It was all so hateful! Her only problem with money had been the lack of it, until she married Luke. Now, thanks to James, she had enough to live comfortably and see that her girls were well provided for. That was what James had wanted for her.

Fran stood up suddenly and gazed down the deserted street, seeing four happy young girls in her mind's eye. Yes, that was what James had intended: that she should go back to Brimdene to take her rightful place as mother. She could make her own decisions now. Hadn't the solicitor said that James had indicated that at some time in the future she might wish to leave her husband? 'Oh, dear God!' she cried. 'But I don't, I *don't*!'

Fran paced the floor for what seemed like hours. She ate little, slept even less, her mind in total confusion, and this continued for several days.

Nanny brought Gordon to her every evening at five o'clock and that was the only time she managed to come back into the real world.

Even Hilda gave up trying to discuss anything with her mother. She finally yelled one day that she wanted to spend the Easter holidays with one of her school friends.

'You don't seem to hear anything I say, Mum,' she said as patiently as she could. 'I know you're upset about Daddy being away at sea, and old Mr Hammond gone, but any other time you'd be getting ready to go to Brimdene, and I'd rather not go with you this time.'

Fran blinked at her daughter. 'Well, you're coming with me. We're going back to Brimdene – for good.'

Hilda stared in shocked disbelief.

'W-we – we can't to that, Mum,' Hilda said. 'There's school. Daddy went to great lengths to get me into this grammar school. It would be letting him down.'

'What's the difference between one school and another, Hilda?' Fran braced herself, feeling much more confident. 'James Hammond left me some money, which he wanted me to use wisely. Not only for myself, but to help make up to all of you for – well – losing your own father. Being separated, leaving Gran to take care of things in

Brimdene.' Weakness prevented her from continuing and she rushed away to her bedroom, where she lay on the huge double bed and cried away her guilt and regret. She couldn't turn the clock back, but she could endeavour to make amends. Wasn't Easter a time of passion and sorrow, to be followed by great rejoicing at the resurrection?

The Rudgwicks and Nanny Marlow weren't able to hide their relief that Fran was emerging from what they thought was a period of deep mourning for her father-in-law. If they noticed an absence of letters from abroad, they chose not to comment upon it — after all, the country was expecting a war, and yet people seemed hell-bent on having as good a time as they could before their lives were turned upside down. Perhaps their mistress was going to make the best of the way things were.

'I don't know when I'll be back — *if* I'll be back,' Fran said. 'Nanny, you can return here with Hilda after the holiday, but I shall try to place her in a school in Brimdene in readiness for the new September term. My mother is seventy-eight and I should be there to look after her now. I want us to be all together if there's going to be a war.'

'Will Captain Hammond return here, Ma'am, or to Brimdene?' Edie Rudgwick asked hesitantly.

'I dare say he'll come here when his ship docks,' Fran said. 'If he wants to see us he'll have to come to Brimdene — but I'm sure he'll agree that Brimdene is likely to be a safer place than here. I expect you'll want to discuss your future with him, but if he doesn't come home for some time, then I suggest you think of going to the country, too.'

Their expressions registered surprise. They had never known any discord within the family. Mrs Hammond had been easy to work for and mild in manner, but now she was showing unusual decisiveness. They put it down to the worry of her husband being on the high seas, and made allowances for the obvious anxiety caused by the daily news of gloom on the continent and elsewhere.

They felt somewhat sad as they helped with the packing of cases and trunks, and there was much speculation about their own future employment. By the time Hilda broke up from school, Betty, the housemaid, had been given a month's notice, and Nanny Marlow informed Fran that she would probably try to join the WRENS if she was no longer required to look after Gordon by the autumn.

'Everything is uncertain at present,' Fran said. 'I'd like to have you stay with us in Brimdene, Nanny, but there just isn't enough room. Besides, I shan't be short of helpers when I get settled in at home.' She sighed. 'I've been away too long. I've neglected my girls and now I must work towards getting the family reunited.'

The Rudgwicks were sorry to say goodbye, especially to little Gordon, who was a happy child and fresh as a summer breeze. They admitted to having been in something of a rut before the new Mrs Hammond had come to Southsea. For the past two years, though, there had been laughter and life in the house. Where young Hilda was concerned you never knew what to expect, and when Mrs Hammond's mother and other daughters came to stay there had been plenty of extra work, but an abundance of fun as well. They waved the family off and watched the taxi until it turned the corner out of sight. Sidney Rudgwick placed his arm round his wife's shoulder as she dabbed at her eyes with her handkerchief.

'There's something not quite right, if you ask me,' he said slowly. 'Can't put me finger on it, but there's changes afoot.'

'Change all right,' Edie retorted. 'A blinkin' war. Goodness knows where we'll all end up − dead, I shouldn't wonder.'

Sidney tried to comfort his wife. He just wished the master would turn up, and jolly quick too. He had a nasty feeling in his bones that the mistress had left Southsea without her husband's knowledge, and Captain Hammond didn't like folk doing things on the sly. Still, there was nothing he could do. Mrs Hammond seemed in a very determined frame of mind.

Ma and Ruby stood and looked at the huge amount of luggage that was plonked in the hall by the taxi driver. He touched his cap politely at Fran's generous tip, then she closed the door after him.

'Well,' she said at last, 'it's nice to be home − and for good.'

'For good?' Ma echoed.

'You mean you aren't going back to Southsea? Ever?' Ruby said.

'I don't know about never, dear, but for the foreseeable future we're home to stay.'

The announcement was received with polite silence. Gordon ran off to find the toys that the girls always kept at hand for him to play with, and Hilda picked up her bag and carried it into the living room.

'Just when I'd really got used to the school,' she grumbled to Ruby, who seemed to be looking to her for an explanation.

'Why? What's happened?' Ruby asked wide-eyed.

'We've just come home,' Fran said, as if they should have known it had only been a matter of time. 'If there is going to be a war, we should all be together.' She burst into a flood of tears as she hugged Ma closer to her.

Gran Brown seemed perplexed by the news, and Ruby felt as if the war had already begun. Fran was too tired to explain the whys and wherefores of her decision. There was time enough to give account of her actions when they were all together. And this time she meant *all* together. She had contacted Prue and Sam, requesting that Babs come to Brimdene to spend some of the holiday with the family. Now it was with trepidation that she opened the envelope propped up in front of the clock on the mantelpiece. She recognised Prue's handwriting. Inside were two Easter cards, one from Prue, Sam and Marion, and the other a hand-drawn one from Babs.

Prue's note was short but to the point, saying that Babs had reluctantly agreed to visit for a couple of days during Easter week, but she was adamant that she should remain in Sherbrook to take part in the Easter pageant which was to take place in the church there. Fran pursed her lips. More than anything she wanted to go to Sherbrook herself. Her mind was set on finding out if there was a vacant cottage anywhere in the area. In her heart she knew she was being optimistic, for there was never enough accommodation for farmworkers as it was. If trying to return to the life she had known before Luke was a means to getting the girls back, then she must do it. She was desperate to make everything right again. If Babs wouldn't come to Brimdene to settle then she − they − must all go back to Sherbrook.

When Fran laid her head on the pillow in the familiar bed in the front bedroom, she knew she was searching for an impossible redemption. She lay awake for hours listening to noises which were strange to her now after five years away. The groaning chains on the grandfather clock, the whirring mechanism and the constant chimes every quarter of an hour. She could hardly believe the way life had changed. Inevitably they had all changed too, so what was the point of trying to regain favour within her family unit? But try she must, and she hoped that James's legacy might tip the balance.

Over the bank holiday period the girls accepted Fran just as if it were any other holiday. They went to church on Easter Sunday, and afterwards visited the other grandparents and Aunt Sissy. Nathan, Laura and the cousins all came to tea on another occasion, but Fran made light of the fact that she had come home for good. They all gawped at her in astonishment, and she suspected that they thought she and Luke had quarrelled. No doubt they assumed that when the rift was patched up she would be off again with her husband. Fran was genuinely disappointed that they didn't trust her. She realised that not only had she lost face with her girls, but that they too were now suspicious of anything she might do or say.

It was a cold, wet and windy day when Prue and Sam arrived with Babs. They stayed for a meal before returning to Sherbrook.

'It'll be quiet without Marion and Babs,' Prue said with an awkward laugh. 'Marion doesn't need us now. She likes to go places by herself, or at least with friends of her own age.'

'She's settled and happy in her job?' Fran asked.

'We didn't like her having to cycle into Blandford every day, Fran, as you'll appreciate,' Prue said. 'But she's eighteen now and you have to let them learn their independence some time.'

Fran knew they were reminding her of the trouble Kate had got into, cycling along the lonely road from Blandford station to Sherbrook when she was eighteen.

'We must be satisfied that she's got a good job in the offices of the Town Hall,' Sam said. 'And you must be very proud of your Ruby doing so well at the telephone exchange.'

'I still feel guilty at leaving them,' Fran said. 'But maybe it gave them the chance to grow up and prove themselves.'

'It isn't going to be quite so simple with Babs,' Prue said. 'She says she wants to stay in Sherbrook with her friends.'

'I shan't pressurise her at all, Prue,' Fran said. 'I just want to talk to them − if only to try to make them understand why I did what I did.'

Sam laid a gentle, understanding hand on Fran's arm. 'You did what you thought was best at the time,' he said. 'Everything is all right between you and Luke?'

Fran sighed. 'Things are a little strained since Luke's father died. He's worried about the war, too − like everyone else − and at present I don't even know where he is. With things in the world the way they are, I just made my own decision, and that's to be where my girls are.'

Prue and Sam nodded their assent and very soon went on their way, leaving Fran to reacquaint herself with her youngest daughter, now eleven years old. Gordon was besotted with Babs, and it seemed to Fran that when Hilda was in the company of younger children, she lost some of her pretentiousness, and all three were soon playing lively games.

After dinner, Ma went to her room to rest, and Gordon had his nap too. Fran watched the clock. Kate was due home at about four o'clock, and Ruby finished work at six. The hour of reckoning was drawing closer, and she began to feel nervous. Nervous! she thought. Of her own girls? She tried in vain to put her thoughts into words but her head started to ache with the mental struggle. She would have to play it by ear.

It was gone five o'clock when Kate walked in. She hugged her mother affectionately and was soon making tea. Fran marvelled at her efficiency. Her lovely hair had grown darker and was almost chestnut colour now. It was plaited and wound round her head in a very neat style, suitable for the work she did in the hotel catering trade. She had brought some scones with her and some leftover steak-and-kidney pie. 'Are you allowed to do that, Kate?' Fran asked.

'I didn't pinch it, if that's what you're thinking, Mum,' Kate said indignantly. 'It's been kept in the big fridge at work, but it can't be served to the guests. I made the scones myself specially to bring home. My boss knows I like to cook for the family sometimes, and it's quite all right. They're very good to us, aren't they, Gran?'

Kate had matured and was quite the businesswoman. As well as doing her catering and book-keeping studies at night school and working in the hot kitchens by day, it appeared that she also managed the home. Fran's guilt magnified. She felt as if she were an outsider, but she vowed she would make it up to them. From the kitchen window she could see Kate's old 'sit and up and beg' type of bicycle propped up against the wall outside. She would use some of James's money to buy her a new one. A nice modern one with three gears and a dynamo light. Never again would she have to walk lonely lanes because her lights had failed.

Ruby arrived home from work soon after Kate had made the tea. They were all sitting round the table enjoying the pie when Kate said: 'How long are you staying, Mum?'

'Mummy and Gordon are staying for good,' Hilda announced. 'I'm going back to Southsea with Nanny. I jolly well hope you can't get me into a school here. I like living in Southsea.'

Kate's fork was poised halfway to her mouth. She stared across at her mother. 'You've come home for good?'

'Yes, dear. You always knew it was only a temporary separation because of Luke's work in the Royal Navy.'

'Where is he now, then?' Ruby asked.

'At sea, of course, and goodness knows when he'll get home if this wretched war starts.'

'Well, I don't want to come back here to live,' Hilda said.

'I'm afraid you'll have to do whatever's best. The grammar school here is very good, and there's talk of evacuation anyway.'

'Too posh for us now, I suppose?' Ruby taunted her sister. 'I don't know that we want you here.'

'That's enough, you two. We'll have a talk after tea.' Fran decided she had better call a halt to the conversation for the present, and as soon as tea was over she prepared Gordon for bed. Usually the girls were all eager to assist her, but tonight they seemed to prefer to help Gran with the washing-up.

There was tension in the room when she returned downstairs. Ruby was sitting at the dining table in front of a mirror, painting her lips with red lipstick.

'I don't think your father would like to see you doing that, Ruby,' Fran admonished. 'And it looks to me as if you've been bleaching your hair. It always looked so pretty before. Daddy would be vexed.'

'He'd be more vexed at the way you left us all,' Ruby snapped. Her eyes burned with defiance. 'And if you think you can bring your husband here to live, then I shall leave home for good.'

'That's no way to speak of Luke,' Fran said. 'He's been good to us all, providing you with a home.'

'And taking you away – as far away as possible, it seemed to us.'

Fran paused, pain in her expression as she looked at her rebellious daughter.

'I – I wanted to talk ... I need to explain that I didn't intend to leave you all in the lurch. It was the hardest thing I've ever done in my life, but I doubt that any of you can understand how difficult things were getting here. It was a real job to make the money go round.'

'We've managed, Mum,' Kate said. 'That's all over and done with now.'

'But I shouldn't have left you at Sherbrook, Kate. I'm sorry about that – it must have been awful for you.'

'Not as awful as it was for Gran and me here, having to do everything,' Ruby snapped. 'And when other parents went to things at school I had no one. You might as well have been dead – the same as Dad!'

'That's a hateful thing to say,' Hilda yelled at Ruby.

'It's all right for you – she made sure you weren't left behind. You've had the best of everything,' Ruby said.

'No, I haven't. Luke made me feel special to begin with, and I liked him, but they soon got fed up with me around so I had to go away to school. Miles away to Aberdeen where I didn't know anyone at all. At least you and Kate had Gran, and Babs was happy enough with Aunt Prue and Uncle Sam.'

'No, I wasn't,' Babs said in a soft tone. 'I hated it at first. I cried myself to sleep every night, and Auntie Prue got cross because I wanted to sleep in their bed all the time.'

283

'Then you'll be pleased to be back with me and your sisters, darling?' Fran said.

Babs sat on the edge of her chair, her two palms together as she rubbed her hands slowly back and forth in the crease of her warm dress, between her knees.

'It . . . it isn't that I don't love you all, Mummy, and Auntie Prue and Uncle Sam.' She glanced up at Fran, liquid fear in her big brown eyes. Fran remembered that Luke would have been happy to have Copperknob accompany them to Scotland, but she had chosen Hilda at the expense of Henry's Babe. Fran's heartbeat thumped against the wall of her chest. She felt that at any moment she might stop breathing, but Babs went on falteringly: 'But − but my home is in Sherbrook, and I don't want to live anywhere else.'

'Prue tells me that you want to be a nurse like her when you're old enough. You've got to have had a good education for that, Babs. I thought that maybe you'd like to go to the grammar school here with Hilda?'

'I might not pass the scholarship,' Babs said.

'That doesn't matter. Luke's father left me some money when he died and I can afford to pay for your education now.' Fran hesitated. 'That's if you'd like to. Maybe you can think about it. If you like you could live here during school termtime and go to stay with Prue and Sam in the holidays?'

Babs glanced at her mother, tears threatening. 'But you might go away again and − and I couldn't bear that.' She burst out crying.

'Now see what you've done,' Ruby accused. 'We were all right as we were. We had to be, because you didn't care − and Daddy would have hated you for what you did. Money won't make up for it either. You can't just walk out on us one minute and come back the next as if nothing has happened.'

'How dare you speak to Mummy like that?' Hilda shouted. 'You don't know what she's had to put up with. It wasn't easy for her − and there have been times when she's been unhappy too.'

'Serves her right for going off with that man,' Ruby shouted. 'He was much more important than us. She never liked *me* anyway.'

'Then we'd best go on back to Southsea, Mum,' Hilda said triumphantly. 'They don't want us here − Ruby said so.'

'Ruby! Oh, dear Ruby, it wasn't that I didn't like you, darling,' Fran pleaded. 'You and me − well, I suppose we're alike in some ways. I know I was too hard on you, but you were always the obstinate one, and I had to correct you. I'm sorry if I ever gave you the impression that I didn't like you. I love you. I love all of you very much. You're Henry's girls as well as mine.'

284

'Then you know how angry Daddy would have been at you getting married again to that – that *sailor*! I don't want you and Hilda coming back here and ruining my life.'

Gran Brown had listened to the rumpus without interfering. Now she stood up, slightly tottering, and said clearly: ' "Honour thy father and thy mother that thy days may be long upon the land which the Lord thy God giveth thee." That's what the Bible says, and you girls had better just think about that. I'm ashamed of you, Ruby. Your mother had a difficult decision to make five years ago. She did what she thought was best for all of you and a lot of thanks she's getting. You'll know when you get married and have babies of your own how hard life can be – cruel too. Bad enough to lose Lennie, then to lose her father and husband on one day – you may feel hurt, what d'you think your poor mother felt?'

'Oh, Ma!' Fran cried, burying her face in her hands on the table. 'I know I did wrong. I shouldn't have married again so soon. I should have kept us all together however poor we were. I was weak where Luke was concerned. I let him persuade me. I didn't want to split up my family – I never meant to treat you all so shamefully.' She wept uncontrollably, unaware that Ma had made her way out of the room.

'I'm sorry – all of you. I'm dreadfully sorry,' Fran wailed. 'Please at least try to forgive me. I'm sure Daddy would have done. Wherever he is, I feel that he understands. You can't know how I've hated myself. The anguish of knowing how I deserted you ...'

Ruby rushed to her mother. 'I didn't mean all those nasty things, Mum. Really I didn't. It would be lovely to be all together again. But Luke will come and take you away – I just know he will – and I hate him!' She buried her face in her mother's neck and cried loudly as only Ruby could.

'No, no!' Fran said. 'I promise you that I'll never go away again unless you want me to. The money Luke's father left me has given me independence, freedom if I want it.'

'You mean you've left Luke?' Ruby asked.

'No, but I'm in a position now where I can choose where I want to be, and that's here with my girls. You're so special to me – more now than ever before. We've all got such happy memories of Daddy, we must never do anything that he wouldn't approve of. We can't be sure what the future holds but we must all stick together. Gran's getting old, and it's my job to care for her now.'

'And we'll all help with Gordon,' Babs said. She had been crying quietly. Now she went to Fran and put two arms tightly round her mother's neck. 'I love you best of all, Mum,' she whispered.

'And I really won't mind too much if I have to go to school here,' Hilda said condescendingly.

Fran dried her eyes. 'Put the kettle on, Hilda,' she said.

No one had noticed that Kate was missing until she collided with Hilda at the door.

'Here's a cup of tea, Mum. I've taken one up to Gran — she's pretty upset too.'

'I'll go to her. I just want you all to know that I'll always want to be a part of your life, wherever you go. You're all growing up and you'll go your own ways, but I hope you'll want to come home sometimes, and look upon me as your friend.' Fran stood up quickly. Drying the deluge of tears away as she went, she hurried to her mother's room.

Ma was standing by the window. There was no light in the room save for the moonlight, which made a pale beam across the uncurtained window.

Fran placed her arm round her mother's shoulders. 'Ma? You've never condemned me for what I did — and I must have hurt you most of all.'

'I'm an old woman, my dear. When Henry was taken you were in the prime of life. You deserved better than a life of mean drudgery, and that's all I wanted for you — happiness. The girls may feel insecure now. They're frightened, and you can't blame them for worrying that you might up and leave them again. But they're old enough now to understand a bit of what you went through.'

'But you've suffered too — it was so thoughtless of me, Ma. How can I ever expect you to forgive me?'

'There's nothing to forgive, Fran dear. But I fancy there might be some forgiveness needed where you and Luke are concerned. You said in your letters that he was upset because his father left you a legacy and not him?'

Fran briefly explained the details of the will to her mother.

'James knew that I had seriously considered leaving Luke when he insisted that Hilda be sent away to boarding school, but I had no money of my own. I don't mean that Luke kept me short exactly, but I reckon he knew what was in my mind. It was a risk he couldn't take by being over-generous. My loyalties were divided, but I stuck it out, and everything changed when James had his accident. James left me the money so that if I wanted my freedom I could have it.'

'And do you, Fran? Want your freedom? Or is Luke coming here to live?'

'He'll come here. He'll have to if he wants to share his father's money. He can only get any through me.' She sighed and gave Ma a squeeze. 'No, Ma, I don't want to be free of Luke. He's got his faults the same as the next man, the same as me, but I do love him. Like father, like son – they're both lovable rogues. But,' she added solemnly, 'I'll be stronger from now on. Heaven knows I thought I was fairly strong-minded before, but now, if – *when* Luke turns up again he'll come to me on my terms. I know where my duty lies, and firstly it's to you and the girls. I know I've got to earn their love and respect. I must try to persuade them to at least listen to my point of view. It was awful hearing their accusations against me, and they were all true. I know I've been utterly ruthless and selfish. I can understand why Ruby hates Luke – because she loved Henry so much. Tomorrow we'll begin again. And I must begin by making a confession to Kate.'

'A confession, Mum – to me – why?'

Fran turned in surprise. She thought she was alone with Ma. She kissed her mother's cheek. 'Night, Ma, sleep well.' With her arm round Kate's waist she ushered her out of the room and they went along to Kate's small bedroom, where they sat side by side on the bed.

'When you were so ill, dear, Maurice did write to you. I did a terrible thing, my Katie, and burnt his letter. You see, I really thought it was he who had raped you, and I could never forgive him for that. If only I had waited! It was all a misunderstanding, Kate – I did it because I couldn't bear your hurt.'

'That's all in the past, Mum, and anyway, I've seen Maurice when I visited Sherbrook to see Babs. We had a long talk. He said he'd written. I told him that I'd waited ages on the station for him to come to Brimdene. We soon realised that something had gone wrong and I guessed that you might have intercepted his letter.' Kate laughed. 'It was our first love, Mum. We've both changed and our feelings have cooled. Men only seem to want one thing so I'm concentrating on my work. I'm glad you're back – I just want us all to be happy.'

They hugged each other warmly. 'We will be, Kate. We'll go back to being a house full of women,' Fran said.

'We'll never be that again, Mum. Don't leave Gordon out – and when Luke comes home we'll give him the best welcome he's ever had.'

Three weeks went by while Fran settled down with the family in Brimdene, but no word came from Luke. She wished she could visit him, but his ship was on the high seas somewhere. Military establishments, airfields and dockyards were all under strict security. Everyone was issued with gas masks – war was becoming more than a threat, it was imminent. Fran couldn't bear the thought that something might happen to Luke without a reconciliation between them. She decided it was time to act.

When everyone else had gone to bed one evening she sat at the kitchen table and began to pen the words that had been going round in her head for the past few weeks.

'My dearest Luke, she began.
I am writing from Brimdene, which is where I want to be with my girls and Ma. It is my duty to be here now in these troubled times, and safer for Gordon too. I can hardly believe you went away without so much as a goodbye, especially to Gordon, and no word since. I miss you terribly, darling, and need you. Please forgive me for my part in the deception. I meant to tell you about Gordon's adoption, I tried to, but you made it so difficult. James was very persuasive, and I only agreed because of your obsession that Lennie was yours. I know you think I cheated you, and I'm sorry. Surely it was worth it to have a lovely little boy like Gordon to bear your name? He misses you and asks every day when you are coming home. I nursed him from the tiniest mite and he has always seemed like ours. You thought of him as ours too.

Fran paused to wipe away a tear of regret. Not regret at having adopted Gordon, but regret that such a letter as this was necessary. She went on:

We've both made mistakes, Luke! You can't deny that you deceived and used me. Isn't it time to forgive and forget? Surely we can come together with mutual contrition now? I want you to try to understand how important it is for me to atone for deserting the girls and Ma. I left them for you, darling, as well as for my own selfish reasons, after those two dreadful years following Henry's death. Your father realised how necessary it was for me to return to Brimdene, and, bless him, he made it possible, though I swear I had no idea prior to his death.

But I want our marriage to continue as it was in the best of times. Can't you see how much I need your help to rear Gordon and prepare him for a future in the foundry? It's so long since Lennie died, but the pain never quite goes away. Never in my wildest dreams did I ever expect to be given a second chance, not only to have the support of a loving husband but to bring up a son just as I would have brought up Lennie. But I can't do it alone, darling.

Please write to us if you are able. The girls are ready to accept you now. They send their love and pray for your safety just as I do. Hilda's school is being evacuated to Brimdene so it seems sensible to remain here all together, a house full of women again, except for Gordon. We hope that it won't be too long before the empty chair at the head of the table is occupied by you.

The next day Fran posted her letter with renewed hope.

The waiting seemed interminable. Still no news as the gloomy clouds of war darkened the summer sky.

Fran was standing at the kitchen window one afternoon watching Gordon playing with a box cart on wheels which Nathan had made for him. Ma was having her rest, and Fran decided it would be pleasant to take Gordon to the nearby park before meeting Babs from school.

The sound of the doorbell echoed through the hall and she wondered who it could be. The postman? Rather late for him, but maybe a telegram? She found herself clutching at the front of her dress as she willed herself to go to the door. She couldn't see anyone through the glass panel. Cautiously she opened the door a crack, then wider when the porch appeared to be empty. Was it Babs home early from school, playing one of her tricks?

But it was Luke who bobbed into view. As ever his dark eyes were mischievous, and then warm with love and longing as he dropped his suitcase and gathered her into his outstretched arms.

'Luke, Luke! You're suffocating me,' Fran protested, even though she was loath to break free.

Luke drew back an inch or so, looking down at her with an intensity that made her gasp.

'Darling,' he breathed. 'I've been a fool! Such foolish pride – which only caused both of us needless pain.' He hugged her close to him. 'I love you so much . . .' He kissed her passionately, and they clung together with wild abandonment right there in the porch for the world to witness. 'Out there with nothing but miles of ocean to look at gave me time to think,' he said huskily. 'Time to come to my senses and realise what I had left behind – what I might lose if this war can't be avoided.'

Fran felt choked. Stunned by this unforgettable moment of reunion.

'Come inside, for goodness sake,' she said after several seconds.

As they closed the front door, Gordon came running through the hall.

'Daddy! Daddy! You're back, you're back!' With a whoop Luke swung the excited boy up into his arms, kissing him and hugging him. At the sound of a slight movement he let him slither to the floor as he saw Babs shyly watching the reunion. Luke didn't wait for her reaction but hurried to embrace her too.

Fran felt a moment's jealousy at the attention Luke showed the girls as each one arrived home for tea, and when she went to the kitchen to help Ma prepare the meal she was sure she saw tears trickling down her mother's cheeks. Luke joined them and stood with an arm round each of them.

'It's great to be home,' he said with an emotional sigh.

'If only there wasn't going to be a war,' Ma said despondently.

'But it hasn't started yet, Ma, and we aren't going to even think about that for the next few days,' Luke said, giving her an affectionate squeeze.

He took his place at the head of the table. Already Gordon had his two small hands together in readiness for grace to be said, which was usually Ruby's prerogative. Ruby glanced towards her mother, and Fran felt her stomach muscles tighten briefly. Ruby smiled and looked directly at Luke.

'Whoever's at the head of the table says grace,' she said, with the kind of impish grin Henry was renowned for when he was making peace.

Luke stood up and looked at each one of them in turn before closing his eyes. Then in a clear, strong voice he said: 'Dear Lord, I thank thee for bringing me safely into port, into the harbour of my beloved family to whom I owe so much. Grant us all pardon for those deeds which have displeased thee, give us grace to be humble before thee and to love and honour one another. Oh, and a special plea from Gordon and myself, Lord, that the sun may always shine on our house full of women.'

All the family joined together in the loud 'Amen'.